Praise for Kelly Irvin

The Year of Goodbyes and Hellos

"Kelly Irvin has crafted an emotional and moving story of family, grief, and forgiveness, and reminds us of God's unfailing love, even in the midst of the storm."

—Sheryl Lister, author of *A Table for Two* and *A Perfect Pairing*

"A heartbreaking, truth-telling look at the ravages of cancer on the body and soul. Kelly Irvin's tale will resonate with anyone who has been affected by this terrible disease. Told with compassion and love, *The Year of Goodbyes and Hellos* is a perfect fit for fans of Tosca Lee, Patti Callahan Henry, and Allison Winn Scotch."

—Aimie K. Runyan, bestselling author of *A Bakery in Paris* and *The Memory of Lavender and Sage*

Every Good Gift

"A beautifully crafted story of mistakes, redemption, healing, and grace. Kelly Irvin's *Every Good Gift* will captivate readers and tug on the heartstrings as characters brimming with real human frailty try to work through the consequences of their lives and choices with love and faith."

—Kristen McKanagh, author of *The Gift of Hope*

Trust Me

"Irvin follows the characters through twists and turns, writing through the lens of faith and broken faith, while illuminating a bridge across shattered relationships to second chances. This one's an emotional roller-coaster."

—Publishers Weekly

Her Every Move

"Though it includes a slow-burning romance and gripping details of chaotic explosions, the novel is, at its core, a heartwarming exploration of faith and friendship."

—BOOKPAGE

"Gripping suspense novel . . . Well-paced plot . . . Irvin consistently entertains."

—PUBLISHERS WEEKLY

Closer Than She Knows

"Teagan and Max feel like complex human beings with strengths, faults, and doubts. The faith of the main characters guides them and their decisions. It doesn't keep them from harm but gives them strength and hope, resulting in a relatable picture of Christianity."

—LIBRARY JOURNAL

"This brisk, smoothly written thriller from Irvin (*Tell Her No Lies*) pits court reporter Teagan O'Rourke, a murder mystery lover, against a cunning and vicious serial killer . . . Irvin keeps readers guessing the killer's identity—and motive—to the climax . . . Fans of serial killer fiction with a Christian slant will be satisfied."

—PUBLISHERS WEEKLY

Mountains of Grace

"With a lovely setting, this is a story of hope in the face of trouble and has an endearing heroine, and other relatable characters that readers will empathize with."

—PARKERSBURG NEWS & SENTINEL

Tell Her No Lies

"Irvin grips readers' attention page after page . . . Vibrant real-world characters and an unpredictable plot keep the adrenaline level high while gentle nudges guide Nina to truth, faith, and love."

—HOPE BY THE BOOK

"In a world where so many present one facade externally and another inside their homes, this novel shines a light on the power of truth to cut through the darkness. This is a keeper of a story."

—CARA PUTMAN, AUTHOR OF THE HIDDEN JUSTICE SERIES

Upon a Spring Breeze

"A moving and compelling tale about the power of grace and forgiveness that reminds us how we become strongest in our most broken moments."

—LIBRARY JOURNAL

"Irvin's novel is an engaging story about despair, postnatal depression, God's grace, and second chances."

—CBA CHRISTIAN MARKET

The Beekeeper's Son

"Irvin writes with great insight into the range and depth of human emotion. Her characters are believable and well developed, and her storytelling skills are superb."

—CBA RETAILERS + RESOURCES

"The awesome power of faith and family over personal desire dominates this beautifully woven masterpiece."

—PUBLISHERS WEEKLY, STARRED REVIEW

THE
YEAR OF
GOODBYES
AND
HELLOS

Also by Kelly Irvin

Tell Her No Lies
Over the Line
Closer Than She Knows
Her Every Move
Trust Me

Amish Callings Novels
The Heart's Bidding
Matters of the Heart (available July 2024)

Amish Blessings Novels
Love's Dwelling
The Warmth of Sunshine
Every Good Gift

Amish of Big Sky Country Novels
Mountains of Grace
A Long Bridge Home
Peace in the Valley

Every Amish Season Novels
Upon a Spring Breeze
Beneath the Summer Sun
Through the Autumn Air
With Winter's First Frost

The Amish of Bee County Novels
The Beekeeper's Son
The Bishop's Son
The Saddle Maker's Son

Novellas
To Raise a Home included in *An Amish Barn Raising*
Holiday of Hope included in *An Amish Christmas Wedding*
Cakes and Kisses included in *An Amish Christmas Bakery*
Mended Hearts included in *An Amish Reunion*
A Christmas Visitor included in *An Amish Christmas Gift*
Sweeter than Honey included in *An Amish Market*
One Sweet Kiss included in *An Amish Summer*
Snow Angels included in *An Amish Christmas Love*
The Midwife's Dream included in *An Amish Heirloom*

THE YEAR OF GOODBYES AND HELLOS

A Novel

KELLY IRVIN

THOMAS NELSON
Since 1798

Published in Nashville, Tennessee, by Thomas Nelson. Thomas Nelson is a registered trademark of HarperCollins Christian Publishing, Inc.

Thomas Nelson titles may be purchased in bulk for educational, business, fundraising, or sales promotional use. For information, please email SpecialMarkets@ThomasNelson.com.

Scripture quotations taken from the New King James Version®. Copyright © 1982 by Thomas Nelson. Used by permission. All rights reserved.

Publisher's Note: This novel is a work of fiction. Names, characters, places, and incidents are either products of the author's imagination or used fictitiously. All characters are fictional, and any similarity to people living or dead is purely coincidental.

Any internet addresses (websites, blogs, etc.) in this book are offered as a resource. They are not intended in any way to be or imply an endorsement by Thomas Nelson, nor does Thomas Nelson vouch for the content of these sites for the life of this book.

Library of Congress Cataloging-in-Publication Data

Names: Irvin, Kelly, author.
Title: The year of goodbyes and hellos: a novel / Kelly Irvin.
Description: Nashville, Tennessee: Thomas Nelson, 2023. | Summary: "Two sisters come together and reevaluate their priorities when one sister receives a terminal diagnosis"--Provided by publisher.
Identifiers: LCCN 2023020628 (print) | LCCN 2023020629 (ebook) | ISBN 9780840709202 (paperback) | ISBN 9780840709219 (epub) | ISBN 9780840709219
Subjects: LCSH: Sisters--Fiction. | Terminally ill--Fiction. | Families of the terminally ill--Fiction. | LCGFT: Domestic fiction. | Novels.
Classification: LCC PS3609.R82 Y43 2023 (print) | LCC PS3609.R82 (ebook) | DDC 813/.6--dc23/eng/20230508
LC record available at https://lccn.loc.gov/2023020628
LC ebook record available at https://lccn.loc.gov/2023020629

Printed in the United States of America

23 24 25 26 27 LBC 5 4 3 2 1

In memoriam
To Rosenda, Mary Sue, Gloria,
and to all the cancer patients who didn't get enough time.
Dedicated to Dr. Irene Kazhdan and all the doctors,
nurses, and researchers who specialize in oncology,
thus making more time for their patients.

one

KRISTEN

Delivering the news required a certain finesse combined with brutal honesty. My technique had been honed over the years. *Lean into it. Do it fast. Make eye contact. Adopt a kindly, caring tone.* Because I did care. Because it sucked. Then brace for what came after the words that would irrevocably change a patient's life.

"You have uterine cancer, Mrs. Sedaris."

Pausing to let the diagnosis sink in, I laid the PET scan report on my desk. My words rattled around in the tiny exam room. Angst sucked up all the air, making it hard to breathe.

My patient, a physical therapist, avid cyclist, and vegan, who glowed with health, stared at the framed North Dakota Badlands photo on the wall behind me. Red blotches blossomed on her throat. She tugged her jean jacket tighter and buttoned it. It provided poor protection against a cold draft. It was a mere sixty-six degrees in San Antonio on the springlike first day of February, so the arctic air temperatures maintained in the Texas Cancer Care Clinic couldn't be excused.

Still, she said nothing. There were no words to be had.

Mrs. Sedaris's husband, seated in the chair next to her, clasped her hand. His big fingers, covered with fine blond hair, entwined with her thin ones. "So what now, Dr. Tremaine?" Only a slight quiver in his deep bass voice gave him away. "Will she have to have a hysterectomy?"

She was twenty-six years old and the mother of an adorable toddler with the same silky blonde hair and indigo eyes. She'd shown me pictures of the little girl named Shiloh on her phone the first time we'd met after a referral from her gynecologist.

"Yes. Given that the cancer has metastasized, the surgeon will remove your uterus, ovaries, and fallopian tubes." She would be thrown into early menopause. Sugarcoating the situation would not help. Most of the time it made things worse. "We have three gynecological oncology surgeons on staff here. An appointment with one of them is next. After you've met with him, we'll map out a treatment that could include radiation and likely chemotherapy once you've recovered—"

"But we want another baby. We're trying . . ." Mrs. Sedaris's voice broke. "We were trying when the bleeding started."

"I'm sorry."

Sometimes those were the only words I could offer. Leaving the uterus and other female organs intact and hoping chemotherapy would eradicate her cancer wasn't an option—not in my book. Mrs. Sedaris's symptoms of breakthrough bleeding and abdominal pain didn't necessarily point to cancer. Her menstrual periods had always been irregular and painful. By the time her ob-gyn sent her for a CT scan, the cancer had spread. Now my job was to utilize all means available to keep my patient alive.

But you'll be alive, I wanted to say. *You'll be here for little Shiloh and your husband, and all those who love you and whom you love.* But I didn't. Because no oncologist could guarantee that. Not with a sneaky, insidious, smarmy disease that constantly reinvented itself, overcoming every medical tool devised to destroy it. Not when her cancer had spread. She would be in treatment for the rest of her life—however long that might be.

I held out a clipboard with a form that would allow us to send a tissue sample to a company for molecular profiling after her surgery. "With that information we can determine the best treatment options following surgery."

Mrs. Sedaris didn't take it. Mr. Sedaris, also blond and blue-eyed but tanned the way a coach who spent his afternoons on the football field would be, did it for her. His chair creaked under his brawny weight, the legs spindly behind his massive calves.

My phone dinged. I took a quick peek. Maddie. When was the last time I talked to my oldest daughter? Our weekly calls had turned into sporadic texts sometime last semester—or maybe it was the semester before. Guilt's sharp arrow tips tried to pierce my thick physician's hide and then fell, broken, to the ground. She needed help with her rent after her apartment roommate bailed out at the last second to live with her boyfriend. Which was why I'd been in favor of dorm living. My husband, Daniel, had sided with Maddie. Something he'd done a lot lately.

Think about it later. Later would come in the middle of the night. I added her request to my mental to-do list without responding.

"It's highly treatable," I offered as I handed Mr. Sedaris a pen. "We should get started as soon as possible, though. When we finish here, my medical assistant will take you to the surgeon's scheduler. I've already talked to him. He's expecting to do a preliminary evaluation early next week or as soon as he can squeeze you into his schedule."

"That's good." He laid the clipboard in his wife's lap and placed the pen in her hand. She scribbled her signature without reading the form. He patted her arm. "That's good."

In time they would realize that *highly treatable* didn't equate to *highly curable.* Patients could only take so much in one sitting. "Give me your phone, and I'll put my cell phone number in it. Call me if you need me."

She met my gaze for the first time since I'd said the words *uterine cancer.* "You'd do that?"

The clinic where I practiced had a terrible habit of making it difficult for patients to reach their physicians. Messages disappeared into great voids. I needed to be accessible to my patients. It was my job. "Put yours in mine too. That way I'll recognize it when you call."

My phone dinged again. Not Maddie, surely. She knew better.

No, it was Daniel. My husband wanted to remind me we were attending his mother's seventy-fifth birthday celebration that evening. He'd reminded me three times before I left the house at seven earlier in the day. And two times the previous night after I'd turned off the reading lamp, rolled over with my back to him, and tugged the sheet up around my shoulders.

I ignored his text. Ignored him. That's what he'd say. But I wasn't ignoring him, just leaving my response for a more appropriate time. I was with a patient. I'd respond later. Which would be about the time I arrived at the house and found him pacing, ready to go.

The door opened. My medical assistant, Shay, stuck her head in. "Sorry to interrupt. Methodist is calling about Mr. Chavez."

My hospitalized patient with late-stage colon cancer. I took the phone. "Shay, please take Mr. and Mrs. Sedaris to see Dr. Rodriguez's scheduler." I turned back to the couple. "Once we have a date set for your surgery, we'll schedule you back with me."

Mr. Sedaris stood. He took his wife's arm and helped her up, like she was an elderly woman in need of a cane or a walker. I held out my arms. "See you soon."

She accepted my offering and walked into them. I hugged her tight. Her thin body shuddered. I heaved a breath, let go, and stepped back. "See Dr. Rodriguez and then we'll make a plan, okay?"

"Okay." She gave me a watery smile, the first since I'd come into the room. "See you soon."

Trust and hope lived in those words. The seeds had been planted. By our next appointment she'd be over the shock and ready to participate as a member of the team responsible for keeping her alive.

At least I hoped she would. I wasn't a big proponent of the so-called power of positive thinking, but a patient determined to fight for survival often fared better. I didn't know why. I didn't really care why. Only the results mattered. "See you soon."

I stepped out into the hallway with Shay. She beckoned to the couple. "This way." She glanced back at me. "You're about an hour behind now."

The clinic insisted on scheduling my patients fifteen minutes apart. "How bad is it?"

"Mrs. Cochrane says she's bringing her sleeping bag next time, and Mr. Johnson thinks we should provide a lunch buffet."

"I'll catch up."

"Uh-huh." Shay had been my medical assistant for five years. She knew better. "Take your call. I'll bring Mrs. Cochrane back as soon as I finish with these folks."

Shay knew I would do my best for the sake of my patients sitting in a crowded waiting room, watching the minutes tick by, some fuming, some numb, some resigned. It shouldn't be like that, but I couldn't fix it. This was the price I paid for practicing in a large corporate clinic.

As soon as I finished with the situation at the hospital, I double-timed to the next exam room where a patient with pancreatic cancer had been waiting for half an hour. I put my hand on the knob. My phone dinged. Not Daniel again. He knew better. I let go of the knob and checked.

My sister, Sherri. When was the last time I'd talked to her? She texted me on New Year's Day from her son Cody's house in Fayetteville, where she was spending the holidays. We used to talk more, but time seemed to get away from us—or me. I glanced at my smartwatch. Ten thirty. She should be sitting crisscross on the rug in her kindergarten classroom in Kerrville, reading *Little Blue Truck* to her students. Or trotting in a single-file line to recess. Her life as a teacher had always struck me as idyllic. Not fair, I knew, but so hopeful and full of tomorrows. She gave her students the key that opened the door to a lifelong love of reading. What a gift.

Know yr busy but need to talk. When u can

Tonight? No. She went to bed so early, and I worked. I stabbed a response with my rapid-fire index finger.

Will try to call u on lunch break. are u on cafeteria duty today?
Not at school. In car. Doctor's office parking lot

The hair on my arms prickled. A cold breeze wafted over me that had nothing to do with the overactive AC. My older sister had always been the picture of health. She loved Zumba, Billy Blanks Tae Bo, and spin classes. Her weight was perfect for fifty-two, likely so were her cholesterol and blood pressure. Last year she finished fourth in the San Antonio Rock 'n' Roll Marathon's female fifty to fifty-five age division.

Why? what's up? are u sick?

Suddenly light-headed, I waited, staring at the little twitching bubbles that meant she was typing a response.

Not sick. Have cancer

SHERRI

I didn't mean to blurt it out like that. Bitter bile rose in my throat. I leaned into the heat blasting from my Equinox's vents. February in South Texas was mild compared to the rest of the country, but I still shivered. The numbness receded, leaving room for a wave of nausea. The sense of unreality that had set in when the oncologist told me I needed to have a biopsy two weeks ago had painted the world in drab grays and bruised blues. It never really abated, even though I'd been sure the masses revealed in the pleural lining of my lungs by the CT scan would be benign. CT scan results could be wrong or simply confusing. *Web*MD said so.

Biopsies apparently were less so. *Adenocarcinoma.* I had to google that word. But the chest CT scan didn't reveal the whole story. We still needed to know where the cancer originated. Thus the PET scan. I'd had so many medical appointments and missed so much work, my munchkins were starting to ask me questions. Questions I didn't want to answer. Did kindergartners really need to know their teacher had a life-threatening disease? Did their parents want them to learn about death and disease at the tender age of five?

Not likely.

I leaned forward. My seat belt fought me. I fumbled with it. Finally, it complied and disengaged. I laid my forehead on the wheel and closed my eyes. Another wave of nausea ripped through me. I jerked upright, frantic, shoved open the door, and heaved onto the asphalt. Heaved until nothing more came up.

I glanced around to make sure no one had witnessed my ignominious display of weakness, then closed the door gently. The parking lot hummed with activity. Business was good at Kerrville's medical arts building. Fortunately, none of the patients trotting through the lot were close enough to see my impromptu performance.

The smell. The taste in my mouth. The memory was so vivid, I gagged again and again. I grabbed a tissue and held it to my mouth.

My stomach lurched at the sound of retching. The grilled cheese sandwich and strawberry milkshake I'd eaten for lunch threatened to come back up. Mom didn't have much in her belly. A few swallows of the milkshake and toast I'd made and insisted she try to eat. They both came up.

Her face gaunt and her skin an ugly green, she leaned back against her pillow and handed me the red plastic beach bucket. Breathing through my mouth, I gave her a tissue. I would never drink a strawberry milkshake again.

She dabbed at her mouth. The tissue still clutched in one hand, she pushed the scarf that covered her bald head back into place with her other hand. "Sorry, baby. I know this is not how you planned to spend spring break."

It wasn't like I planned to go to Corpus with my friends. A bunch of seniors on their last spring break before graduation. I had a job at Dairy Queen. We needed the money. A guy I hardly knew had agreed to cover my shift. "It's okay, Mom." I offered her a sleeve of saltine crackers. "Try to eat a few crackers. They'll settle your stomach." Now I sounded like a nurse.

Her mouth worked. She closed her eyes. She was so skinny that her high cheekbones looked sharp enough to cut wood. Her long-sleeve Henley shirt, big enough for two of her, hung on her body. "Maybe in a while."

"Drink some Sprite then."

She managed a few swallows. Two minutes later it came back up.

"Let me call the doctor, Mom."

"He'll just want to write another prescription we can't afford to fill. Let me sleep. I'll feel better after I sleep."

She closed her eyes. I climbed onto the bed and snuggled close, my arm around her shrunken body as if I could somehow infuse some of my healthy cells into hers. Please, God, let it be true. Let her feel better after she sleeps.

Bong, bong, bong.

The grandfather clock's chimes in my head struck again and again. The sound reverberated. I clasped my hands to my ears. It didn't help. It first started doing that when Mom was diagnosed with cancer. I'd learned at fourteen that time was finite.

Bong, bong, bong. Not the pretty tunes one would expect. More the "Don't Ask for Whom the bells Toll, they Toll for Thee" vibe.

They woke me in the middle of the night. While watching my children play on the beach or walking across the stage to get their high school diplomas. Time simply ran out while we were busy doing something else—usually something mundane like flossing our teeth or trimming a brisket.

Bong, bong, bong.

Seriously, God? Dad left us when I was ten. Mom died when I was eighteen. I took over as mother and father to Kris. Wasn't that enough? I squinted against the afternoon sun beating through the windshield. Are You listening?

Of course He was listening. And biding His time. He had a plan. Do You mind sharing it, Mr. Yahweh?

I knew what He was thinking. Getting mighty big for your britches, blondie.

9

Kris's ringtone blared Bruce Springsteen's "Born to Run." I jumped. The memories sank into a bottomless chest filled with everything from a first lost tooth to fender benders to a single DUI (son number two) to weddings and the births of my grandchildren.

I sucked in air and let it out slowly. *Get it together, blondie. You can do this.* I stabbed the green circle on my phone. "Hey."

"Don't 'hey' me. What do you mean, you have cancer?"

"You're an oncologist. I'm sure you're familiar with the disease."

"*Sherri Anne.*"

Kris filled those three syllables with forty-plus years of good times, bad times, and everything in between. The two of us against the world. When Dad left. When Mom got sick. When Mom died. Kris and I had each other when we had no one else. I was the big sister. I took the lead. "Sorry. Yes. Ovarian cancer." I resorted to my big-sister voice. My everything-will-be-all-right voice. "I just came from reviewing the PET scan results with my oncologist."

The silence that followed was fraught with meaning. The bewilderment, anger, disbelief, and outrage would boil over no matter how hard Kris tried to harness it. Not because I had cancer. But because I'd failed to tell her earlier. "What the . . . ? How am I just now hearing about this? You've had a PET scan and didn't tell me? Which means you had any number of exams and appointments leading up to the scan and the appointment today to get the results."

Her voice didn't rise. Kris wasn't a screamer. It went deadly quiet, lower and lower, until it became a whisper so loaded with pent-up emotion that it's a wonder my phone didn't melt in my hand. "You didn't tell me. You went through this alone. You never said a word. Why?"

"Why? You know why. Because I—"

"You didn't want me to worry? I'm your sister. It's my job to worry about you. It comes with the territory—"

"Okay, I wanted to wait so as to have as much information as possible before I told you. And you're so busy with your patients. You don't need another one." I leaned back against the headrest and closed my eyes.

The memories, like a movie whirring on old-timey film on a reel, threatened to resurface. Mom's friend shaving the few wispy hairs left on her head while Mom told us how cool she would be when the dog days of summer hit.

Mom assuring us she'd be fine. We'd be fine. We'd all be fine.

Mom crying out in her sleep when the morphine drip wasn't enough.

Mom whispering our names before she closed her eyes and never opened them again.

We weren't fine. I was eighteen and Kris, fourteen. Not even close to fine.

"Did they give you a copy of the results?"

The two offending pages with their damning words laid on top of my copy of Louise Erdrich's *The Sentence*, like silent, accusing passengers I wanted to drop off at the next bus stop, sending them to a destination far, far away. "Yes."

"Read me the impression on the last page."

"Kris."

"I know, honey. Do it, please."

The anger had leaked from her voice, replaced with a tenderness that brought the tears I'd been fighting all day—for weeks—to the surface. *"There's no crying in baseball."* It was a line Kris and I used to throw at each other when we were young, married, and raising kids, trying to navigate being wives, mothers, and professionals. We had no role models for parenting. Kris called me late at night after everyone was in bed so she could quote lines from the last movie we'd seen in the theater together, *A League of Their Own.*

We were baseball fanatics—the one thing we'd inherited from a father who'd been a semipro baseball player more absent than present in our lives. Kris had a gift for mimicry. She could do Tom Hanks's Coach Jimmy Dugan at the drop of a hat. I'd answer the phone, exhausted from a day of teaching, feeding my kids, bathing them, putting them to bed, packing lunches, cleaning up the kitchen, and hear Coach Dugan's voice: *"It's supposed to be hard. If it wasn't hard, everyone would do it. The hard is what makes it great."*

Words to live by.

I swallowed hot, salty tears, sniffed, and picked up the report.

"'Hypermetabolic adenopathy consistent with metastatic disease involving the subcarinal . . .'" A medical degree came with a minor in a foreign language that no patient could be expected to pronounce, let alone understand. Was it intentional? To give it mystery or make it worth the prices they charged? Now I would have to learn this language, whether I liked it or not.

I cleared my throat. "'Cardio . . . iphrenic angle, upper abdominal, retroperitoneal levels—'"

"Just a minute." Shuffling sounds, muffled talking. Seconds ticked by. More shuffling. "Okay, go on." Now she sounded breathless, agitated. "Is there more?"

"Yes." Unfortunately. This part I could translate, even with my meager knowledge of this foreign language. Big honking tumors on my ovaries. Why didn't they simply say that? "'Large bilateral adnexal hypermetabolic masses concerning for ovarian primary. End of impression.'"

"All right. Got it. Give me your oncologist's name and number."

I'd heard this Kris voice before, when she took a call from a patient in the old days when we used to get together on weekends: two married couples with kids. It was her medical professional voice.

"I don't understand. I did my annual pelvic and pap smear religiously." We both did because we knew our family history put us at greater risk. "I did all the right things. How did this happen?"

"Because pap smears don't catch ovarian cancer. There is no

reliable diagnostic tool for it. Doctors tend to diagnose the symptoms as everything else first. Sometimes they think—the men at least—that women have PMS or bad periods."

"My doctor thought I had IBS. Then I started losing weight, even though I felt full when I wasn't eating that much. Plus, I had to pee all the time. Then he thought it was diabetes."

He'd considered a boatload of possibilities before he sent me to my gynecologist.

"Classic ovarian cancer symptoms, yet most doctors don't even have it on their radar."

"Tell me about it."

"So give me your oncologist's name and number."

"Why?"

"Give them to me. Please."

Despite the *please*, Kris's tone had an edge. Doctors were used to getting their way. But I was the older sister. "I'm a big girl. Your plate is already full. I don't need you to ride to my rescue."

"Don't be ridiculous. This is my world and now you're living in it." Kris was definitely headed toward a snit. "Shut up and give me the name and number."

Tears mingled with the snit. Kris simply did not cry. *There's no crying in baseball or cancer.* I complied.

"I'll call her and ask her to do a referral to an oncologist and a gynecological-oncology surgeon at my clinic here in San Antonio." Her doctor voice made another appearance. "We'll need your medical records transferred here."

"Why?" I sounded like a broken record. "I can't run back and forth to San Antonio for my appointments. I have a job to do here. I have students—"

"You have stage 4 ovarian cancer, sissy. Didn't your oncologist tell you that?"

No. She'd given me the results in an earnest, concerned voice, like a parent reviewing a child's less-than-stellar report card. "She said it was highly treatable."

A sound like a snort or a cough reverberated over the line. Or was it a muffled sob?

I stopped breathing. The three-story stone-and-glass building and everything else in front of me blurred. The grandfather clock's *bong, bong, bong* in my ears made it hard to think. My hands hurt. I focused on my fingers. They gripped the steering wheel so tightly that my knuckles had turned white.

Breathe through your mouth—one, two, three, four. Hold, one, two, three, four. Breathe out through your mouth—one, two, three, four. Again. Again. Again.

"Sherri?" Kris's voice penetrated the thick wool that encased my head. "Sissy? Stay with me."

"I'm here."

True, but I wanted to be somewhere else. Sitting on the beach, sand between my toes, sun on my face, feeding bread to the seagulls, listening to their calls over the steady, roaring ebb and flow of the waves. Or sitting in a rocking chair in my daughter's living room, my grandkids crowded on my lap, reading *Llama Llama Red Pajama*.

How many more times would I be able to do either one?

"That means we need to move quickly." Kris was talking.

I tried to make sense of her words. *Keep up, keep up.* She was always smarter than I was. Smart was good. Smart was what I needed now. She excelled at math and science while I buried myself in books. She had a full-ride scholarship to UT-Austin. Blew the wheels off everyone else in medical school. "You'll see one of my oncologist colleagues so we can get your port installed early next week. You'll do three rounds of chemotherapy followed by the surgery and then three more rounds—"

"We can do that here in Kerrville." My three-bedroom Hill Country house on a quiet street a few blocks from school was old and in need of renovation, but it was all mine. I bought it when my ex-husband, Chance, and I sold our house and split the proceeds. "I live here, remember?"

"The statistics are clear. Having the surgery you need performed by a gynecological-oncology surgeon greatly improves your chances of survival. Dr. Rodriguez is a rock star in this field. He specializes in robotic surgery."

Rock star. Now I had a rock star doing my surgery. Did he play heavy metal while he snipped out my female organs? Did he don leather pants and a vest under his scrubs and wear his hair in a ponytail?

Thank goodness I didn't need those ovaries anymore. "I want them out as soon as possible. The ovaries, I mean. I don't need them anymore. Why not take them out right away?"

"Because then you have to recover from the surgery before we can start chemotherapy. And in the meantime, the cancer outside the ovaries continues to progress."

So logical. "Sorry, I'm having trouble applying reason to this situation."

"You'll get there."

Would I?

Her words penetrated my dizzying kaleidoscope of disconnected thoughts. *Chances of survival.* My mouth was so dry that I couldn't swallow. I tried to drink from my travel mug. It was empty. My lips were chapped. I dug through my purse, searching for my ChapStick. My three kids and my grandkids lived in Chicago, Fayetteville, and Germany. I rarely saw them in person. Would they remember me when I was gone?

Kris was talking again. "Right now, I want you to go home, pack a bag, and come to San Antonio. You can stay with me while we work out the details."

That sounded so good. To rely on my sister, just for a few days, just until I got the hang of this bizarre new reality. But it wouldn't work. I was the big sister. I did the heavy lifting. "I can't. I have work. I've missed so much work already."

"My recommendation is that you ask for a leave of absence. Starting tomorrow."

"But my students—"

"Twenty-two five-year-olds in one room is a petri dish recipe for colds, flu, ear infections, COVID, and viral infections. You name it, they get it. Chemotherapy will wreak havoc on your immune system. The school can get a long-term sub. You need to focus on your treatment."

"I love my job. It keeps me sane." Not many people could say that. Instilling a love of learning and reading in a bunch of kids who were like sponges absorbing everything I taught them—who could ask for a better job? Kids soaked up everything—good and bad—and I wanted to be the one who filled them up with so much good, the bad couldn't squeeze in between the cracks. "The kids love me and I love them. I need to work."

Not sit around thinking about this unfathomable new reality. Besides, I needed the money. *I'm not a physician married to an architect with his own successful firm.* I blinked. Did I say that aloud? No, thank goodness. I only thought it.

"Don't worry about the money." That didn't mean Kris couldn't read my mind. She was good at it. "I'm sure you have short-term disability insurance with the school district. You'll need to submit the paperwork for FMLA. That way they'll have to hold your position for you."

FMLA. Family and Medical Leave Act. I tried to keep up. I was still back at short-term disability insurance. I vaguely remembered paperwork during the open enrollment period for insurance. Where were my copies?

"But not today." Kris was still talking. "Go home. Eat something. Get some caffeine in your system. Call your principal. Pack your bag.

Come to San Antonio. I'll be waiting for you. We'll make a game plan, and tomorrow we'll start on it."

"But your patients—"

"Shay will schedule them with my physician assistant until I know when your appointments are. If it's something she can't handle, my other colleagues will pick up the slack. See you in a couple of hours."

"Cleo. What about Cleo?"

"Cleopatra can come too."

Cleopatra, the queen of cats, queen of my house, and queen of my heart, would not be happy. She didn't like any change in our routine. "You have dogs."

"They'll love the company. I promise. Just come, honey."

Honey. That was my endearment for her. She didn't play fair. I took care of her while Mom and Dad had worked—and then when Mom worked—when Kris had mono in fourth grade, a broken arm in sixth grade, appendicitis her freshman year, a broken heart her sophomore year, and her wisdom teeth out as a senior. And a hundred other moments in time when she needed her big sister—really she needed her mother, but that option was off the table. That left me. Now I had her.

"Sissy?"

"Yeah?"

"It won't be like Mom. It's not like that anymore."

She was my sister. She was the only one who knew what was going through my mind. Because it was going through hers too. "Promise?"

"Promise. See you soon."

"See you soon."

three

KRISTEN

Don't make promises you can't keep. A cardinal rule in the practice of oncology and I'd broken it with my own sister. One of the many reasons a medical professional shouldn't treat a family member. After our call, I'd managed to retrieve my focus and treat my remaining patients for the day without further interruption. To Shay's surprise, I almost finished on time—a rare treat for my staff.

I answered one last email, perused my schedule for the next several days, logged off my computer, grabbed my bag, and took a last look around my office. How I would balance my responsibilities here while guiding Sherri through her treatment escaped me at this moment. Guilt settled in my stomach like toxic sludge. My patients counted on me. Some had been seeing me for years.

I'd figure it out. Just like I'd figured out how to divvy up my time among my daughters, my husband, and my practice. I always did, never losing sight of the fact that I had to do better for my patients than my mom's oncologist had done for her.

I could almost hear Daniel's response to that sentiment. *Ha. Ha. Ha.* With an exaggerated sigh and an eye roll equal to any our two daughters could muster. He didn't understand what drove me. Mostly because I had never articulated it to him. This time he didn't need me to spell it out. This was Sherri. He'd understand.

My conversation with Sherri's oncologist had been short and less than sweet. She took umbrage to the idea that we could do a better job treating her patient in San Antonio than she could in Kerrville. In theory I agreed. Just not when the patient was my sister. I tried to smooth her ruffled feathers by explaining that I wanted to be Sherri's support system, and to do that she needed to be here. Because of my practice. I tossed in words like *professional courtesy* and *patient's quality of life* and *twenty-plus years of experience*.

She unbent enough to agree after a few minutes that a support system was paramount in a situation such as Sherri's. Especially since she was divorced and lived alone. Her oncologist would make the referral.

I barely had the words *thank you* out of my mouth when she hung up. It had been a tough day for everyone, it seemed.

Next step was to talk to Shay and my physician assistant, Tasha. They were huddled behind the counter in my medical assistant's workspace, poring over a fax.

"Just the two people I need to see."

Grinning, Tasha nudged Shay. Both women saluted. They liked to tease me. "Hey, Dr. T., you did an amazing job of keeping up today."

"Thanks. I need your help." I sketched out the situation. "I'm sorry to unload on you with so little warning. As soon as I know my sister's schedule, we'll huddle and make a plan for what I need to handle and what patients you can cover, Tasha. Shay, I need you to send patients messages through the portal, giving them a heads-up. Offer to reschedule anyone who objects. New patients should be referred to Dr. Jensen or Dr. Shumaker. I don't want to postpone their initial consults."

I answered a few more questions and headed for my car, already thinking about what came next. When was the last time the bedding in the guest bedroom had been washed? My brain refused to cough up that information. Had Daniel been to the grocery store recently? I hadn't. My husband did most of the cooking, so I left it to him.

At a minimum the bedroom probably needed tidying. The cleaning lady generally skipped that room unless we were actually having company. Cleo's litter box would go in the adjoining bathroom. My Nissan Leaf EV must've driven on autopilot the twenty-plus minutes it took to pull into our far northwest-side subdivision.

I pulled into the driveway and sat there, staring at the two-story classic Hill Country–style house with its white limestone-and-timber exterior, metal roof, and solar panels. It nestled perfectly in the expansive one-and-a-half-acre yard filled with crepe myrtle, Mexican plum trees, and live oaks. I loved the esperanza, pride of Barbados, salvias, lantanas, mint marigolds, and coral honeysuckle Daniel and I had planted. The native plants reduced the need for watering and fed the hummingbirds and butterflies.

I loved this house with its high ceilings, stacked-stone fireplace, exposed wooden beams, and dark hardwood floors. It was Daniel down to the joists. He'd designed it to be full of light and energy efficient. I trusted him like no other architect. Not because he was my husband, but because he had exquisite taste, a strong sense of place, and the talent to go with it.

I loved it like I loved my husband.

It was a perfect place for Sherri to go through treatment. Not like the drab, airless, cramped apartment where we'd grown up. Mom did her best, and we never complained. We kept the place clean and neat and put supper on the table every night when she came home from work selling clothes to well-to-do women at Dillard's, tired to the bone—until she couldn't be on her feet for eight-hour stretches anymore.

Stooping like an old lady, I dragged my carcass up the winding sidewalk to the porch. Raucous barking greeted my pending arrival. I

shoved open the door to meet Dash and Scout, my welcoming committee of two Australian Shepherds, waiting to herd me into the kitchen
so I could fill their bowls. I shed my slip-on Crocs and dumped my
purse and keys on the table in the foyer. Dash nudged my hand while
his brother headbutted my knees. At sixty pounds apiece, they could
easily knock me over. I knelt and gathered them in my arms. Their
blue eyes were filled with the unconditional love I wish I could bottle
and prescribe for my patients. Scout stood a little taller, but they both
had coats of mottled black, gray, and white patchwork known as merle.
"Long time no see, you dweebs."

"You came home early!"

Startled, I glanced up from scratching behind Scout's ears. A glass
of water in one hand, my husband stood in the middle of the great
room he'd designed. He rarely came home before six o'clock. "So did
you."

He smiled. That knock-your-socks-off smile that never failed to
make my heart do a two-step that would worry my cardiologist friend.
Even after twenty-four years of marriage, Daniel still had that effect on
me. He toasted me with his water. "I told you I was taking the afternoon off. Dad called. They want us kids there early so we can take
family pictures before the guests arrive. Did I tell you they hired a live
band? Bluegrass. Her favorite."

His mother's seventy-fifth birthday celebration. I'd forgotten.

His voice trailed away. His smile faded. "You forgot, didn't you?"

"I didn't—"

"Don't deny it. I can read your face like an open book, you know
that." Daniel took a long swallow of water, then set the glass on the
coffee table in slow, deliberate movements. "I guess it doesn't matter
if you forgot. You're here. You have plenty of time for a shower before
you get dressed. It's casual."

He clipped the words the way he did when he was trying not to
show his anger. He eased onto the couch. He was as trim and fit as he

had been when I married him at twenty-three. His dark, almost-black curls were as thick as ever, even with the occasional strand of silver. He'd already changed into tan Dockers and a white, long-sleeved dress shirt. His huge ochre eyes were his best feature. Right now they were somber. Disappointed. "What's going on? Why are you home early? It's obviously not for Mom's party."

I straightened. Scout whimpered. He was more tuned in to the temperature in the room than his brother. "It's okay, sweet pea." I padded barefoot into the great room and sat on the settee across from Daniel. The dogs settled at my feet, panting as if they'd hiked Death Valley to get there. "I got some bad news."

"I understand how bad you feel when you realize a treatment isn't working and a patient's only option is hospice." That he managed to keep his voice level spoke well of Daniel's character. He'd taken a back seat to my patients for most of our marriage. He didn't always like it, but he acquiesced to it. "Come to the party. You love ribs. Eat ice cream and cake. They're having carrot cake and German chocolate—your favorite." He approached, knelt at my feet, and took my hands in his. "Talk to people about something besides disease and death."

It did sound nice. But no amount of discussions involving politics, wars, weather, or whose child received a full ride to what university next fall would drown out the droning of the digital recordings used by medical records transcribers. Nothing could stifle my brain's endless efforts to devise a new treatment regimen that might be the one to make the difference for this patient or that one. "It's not—"

"We could dance a slow dance. Remember how we used to dance to Coltrane in our old apartment when you were doing your residency?" His disappointment had been replaced with a tender tone that begged me to join him in this jaunt down memory lane. Today's reality kept intruding.

Daniel laughed softly. "The living room was so small we kept bumping into furniture."

I did remember. The feel of his hands on my lower back, holding me close to his warm, solid body. His smell of Polo, oregano, and basil. The roughness of his five o'clock shadow when he nuzzled his chin against my cheek. The sound of his laugh when I stepped on his bare foot. I was—and still am—a terrible dancer. "You still make the best spaghetti sauce—better than your mother's."

"I won't tell her you said that." He rubbed his thumb over my palm. "Come."

"It's not a patient. It's—"

The doorbell rang. Dash and Scout barked—in case we weren't aware that friend or foe approached. They raced to the foyer and back. "Hush, hush, you two. That's enough." Daniel let go of my hand and straightened. I beat him to the door. I grasped the doorknob and swiveled for a second. "It's Sherri."

"What's Sherri doing here in the middle of the week? That's why you can't go to Mom and Dad's? I don't get it. What's going on?" He grabbed Scout's collar and pulled him back. The dog was still enough of a puppy that he wanted to jump on our guests. "She can come. Mom and Dad love your sister. No RSVP required. They'll have enough food to feed Canada."

"She won't be up to socializing. I tried to tell you." I shooed Dash back from the door. His MO was to sniff, bark, wag his tail, and then jump. At least the guest had a chance to brace herself. "I have to let her in."

"Yes, of course."

I opened the door. Sherri stood on the porch, a suitcase in one hand, the long strap of her purse over her shoulder, her bulging canvas book bag hanging from her other shoulder, and a bag of cat food under her arm. She clutched Cleo's pet carrier in her other hand. Her face was red and damp with perspiration. "I know it's a lot of stuff, but I'm not moving in, I promise. There's a bag of cat litter in the car."

"No worries. Let me help you." Daniel relieved her of the pet carrier, from which yowls and hisses announced Cleo's unhappiness with her current circumstances. Daniel also took the bag of food. "It's good to see you, Sher. It's been months. I was so busy yapping, Kristen couldn't get a word in edgewise to tell me you were coming."

"It was . . . last minute." Sherri set her suitcase aside. "It's good to see you too. Thanks for letting me stay a day or two."

A day or two? Wishful thinking.

Daniel did what he did best. He set aside her burdens—out of the dogs' reach—and gave my sister a hearty hug. "I'll get the cat litter in a minute. You're always welcome here. Come in, come in. We were just talking about my mom's seventy-fifth birthday blowout. It'll be epic. You should come."

Sherri took a step back. Her cobalt-blue eyes were wet, but no tears fell. "That's sweet of you to invite me, and I'd love to see your family, but I'm . . . I haven't . . . I don't feel very well."

Daniel's gaze bounced from Sherri to me and back. "I'm sorry to hear that. Come in, come in. Sit down."

"I have to get Cleo situated. She had one hissy fit after another the entire way here. Not even Kenny G made her happy."

Usually smooth jazz calmed the persnickety feline. The dogs weren't helping either. Scout had his nose thrust against the carrier's mesh. I dragged him away. "I'll take her to your bedroom—"

"Let me do it. I'll get the litter first." Daniel dashed out the door and was back in less than ninety seconds. Murmuring sweet nothings, he carted Cleo down the hallway that led to the guest bedroom.

I turned to Sherri. "How did the conversation with your principal go?"

"She told me to take all the time I need." Sherri kicked off her flip-flops. Her pale-green BLOOM WHERE YOU'RE PLANTED T-shirt hung loose on her angular body. So did her white slacks. "She said she would ask the district's HR folks to email me the paperwork to fill out, not to worry about a thing."

Kerrville wasn't a big town, but big enough that the school district and Sherri's principal would have plenty of experience in dealing with leave issues. No matter how guilty Sherri felt about it—and guilt was written all over her face. "Good. I'm glad you were able to start the process so quickly."

It would take time to complete. The FMLA red tape was massive.

Sherri pulled a tie from her ponytail and let her blonde hair—now streaked with big swathes of silver like the highlights most women paid their hairdressers for—fall to her shoulders. "I suppose. I'm going to miss my munchkins. I plan to go back to teaching the second I'm able."

"Of course you do."

I understood. My eyelid twitched every time I thought about the patients getting the word tomorrow that I wouldn't be sitting with them in the exam room, walking them through next steps, advising them, and treating their side effects. "You can reassess in the fall, depending on how you do with chemotherapy."

She would learn no one is indispensable. Daniel's voice reverberated in my head. He said that every time we argued about why I couldn't take time off for a weekend trip to the beach or even a movie. Those arguments had become more frequent after the girls left for college. He wasn't handling our empty nest well.

"You didn't tell Daniel I was coming?"

Sherri obviously intended to move on. So I followed. "He didn't give me a chance. He's totally wound up about his mother's birthday. Not that I blame him." I linked arms with her. I might be four years younger, but we'd been the same five feet, eight inches tall since my last growth spurt in eighth grade. We trudged into the great room, where we settled side by side on the most comfortable couch in the universe. "With her heart attack and quadruple bypass last year, they weren't sure she'd be around for this birthday."

Not to mention the breast cancer diagnosis five years earlier. She'd been diagnosed stage 1. A lumpectomy and radiation had successfully treated it with no recurrence. Everyone had breathed a sigh of relief when she hit that critical five-year mark. Chances of a recurrence were small—not zero—but small.

"And they're having a big celebration. You should go. Don't miss it because of me. I don't want Angela giving you demerits because of me."

"Angela gave up on me years ago." Daniel's mother loved her five progeny fiercely and expected their wives to put them first, as she had done throughout her life. "I doubt she'll even notice with a hundred of her closest friends invited to the soiree."

"Can you call a Texas barbecue a soiree?" Sherri tucked her hands under her armpits and leaned her head against the couch. "I bet Daniel's dad will wear a white cowboy hat and ostrich-skin cowboy boots."

Daniel's parents were the king and queen of country with a massive ranch south of San Antonio. Four of their boys grew up in 4-H, Future Farmers of America, rodeos, and country music concerts. Only Leonard Tremaine could be disappointed in a son who chose architecture at the University of Texas at Austin as his college major instead of agricultural business at Texas A&M in College Station.

"They'll probably barbecue an entire cow. And there will be homemade ice cream and two kinds of cake."

Sherri had been to enough Tremaine family events to know they never failed to send their guests home stuffed to the gills and teetering on a food coma. "I'm sure you're right. I happen to have the makings for ice cream sundaes and banana splits in my kitchen for just such an occasion as this. Besides, Angela will understand when she hears about the cancer."

"The cancer? What cancer?" Daniel strode into the room. "Who has cancer? Which one of you?"

The fear that etched lines in his face was so familiar. No one was immune to it, least of all a man married to someone who spent every day trying to rescue people from the disease's clutches.

"It's me. I have cancer," Sherri said in a rush to end his panic. "Ovarian cancer."

Daniel didn't curse much. He did so now as he eased onto the settee. "I'm so sorry. No wonder you're here." Scout, finely tuned to Daniel's every emotion, propped his head on his knee. Daniel scratched behind the dog's ears. "This is exactly where you need to be. I'm sure Kristen has made it clear, but I second it. Stay here as long as you like. We're here for you. I'm here for you."

Sherri clenched my hand so hard my fingers hurt. "Thank you. I appreciate that so much. We'll see. I want to get back to teaching as quickly as possible."

"I set up Cleo's litter box in the guest bathroom and put out her food and water. Then I released her from the carrier." Scout sneaked up onto the settee next to Daniel. He slid an arm around the dog's shoulders and pulled him close. It wasn't clear who comforted whom. "She wandered around for a bit, yowling and complaining, but then she lapped up some water and took a seat on the windowsill."

Daniel's love language was doing things for people. It took me a while to figure that out. I wanted him to tell me he loved me with words. He preferred deeds. In this instance it also took the pressure off Sherri to talk with him about her situation.

"Thanks." She heaved a sigh. "Thanks for doing that."

"No problem." He ran his hand down Scout's back, planted a kiss on the dog's nose, and stood. "I better get going and let you get settled in. My dad's probably paying the photographer big bucks for the family photos."

"Tell your mom I send my regrets." I stood and followed him out to the kitchen and the door to the garage, where he'd parked his F-150 EV. He turned and paused, his dark eyes full of pain. "I'm really, truly sorry about this. I would stay, but I figure Sherri needs some time to decompress. So do you. You don't need me around, getting in the way."

His arms came up as if he would hug me, then dropped. "Unless you want me to stay. You know I will."

"No, no, go." When was the last time we hugged? I couldn't remember. Now wasn't the time to pull that thread in our unraveling relationship. What I wanted to say was never take for granted that there would be another birthday to celebrate. Savor those moments now. "This is your mom's day. Don't disappoint her. We'll be fine."

He kissed my forehead and stared at me for a long moment. The pain faded into resignation. "See you . . . tomorrow . . . or sometime . . ."

"Tonight when you get home." It would be late. "Wake me up and tell me all about it."

When was the last time we'd done anything together, just Daniel and I?

Probably the last time we hugged. A parade of memories marched by. His invitation to go to a movie, a comedy club downtown, a Spurs game, a Christmas tree lighting, a play at the Majestic, a concert at the AT&T Center. Invitations abounded. Memories of togetherness not so much.

Bitterness tinged his smile. "I'll probably be back late."

"Tomorrow then, for dinner."

But he was gone.

Relief swept over me. Followed closely by guilt. He was my husband. Did I take him for granted? Did I shortchange him in my balancing act? No. No. I tried to dredge up righteous anger. How dare he try to guilt-trip me in the middle of my sister's crisis? He was being selfish.

Daniel was the least selfish person I'd ever known.

Like Scarlett O'Hara, I'd think about it later. Tomorrow.

I found a tray and loaded it up with all the fixings for an ice cream extravaganza. In South Texas, ice cream was a year-round treat. Sherri would have her choice of a sundae, a root beer float, or a banana split. Or all three. Chemotherapy would come later. Tonight the patient needed ice cream therapy.

I deposited the tray on the coffee table and bowed like a butler. "Ice cream eaten on your diagnosis day has no calories." With a flourish I listed ingredients that included chocolate, caramel, or strawberry syrup, bananas, whipped cream, chopped nuts, candied cherries, root beer, and three flavors of ice cream. "I'm happy to do the honors, or if you prefer, you may serve yourself, which allows you to double up on your choice of ingredients."

Sherri struck the thinker pose. "Decisions, decisions, decisions." Then, with quick, efficient movements born of much practice, she assembled a banana split, heavy on the whipped cream. She leaned back, took a bite, and mimed a swoon. "A masterpiece, if I do say so myself."

"You're so predictable." I went with my usual. A sundae, heavy on the chocolate syrup. "Chocolate is better."

"You're the predictable one." She took another bite and savored it for a few seconds. "At least mine has bananas. Potassium and fiber."

"Hey, mine has cherries. They're full of antioxidants. Besides, ice cream is made from milk. Therefore it's full of calcium. So it's healthy, right?"

"Mmm, no. Wishful thinking and maraschino cherries don't count." Her smile faded. "Is it just me or is it ironic that I've spent so much time working out, eating healthy, and avoiding alcohol, only to end up with cancer anyway?"

I concentrated on the creamy chocolate delight on my tongue for a few seconds, searching for an answer. "You can do all the right things and get cancer. That's a fact. The fact that you're in good health, not overweight, and you exercise gives you a leg up in withstanding the treatment and its side effects. This little pity party tonight is the exception, not the rule. Don't stop exercising—unless your body tells you to rest, then rest."

"Good to know."

"Sorry, I didn't mean to lapse into doctor mode. Tonight I'm in sister mode."

"I appreciate both more than you can possibly imagine. Especially when sister mode means all the ice cream I can eat." She licked her lips and sighed dramatically. "Now all we need is a rom-com flick."

"That can be arranged." I picked up the TV remote but didn't push the power button. "Before I slide completely into sister mode, do you want to know about the call I had with your oncologist?"

Sherri whipped her spoon in the air like a fencer with a sword. "Cancer talk is off the table for the rest of the evening. Tomorrow we face reality. Tonight we eat junk food and entertain ourselves with unrealistic but extremely satisfying romances."

Sounded like the perfect plan. "*You've Got Mail, Sleepless in Seattle, Sweet Home Alabama, Ghost, The Wedding Planner,* or *Twister*? Or the usual?"

The usual was Kevin Costner's baseball trilogy: *Field of Dreams, For Love of the Game,* and *Bull Durham*. They had the advantage of being about baseball and featuring our favorite actor.

"You've got *Ghost*? I'm in awe." Chewing her lower lip, Sherri shook her head. "Let's start with *Ghost*, but we have to watch *Sweet Home Alabama* after that. We save Kevin for when we're really in the dumps."

It didn't matter which one we watched. We knew their dialogues by heart.

"'Why would you wanna marry me, anyhow?'" we recited together. "'So I can kiss you anytime I want.'"

Laughing, I stood and rearranged pillows and grabbed an afghan from the back of the sofa. Sherri snuggled under it with me. I pressed the power button and navigated my way to the DVR and the folder where I kept all the movies Daniel never wanted to watch with me. I leaned my head on Sherri's shoulder. She patted my knee. "Just so you know, I'm so glad you're my sister," she whispered.

"Ditto," I whispered in my best Patrick Swayze imitation. "Now shut up, Patrick's talking."

We both knew Patrick died of cancer. So maybe it wasn't the best choice of movies. Halfway through the scene where Demi Moore was watching the penny slide up and down the door like magic while Patrick Swayze and Whoopi Goldberg waited on the other side, Sherri grabbed the remote and paused the movie. "Just so you know, I bought a cremation plan."

"Which you won't need for years, Ms. Marathon Runner." I tugged the remote from her hand and pressed Play. "Watch the movie."

She tugged the remote back and put the movie on pause. "You need to know this. Chance and I have living wills. He has medical power of attorney—"

"You gave your ex-husband medical power of attorney? Are you nuts?"

"Hush. I have a DNR. I didn't want you to have to make the decision to unhook me."

"Which isn't going to happen." I understood the need to feel in control. I knew when to recommend to patients to get their affairs in order. But not my sister. Not yet. Surely not yet. "Let's not assume the worst. New treatments are getting approved every day."

"I'm not assuming the worst, but I am being realistic—at least about that part."

"What do you mean, that part?"

She grinned. "I want my ashes tossed from Machu Picchu. You know, in the Andes Mountains in Peru."

"Seriously?" I groaned. "Fine. But if I go first, I want mine spread from the Egyptian pyramids. You have to climb every step."

"I'm obviously going first. I'm the older sister. I have cancer."

"I smoke."

"So you admit it—"

I turned the movie up. Demi Moore was such a good crier. I wanted to cry with her. Instead, I ate more ice cream.

four

DANIEL

Mom accepted my hug and birthday wishes with her usual elegant aplomb. Her scent of roses, lilies, and sandalwood always reminded me of car rides to church and then to Grandpa and Grandma's house for Sunday dinners. White Diamonds. Classy, like her. She made a production of peering left, right, then over my shoulder. "No Kristen?"

"I'm sorry, Mom. She sends her regrets." I'd spent the better part of the thirty-minute drive to my parents' house debating how much to say. I didn't want to throw a damper on the party with Sherri's cancer diagnosis. Nor did I want Mom to think less of Kristen than she already did. "A pressing emergency came up."

"As per usual." Her expressive shrugs used to amaze me as a kid. How a woman could say so much with a simple lift of her shoulders boggled the mind. Get a C in math? A shrug conveyed disappointment, disapproval, disbelief, and anger in one fell swoop. Fender bender in the family car? Fear, concern, relief, and disapproval in one rise and fall. "There's always next year." Which was her way of saying she might not be around another year. Never mind that at the moment she looked as if she might live forever—certainly longer than I would. She'd weathered her share of health crises, but tonight she glowed with health in a shimmering red dress and silky black jacket. Hair in an attractive silver bob. Classy sapphire pendant earrings.

I took her arm and matched my stride to hers toward the gathering of the Tremaine clan in front of a stand of heritage oaks. "She got some bad news today. I'll tell you about it later. Tonight's your night."

Yes, it was a base appeal to her desire to be the center of her son's attention, and I played it to the hilt. Her billion-dollar smile widened as her sons, daughters-in-law, and a multitude of grandchildren—although not my daughters—took turns embracing her and then me. Without fail, each one asked for Kristen. Without fail, I made vague references to a pressing emergency. Without fail, they nodded knowingly. They were used to it. As was I.

Finally, the agony of posing three dozen adults and children for a portrait came to an end after much pulling of hair and gnashing of teeth. My dad threw his arm around my shoulders and walked me toward the massive pavilion where catering employees put the final touches on an array of food that would feed most of Texas. My brothers and their wives assumed their posts, greeting guests just beginning to stream through the fence gates.

Dad wore his usual attire of pressed, creased blue jeans, a long-sleeved Western-style shirt, a sports coat, Tony Lama cowboy boots, and a white Stetson cowboy hat that didn't quite cover his mass of snowy-white hair. "Your mom tells me Kristen won't be with us tonight."

"That's right. She has—"

"A pressing emergency, I know." He paused long enough to straighten a slightly cockeyed pile of napkins next to a stack of earthenware plates—no Styrofoam for this shindig. "Is everything all right between you two? I don't remember the last time I saw you both together. Or Maddie and Brielle."

How quickly they forgot. "The girls were with us when we came over for Christmas Day brunch."

Over a month ago. Not so long.

"And Kristen barely spoke. She spent the entire time on her phone." His tone matched the disdain on his weather-beaten face. Mom might look fifty, but years of working in the sun on the ranch had given Dad the deep wrinkles of a man midway through his seventies. "She's worse than the grandkids."

Not fair. One of her patients ended up in the hospital on Christmas Eve. He died on Christmas Day. Neither of us shared that news in the interest of not casting a pall over the festivities.

Dad snagged a tortilla chip and dunked it in a steaming vat of chili con queso. "Your mother's going to faint when she sees her birthday gift."

I froze. Birthday gift. In the midst of Sherri's chaotic arrival, I'd left the simple silver-and-turquoise James Avery bracelet I'd picked out for Mom on the kitchen island. "You never said what you got her."

"A European cruise with stops in Austria, Germany, and Sweden."

Mom loved cruises. Dad would prefer a trip to Canada to hunt elk. "She'll love it."

"It's not my thing, but it's hers. That's what counts. Romance is never dead, no matter the age or the number of years married, son. You should try it. Maybe Kristen would pay more attention to you if you swept her off her feet with a big romantic gesture."

Romantic advice from my father. I veered toward the bar. "I need something to drink. Do you want anything?"

"I better circulate and greet our guests." He slapped me on the back. "We'll talk later."

I sank onto a barstool. The bartender laid a napkin on the bar in front of me. "What'll it be?"

I ordered a Diet Pepsi and contemplated a basket of Texas-shaped tortilla chips surrounded by small bowls of green salsa, red salsa, pico de gallo, and queso. The scents of chopped cilantro, onion, garlic, and lime were as familiar to me as Mom's perfume. Dad married a stay-at-home mom in an era in which she would've been called a housewife. And she liked it. He knew nothing about being married to a professional, career-track woman.

I wasn't a quitter. Twenty-four years married to Kristen proved that. Sherri's diagnosis broke my heart. But it was only the latest in a never-ending series of crises that kept Kristen from focusing on our marriage. She was so oblivious that she didn't even realize our relationship was broken. It took two people to make a marriage work. I'd been alone in this relationship for years.

When was the last time we'd gone anywhere together? I searched the far corners of my memory until I stumbled onto it. We'd gone to Brielle's high school graduation, out to a family dinner, and then had a drink at our favorite piano bar while Brielle went out to celebrate with friends. Almost two years ago.

I dipped a chip in the pico and savored the crunchy chip, the salt, and the fiery bite of serrano pepper. It seemed wrong to enjoy anything when a person I knew and loved had received a cancer diagnosis only hours earlier. I gulped down soda, trying to wash the bitter taste of reality from my mouth. Kristen's worst fear had come true. It sucked. Absolutely sucked. For Sherri. For her kids and grandkids. For the children she taught. For Kristen.

And yes, for me, if I was allowed to say that.

A few notes from an Ed Sheeran song emanated from my phone. The air around me lightened. "Hey, Maddie, did you decide to live at home and finish college at UTSA?"

My oldest daughter laughed—she sounded just like her mother. *Chuckle, chuckle, snort, chuckle.* "And you call me the eternal optimist."

"So what do you want?"

The going gag was that she never called unless she wanted something, which couldn't be further from the truth. She called me at least twice a week, sometimes more. "I sent Mom a text this morning about help with my rent. She didn't answer." The laughter had faded from Maddie's voice, replaced by concern mixed with hurt. "I know she doesn't have time to call me like she used to, but she usually answers my texts—eventually. Is something wrong?"

Maddie was empathetic and discerning. She would make a great psychologist one day. I stirred the ice in my glass and contemplated whether it was my place to tell her aunt Sherri's news. "Your mom's been up to her ears this week, especially today."

"When isn't she? She used to make it work. We used to talk on the phone all the time. Now I don't even rate a text?"

"I'll transfer the money to your account."

"That's not the point and you know it. Mom used to make all our games and recitals and stuff. Now that we're not at home anymore, did we stop being her daughters? Brielle has noticed it too. What's going on? You're being weird."

I couldn't talk to her about the bigger picture. It would be a betrayal of her mother. I swallowed all my own feelings. They made a huge, twisted hunk of sharp, broken metal, dreams, and feelings in the pit of my stomach. "She had a bad day today, ladybug. Your aunt Sherri got some bad news."

"Oh no. Tell me. Who knows when Mom will get around to it."

I spilled the news.

The intake of breath reverberated in my ear. It was the same sound I'd made when Sherri told me. "She'll be okay. Your mom will do everything in her power to make sure."

"She'll do her best." Maddie's voice held tears. A child who grew up with an oncologist for a mother knew what the facts were. Kristen never hid her defeats—or her victories—from the girls. Nor did she sugarcoat the facts. Maddie sniffed. "I'll come home."

"You have classes. Give it a few days and then call both of them. I know your mom will appreciate it, and so will Sherri."

"I should be there for Aunt Sherri. She's always been the best aunt ever."

"She's in good hands with your mom." I struggled for a way to capture Sherri's immediate future without making my daughter feel worse—or hurt her feelings. "She'll start chemo quickly and then she'll have to be careful not to be exposed to any bugs. Her immune system likely will crash."

"I didn't think about that." Maddie's voice quivered. "If you would take care of the money thing, that would be great, Daddy. That way I won't have to bother Mom about it."

"I'm on it."

"Thank you. Love you."

"Love you more. Later on, you can come down for a weekend and stay with Grandma. She'd love it, and that way we can see each other."

"Talk to you soon."

Then she was gone.

It still boggled my mind how one minute my daughters were blowing bubbles and squealing on the back patio, and the next they were unpacking boxes in dorm rooms. I opened my banking app and took care of the money transfer.

"So, you said you were going to call it quits with Kristen if she stood you up one more time. Did you tell her it's over?" Andrew, my second-oldest brother behind Leonard Jr., snagged the barstool next to mine and crooked a finger toward the bartender. She nodded but continued preparing margaritas for the over-seventy crowd. "Obviously not. What happened?"

I scratched my forehead and cranked my head side to side. The words I'd spoken only a week ago over drinks at a sports bar watching a Spurs game finally came back to me. Sherri's diagnosis had changed the course of action open to me—at least for now. "Unforeseen circumstances."

"So much for drawing the line in the sand. 'Put time and energy into our marriage or I walk.' You even practiced that line ten or fifteen times." Andrew pulled the basket of chips closer. "I knew you'd chicken out. You've been putting up with her for so many years, you've forgotten how to stand up for yourself."

I didn't recall practicing. People used to say Andrew, with his dark hair and ochre eyes, and I could be twins. We looked so much alike growing up, but our personalities were completely different. Andrew was a big talker and prone to hyperbole. "You don't know what you're talking about."

"Sure I do. You've been unloading on me forever."

He was right. I needed to be able to talk to someone. The few times I'd tried with Kristen, she'd blown it off as me being in a bad mood. After all, who could blame an oncologist for putting patients first? She was trying to save their lives. I couldn't compete with that. I shouldn't want to compete with that. And I didn't.

"Andrew's right." William, my youngest brother, plopped onto the stool to my right. He had won the handsome sweepstakes, taking after Mom with her high cheekbones, dimples, and crystal-blue eyes. "You gotta stand up for yourself, dude. The martyr-for-a-cause thing doesn't suit you."

"Easy for you to say. You have a stay-at-home wife who home-schools your kids." William had married a chef who chose to give up her career to be a full-time mother to their three kids. I concentrated on loading a chip with guacamole. "That's an important job, but it lends itself to being available to you as needed."

"Seriously? You haven't seen Hope's dry-erase board calendar. Baseball practice, dance lessons, art camp, swim meets, birthday parties, doctor's appointments, orthodontist appointments, driving lessons. She needs a chauffer's license. Hope works full time. She just doesn't get paid for it."

True. Hope was blessed that her husband recognized this fact. Many husbands didn't. "When the girls were young, Kristen handled all those duties *and* worked full time."

"Supermom." We recited the words in unison. "Superhero."

"Talk about a martyr complex. Kristen loved showing off her Supermom skills." William ordered a Bloody Mary and a shot of tequila. At my raised eyebrows he shrugged. "Hope is my designated driver tonight. I'm celebrating Mom's birthday. She made it—in spectacular fashion, I might add."

Andrew and I raised our glasses. "Here, here."

"So we're way off topic now." Andrew drew circles in the condensation on his glass of iced water. "What happened to telling Kristen you're considering filing for divorce?"

Hearing the words *filing for divorce* spoken aloud—even by someone else—made the hair on my arms stand up. I took another slug of soda. "I can't. Not now. It wouldn't be right."

"Bawk, bawk, bawk!"

"Sherri has cancer."

No one spoke for several seconds. Banjo, steel guitar, and mandolin riffs in the midst of mic checks signaled the impending start of the band's performance.

"That sucks." Andrew spoke first. "Really sucks."

"That's the understatement of the century."

"Did they catch it early?"

"That rarely happens. There's no diagnostic tool for ovarian cancer."

"At least she's already had her kids."

People always said stupid things when confronted with a cancer diagnosis. I'd learned that from Kristen. She said it was a reflex action. They didn't know what to say so they said the first thing that came to their minds. Invariably something stupid. "I think she'd like to be around to see her grandkids grow up."

"Sure, sure."

We sipped our beverages in silence for a few moments.

"Hey, it's the Tremaine boys. Three of them anyway."

I swiveled at the sound of Matt Caine's voice. Matt had been my best friend since college. He was also my partner in our architectural firm. A woman I hadn't met accompanied him. She was a looker with onyx-black hair that hung loose on her shoulders. She leaned against the bar and offered us a confident smile. Her turquoise eyes matched the color of a form-fitting dress that showed off her physical attributes.

I nodded to acknowledge her presence before I turned to Matt. "Long time no see, partner."

We'd met earlier in the office conference room over a Grubhub-delivered lunch of Thai curry to discuss preliminary plans for a new building on the UTSA downtown campus.

"We can never see enough of each other, I'm sure." Matt shot me a lazy grin, softening the sarcasm. With his dark-brown hair and brown eyes, he could've been mistaken for the sixth Tremaine brother—except for his shorter stature. He definitely had the confidence. "I wanted to introduce you to a friend, Pilar Lozano." He waved in his guest's general direction. "Pilar just moved down here from Chicago. She's an architect in the market for a job. She specializes in green architecture. I've scheduled her for an interview early next week."

Our firm specialized in environmental architecture—the kind that required zero-carbon buildings that would not negatively impact the environment. Was this some kind of off-the-cuff job interview? We'd hired three new employees in the last month, and we still had more business than we could handle. A good architect grounded in our specialty would be welcomed. "Great. I'll look forward to it."

"Me too." She held out her hand. I hastily wiped mine, damp from my drink, on my pants and shook it. Her smile widened in amusement. "It's good to meet you. I'm excited about the opportunity to interview."

An awkward pause followed—likely only awkward for me. I'd never been good at chitchat. Especially with women I didn't know. Fortunately, my brothers welcomed the new guest and made desultory conversation for a few moments.

"I'm starving." Andrew stood and pushed away from the bar. "Bring you a plate, bro?"

My appetite had fled when I learned of Sherri's diagnosis. "I'll grab something later."

William followed his big brother into the growing mass of people lined up at the tables where waiters filled their plates from warming pans. "I could eat." Matt took off after them. "You two get acquainted. If you have questions, Pilar, now is the time to ask them. Get a leg up on your interview. Daniel is no pushover. He likes to grill job applicants until they feel like blackened fish."

"My partner likes to overstate things." I studied my now-empty soda glass. "But I'm happy to answer any questions you might have."

"That would be nice, really, but I don't want to impose." Pilar moved to the stool closest to me. "I've done a few job interviews in my time. I'll figure it out."

Work-related questions would be easier than social banter. Pilar had to fall into the thirty-five to forty age range, so she'd been in the workforce for a reasonable chunk of time. "I don't mind. Tell me about yourself. Where are you currently employed?"

"You're here to enjoy your mother's seventy-fifth birthday, not conduct a job interview." She waved at the bartender, who nodded and went back to the margarita he was mixing for one of Mom's book club friends. "I'm perfectly happy to just chat the way one does at a party when you don't know anyone."

She was right, of course. I waited while she ordered a glass of Chardonnay, and the bartender refilled my glass with Diet Pepsi. "Matt said you were a friend, but you're interviewing for a job. I've known him since college, but I don't recall him mentioning your name. How do you know each other?"

"Actually, I'm his wife's second cousin. I grew up in Chicago so we're not that close. But when I realized I needed a fresh start, she invited me to stay with them while I scouted opportunities. Matt treats me like I'm his protégé." She rolled her eyes and chuckled. "I can handle myself professionally, but I do appreciate the social invites. Plus, they're both determined to cheer me up as my marriage had a nuclear meltdown."

That kind of fresh start. "I'm sorry about the nuclear meltdown. That must be hard."

Her eloquent shrug showed off muscular—yet elegant—bare shoulders. "Gorgeous weather for an outdoor party. February can be cold. Your parents lucked out."

Too personal, too quickly. Weather was a much better topic. "You never know in South Texas, but Dad was prepared to put up tents and have heaters, if need be."

"I understand you designed this house for your parents."

Another safe topic. "I did."

"It's beautiful. Clean lines. Fits seamlessly into the landscape." Pilar waved her hand with its long, delicate fingers toward the pool. "I haven't seen the inside, but I could live on this patio with the saltwater pool, hot tub, the full kitchen, and that view of the foothills."

"Thanks. This piece of land made it easy. Locally sourced materials are relatively easy to find here."

"Some architects would've tried to make the site fit the house."

"If my parents had wanted that, they would've found themselves another architect."

"How was it working with your parents?"

"It had its moments, but fortunately, my dad let my mom handle it. He gets what he wants at the ranch. And my mom is like me, a collaborator."

Or I was like her.

"I also saw the building you reimagined at the Pearl. Gorgeous."

We'd turned a stable into a music venue and bar without losing any of its historic features or charm. Or so said the owners. And I agreed. "One of my favorite projects."

"Did you always want to be an architect?"

After an astronaut phase followed by a brief flirtation with becoming an artist. "I think so. I just didn't know what it was called. I liked to draw. I was interested in ecology, botany, and history. I was a nerd. My brothers played football and did FFA and 4-H. I had two left feet and no interest in ranching. They insisted I was adopted. I'll give my dad credit. He tried to hide his disappointment, but I could see it."

"I get that. My siblings are all in the medical profession, like my dad and mom." A faint bitterness imbued her words. It matched her downturned lips. "My parents were actually disappointed I chose architecture."

"I was lucky. Mine hid it well."

"You've done well. You have your own firm." The hard lines of her own disappointment in her parents disappeared. "No one argues with success."

Mom and Dad hadn't tried—much. Especially when we opened a second office in Austin, where we now had twenty-plus employees.

"For the most part. It took a lot of years to get here." I'd done fifteen years with an excellent local firm. When Matt came to me with a proposal to join forces in a firm dedicated primarily to green architecture, I'd jumped at the chance. "San Antonio's very different from Chicago. That's quite a fresh start."

Her smile fading, Pilar sipped her wine. Another awkward pause.

"I'm sorry about your marriage. It must be incredibly painful."

"Thank you. We've been married seven years. Not that long when you think about it. We don't have any kids, no joint property, not even a pet in common. Yet somehow, Chicago doesn't seem big enough for the two of us. I couldn't get far enough away."

I could see that. How far would I have to go to leave behind the shadow Kristen cast over my life in San Antonio? To the edge of the earth.

"I'm sorry it's not working out."

"Thank you." She ducked her head and studied fingernails painted a shiny pearl color. "He's always working. He's a security consultant. He says his work is really important. Like mine isn't. His boss wants to know he can depend on him to make sure their clients' buildings are safe, their proprietary property is safe, whatever. He loves his job . . . I'm glad he does. So many people hate their jobs. I love what I do too. Just not . . ."

"Just not more than you love him."

"Exactly."

"I'm sorry about that too." Such lame words. I hardly knew Pilar, but her situation resonated. Too much. She had only seven years invested. I had twenty-four in my marriage, more in the relationship. Maybe she was right. Maybe getting out now would save her years of feelings of neglect, hurt, and bitterness that grew and grew until they overcame love and the willingness to overlook them in order to stay together.

"Don't be so sad." Pilar nudged me with her elbow. "I'm sorry. I shouldn't have unloaded on you. I don't know why I told you all that. Come on. This is a celebration. It's your mother's birthday. She's here, she's healthy, and she loves you."

Pilar motioned for the bartender, who came over with the bottle of Chardonnay. "My friend here will have what I'm having."

I shook my head. "I'm driving."

"Fine, then I'm going in search of ice cream." She stood. At six feet I'm fairly tall for a man. She matched my height. "This lady can fix you a root beer float. How does that sound?"

The bartender nodded. "Sure thing. Our motto is what the customer wants the customer gets—within reason."

"More my style," I conceded. "My girls always have root beer floats on their birthdays."

Kristen preferred hot fudge sundaes, heavy on the hot fudge. Knowing her, she and Sherri were eating them right now.

Pilar tossed her hair over her shoulder, cocked her head, and squinted at me as if taking a second or third gander. "You sure you don't want real food first?"

"Root beer floats *are* real food."

She grinned. "I knew I liked you. I'm on it. I'll be back with vanilla ice cream. I might even have some myself."

I swiveled on the stool so I could watch her thread her way through dozens of tables decorated with bouquets of sunflowers. Matt sat with his wife, who was drinking a humongous margarita. He cocked his head, his expression a question mark. Did he really think I could take stock of a potential employee at my mother's birthday party? So far, I liked what I'd heard, but I hadn't seen a résumé or checked references or talked architectural philosophy. I shrugged.

He nodded and went back to sipping on his wife's drink when she wasn't looking.

William and Andrew were seated at tables with their spouses and children. My other brothers, Leonard Jr. and Robert, and their broods chowed down across the aisle. Mom and Dad had the places of honor at the head table. Their best friends took turns toasting them. The only people missing were my wife and kids. Loneliness grabbed me in a headlock.

Around me everyone talked and laughed. At least a hundred people, probably more, eating, drinking, and making merry. The sounds faded. The images blurred. A person could be alone just about anywhere.

Get over it. This is Mom's day. Be happy for her. It's not about you.

Pilar returned, loaded down with two bowls of homemade vanilla ice cream, which our bartender turned into floats in a matter of seconds.

We alternately slurped and spooned while she plied me for stories she could later use against Matt. Given we'd roomed together throughout our formative college years, I had plenty, and given his decision to introduce me to Pilar, I was completely within my rights to share them.

"He really passed out in front of a bar on Sixth Street in the middle of the sidewalk with no pants on?"

"Yep. One of his finer moments. Or there was the time he tried to break into the dorm's cafeteria because he had the munchies at two o'clock in the morning. Fortunately, a custodian caught him before he actually could've been charged with breaking and entering and theft."

"My cousin knows about all these escapades and she still married him?"

"I think she figured if he survived all those crazy nights and near-death experiences, he must be good luck." I savored sweet melted ice cream mixed with the fizz of root beer. Kids had it right. Sugar highs were the best. "Plus, he was never a total screwup. He partied hard, but he studied harder. Architecture school is no cakewalk. He graduated with honors."

"And he had a good friend who had his back."

"Maybe."

"You're fortunate to have made a friend you've kept all these years. So much so you've gone into business together."

"No such friend for you?"

"My college roommate grew pot on the windowsill in our room. She majored in frat boys and beer pong. I had friends, but they got jobs in other cities. Or we grew apart. I guess that's why it'll be easy to leave Chicago."

Loneliness reverberated in her voice. How could a gorgeous, smart, funny woman like her be lonely? Easy. I was a smart, well-educated, semi-funny guy. I didn't claim to be good-looking, but I was passable. I was married yet I was still lonely. Maybe it was the world we lived in. Or maybe it was the choices we made.

I didn't want to know which.

The music died away. A squawk announced a newcomer at the

microphone. Pilar and I turned to face the portable stage. Andrew had the mic in his hand. The speechifying was about to begin.

At least I could offer her a friendly hand-up in the professional world—if she was indeed a qualified applicant. The firm was full of young, single architects who would welcome Pilar with open arms. She wouldn't lack for social opportunities or the chance to meet someone new. "I'm looking forward to interviewing you. I think you'd be a good fit."

She swiveled and looked me in the eye. "I'm so glad to hear that. Matt said the same thing. I'm coming by tomorrow to drop off my résumé and application."

I envied her, in a way. A fresh start sounded good. So good.

five

SHERRI

Any discussion of forgiveness would require a strong dose of caffeine first thing in the morning. Especially after a night filled with nightmares involving cemeteries and open graves. I poured coffee made from my favorite Costa Rican dark roast into a Minnie Mouse mug, added almond milk and stevia, and took it to the counter where Kris sat on a barstool, rubbing her baby-blue eyes. With her tousled pixie-cut blonde hair, UT T-shirt, and leggings, she could've been the college kid I shared an apartment with in Austin when we were both students, struggling to make ends meet. I set it in front of her. "So, I want to see Dad after I call the kids."

"Why?" Her tone was flat. "What does this have to do with him? And how do you even know where he is?"

Dad had bailed when I was ten and Kris six, only to reappear periodically after Mom died, acting like an avuncular friend offering unsolicited dating advice and the occasional check "to help out." He'd show up at our door with a pizza and Rollerblades in the wrong size or tickets to a baseball game on a school night or Barbie dolls for kids who'd outgrown them long ago. Mom's best friend, Tricia, who'd graciously taken us in at Mom's request, tolerated him because she thought we needed a father after losing our mother so young and so cruelly.

That was thirty-four years ago. I'd worked long and hard to forgive him. Where Kris stood on the subject was apparent. "He contacted me a few months ago after he fell and had to move into an assisted-living place on Stone Oak Parkway."

"And you raced right over there to hold his hand? Seriously?"

"He said he called you too."

"I was smart enough to ignore his voice mail. Why do you feel the need to tell him about this?"

Cleo rubbed her slinky body against my bare legs. Apparently, she'd forgiven me for uprooting her so abruptly and subjecting her to the hulking monstrosities known as Scout and Dash. The two offenders currently patrolled the backyard for birds. I swooped down and ran my hand down her sleek back. "Love you, too, Cleopatra Queen of Cats."

I straightened and turned to Kris. "Because no matter what happened in the past, he's still our father. The only one we've got. Do you want some toast? Do you have crunchy peanut butter?"

Kris set her mug down and scrutinized me like a tissue sample under a microscope. "A bagel."

"Peanut butter?"

She pointed to the pantry. "Crunchy and smooth with honey. If you want to get your heart broken again by him, that's your call, I suppose."

I swiped a Costco-sized jar from the shelf, grabbed a loaf of whole wheat bread along with a package of cinnamon-raisin bagels, and trotted back into the kitchen. "So you won't come with me?"

Kris studied her coffee like a fortune teller reading tea leaves. "If you need me to."

Her grudging tone notwithstanding, Kris meant it. She was a pro at gritting her teeth, lowering her head, and bulldozing through unpleasant tasks. An oncologist didn't have a choice. "It's not a matter of whether I need you to. When was the last time you saw him?"

She pursed her lips and rubbed her forehead.

I popped bread and bagels into the appropriate toaster slots and shoved the lever down. "If you have to think that hard, it's been too long." The scent of toasting bread soothed my soul. Mom considered bagels a food group. My throat ached at the thought. *I could sure use your company now, Ma.* "He lives thirty minutes from here."

In an assisted-living center where he had a degree of independence, but enough oversight that he wouldn't take a fall and lie on the floor for days before someone noticed.

"I sent him a birthday card in November."

"His birthday's in October."

Kris shrugged. "Close enough. It's the thought that counts."

"That's cold."

"Cold is never paying child support and letting her work herself to death to support us. Cold is—"

"I get it. I understand you're bitter—"

"And you aren't? Talk about forgetting birthdays. When was the last time he remembered yours or mine? Or one of his grandkids'? I'll bet you a weekend stay at a condo in Aransas Pass that he can't remember the names of both your nieces or all three of your kids."

"He's old and sick." Why was I defending him? Literally, because he was the only living relative left from our childhood. Because he was a fallible human being who was miserable in his old age. Because he knew he'd made mistakes, and it was too late for him to go back and fix them. I had some of those in my past as well. Because no one deserved to die alone.

The toast and bagels popped up together. I jumped up. "Peanut butter or cream cheese?"

"Half of each."

"That's how I know we're related." I offered her an air high five, which she returned with less enthusiasm. "Strawberry jam? Honey?"

"Both." Definitely my sister. We'd be twins if it weren't for the four-year age difference. "What was his excuse when Mom died?"

Kris refused to be distracted from the topic at hand. Also a trait I shared with her. "Wow. Have you considered that forgiveness tends to be as beneficial to the forgiver as the forgiven?"

"Save it for your Sunday school." She poured herself more coffee, added almond milk, and stirred. "Has he sought forgiveness? Is he repentant? Will he go and sin no more?"

"Tsk-tsk." I clicked my tongue against my teeth as I added another heaping spoon of stevia to her coffee. "Such cynicism. I definitely need to sweeten you up."

"I'm sorry. I don't mean to make fun of your faith. I'm hoping to ride your coattails into heaven someday. Someday far, far from now."

"It doesn't work that way." I loaded our goodies onto plates and settled onto a stool next to hers. "Where's Daniel?"

"Up and out the door for an early morning meeting." She carefully smoothed the cream cheese to the edges of her bagel. She was like that. Anal about the details. "Despite the fact that he didn't get home until after I was asleep last night. Did he seem . . . different to you?"

"Different how?" Happy to let the subject of our father simmer on a back burner—at least for now—I sipped my coffee and contemplated for a few seconds. "He has a few more gray hairs, and his teeth are so white they blind me. He should lay off the whitening trays."

"I don't mean like that." She fiddled with her T-shirt sleeves. "Like distant. Distracted. Cool."

"He almost broke my ribs with his hug." Daniel was an expert hugger. He'd been the one to teach Kris the art of hugging. We hadn't learned it at home. "He engaged with me. He took care of my baggage." I ticked each item off on my fingers. "He settled Cleo in my room, gave her food and water, and set up her litter box. He invited me to the birthday bash. Not distant, no ma'am."

"He seems different to me." She dabbed peanut butter from her bagel onto the cream cheese, swirled it around with a butter knife a few times, and added honey. Then she held the knife in the air, pausing in midswirl. "Like he has something to say, but he's not saying it. Like one of these days he might erupt like Mount Vesuvius and bury us both in searingly hot lava."

"That's quite a picture you're painting." If Daniel was harboring pent-up hostility, he hid it well when I landed on his doorstep. "Have you asked him about it?"

Dash and Scout appeared at the sliding glass doors. A polite *woof* was all Dash allowed himself. *Please, let us in.* Scout was more vociferous with a sharp bark that sent Cleo darting down the hallway toward the bedroom, clearly in a snit. Kris took her time letting them in. Both dogs headed for their water bowls and proceeded to sling liquid in all directions in their enthusiasm for quenching their thirsts. Her back to me, Kris watched them, head bent, for a few seconds. "He always says the same thing."

"What's that?"

"He says he wishes we had more time together."

My stomach clenched. I dropped my half-eaten bagel on the plate next to the toast. Time. *Bong, bong, bong.* "We all do."

"He means him and me. He thinks we don't spend enough time together. I think it's an empty-nester thing. The girls aren't around the house anymore. He misses them so he wants to fill his free time with me."

"Or maybe he really does miss spending time with his wife."

"He knows how all-consuming my job is."

"He's lived with it for twenty-four years."

"What's that supposed to mean?"

"Nothing. Nothing." Kris tended to be the center of her universe. It probably never occurred to her how hard it was for me to be single and alone at my age. Chance, my ex-husband, liked a twirl on the dance floor at his favorite honky-tonk bar or front-row seats at a monster truck rally. Not necessarily my idea of a good time, but he'd tried. Another person I needed to tell about my diagnosis. "Talk to him. Carve out a week in Cancún. You work too hard. So does he. Some R & R would be good for both of you."

"We'll see." Her somber gaze bounced from mine. "When are you going to tell the kids?"

Deflecting. Classic Kris.

"Soon. Today, I guess. Is it something you tell your kids over the phone? I'd like to have some time to eat a meal with them, visit, chat, then ease into it. A phone call seems so cold."

I wouldn't be there to hug them, reassure them, love them.

"You can't fly to Chicago or Fort Bragg or Germany right now." Ever the practical one, Kris pointed out the obvious. "I know you still think of them as kids, but they're adults. They can handle it."

A bite of peanut butter toast turned dry and thick. I struggled to swallow it. "Being an adult has nothing to do with it. Telling you sucked and you're an oncologist."

"Telling people about your diagnosis is hard. Pace yourself." Kristen had slipped back into doctor mode.

I turned my back to her and went to freshen up my cooling coffee. I needed to fortify myself.

six

SHERRI

I started with child number one because Noelle would be the easiest—and the hardest—to tell. Her smiling face and dimples filled my iPad screen on the first ring. A wonderful sight to be sure, but it would've been easier if she hadn't answered. *Coward. Better to get it over with. For whom?* I plastered a smile on my face. "Hey, how's it going?"

"Going good, for the most part, Ma. Your timing is perfect. Max just woke up from his nap."

Noelle grinned, showing off a set of even, straight teeth made possible by two years of megapayments to an orthodontist. Like her younger brother, Cody, Noelle favored Chance with his chestnut hair—before it had turned gray—fair complexion, brown eyes, and lean body. She wore her usual attire of a T-shirt stained with paint and leggings—not that I could see her legs on the screen.

"Gracie's at Mother's Day Out." She glanced at her smartwatch. "For another hour and ten minutes. Thank goodness. That girl was in a mood this morning. Max, say hi to Grandma."

Noelle held her phone so Max's face filled the screen. His wild brown locks, sleepy eyes, and pink cheeks attested to her statement that he'd just woken up. "Hi, Granmol." He laid his head on Noelle's shoulder. "It snow here."

He was so stinking cute in his fleece dinosaur jammies. I couldn't stand it. Grief gutted me. All the memories we might not make together. *Stay positive. Be realistic. Pray. Hope. Keep it together.* I sucked in a breath. *Get a grip.* "Hey, Max. Snow is fun. Did you make a snowman with Gracie?"

Rather than responding, he hid his head in Noelle's chest.

"He's been running a fever off and on, so he's not his usual sunny self. We haven't been doing any playing outside. It's only eight degrees." Noelle rubbed his back and kissed his cheek. "You want some water and some Goldfish, Max?"

Max straightened, suddenly looking more chipper. The screen wobbled as she stood, hefted the three-year-old on her hip, and trotted into their breakfast nook. The phone swung dizzily in Noelle's grasp, quickly showcasing the tile floor, the table covered with Noelle's art supplies, and finally, the booster seat attached to a chair pulled up to the table.

Noelle filled Max's Paw Patrol bottle with water and dumped cheddar Goldfish onto a napkin. She grabbed a travel mug and took a long swig. "I need my caffeine by the gallon when a sick baby keeps me awake half the night. Of course, Zach has no trouble sleeping through both kids' nighttime sniffles." She ruffled Max's hair, then collapsed into a chair.

"I'm so glad you called. I got a contract with a local nonprofit agency to do a mural in their lobby. I'm so psyched. They want something big and splashy and vibrant with wild animals and jungle plants. I'm chomping at the bit to get started."

"That's fabulous." She was the creative one among my children. "You'll have to send me photos as you work on it so I can see your progress."

"I'll post them on Facebook. I'm up to ten thousand followers now. The cool thing is the agency is good with me bringing the kids. They have space for kids to explore their own artistic talents." She took another swallow of coffee. Her smile faded, replaced with a slight frown. "Today's Wednesday, isn't it? I lose track of the days. Yes, it's Wednesday because Gracie's at Mother's Day Out. Which means it can't be a holiday. Why aren't you at school?"

I heaved a breath. My heart tripped and sped up. My mouth was so dry, my tongue stuck to the roof of my mouth. The phone weighed a hundred pounds. Max's tuneless rendition of "The Itsy Bitsy Spider," missing words here and there, filled the space.

"Mom?"

"I wanted to tell you something." I shifted in the office chair. Its wheels squeaked. I studied the framed photo of Kris, Daniel, Brie, and Maddie, with the Gulf of Mexico crashing against the beach behind them. *Stop stalling.* "I had some medical tests done and the results came back yesterday—"

"Wait. This sounds like a grown-up conversation." Noelle sprang up and strode away from the table. She disappeared for a second, then reappeared with the kitchen sink behind her. "Okay, what's going on?"

Like a three-year-old would understand the word *cancer*. I was thankful Max and Gracie would be spared that worry. I cleared my throat and delivered the news. "I don't want you to worry about me. I'll be fine. My oncologist says it's highly treatable. So does your aunt Kris."

"I knew something was up when you didn't text me back yesterday." Noelle's face crumpled. She shook her head. The screen tilted crazily, then righted. "So they caught it early then?"

Noelle texted or called me every day. It was rare that a day went by when we didn't communicate in some form or fashion. She was my best friend. Right now, she needed her mother. "Not exactly, but they've made huge strides in cancer treatment in the last ten years." Every muscle in my body fought to escape these four walls and race to

Chicago to deliver a hug. Telling her over the phone was wrong. "Plus, I have Aunt Kris to help me. You know she's at the top of her game on the latest treatments and clinical trials."

"Clinical trials?" Noelle's sobs exploded. "Are you gonna die, Mom?"

"Whoa, whoa!" I clutched the phone closer as if she could feel my hands and find solace in my touch through that small, rectangular device. "Nobody said anything about dying. Clinical trials aren't a last resort anymore. We don't have to talk about all the nitty-gritty stuff right now. Aunt Kris has it all mapped out. She's found me a great surgeon here in San Antonio. And an oncologist. I'm seeing her Monday, so I can start chemo as soon as I get my port installed—"

"Port? What's a port?" Noelle wailed. Max's cries mingled with hers. She clasped her hand over her mouth for a second, shook her head, then removed it. "It's okay, Bubbas, Mommy's fine."

More fumbling with the phone. Then Max reappeared. "See. Grandma's still here. Tell her how old you are."

She blew her nose in the background while Max contemplated the question. He popped a Goldfish in his mouth and chewed. "I don't know."

"You do too. Tell Grandma how old you are."

"Three." He held up the requisite number of chubby fingers. "Baby three."

"How old is Mommy?"

"I don't know."

"I think you do. How old is Mommy?"

"Three."

"How old is Grandma?"

Max cocked his head and grinned at the screen. "Granmol three. Like baby."

"You're not a baby. You're Max."

"Not Max. Baby."

"For now. Do you want some more Goldfish?"

"Cookie."

"Cookie wasn't the offer."

"Cookie."

Noelle reappeared on the screen. "I think we could both use a cookie. Don't you, Grandma?"

I didn't tell her I'd eaten a banana split and a fudge sundae the previous evening. "A cookie might be just what Grandma ordered." I was the mom who baked for every Girl Scout meeting, birthday party, bake sale fund-raiser, team party, and broken-heart pity party. "I'm partial to snickerdoodles myself."

"Max likes peanut butter." Noelle blotted her eyes with a balled-up tissue. "You seemed great at Christmas. Like, in perfect health. Same as always."

We'd all converged at Cody's house in Fayetteville for the holidays: Cody, his wife, and their two rug rats; Noelle and Zach and their two kids; even Jason had managed leave before deploying to Germany. "I've been having stomach troubles and bathroom issues. The doctor thought I had IBS. Turns out he was wrong. But I feel fine. I feel good."

"I'll come home. I'll have to bring the kids, though. Zach is working a lot of hours at the base."

Her husband was in the U.S. Navy. He did something with new recruits at the base outside Chicago. "It's not necessary." I loved visiting them. But not now. Not while I was in treatment. That could be six months at a minimum. "You take care of my grandkids and your husband. I have your aunt and uncle and my friends from school and church. I have a support system."

"I'm your daughter. I should be there for you." Noelle handed Max a cookie. She placed a second one on a napkin on the table. "You've always taken care of me. It's my turn." Her voice broke.

"Please, honey, don't cry. It'll be okay. I'll be fine." One way or another. That's what my Sunday school leader, Mona, would say. If I didn't get healing on earth, I would experience complete healing in heaven. That should be comforting, but all I could think of was Max and Gracie forgetting me after a few years. "I'm not going anywhere. I plan to watch Gracie and Max grow up."

"So come here. Let me take care of you. I know Aunt Kris is an oncologist, but she's got her hands full with her practice, and there are outstanding oncologists in Chicago—some of the best."

"I appreciate the offer, but I have a job in Kerrville, and I plan to return to it."

"You could get certified to teach here. They're desperate for teachers. Even taking alternative certification."

"I could, but this doesn't seem like the time to reinvent the wheel."

"Yeah, but you'd be able to spend your free time with your grand-babies. Both of them, maybe even more in the future."

"What do you mean more?"

"Zach and I were talking, and suddenly we realized that we both aren't ready to be done having babies."

"You have two, a boy and a girl. You said one of each was perfect."

"Yeah, well, Zach has two brothers and sisters. I had two brothers. We just realized we want Gracie and Max to have more siblings."

"More siblings, as in plural?"

"I don't know. You know how I love being a mommy. Anyway, we're having fun trying again, and we'll just see what happens."

Max whimpered. She undid the strap on his booster seat and swung him into her arms. "It's okay, Bubbas. It's okay. Mommy's fine. I'm happy."

More grandbabies. Nothing would make me happier. I clenched my jaw to keep from sobbing. I would wait until another time to tell Noelle she was now at far greater risk for getting ovarian cancer, as was Gracie and any future daughters. "I have to agree that making babies is fun, but paying for them, not as much. Not that I want to think about my daughter and her husband—"

"Eww. Enough said, Ma."

We both giggled.

"I really want you to come stay with us, Mom. I miss going to the movies with you and hunting for clothes in the vintage shops and planting wildflowers."

"Then you need to move here. We could plant wildflowers until the cows come home."

Something more likely to happen in Texas than Chicago.

"Zach's family is here. He'll never live in Texas. He says he doesn't want our kids educated there either."

Not having that conversation. "Then we'll have to make do with visits, my friend."

"When?"

"It all depends on my treatment schedule."

And my counts. I was about to enter the immunocompromised club.

"Have you told the boys?"

"They're next. Have you talked to them recently?"

Noelle switched the phone to her other hand. She stood and wandered into the living room. Max made *choo-choo* noises interspersed with crashes and bangs. Noelle sank onto the floor next to him, her back against the couch. "Not Jason since Christmas, but I talk to Cody all the time."

"How is he doing?"

"He sounded good. Upbeat. You know Cody, he never has much to say." She picked up a Matchbox car and ran it across the tile so it bumped into Max's legs. Giggling, he added it to a row of them on his train track table. "He says he'll be stationed at Fort Bragg for at least another two years. Cais may have to deploy again before that."

Having both spouses in the military was a challenge, but Cody and his wife handled it well. I was the one who worried. It was like having another child at risk when the mother of my grandchildren deployed. "I hope not. The kids are so young."

"They've never known anything different. They're military brats. And they love Cais's parents." Noelle scooped up Max and pulled him into her lap. He complained, but she smothered him in kisses anyway. "Just say the word and I'll come home."

"I know you will. You just take care of my grandkids. I better be the first one you tell when you get pregnant with number three—after Zach, of course."

"Max, can you tell Grandma you love her?"

"Love you, Granmol."

"You're so sweet. Love you too." I threw him kisses. He returned the favor. Grandbaby kisses were the best. "Be good for Mommy. Feel better."

"I love you, Mom." Noelle's voice quivered. She blew me a kiss too. "Call me after you see the oncologist in San Antonio."

I kept blowing kisses until the screen went black.

I would live for baby kisses.

seven

DANIEL

Still mumbling to myself about the skyrocketing cost of chicken breasts, I juggled two canvas bags of groceries and managed to shove open the door from the garage to the kitchen with my elbow. Between avian flu and pervasive inflation, groceries were getting almost as ridiculous as the price of gas. Fortunately, somebody— meaning Kristen—hadn't pushed the door completely shut at some point during the day. Which meant she hadn't set the alarm either.

"Kristen?" I called as I turned to set the bags on the granite-topped island that held the place of honor in the kitchen I'd designed for myself—since I did all the cooking. Double ovens, stainless steel, mammoth refrigerator, a sink in the island, a pot-filler faucet over the gas stove, a high-end dishwasher—everything a would-be chef could want. "Kristen, where are you? I need to know what time you want to eat . . ."

My voice trailed away. She had to be here. Her SUV was in the garage. Plus, the scintillating aroma of beef and possibly ginger mingled with onion and garlic was tickling my nose. I marched over to the stove where my favorite wok held chunks of beef, bok choy, green beans, mung beans, carrots, broccoli, and porcini mushrooms. "Kristen? Where are you? You won't believe how much—"

"Here! I'm here!"

Her voice and the dogs preceded her actual appearance. Dash and Scout charged into the kitchen, tails going wild, their nails clicking on the dark hardwood floor. They didn't bark. They were far too well-behaved for that, but they did lick and nudge my hands. I knelt to wrap them in body hugs. "Hey, boys, I missed you too. You're such good dogs, guarding the house all day long. I'm so glad to see you."

All smiles, Kristen padded into the kitchen barefoot, dressed in an oversized burgundy T-shirt and black leggings. She looked every bit as enticing as she had when I turned around and accidently whacked her with a two-by-four at a Habitat for Humanity build almost twenty-six years ago. "Dinner is almost ready. The rice needs to finish steaming. I fixed a fruit salad. I think we have some spring rolls we can heat in the microwave."

"Dinner is almost ready?" I rose and cocked my head toward the bags. "I braved the after-work crowd at H-E-B for the stuff to make Caesar salads. I planned to cook the chicken breasts on the grill."

"Sherri's in the mood for Chinese stir-fry. She hasn't had much appetite, and she's lost ten pounds, so I thought it would be best to make something that sounded good to her."

Whatever Sherri needed was fine by me. I let the dogs out before they decided to plant themselves next to the stove in hopes that a tasty morsel would fall to the floor. "I wish you would've let me know. I could've picked up the stuff when I stopped at the store. I love my H-E-B, but man, it was a zoo this evening."

"I tried to call you, but you didn't answer, and it said your voice mail was full."

"My bad. Shall I freeze the chicken, or do you want me to make the salad tomorrow night? I bought two bags of precut romaine. We need to use it pretty quickly."

"Let's play it by ear, shall we?" She stirred the veggies and beef, then took a bite of the beef. "Yum. Sherri will love this. She's a big fan of fresh vegetables."

While Kristen was *not*. Her idea of a good meal with a vegetable was a BLT—heavy on the bacon and mayo, light on the lettuce. The tomato served as her fruit for the meal. Maybe because of her chosen field, she seemed to take a fatalistic approach to diet and exercise. "Where's Sherri? And who are you and what have you done with my wife?"

"She went for a run. She's been gone for almost an hour." Kristen peeked at the steaming rice by lifting the lid just a tad and lowering it before all the steam escaped. "She should be back any minute. I can cook. I've also been known to eat vegetables if they have enough spices and soy sauce on them."

In the early years we had a deal. Whoever arrived home first cooked. That was almost always me. When Kristen knew she'd be home first, her MO was to pick up takeout—mostly pizza. After the kids were born, I handled drop-off and pickup at the day care and much of the cooking, while Kristen did baths, story time, and bedtime. "Not really. At least, not so I've noticed."

"I'd think you'd be happy to have a break." She grabbed plates from the door-less cabinets that lined the walls between the refrigerator and the dishwasher. "I thought we'd eat in the breakfast nook instead of the dining room. Cozier and easier for cleanup."

"Fine by me."

"Are you mad that I cooked?"

I unloaded the chicken into the freezer before I answered. "Not at all. Just surprised."

"You sound a little jealous that I never found the time to cook for you."

"That might be your guilty conscience talking." I stowed the lettuce in the vegetable bin and the shredded Parmesan with the other cheeses. "I knew going in you weren't Martha Stewart."

"What's that supposed to mean?" Now she sounded PO'd. "I decorated the bedrooms, didn't I, and planted the garden?"

"With my mother's help. But that's neither here nor there. We're way off topic." I reined in a sudden rush of irritation that came out of nowhere. Was she right? Was I jealous because my wife was cooking for her sister, who had a deadly disease? That was ludicrous. *Get your act together, bud.* "I didn't mean to insult you. If cooking for your sister makes you feel good, I'm all for it, but pace yourself."

She slapped napkins on the table and added forks. "What's that supposed to mean?"

"You're coordinating her medical care, navigating for her, right?"

"Absolutely. That's my area of expertise—"

"Exactly. So let me help by doing what I can do, which is get groceries, cook, and take care of the dogs."

"You worked all day. I didn't."

"Are you taking a leave of absence?" Something else she hadn't communicated to me. "Is Texas Cancer Care Clinic okay with that?"

"Not exactly. I'm doing a sort of half-on, half-off thing. Tasha's covering some of my patients, and new patients are being referred. I'm still figuring it out. I'll know more when we get a schedule for Sherri's treatment and her surgery. Then I can work around it."

Still determined to keep all the balls in the air—except the one with *wife/marriage* written in pencil on it.

She slipped past me, close enough to touch my arm or stop off for a kiss, but she didn't. Gone were the days when she kissed and hugged me every time our paths crossed after being apart. Gone were the days of holding hands at the farmer's market where we thumped melons and squeezed grapefruits to the sound of homegrown blues from a live band. I was to blame as well. I could've caught her arm and drawn her close for a hug. But I didn't. Why not? For fear of a rebuff? Or to find no heat in that long-overdue kiss?

She took a pitcher of tea from the refrigerator and turned to drill me with a frown. "Surely you don't mind not having to cook for a change. I would think it would be a nice reprieve."

I enjoyed cooking for family dinners in the early days. Then Maddie had softball, basketball, and track. Brielle had dance, theater arts, and orchestra. Then they got cars and jobs. The more they bowed out, the more Kristen felt free to work late. On average, the four of us ate together two nights a week—or less during UIL competition, finals, recitals, plays, performances, and state tournaments.

"I enjoy cooking." I snatched some grapes from a bowl of fresh fruit on the island. They were plump, fresh, and sweet. I focused on their taste for a few seconds while I gathered my wits. "I also enjoy traveling with my wife."

"What? That's what they call forcing a segue." She spooned the stir-fry into a large serving bowl. "Will you bring the rice? There's soy sauce and hoisin sauce in the fridge."

Taking care of the rice gave me something to do while I marshaled my arguments. "We talked about doing something special for our twenty-fifth anniversary."

"Do we have to talk about that right now? Our anniversary isn't until September." She ran her free hand through her short hair in an impatient gesture as she turned to face me. "As you just pointed out, I have a lot on my plate. So much depends on how Sherri's cancer responds to treatment and how optimal the surgery is."

"I totally understand that. It's just that we have to book the trip now or the hotels will be full and the flights will be more expensive." Dad's advice echoed in my ears. Big romantic gestures. Maybe we needed to get jolted from our rut. "I thought instead of going to Cancún like we always do, we could try a European cruise. Or a tour of England, Scotland, and Ireland. You've always wanted to go to Ireland."

"That sounds like more than a week's trip." Her nose wrinkled, Kristen again brushed past me without a second glance, headed toward the table with the pitcher. Her tone was skeptical. "I really can't take off more than a week. You know that. Especially now."

"Take off a week for what?" Sherri trotted into the kitchen. Her face shone bright red. Sweat soaked her blue CHRIST IS RISEN T-shirt and white spandex running shorts. For a woman facing down stage 4 cancer at age fifty-two, she glowed with health. She slowed, then started backing up. "Am I interrupting something? I can take a shower—"

"No, you're fine. Dinner's ready. Chinese stir-fry." Kristen gestured toward the table with an elaborate flourish. "It's hot and it's on the table."

"Are you sure you don't want me to clean up first?" Sherri wiped her face with a sodden towel, then took a swig from her neon-green water bottle. "I'm sure I stink to high heaven."

"We'll use clothespins on our noses." I pasted a smile on my face. "Kristen's made a feast. Let's eat while it's hot."

So we did. Kristen went out of her way to be chatty—also not her norm. She ignored consecutive *dings* from her smartphone telling her she was getting texts. All this effort was for her sister. She of all people knew how short time was. Yet she had none for her husband.

I drank half a glass of tea. This was not the time or the place to air my grievances. "How was your run, Sher?"

"Good, good. I wondered if I would have the energy and stamina I've always had." She heaped veggies and beef on her plate but let the rice bowl go by without serving herself. "I was afraid of the power of suggestion. I have a horrible disease ravaging my body. Shouldn't I feel like it? But I don't have any symptoms to speak of—other than being a little short of breath."

"That's why ovarian cancer is so often diagnosed in late stages." Kristen pushed her veggies around on her plate but didn't actually move the fork to her mouth. "Or is misdiagnosed. It's good that you feel like exercising, though. It's a fantastic way of beating stress. Keeping your body strong will help for the long haul too."

"Yes, Doctor." Sherri's grin took the sting from her sarcasm. "You should eat your vegetables. When was the last time you worked out? Or had a physical?"

Kristen selected a chunk of beef and popped it in her mouth. She took her time chewing and swallowing. "Don't turn this around on me, sis. I had a clean bill of health from my PCP on my last physical. He said I'm the picture of health, in fact." She shot me a warning sign. I closed my mouth. She had failed to mention that physical was two years ago. "I walked the dogs this morning, remember? While you were making your phone calls, I was endeavoring to restrain one hundred forty pounds of canine instinct from chasing squirrels, annihilating a rabbit, and sniffing every fire hydrant, tree, and bush on a four-mile circuit."

"I suppose that counts. Enough about us." Sherri waved her fork toward me. "How goes it in the land of architecture? How was your day?"

"Good. We landed another client—a big one. A local corporation is expanding their footprint downtown with a second headquarters. They want a zero-carbon, LEED-certified building." Their eyes quickly glazed over. Not everyone could muster my excitement over local sourcing. "It'll be a challenge in that location, but it's exciting. Thanks for asking."

"That's right down your alley." Kristen picked up her tea glass and toasted me. "Congratulations. I guess you'll be super busy for the next several months—or years."

"Not so busy I can't book a trip." I was adept at catching Kristen's thought waves, even when we weren't on the same one. "This is our silver anniversary. It's a big milestone, worthy of celebration. And we can afford to take a real honeymoon. I think twenty-five years is long enough to wait."

"Is that what you were talking about when I so rudely interrupted?" Sherri's gaze bounced from me to Kristen and back. "Definitely. It's in September, right? You had such a beautiful wedding."

Because Kristen had no family other than Sherri and an absentee father, my parents insisted on paying for the wedding, and they never do anything halfway. Kristen's memories were less shiny, mostly along the lines of having little or no say in any of the details. We were married at the ranch on a warm fall afternoon under a pergola decorated with honeysuckle vines followed by a massive dance and reception under twinkling lights in an enormous white tent.

An endless supply of champagne and wine, a menu of filet mignon, lobster, baked potatoes, and myriad other side dishes, followed by the cutting of a five-tier white wedding cake surrounded by smaller cakes in every flavor. Then it was time to dance to a band that played everything from Sinatra to Springsteen to Whitney Houston. The evening concluded with a fireworks display that lasted twenty-five minutes.

Memorable? Yes. Overwhelming? Possibly. Likely for Kristen, who knew me and my family and a few of her friends from medical school but none of the other more than one hundred guests. Her father had been a no-show. Sherri had walked her sister down the aisle.

"It is and it was," I answered when Kristen didn't. I patted my mouth with my napkin and dropped it on my plate. The expression on my wife's face made my appetite wither. "We were trying to decide where to go."

Or whether to go at all.

"Have some more stir-fry, sis. The fresh ginger is good for what ails you." Kristen nudged the bowl in her sister's direction. "But leave room for the fruit salad. The blueberries, strawberries, and raspberries are full of antioxidants. They're great disease-fighters."

"Yes, Doctor."

Sherri and I chuckled. Kristen didn't. I shook my finger at her in mock disgust. "You need to eat your vegetables and your fruit, little girl, or no dessert for you."

"I can live with that." She pushed her plate away. "I cooked. You get cleanup duty."

"You're not getting away with changing the subject that easily." Sherri mimicked my finger-shaking routine. "You need to clear your schedule in September. Celebrate twenty-five years! I wish Chance and I had made it that far—or farther. When so many of your friends who married around the same time as you have been divorced for years, you're still hanging in there. That deserves a celebration."

"Who said we weren't celebrating? We'll celebrate, I promise." Kristen shoved her chair back and stood. "I forgot something in the car. I'll be back."

She slipped through the garage door and disappeared.

"Was it something *I* said?" Sherri grinned at me like a co-conspirator. "She doesn't like for us to gang up on her—about her eating habits or her workaholic habits. I guess you put up with a lot of that doctor-knows-best talk from her. You must be used to it."

"Yep. It doesn't have much effect on me since I'm the one who eats healthy and works out in the first place." I cocked my head toward the garage door. "Just so you know, she didn't leave anything in the garage."

"I know. She's having a smoke."

The most egregiously incomprehensible fact about my oncologist wife? Her secret smoking habit. She didn't partake on the regular—only when she got stressed. She claimed she'd quit when we got married, but I still smelled it on her clothes and tasted it on her lips more often than I should. "You knew she still smokes?"

"She insists she quit and that having a cigarette once in a while doesn't count." Sherri nibbled at a strawberry. "I smelled it on her yesterday when I got here and today when she came back from her walk with the dogs. So much for a healthy activity."

"She would tell you that the walk cancels out the ill effects of the cigarette."

"Our grandpa on our mom's side died of lung cancer. I bet she never told you that."

I shook my head. "Nope. She didn't talk much about anything or anybody prior to us meeting—except you. It's like she came into existence when I smacked her with the board."

"Such a romantic meet-cute." Sherri leaned back in her chair and sighed. "I tried so hard to make her life normal after Mom died. So did Tricia. Maybe because she was younger, Kristen didn't bounce back as easily as I did."

A bit of revisionist history, I suspected. Sherri had a tender heart, one of the reasons she made such a great kindergarten teacher. She'd shouldered the brunt of caring for her mother during the last days of her illness. The wounds likely healed slowly. "You did your best. Kristen was blessed to have you."

"That's nice of you to say." Sudden tears wet her eyes. She shook her head. "I'm so emotional, it's ridiculous. Sorry."

"Don't apologize. You've had a hard day. I can't imagine having to break that kind of news to our kids. How'd it go?"

She shrugged, but those tears teetered and threatened to fall. She dabbed at her eyes with her napkin. "I'm a mess. I've only talked to Noelle so far. She cried. She wanted me to come stay with her. Then she wanted to come here. Of course, I told her no. She has a life up there."

Her head bent, and she picked at the remaining fruit on her plate. "I had to wait for Cody to be home tonight and figure out the time difference for Jason in Germany."

"I told Maddie. I hope that's okay."

"Of course."

"She wanted to come home too."

"I know it's because they care, which means the world to me. I feel like a jerk for telling them to stay away." Sherri studied her plate as if she would find answers to a world of problems there. "I've always wanted them to live closer. I want to see my grandkids ten times a week. I practically beg them to come. I go visit them every chance I get. Now I'm telling them to stay away. Thank you for opening your home to me. I know it's an inconvenience."

I didn't need thanks for doing the right thing. "Are you kidding? I'm glad you have Kristen to help you with this. I would've insisted you stay here."

"You haven't cleaned up yet?" Kristen barged into the kitchen, bringing with her the distinct stench of cigarette smoke. Her cool gaze traveled to Sherri. "I thought you were going to take a shower so we can finish watching *You've Got Mail*."

"Actually, I need to call Cody before the kids go to bed, but I want to clean up first." Sherri grabbed Kristen's plate and stacked it on top of hers. Neither woman had eaten much. "It's only fair. You cooked. Dan worked all day. I loafed. You two go spend some time together."

"Thanks, but I'll do the cleanup. Maybe Kristen and I can do it together. It'll be like old times." I stood and tugged the plates from her. We used to talk over our days while loading the dishwasher when the kids were little and went to bed early. Did that qualify as the good old days? "You've had a stressful day. I like cleaning up."

"You married a good man, sis."

Sherri's words lingered in the air a few seconds too long—long enough to be classified as an awkward pause. "Yep." Kristen's lips barely moved to allow the single-syllable response to pass through them.

"I need to shower and make that call." Sherri edged toward the hallway. "Thanks for cooking, sis. After I make that call, I think I'll read. I have a William Kent Krueger mystery calling my name."

She hightailed from the kitchen without a backward glance.

"I guess I'll take the dogs around the block one more time." Kristen grabbed their leashes from the hooks next to the back door. "Unless you want me to help load the dishwasher."

Her tone was stiff and polite. I surveyed the counters. She'd dirtied an inordinate amount of pots, pans, and dishes, but she had cooked.

Our pact was a time-honored tradition. "No, go on, take a walk . . . unless you *want* to help."

Kristen shoved open the French doors that led to the terrace. "I need to stretch my legs."

And she was gone too.

"Love you too." My voice reverberated in the emptiness. Or maybe that was my overactive imagination. "See you around."

eight

KRISTEN

"How does Roy afford to live here?"

I posed the question as I maneuvered my Leaf into a parking space several rows back from the entrance to Gardenside Manor. Dad's latest residence lived up to its name. Showy pride of Barbados, esperanza, and Texas sage mingled with coral honeysuckle and vincas. A person might not even notice ASSISTED LIVING COMPLEX in smaller letters under the fancy font announcing the facility on a huge stone-framed sign. I really wanted to know how our dad afforded the place, but my question also forestalled further questioning from Sherri regarding the chill in the air during the previous evening over dinner.

I'd been unduly prickly, I was willing to admit, during dinner. I preferred not to delve into why. Daniel had been asleep—or was pretending to be—by the time I showered and went to bed.

"Stop calling our dad Roy." Sherri let go of the door handle she'd clutched much of the drive on Loop 1604 to Stone Oak Parkway, where the facility was located. She'd never appreciated my efficient driving techniques. "I have no idea what his financial situation is. Until I called him yesterday, I hadn't spoken to him since he got in touch to tell me he was moving into assisted living, but he's still our father."

I contemplated that fact. Something about a bad fall and a motor neuron disease diagnosis. I hadn't listened closely when Sherri shared that information with me more than a year ago. Dad knew better than to call me. "There's a difference between being a father and being a sperm donor."

"I'm aware. I have three kids, remember." Sherri's tone was weary. She rubbed her eyes. "Being a father involves having a relationship with the child. The kind of relationship Dan has with your daughters."

Now she sounded angry. At me? Or at the way her life had turned out? Her divorce from Chance had taken everyone by surprise. They had seemed happy. After more than eleven years, surely the demise of her marriage didn't rankle as much as it once had. "Your divorce aside, I always thought he was a good dad." Chance was a decent guy. At least he appeared to be, but a sister always took her sibling's side. "He coached Little League. He attended every recital and every play. He insisted on joint custody when you two split. He stuck around."

"He was. He still is. The kids adore him." She leaned her head against the passenger-side window. She claimed to have slept fine, but the dark circles and bags under her eyes told a different story. "He taught all three to hunt and fish. He coached baseball teams. He taught them to drive. He was present."

Yet he'd bailed on her.

"Are you sure you're okay? You seem out of sorts this morning."

"The calls last night were tough. Both Cody and Jason wanted to use emergency family leave to come home. I told them no."

"Are you regretting that?"

"No. They may need it later. But I talked to Xander and Lucas. They're getting so big. They're crazy funny." Sherri's grandsons were five and seven, if memory served. "They want me to come back to Fort Bragg and play games with them like I did at Christmas."

"And you're wondering if you will get that chance."

"Yes, I'm wondering."

"I try never to make promises to patients I can't keep. But this I can promise. You will see them again. You'll play games with them again."

Even if she didn't live to see them grow up. No one had that guarantee—cancer diagnosis or not.

At the facility's glass double doors, I posed my original question again. "Tell me again how he affords this. He always claimed to be penniless when the attorney general went after him for child support."

"That was a long time ago." Sherri stepped aside and held the door for a young guy in jeans and an Ed Sheeran T-shirt, pushing a white-haired woman's wheelchair into the building. "Try to remember that, okay? For me. After baseball, he worked in the oil fields, he drove trucks, he sold cars. He did a lot of different things to make a living. He always worked hard."

"How do you know?"

"Grandma Miller told Mom who told me."

"How come no one told me?"

"You were a kid. I think Grandma Miller felt bad about Dad walking out—"

"He didn't walk; he ran like a guy stealing home on a wild pitch."

"He'd call her and then she'd call Mom. She said she tried to get him to come home. She tried to get him to call Mom, but he said he couldn't. He was ashamed he couldn't do better by us."

"What a coward."

"Not a coward. Just not meant to be a parent, I guess. The best thing you can do for yourself is forgive him. You'll feel better. Why carry that baggage around?"

"Yes, Saint Sherri."

"Stop. Be civil."

Mom had named Sherri and me the beneficiaries on a small life insurance policy that helped us get our start in the world without her.

She'd even taken care of her own arrangements. Mom had known we wouldn't be able to depend on Dad. He'd moved around, which made it hard for the Texas attorney general to track him down and throw his behind in jail for being in arrears on child support. "Like I said, I'll try."

The foyer opened up into a spacious lobby with seating areas with sofas, overstuffed chairs, and round tables on both sides. Four men engaged in a spirited card game at one table. A woman dressed to the hilt in a two-piece suit, pearls, and a matching hat sat at a piano, fingering the keys and humming. I sniffed the air. No smell of cleanser or urine—the two smells I associated with nursing homes. "This is nice. Too nice for Roy—Dad."

"Stop."

We signed in and followed the receptionist's instructions to find Dad's one-bedroom apartment down a long hallway painted a cheerful blue and with a vinyl floor with a geometric design in a variety of matching shades. ROY MILLER in an ornate calligraphy on the door told us we'd arrived.

No one answered Sherri's knock.

Woot! "He's not here. Let's go."

"He's here. I told him we'd be here around nine. Give him a minute."

Sherri knocked again. "Dad? It's me, Sherri."

"Coming."

Not anytime soon. After several minutes, the door opened.

The man standing in front of me was a stranger. The larger-than-life guy who lived in my memories was gone. This guy wore gray sweats and a Texas Rangers muscle shirt. He hunched over a metal walker. His lined face, half hidden by a white beard, was pale, making his slate-blue eyes seem even bigger. An old bruise on his cheek had turned yellow and green. The tanned six-pack, pecs, and biceps he'd relished even as an aging athlete were long gone, replaced with white, hairy flab and loose skin. "Blondie, you're here." The gravelly voice of a smoker greeted us. "I can't believe it. Come in, come in."

Dad let go of the walker and held out his arms. Sherri accepted a quick hug. I ducked and two-stepped my way past his offering.

"You look great, Krissy." He manhandled his walker into a turn with ease for a man diagnosed with a motor neuron disease. "You look so much like your mom. You and Sherri both do. You're lucky you didn't get my ugly mug."

Krissy. Again, only him. "You really don't get to talk to me about Mom."

"Yep, yep, I get it. Have a seat." As usual, he chose to fold at any sign of hostility. He motioned toward the couch. I perched on the edge of a recliner so used, the cushions held his body's shape. The chair and the sofa were angled to have a good view of a large TV hanging on the far wall.

The White Sox were playing the Tigers. Baseball season didn't start until April. Dad's smile didn't waver. "It's a taped game. I get the DTs during the off-season so I replay games." He cocked his head to his left. "I got coffee and some of those frosted circus animal cookies you like."

"That was forty-five years ago—"

"Thanks, Dad." Scowling, Sherri interrupted me. "What happened to your face? How'd you get that bruise?"

"Took a little tumble, that's all. No harm done."

"They're supposed to be helping you—"

"They are. My fault. I thought I could get along without the walker after so much PT. Bad idea."

"Other than that, how are you feeling?"

"Doing good." He eased onto the couch next to her. "I go to PT in the rec room three times a week and do all my exercises here every day. I take three kinds of muscle relaxants for the spasticity in my legs and a med for the nerve pain on schedule like clockwork. My home health aide gives me gold stars—except for the fall, of course. They don't like it when you fall."

He said it like a kid seeking praise from a parent. At his age, he was lucky he hadn't broken a hip. A sliver of concern wiggled its way into that space where my heart resided. I shooed it away.

I stood and turned my back. Memorabilia from his minor league baseball days covered the living room wall. A framed jersey from his season with the Durham Bulls—yes, the team made famous by the Kevin Costner movie. A baseball signed by a bunch of LA Dodgers on a shelf next to photos of him with various semipro teams. A framed eight-by-ten photo of him making a one-handed catch in deep center field during the one season he played with the San Antonio Missions before getting cut from the team.

The scent of hot dogs and popcorn replaced floral air freshener and coffee. The July sun blazed overhead in the first game of a doubleheader. I wore a Missions ball cap, a pink gingham sundress, my favorite pink cowboy boots, and a well-oiled glove. I was six; Sherri, ten. Dad sat between us watching the Missions play Midland.

He practically quivered with excitement during the playing of the national anthem. When the umpire shouted "play ball," he whooped and hollered. His voice joined with ten thousand other die-hard Missions fans singing "Take Me Out to the Ball Game." He was on his feet cheering every time a Mission bat connected with the ball.

I loved the game, but I loved being there with my dad more than anything.

"Did you see that? Did you see that swing, slugger? I knew the minute I heard that sound of ball on bat they could kiss that baby goodbye."

He picked me up and stuck me on his hip. "When we get home, I'll show you how to hit a slider. It's easy to hit a fastball, but a player who can hit a slider, a curveball, and a changeup, that's a player who'll make it in the bigs."

The player at the plate swung and missed.

"That guy's going nowhere fast."

"Strike him out, strike him out, strike him out!" the crowd chanted.

"Hey, batter, batter, batter, swing, batter!" Sherri and I yelled, just the way he'd taught us.

The batter swung so hard he tripped over his own feet and nearly fell down.

"Missed by a mile!" Dad whooped along with the crowd. He hugged me so hard my ribs might've cracked. "He's out of here."

"How 'bout them Astros, huh? You think they'll make the series this year?"

I jumped. I'd tunneled so deep into that memory, I hadn't heard him approach. I studied his wrinkled face, so different from the one that peopled my memories. Not a single family photo graced his wall. "Where did you go?"

"What do you mean?"

I ran my finger across the assortment of signed balls. "You took us to a Missions game, remember? I think I was six. All the way home in the car you talked about signing us up for a girls' softball team. You said you would coach." The words and the memory stuck in my throat. I swallowed hard against them. "The next day you were gone."

"Yeah, yeah. I remember that. I got a call." He tugged on his beard, his face scrunched up, whether in an effort to remember or to come up with a plausible lie. Only he knew which. "A buddy said the Elizabethton Twins had a spot on their roster for an outfielder."

"So you made the team?"

"Naw. The Pirates sent down some rookie who needed more grooming before he was ready for the majors. I was too old by then anyway."

"So why didn't you come back?"

He scrubbed his face hard. "The Missions moved to Midland and changed their name to the Bullets."

Later, the team returned to San Antonio, but Dad didn't. "You left us because there was no minor league baseball team in San Antonio?"

"No. I love baseball, but I'm not that crazy." He picked up a ball autographed by Sandy Koufax and thumbed the stitching lovingly. "I had an itch that I kept trying to scratch."

"You didn't have an itch to be a parent then?"

"Slugger, I was no good at it."

"Don't call me that. How do you know? You never tried." I tugged the ball from his hand and returned it to its place of honor. "I waited for you. I watched at the window. I listened for the sound of your old Capris. After a couple of weeks, I gave up. I threw my glove in the trash and asked Mom to sign me up for basketball."

I left out the part where I hid in my closet with my Tigger and my Pooh Bear as my only witnesses while I bawled into a blanket I'd stopped carrying around at age four.

"I'm sorry."

"Not good enough."

"So is that why you came here today? To remind me of my short-comings? Believe me, I'm aware of them." He dropped into a chair. "Go ahead, Sherri, your turn. Let me have it."

"It was a long time ago." Sherri drilled me with a scowl. *You promised to try,* her fierce gaze said. *Be civil.* "I didn't come here to dredge up old hurts. There are plenty of new ones to deal with."

"I'm sorry." Dad tossed the words like a bunt down the first base line into the space between Sherri and me. His expression doleful, he shrugged. "I can't change the past, but I gotta say I'm glad you're here now. Real glad."

"Me too." Sherri picked up her phone. "I don't follow sports much anymore, now that my kids are grown. All three kids played baseball and basketball, thanks to my ex-husband, who did all the sports with them. Noelle was also a great volleyball player—good enough for a college scholarship, but she was more into art by then. She has an MFA in visual arts and art history."

"I'd love to see her and the boys."

"Unfortunately, none of them live close by. I wish they did." Sherri held out the phone. "But I have a ton of photos of them and the grandkids."

"I'm a great-grandpa?" He crowed like a proud rooster. "Dang, I feel old."

Dad oohed and aahed like a drunk guy at a fireworks display. Videos and photos of the kids playing in the ocean, water balloon fights, Christmas, cookie baking, pre-K programs, first days of school, graduations, military uniforms. I had just as many on my phone, but scrolling through a camera roll on a smartphone was a poor substitute for being there. He knew it. She knew it. I knew it. So why pretend?

I couldn't make myself sit down. Or talk about my girls. This wasn't why we'd come. But it seemed part and parcel of what Sherri had come to do. Like a prelude to the lesson Dad was about to learn. He'd wasted most of our lifetimes not being a part of Sherri's life, the lives of her kids and of her grandkids. They were blessed with Chance's grandparents. My girls had Daniel's parents, the ideal grandparents. Leonard taught them to ride horses. Angela did their hair, taught them to put on makeup, took them to art museums and plays. As a high school graduation gift, each girl received a trip with Grandma to the destination of their choice in the continental USA. Brielle chose New York City; Maddie, Washington, D.C.

From Grandfather Miller they'd received even less attention than his daughters had.

Why is it so hard to see how we've squandered time until we can see it all in hindsight?

Sherri and Dad huddled together, their heads almost touching. So father-daughter. She started working at age fifteen, ending her days of playing sports, but she insisted I keep playing. She never missed my basketball games or track meets. She told me about sex. She went to the plays and the debates. She gave her shoulder to cry on when the first boy broke my heart. She helped me fill out college applications, financial aid, and scholarship applications. Sherri shouldered both mom and dad roles for years.

Did Dad understand what that cost her? Did he care?

I opened my mouth. Sherri glanced up at that moment. She shook her head. "Max has Dad's chin. And his eyes."

She was a better person than I was any day of the week. I tried to up my game. "Strong genes."

Her smile slipped away. She leaned back. "Dad, there is something I wanted to talk to you about."

"I figured as much." He handed the phone back. "But let me get the coffee first. You have to eat those cookies. The PA is always telling me to cut back on sugar."

I edged away from them. "I'll get the coffee. You two talk."

Now who was the coward? The coffee was already made in the tiny, spotless kitchenette. He'd set out three mugs on a tray with sugar, a pint of milk, and the coffee. The bag of pink-and-white-frosted animal cookies lay on a stack of napkins. It didn't take nearly long enough to pour the coffee and carry the tray to the living room.

"It's stage 4," Sherri said. "But my oncologist in Kerrville said it's highly treatable. And Kris has me set up to see a surgeon and an oncologist here in San Antonio. I'm in good hands."

Dad said nothing. He rubbed both hands on his sweats, then planted them both on the walker's handles. Ropy veins and age spots covered hands that had once thrown an unerring fastball from center field to home plate. "I'm sorry, girl, so sorry." His Adam's apple bobbed. "Dang it, I don't know what to say."

"It's okay. You don't have to say anything." Sherri patted his hand. "I just thought you should know."

"You got this, Krissy, right?" Dad grabbed Sherri's hand and held on, but he stared up at me, his bloodshot eyes big and wet. "You're a . . . whatchacallit? An oncologist, right?"

"I am."

I set the tray on the table and proceeded to serve the coffee and cookies as if this were a social event. It gave me time to contemplate my response. Did I have this? I teetered between telling the truth and telling him what he wanted to hear. "Sherri will have the best medical care available. Treatment has evolved in leaps and bounds in the last thirty years. Every day, new drugs are approved by the FDA."

"See, Dad, no worries." The smile plastered across Sherri's face was reminiscent of so many of my patients who spent precious energy comforting their loved ones instead of being comforted. "I'm in good hands. In fact, we're headed to the clinic to get the ball rolling this afternoon. You just take care of yourself. I'll be fine. Right, sissy?"

My chest hurt. I couldn't get a breath. Blood pounded in my ears. Adrenaline pulsed through me. All the fight-or-flight symptoms I experienced when introducing a patient to her so-called new normal. Only multiplied by a thousand times. A million times. My heart beat so furiously, it threatened to crack my ribs. My sister was depending on me the way I'd depended on her all these years.

Breathe. Breathe. "Right."

No pressure.

nine

KRISTEN

I tugged a burnt orange UT-Austin Longhorn hoodie from Sherri's bag that also held an envelope with all the new patient paperwork duly completed, a water bottle, snacks, and books—she never went anywhere without them. She knew how to come prepared. I held it out. "You're shivering."

She studied the small triangular ticket in her hand printed with the number 93. She said nothing. The digital sign behind the bank of intake workers at Texas Cancer Care Clinic read 78. Par for the course. Every chair in the outer lobby was taken. A couple stood near the sliding glass doors. A man came in, halted, and went back out. Just getting from the lobby to the lab was a waiting game.

"You should put it on, Sherri."

She nodded and accepted my offering with shaking hands. "The paintings are nice. This clinic is much nicer than the one in Kerrville."

I shrugged, preferring to remain noncommittal. A patient once described the new building as an attempt to smear lipstick on a pig and call it beautiful. It was a million times better than the dark, drab, windowless clinic once housed in a building in San Antonio's

Medical Center area where patients had to park in a parking garage that was always full.

Still, I saw her point. No amount of artwork done by Texas artists of bluebonnets, the River Walk, cowboy boots, and cows could hide the fact that the people sitting in the massive waiting areas were cancer patients hoping for good news, dreading bad news, and steeling themselves for needle pokes, chemotherapy, radiation, and scans. Even so, walking into the front lobby with Sherri sent adrenaline rushing through my body like a hit of speed. My turf, my home base, the place where coworkers understood me because they were like me.

"Dr. Tremaine?" The intake person who called our number fifteen minutes later looked startled, then chagrined. Our paths had crossed many times in the two or three years since she started working here. "You didn't have to take a number."

"This is my sister, the patient." I cocked my head toward Sherri, who nodded with a frozen smile. "She's seeing Dr. Pasternak. I'm here for moral support."

The intake worker nodded and went into efficiency mode. Insurance card, driver's license, co-payment, paperwork. Bam, bam, bam, thank you, ma'am.

"Have a seat. They'll be right with you."

The biggest lie in the universe perpetuated by the medical profession. No matter how many times I suggested at staff meetings that no one—absolutely no one—use that phrase, they still did it. It created an expectation that someone would, indeed, be with the patient soon. It was a falsehood, pure and simple.

Another fifteen minutes went by. I tried to concentrate on the *Journal of Clinical Oncology* in my lap. It seemed like a good time to get caught up. My eyes refused to focus. Sherri read one of the two books she'd squeezed into her bag—something called *The Sentence*. She shifted in her chair, wiggling like one of her kindergartners. She hadn't turned the page in several minutes.

"So what's your book about?"

She stuck the postcard from a van Gogh exhibit she was using as a bookmark in the book and closed it. "Books, the power of words, a ghost that haunts a bookstore, George Floyd, the COVID pandemic . . . love."

"So, light reading?"

Laughing, she tapped my open magazine. "Like yours." She leaned closer. "'Apatinib Plus Pegylated Liposomal Doxorubicin' . . ." She stumbled over most of the words but kept going. "'Yields Significant Efficacy in Advanced Ovarian Cancer.'"

I'd always tried to squeeze in every available minute to keep track of research advances for the sake of my patients. Also, because the possibility existed of becoming a principal investigator for some of the clinic's trials. It took an average of ten years to get a new drug from research and development to the patient. Fifteen thousand women died each year from ovarian cancer. I was terrible at math, but even I knew that equaled one hundred fifty thousand deaths in a decade. I wanted to change that. "The results are promising. New drugs are coming on the market every day. There's every reason to be hopeful."

"I know what you're doing."

"What do you mean?"

"Trying to take my mind off the waiting. Is it always like this?"

"Pretty much. That's why I told you to bring earbuds, a Spotify playlist, a charger, a book, two books if you're a fast reader, and never come without snacks and a lunch if your appointment is in the morning."

"It's okay. It gives me time to think about where I want you to spread my ashes. What about a nice deep-sea fishing boat off the coast of Maui? I hear the water is sparkling blue there and so clear you can see the bottom."

She insisted on being morbid. The clinic social worker in palliative care would call it a coping mechanism. I called it morbid. "Fine, then I want mine tossed into one of the volcanos on the Big Island—"

"Dr. Tremaine! You're here. Oh, thank goodness." A patient I'd been treating for metastatic breast cancer approached, the relief so clearly written across her puffy, pink face that my heart played limbo with my stomach. Chemotherapy, a bilateral mastectomy, and endless rounds of radiation hadn't given us the results we'd hoped for. She was due to start a new drug regimen today. She ran her hands over her bald head. "Shay told me you were out on a family emergency. I'm so sorry about that. I'm just worried about the side effects—"

"I'm so sorry to have to do this, but Tasha will be able to help you with those side effects until I'm able to return." For twenty-plus years I'd kept all the balls in the air—wife, physician, mother, sister. I could do it all. I had done it all. "I promise you it's temporary. I'm still consulting with Tasha and Shay on your treatment. I'll be back in clinic as soon as I can. Right now, I'm here on personal business."

My patient's gaze bounced from me to Sherri and back. Tears in her eyes, she tucked her hands in her jean pockets. "Do you have cancer?"

"No, no, not me."

"You'll be back then? Soon?"

"That's the plan."

She swiped at her face with a sodden tissue. "Sorry I bothered you."

"Don't be. We'll talk soon."

We would talk soon. I'd make sure of it. I could balance Sherri's needs with those of my patients. Just not today.

How well? If I asked Brielle and Maddie to grade my performance in the category of Supermom, what would they give me? And what about Daniel? What would he say? On this day and for as long as necessary, my sister had to come first.

I took a covert peek around the room. Two more of my patients sat at the far end of the lobby. Neither seemed to have recognized me. Maybe I was incognito in my street clothes. One connected with my gaze. Her expression changed. I glanced away.

The door to the sacred inner sanctum opened. Darcy Helm, one of several phlebotomists, peered out. She checked the labels in her hand, then out at the patients. The crowd held their collective breaths. "Sherri Reynolds."

We stood. A collective sigh went up. Envious glances shot our way. I ignored them and hustled Sherri through the door. "What's up, Doc?" Darcy bowed and waved us in with a flourish. It was her favorite line. She used it on all the physicians. "I didn't expect to see you coming through this door."

"I like to keep you guessing, Darcy. I'm loving the purple." An amazon of a woman, Darcy wore purple scrubs, sneakers, earrings, hair extensions, and nail polish—every day. I offered my traditional thumbs-up and introduced Sherri again. "Be gentle with her, please."

As if Darcy wasn't gentle with every one of the patients. Her look of admonishment was well-deserved. "Have a seat, Ms. Sherri."

"Dr. Tremaine."

Oops. Caught before I'd even made it two yards into the inner sanctum. I turned at the sound of a familiar voice. Practice Manager Pamela Kitchens bore down on me with a frown that would melt titanium. "A word, please."

"I'm here with my sister—"

"She's in excellent hands."

"I'll take good care of her." Darcy waved me away. "We're gonna be best buds. I'll walk her over to Dr. P.'s area when we finish here."

I followed in the wake of Pam's *swish-swish-swish* pleated skirt through a door marked EMPLOYEES ONLY and into her office.

"I understand you've handed off your appointments to your PA for the next several days." She plopped into her desk chair and pointed at the one across from her. Pam wasn't one to pussyfoot around. "Without notifying me. Shay simply said you had a family emergency."

Shay wasn't one to violate HIPAA rules. Sherri wasn't her patient or mine, but my medical assistant was hypersensitive to patient confidentiality, as she should be. "I'm sorry. I intended to get with you when I had a better idea of what my timeline would be."

"I'm not trying to be intrusive, but why are you here today, if not to see patients?"

Not intrusive my hind end. Pam was the world's biggest buttinsky, which made her a good manager—much as I hated to admit it. She knew what everyone was doing, all the time. "My sister is now a patient here. I'm getting her oriented."

"Who is she seeing?"

I explained with a minimum of detail.

Pam's frosty blue eyes warmed. "I'm really very sorry, Kristen. If there's anything Texas Cancer Care can do to help, please let me know. If there's anything I can do personally, simply say the word."

Just when I wanted to make her the bad guy. A sob snuck up on me. I squashed it summarily. "Thank you, Pam. If you could run interference for Tasha for a few days, I'd appreciate it. There's no way she can handle all my patients for any length of time. I hope to know more about my schedule after we see Arina today. I'm doing a virtual meeting with Tasha and Shay later. If not today, tomorrow."

"Absolutely. She and I will talk this afternoon. I'll review the patient loads to see who might be able to take some of your more critical patients. We should probably send an email to all your patients, letting them know your status."

"Shay is calling them. I think that's better than an email. More reassuring. Some of them are very fragile." A shudder shook my body. I couldn't imagine being away from these people for an extended period. Some had been my patients for four, five, and six years, or more. Some were nearing that fork in the road where they had to decide whether it was time for hospice. Some needed help deciding whether to stick with standard of care or opt for clinical trials. "I took a laptop home. I'll consult with Tasha via Teams. We can use the encrypted email system to discuss patient treatment plans."

Pam pursed her thin lips. She steepled her hands, her gaze pinned somewhere over my head. Finally, she nodded. "It sounds like you have an adequate plan, but first tend to your sister. No one is indispensable. Not even you. You'll be in and out of the clinic regularly with her. She'll have some long days in the infusion room. There will be time to reassess when the time is right."

The time was right now. "I can handle both."

"We'll follow up on Shay's call with an email stating that you're taking some time off for a family emergency, your schedule is temporarily in flux, but we'll get back to them as soon as possible with an update."

She didn't intend to budge. Neither did I. I would handle this my way. It was better to seem pliable when dealing with the face of Texas Cancer Care's bureaucracy. "That sounds good."

From the patients' perspective, it sounded awful. They experienced so much uncertainty as it was. Daily, they wondered if they would survive the harsh treatments. They wondered if the treatments were working. What would they do if they didn't work? What would life be like if they did? They wondered if they were going to die. Causing them more uncertainty was cruel. I stood. "Let me draft something and send it to you. I don't want them to think I'm abandoning them."

"That's why you're such a good doctor. You care so much about your patients. I'll wait for your draft, but it should go out soon— tomorrow, if possible." Pam took off her black-rimmed glasses, laid them on her desk, and rubbed her eyes. "Arina's the best. You'll go with Salvador for the surgery?"

"He's also the best."

She stood as well. "I won't keep you any longer. Try not to worry—at least not about your patients. We've got you covered. Just keep me in the loop, if you can."

Of course . . . as much as necessary. "Will do."

She followed me to her door. For a moment I thought she might hug me. Instead, she rubbed my back for a brief moment, much the way a mother would comfort a child. That sneaky sob made another run at me. I squashed it again. "Thanks," I whispered.

"Anything you need, remember that."

Did she have a miracle cancer cure up her sleeve?

SHERRI

Dr. Pasternak didn't walk into the exam room. She hustled. Her energy exploded in the tiny room. She pumped my hand, hugged Kristen, and introduced her transcriptionist with barely a pause for our responses. She was a tall, solid, bespectacled woman with short gray hair that curled tight to her head. Her Russian accent enchanted me—along with her total lack of artifice.

"I've reviewed your medical records." She settled into her chair, leaned her elbows on her thighs, and peered at me through her bifocals. "I've already talked to Salvador—Dr. Rodriguez—but there's no rush to see him. We'll get you started on a carboplatin, Taxol, Avastin regimen as soon as you get your port in and do your chemo education. You'll do three rounds, which takes three months, and then we'll see about surgery. I'd like to get you started on Monday—if we can get the insurance approval by then. The scheduler is working on the port thing at Methodist—hopefully tomorrow. Again, depending on insurance."

"If you can't get the insurance approved that fast—"

"We'll do inpatient on Wednesday at Methodist when they do the port if we have to," Dr. Pasternak interrupted Kris. "I can get chemo approved for inpatient. The clinic doesn't like it, but we don't have time to mess around."

I opened my mouth, then closed it. Whatever question I intended to ask had flitted away before I could capture it. The *bong, bong, bong* was back so loud that I couldn't think. Time. The words were jumbled up like jigsaw pieces thrown into a box. Some of the pieces were missing.

Kris had my notebook out. She was taking notes for me. I'd said I would do it myself, but she'd known. I wouldn't be able to speak, let alone write. "Are you doing every three weeks, or three weeks on, one week off?"

"Three weeks on, one week off seems to be easier on the patient. Smaller doses, fewer side effects. It seems to make little difference in effectiveness."

Kris nodded in agreement.

"The port procedure only takes about thirty minutes." Dr. Pasternak paused as if waiting for me to acknowledge her words. "It's simple, quick, but if we need to do the chemo inpatient, then we will. Be prepared to spend the night the first time—not because you need to, but because that's the game insurance forces us to play."

I nodded. At least some part of my anatomy moved.

"Any questions?"

"Will I lose my hair?" Who cared? Was I that vain?

"Possibly."

"Probably," Kris amended. "The ACS offers one free wig to cancer patients."

ACS? It took a minute. American Cancer Society.

"Wigs are itchy. Especially in these hot Texas summers." Dr. Pasternak's tone was blithe. "But one thing at a time, my friend. As soon as our insurance people make headway, they'll let the schedulers know.

They'll call you. If you don't hear from them by Thursday, call me. Right now, I want my MA Cammy to take you down to the infusion room so you can get signed up for chemo education. Insurance won't cover chemotherapy without it."

Everything hinged on my insurance. That wasn't exactly breaking news. Nausea roiled in my stomach. Pain throbbed in my temples. I rubbed my forehead. My throat was too dry to speak. My lips hurt. Where was my ChapStick?

Dr. Pasternak held out her phone. "Put your number in my phone, and I'll do the same for you."

Numbly, I racked my brain. "I don't call myself." My voice was a croak. "I have to think . . ."

"Do you want me to do it?"

Kris's question penetrated the fog. I shook my head. "I've got it." I was a grown woman, for criminy sakes.

While I took care of this simple task made almost impossible by my shaking fingers, the two doctors commiserated over why it was necessary to give out their cell phone numbers to patients. Messages sent to the wrong place or simply lost in outer space. Excessively long hold times.

"I got it." I hoisted the phone over my head in victory, then lowered it. "Sorry, I didn't mean to interrupt."

"You're not interrupting." Dr. Pasternak handed my phone back. "We're just doing the misery-loves-company thing."

She turned to her computer and tapped keys. Then she proceeded to regurgitate our conversation in a singsong voice with a lot of umms whenever she stopped to gather her thoughts. It took a few seconds to realize this was for the transcriptionist's benefit. The young woman nodded and periodically threw in a question. Until then, I'd almost forgotten she was in the room.

"Okay, my friend, you're all set. So to speak." Dr. Pasternak moved her stethoscope from around her neck to her ears and stood. After a quick listen to my heart, she moved on to my lungs, front and back. Frowning, she straightened. "Do you experience shortness of breath?"

"I'm a runner. I've noticed it when I'm running. Also when I sing in church." The only place I sang in public. Kris shifted in the chair next to me. A grin flitted across her face. I stuck my tongue out at her. We were sisters, after all. "Hush, sis. I know I can't carry a tune in a bucket, but God loves a cheerful noise."

"It's a good thing—"

"Hush."

Smiling, Dr. Pasternak stepped back and sank onto her chair. "I can't sing either. I'm terrible at it. Sergei—my husband—covers his ears when I sing along to the car radio."

"How is Sergei? As crazy as ever?" Kris interjected. "I haven't seen him since the New Year's Eve party."

And Dr. Pasternak was off, sharing photos with us of last summer's haul from a vegetable garden she and her husband—also an oncologist—had started as therapy, as well as their two Australian kelpie puppies, whom she said ruled the Pasternak household. If she had any concerns about time or patients waiting, it didn't show.

"Gardening is good therapy." Dr. Pasternak directed that statement to me. "I highly recommend it. Also the pups. They meet me at the door at the end of the day, tails wagging. They let me pet them and cuddle them."

"I have a cat."

"I don't have experience with cats." Her expression turned contemplative. "But whatever works for you. Back to your lungs."

Which apparently weren't working so well. "Chemotherapy, the sooner the better, my friend. We need to get after those masses in the lung's pleural lining."

"I agree." What else could I say? "I'm ready."

As ready as a person scared spitless could be.

"I'll send in prescriptions for anti-nausea meds so you'll have them when you start chemo. Take them as directed. Don't wait until you feel sick. That's an order."

The image of my mother vomiting into that red plastic beach bucket loomed large. *"It won't be like it was with Mom. I promise. Treatments have improved exponentially."* Kristen's words tried to override it. I had better insurance too. More coverage. I hoped. "Got it."

"And the lidocaine cream for accessing the port." Kristen closed the notebook and stuck it in my bag. "I have patients who say it really helps. Apparently, the Huber needle stick feels like getting stuck with a tack."

Dr. Pasternak tapped her computer keys with efficient strokes. "Done."

Having an oncologist for a sister would never stop being a benefit. As a new patient, I didn't even know what I didn't know, which made it hard to ask intelligent questions.

"Let's get the chemo education scheduled." Kris gave me a quick one-armed hug as if she could feel my angst. She probably could. We were connected by the sinew and tissue of shared joys and traumas. "It's bogus, but necessary."

Dr. Pasternak stood. She hugged Kristen again, then turned to me and held out her arms. Suddenly, a hug from my new oncologist seemed like the most natural thing in the world. I walked into it, hungry for contact with this solid, genuine human being. She patted my back and stepped back. "Take care, my dear. We'll talk soon."

I made it through the long trip past waiting areas with names like River Walk and Bluebonnets to the infusion room. It was enormous. Kris said it had ninety chairs. Most of them were full, along with the visitor chairs placed between the recliners. Floor-to-ceiling glass walls took up one entire side, giving patients a view of a patio filled with native plants just beginning to turn green and lush at the end of a cool South Texas winter. A few patients, tethered to infusion poles, sat at outdoor tables, passing the time with friends or family members.

"Not bad," I managed to murmur. "At least they tried."

Kris shrugged. "It is what it is."

An efficient, if cool, scheduler got my chemo education on the books. I surveyed the infusion room once again. *Until next time.*

I made it to her Nissan Leaf in the parking lot before the dam burst and the flood came.

"I'm so sorry." I kept saying it over and over again in a voice so choked I wasn't sure she could understand my garbled words. "I just need . . ."

"Don't be sorry." Kris maneuvered me into the passenger seat and strapped me in. "You're allowed."

"I just need to get it out of my system." I hiccupped a sob, swallowed another one, and heaved a sigh. "I'm fine."

"You don't have to be fine." Kris bit out the words as if suddenly angry. She reached into the glove compartment in front of me, pulled out a package of tissues, and handed it to me. "You don't ever have to be fine for me. Maybe for your kids or for Dad or whoever, but not me. You got that?"

I snatched a wad of tissues and mopped my face. "Got it."

"You can be real with me. I won't fold. I won't run away. I'm the one person you can count on no matter what."

She slammed the door and marched around the front of the car to the driver's side, where she slid in and slammed her door. The role reversal stunned me for a few seconds. I heaved another sigh and sat up straight. "Thank you."

"Don't thank me. I owe you." Kris put both hands on the wheel. She ducked her head for second, then swiveled to meet my gaze. "You shouldered the burden when Mom was sick. You took care of her and me. Then me. You've always taken care of me. I owe you."

"I've never thought of it that way. Ever."

Being Kris's big sister had been a gift from God. Even before Mom died, and certainly after she passed, I needed someone to think about besides myself. I needed the nights we lay on our backs on the grass in Tricia's backyard, staring at the stars, wondering which one was Mom's hangout, wondering if she was watching, wishing for a little hint of things to come. We talked about boys and love and sex and God and the universe and whether Bruce Springsteen's "Born to Run" was a better song than Bob Seger's "Night Moves." I needed to cheer at her basketball games and help with homework. I needed to drill her regarding her whereabouts when she came in late on a school night. I needed to be needed.

I needed her as much as she needed me. As nice as Tricia was, she had her own life, her own kids, a full-time job, and a boyfriend she eventually married. Her life went on.

"It's not a debt you pay." I dug around in my bag, came up with my water bottle, and took a long swallow. The desperate desire to wail subsided. Kris still needed me, whether she liked it or not. "We may not have had a lot of experience with family back in the day, but we knew then and we know now how to act like family."

"Don't you forget it."

"You either." I leaned back in the seat and closed my eyes. For a few minutes it was okay to let someone as experienced as Kris take the wheel.

She'd been a gift from God before. She was now.

ten

DANIEL

I jolted awake. The door creaked. Footsteps. The light came on in the bathroom, a thin line under its door. I glanced at the digital clock on my nightstand. Midnight. I leaned my head on the pillow and contemplated the darkness. Kristen had been Miss Congeniality while serving me dinner—the Caesar salad I'd planned to fix a few days earlier. The romaine was only slightly limp. Kristen assured me Sherri knew how to use my gas grill to prepare the chicken breasts. No harm had come to it.

She and Sherri had eaten Whataburger with fries and onion rings before returning to the house after Sherri's appointment. But they insisted on sitting with me while I ate. They also insisted on cleaning up as well, since I'd worked all day. They were like twins. I had the distinct impression they were putting on a show for me. *Give me an F. Give me an I. Give me an N. Give me an E. What does it spell? Fine! Who's fine? We're fine!*

Not fine. No mention of the appointment at the clinic. Instead, the discussion had centered around Kristen's decision to take up running with Sherri—something she'd never done in her life. And a second walk with the dogs. Basically, they sat at the table, sipping large jugs of water, watching me eat.

Nothing awkward about that.

The bathroom door opened. A shaft of light spread across the salvaged oak floor, covered with a leaf-themed rug, and splashed on our king-sized bed crafted from reclaimed pine. Kristen paused, her body dark and silhouetted. "Sorry. I didn't mean to wake you."

"You didn't," I lied. "You're up late."

"I was too wound up to sleep. I just took a quarter of a zolpidem. I'm hoping it'll help."

As an oncologist, Kristen rarely took sleep aids or drank in case a patient needed her during her off-hours. Even when other physicians were on call. She had trouble turning off the litany of cases in her head at the end of her day. "Want me to rub your back?"

"That's okay. You have to get up early in the morning."

I'd gladly give up sleep to touch her. For her touch. It had been so long. I rubbed my chest. The ache didn't recede.

She turned off the light. A few seconds later she slid under the sheet but stayed on her side. I rued the day we'd upsized the bed from a queen. That two people could sleep in the same bed and never touch hadn't occurred to me until it was too late.

I turned on the reading lamp on my side. "What's going on, Kristen?"

"What do you mean?" She rolled over with her back to me. "Nothing's going on."

"I'm your husband. I'm Sherri's brother-in-law. I care about both of you. I'm part of the family too."

"Of course you are." She rolled onto her back, then faced me, both hands under her cheek. It would be nice if those were my hands touching her soft skin. "We just didn't think it was necessary to get into the gory details at the dinner table. Besides, the details haven't been nailed down yet. Plus, you work all day. You deserve a nice dinner to decompress."

She'd never shown any concern for me decompressing in the past.

"You two do this thing. You always have." I worked to keep my tone conciliatory. Maybe I *was* just tired. It had been a long day that had included a site meeting with a difficult client bent on changing the blueprints and materials again and again. "It's the two of you against the world."

"No we don't. No it isn't."

"Did you see your dad today?"

She rolled over yet again, came up on one elbow, and turned on her lamp. "How did you know about that?"

"That's your first question?" I sat up and propped up my pillows behind me. "I heard you and Sherri talking about it last night. Why wouldn't you tell me?"

"Let's not do this tonight." She ran her hand through her silver-streaked blonde hair cut so short she could pass for a high school boy. When we married it had reached below her collarbone and felt silky in my hands. This was easier to maintain, she'd explained after that first haircut. She wore one of my old, baggy T-shirts. It didn't matter what she wore or how she cut her hair. She still looked as good as she had on our wedding night. "You're tired. I'm tired."

"How did it go?"

She blew out a sigh. "Fine. It was fine."

"You haven't seen your father in, I don't know, how many years? And it was fine?"

"We ate frosted circus-animal cookies, drank coffee, and oohed and aahed over his baseball memorabilia like civilized people do."

"So you didn't confront him about your feelings?"

"He's old. He's infirm. He's sorry." Her voice dropped off in a husky whisper, the way it always did when she was angry. A soft *woof* emanated from the alcove sitting area where the dogs slept. They were tuned in to Kristen's moods—day or night. "It's okay, Dash. Dad wants to make nice and act like he didn't drop out of our lives when the going got rough. He wants to be great-grandpa to the babies and forget that he was never around for our girls or for me and Sherri."

Kristen had always refused to go to therapy. She still carried around baggage from her childhood so heavy that she could barely pull it behind her. Bewilderment at being abandoned, anger, hurt, pain, feelings of inadequacy and blame, feeling unloved—all that stuff weighed a ton. Even when she'd discovered he was living relatively close to us, she refused to see him.

"Things are different. Treatments are so much more effective."

"I know," she whispered, "but she's my sister. She's all I've got."

The knife turned in my gut three or four times before I could get a breath. Which gave Kristen a minute to hear in her own head the words she'd uttered. "I didn't mean it that way. You know what I meant."

"You meant what you said."

"I love you and Maddie and Brielle with all my heart."

No, with the space left after she stuffed in all her other priorities. "You're right. We shouldn't talk about this when we're tired."

"I'm sorry. I only meant that Sherri kept me from spiraling out of control after Mom died. It was us against the world. You have a huge, picture-perfect family. You can't understand."

"I'm capable of empathy. I'm capable of sympathy. I'm capable of being there for you."

"I know you are, and you're so kind and patient with me. I never forget that."

Did she realize how often she took advantage of those qualities? "Don't worry about it. Get some sleep."

"Sherri asked me to be nice, to be civil."

She was making an effort to open up. For Kristen, this was epic. "But you couldn't."

Dash appeared on her side of bed. He whimpered. She patted his muzzle. "It's okay, boy. I'm fine." He nosed at her hand. She scratched behind his ears. "I thought I restrained myself pretty well. Sherri didn't think so. She showed him pictures of her kids and grandkids."

"But you didn't."

"No."

"That's okay."

"He's old and sick. Sherri says my inability to forgive hurts me more than it does him."

Sherri was right, but she didn't allow for the fact that Kristen had been younger than she was when Roy Miller bailed out of their lives. Kristen didn't have Sherri's faith either. While Sherri's faith grew after their mother's death, Kristen's had dried up and blown away. I'd tried many times to talk to her about it, but she refused to engage. "Everybody works through their stuff in their own way and on their own time."

"I know. You're right."

I grabbed my phone from its charger. "Say that again so I can record it."

She dredged up a half laugh. "Very funny."

"Will you see him again?"

"Sherri wants to."

Which meant Kristen would too. "How did things go at the clinic? I imagine Pam took advantage of the appointment with Arina to harangue you about taking a leave of absence."

"I'm not taking a leave of absence. Not exactly."

Here we go. "Come again?"

The long and short of it was Kristen refused to give up control of her patients, even while she intended to serve as Sherri's patient navigator. A position that would be made available to Sherri by the clinic. "How will you work around Sherri's appointments, her surgery, and the long days when she has chemo?"

"I brought a laptop home from work. I'm updating my patients' treatment plans going forward. I have a virtual meeting with Tasha tomorrow morning. Once I have Sherri's schedule, I can figure out when I can be in clinic and when I can work from home."

A whoosh of anger-driven adrenaline flooded me. Blood pulsed in my ears. Kristen was right. We should've left this conversation for another time. In a minute *I* would need the zolpidem. "So you'll try to run Sherri's life and tend to all your patients."

"Just for the time being."

Which left no room for the girls or for me. Again. "The time being? I'm not stupid. Sherri will be in treatment for the rest of her life. God willing, that will be a long time."

"Once she's N.E.D., it'll ease up. She'll be able to go back to work. I'll go back to the clinic full time."

Seriously? Kristen probably thought I didn't pay attention when she used me as a sounding board when some new breakthrough treatment excited her. I had a store of information probably akin to what patients in active treatment had or fresh-faced residents doing rotations in oncology. No evidence of disease had replaced cancer-free in the cancer-space lexicon. No one with metastatic disease could use the phrase "cancer-free." Microscopic cancer cells floated freely in their blood, biding their time, spreading their disease until new tumors or enlarged lymph nodes became visible on scans.

There was no guarantee Sherri would get that coveted status of N.E.D. And if she did, the next step would likely be some kind of maintenance therapy, along with periodic CT scans and lab work. "I hope that's true, babe, but in the meantime, you can't run yourself into the ground. It's not good for you, for her, or for your patients."

"I can handle it." She turned off her light. Dash took the hint and padded back to his bed. Once again, Kristen settled down with her back to me. "The pill will never kick in at this rate. Good night."

I turned off my light and resumed staring at the dark.

I can't. I can't handle it. I didn't say those words aloud. *Don't be selfish. Don't be a whiner.* Kristen had spent most of our marriage

105

working herself into the ground while playing the role of Supermom and wife. Nothing I said or did disabused her of the notion that this was what the world expected of her. Scaling back her practice wasn't an option. Her work was too important. Why didn't I cut back my client load? Because I was an employer who had people depending on me for their salaries. Round and round we went.

When the girls left for college, the hope that there would be more time for the wife-husband part had quickly been squashed.

A wave of loneliness crashed over me so intensely that my lungs refused to inflate. "Love you."

Kristen responded with a soft snore.

eleven

SHERRI

I couldn't help myself. I ran my fingers over the new, tender lump a few inches below my right collarbone. Things were moving so fast. Port today. Chemo tomorrow. The insurance hoops had been cleared. The port was my new best friend, according to Dr. Pasternak. I stared at myself in the mirror. The angry, red incision that ran up and over the bone didn't hurt. The surgeon who implanted the mediport had assured me the most I would need for discomfort would be Tylenol. The kind nurse who rolled me into the imaging room told me the same thing. Her assurance was the last thing I remembered before the sedation drugs took effect.

The next thing I remembered was being wheeled back to the recovery room. How was it possible to plunk a small, round hunk of plastic with a self-sealing silicone cover in my chest wall and connect it to a catheter that snaked its way to my superior vena cava near my heart and not have it hurt? The gizmo allowed chemotherapy drugs to be delivered safely and reduced the number of needle pokes patients endured for lab work and scan contrasts.

"No worries," I said aloud. "Piece of cake."

No worries that this little port would be used to transport

poisonous chemotherapy drugs directly into my body through a vein near my heart in order to kill my cancer.

"Sherri? Are you all right in there?"

Kris's anxious voice filtered through the cracks around the door. I stifled a half-hysterical laugh at the image of her hovering outside the guest bathroom like a mother with a wayward teenager who'd locked herself in the bathroom. As a physician, she knew it was a simple procedure. Her worry focused on *my* state of mind. My state of mind involved getting through it. Put one foot in front of the other. Do this so the next thing can happen.

The next thing being chemotherapy itself.

"I'm fine."

"Someone's here to see you." The timbre of Kris's voice resonated with something akin to surprise.

"Who is it?"

"Chance."

I glanced at my phone. One thirty in the afternoon. Why wasn't he at one of his construction sites making sure the crews that worked for him were doing their jobs? "Coming."

I ran water and washed my hands because that's what a person did in the bathroom.

Kris was nowhere to be seen. Chance leaned against the opposite wall in the hallway, arms crossed, head back. His dark-brown eyes that always held amusement at the world were closed. He was as long, lean, and hard-muscled in his fifties as he had been in his twenties, wearing faded jeans, a blue chambray shirt, and steel-toed Dickies work boots. The bill of his Texas Rangers cap partially hid his thick silver hair. He'd gone gray in his late twenties, long before I had even a single silver strand. "What are you doing here?"

He opened his eyes and straightened.

"When were you going to tell me, Sher?"

Even after twenty years of marriage and eleven years of divorce, his baritone sent a prickle of electricity up my spine. The hair on my arms stood at attention. I headed toward my bedroom. I was tired of talking about cancer. I was already tired of telling people I loved—and yes, I loved my ex-husband—my crappy news. "I was about to go for a walk. I need to change into my sneakers. A run would be better, but Kristen says no running today. Where did my sister go, by the way?"

"She said she had some work to do in her office." Chance followed me, the rubber soles of his boots thudding on the hallway tile. "She said to help ourselves to tea or lemonade or whatever."

"My agenda is to walk, shower, and nap." I silently acknowledged a weird superthin silver lining. I could engage in these activities mid-day because I had cancer. "You're welcome to walk with me or go about your business."

"Answer my question."

"I'm tired, Chance. Could we not do this right now? You can chew me out tomorrow, but I prefer you do it via phone rather than showing up at my sister's house without calling first."

"I just got off the phone with Noelle. She told me."

It would be ridiculous for me to act like I didn't know what he was talking about. "Told you what?"

After all these years, Chance still had the ability to make me act like a rebellious teenager.

"I know we're not married anymore, but I thought we were friends." Genuine hurt bled through his words. That I could still find new ways to hurt this man surprised me. It hadn't been intentional. He picked up his pace until he was even with me. "You used to be my best friend. If nothing else, we still share three kids and five grandkids."

"I'm sorry, Chance. I don't know why I didn't tell you. Now go back to work and let me take my walk."

Just shy of the bedroom door, Chance grabbed my arm and spun me around so I faced him. His tanned face with its crow's-feet around his eyes and laugh lines around his mouth held a tenderness that threatened to dissolve my defenses. I stopped moving. His familiar scowl sent me hurtling through time and space to all our arguments—some ended in prickly, extended silences, and some ended in bed. Neither option would work here. "That's not good enough. What am I, chopped liver?"

I'd told Kris, the kids, my colleagues and friends at school, and my church small group. My diagnosis had been broadcast on the church's email prayer chain. Yet I hadn't told my ex-husband. Why?

Like Kris, he would want to fix me. His love language involved taking action. Which made sense. He owned a construction company. He built houses. Until our divorce, he and Daniel had been buddies. They'd even worked on some projects together. All good.

That wasn't the problem. I tugged free, whirled, and stomped into the bedroom. "I feel like it's just one more way of disappointing you." The words came out before I had a chance to examine them, but they hit the nail on the head—Chance would appreciate the pun, even if it was unintentional.

"You're crazy, girl. What are you talking about? You have cancer. It's not like you did it on purpose." He stomped past me and paused in the open space between the dresser and the queen-sized bed, his arms hanging awkwardly at his sides. "Besides, there's only been one time in all these years when you disappointed me, and we both know when that was. If I still held that against you, I wouldn't be here now telling you that I'll help any way I can."

I swallowed salty tears. I didn't deserve his help, but that wouldn't stop him. Cleo meandered into the room and stopped, one paw in the air, and stared at Chance. A second later she trotted over to him and rubbed up against his pant leg. She'd always liked him. I started to sit on the bed, thought better of it, and chose the recliner next to the window. I tugged on my sneakers as quickly as humanly possible. "Thank you, but you have a business to run."

"And Kristen has patients. Let me help." He stooped to pick up

Cleo. He petted her for a few seconds, then brought her to me. She took this as her due. He reversed until his back was against the wall between two watercolors. "Let me take you to your appointments. I could help you with meals. I'm good at ordering Grubhub. I can run over to Kerrville and mow your yard this spring when it needs it."

I hadn't even thought of that. "I'll take you up on that last item."

"Good. What else? Let me switch off with Kristen when you start treatment."

"I'm capable of driving myself to my appointments. I won't be incapacitated." I'd made that argument with Kristen on the drive home from the hospital earlier in the day. She admitted that not every patient needed or wanted a chauffeur or company in the infusion room, for that matter. *"We'll see,"* she'd muttered.

I couldn't imagine wanting to make conversation. Reading a book was more my style. "But thank you for offering. If I need anything, I promise I'll let you know."

His gaze averted, Chance crossed his beefy arms. Both our boys were his spitting image. Same lean build, thick dark hair, brown eyes, high cheekbones, long noses. Noelle had his chestnut hair and eyes, but she had my build. He glanced up. "What?"

"You were a good daddy. You still are."

"Thanks. What brought that on?"

I snuggled Cleo one last time, stood, and laid her in the chair. She raised her head and meowed plaintively. "Sorry, girl, I have things to do."

I headed for the hallway. Chance followed so close I was afraid he'd step on my heels. "Come on, Sher, what's going on in that brain of yours?"

He always claimed my brain was twice the size of his. He didn't have a college degree. He didn't read—unless it was a car manual. He liked country music, considered steaks to be a food group, and Dr Pepper was his drink of choice now that he was sober. I preferred the blues, veggie burgers, and coffee anytime: morning, noon, and night. "I'm walking, that's all."

"Then so am I."

"You're not exactly dressed for it."

"It's a walk, not a 5k. Besides, it's a nice day for February. We don't get a lot of those."

I picked up my pace. So did he. I stopped on the sidewalk outside Kristen's. Chance's extended-cab, diesel Ram truck with its retractable tonneau cover sat at the curb. It needed a wash. I told him so.

"Sherri."

I started walking. He came along. So I told him about the visit with my dad. He let me talk without saying a word, but his pace slowed. He'd met our father only once—prior to the wedding. Dad had put on quite a display of parental happiness at our news. Then he went off on a tangent about how tough the economy was, how tight finances were, how little there was for a retired baseball player to do in the "real world."

It only took a quick peek at his dilapidated one-bedroom, one-bath rental with its peeling paint, sagging front porch, and scarred vinyl floors to realize where he was going with this monologue. He was afraid we were there to hit him up to pay for the wedding. After all, he was the father of the bride.

It had never occurred to either of us to ask him for money. We had a small wedding at my church with a reception in my in-laws' backyard. My ivory-lace, tea-length dress came off the rack from Dillard's. We served beer, burgers, and brats grilled by Chance's dad along with sweet tea, followed by Tricia's famous red velvet cake and homemade vanilla ice cream.

I would never know if it was embarrassment at not being able to take that traditional role that kept him from coming to the wedding, but the next time I reached out to Dad, he was in Florida on the hunt for a job and wouldn't be back "anytime soon." Kristen gave me away.

"I'm glad you extended the olive branch, I guess," Chance said when I finally shut up. "Maybe he'll see this as a wake-up call and get more involved with you and the kids. And the grandkids."

"I'm not holding my breath."

Although it did feel like I was. The sidewalks in Kristen's neighborhood, located on the edge of the Hill Country's beginning, wound up and down and around legacy oaks, pecan trees, and juniper. The stretch felt good on my hamstrings and calves, but I struggled to breathe. Allergies and humidity. It had to be. "He's good at talking the talk, but he's never walked the walk. I don't expect him to start now."

"I know how Noelle took the news. What about the boys?"

Chance was the only other person in my life who could read my mind the way Kristen did. "Like Noelle, Cody wanted me to come stay with him. Jason wanted to come home from Germany. I just tried to reassure them. I'm not dying. I'm in good hands. No need to panic."

"You always did put on a good show."

"It's not a show. It'll be fine."

He threw out his arm to force me to stop at the corner. A Mercedes SUV careened past us doing at least forty miles an hour in a twenty zone. "You're so fine you just about walked in front of a speeding car." He snorted. "Be Miss Fine with the kids. I understand that. But don't do it with me."

Echoes of Kristen. I closed my eyes and listened to the cardinals, sparrows, and finches arguing over birdseed in a feeder in the front yard of a three-story plantation-style house. "I have experience with this. I took care of Mom. I survived. I can do it again."

Dumping my fears and anxiety on Chance wasn't an option. His response to stressful situations might lead places I wasn't willing to go. It had before. His sobriety had been a condition of our marriage. He'd faltered once during our twenty-year marriage—after a miscarriage between Jason and Cody—and then hopped back on the wagon so fast I couldn't find it in my heart to hold it against him. He faltered again upon our divorce—for which I took the blame.

"But you don't have to do it alone this time while taking care of a younger sister, finishing school, and working." Chance's Adam's apple bobbed. "Kristen's an oncologist. The kids want to help. You have your faith. I know you're praying about this. I might even try it myself."

Chance might pray. If my diagnosis brought him closer to Jesus, then who was I to complain?

We resumed walking. The houses were set back on large lots with plenty of room for trees and landscaping. The next one was a wood-and-stone house similar to Kristen and Daniel's. A mom in leggings and a T-shirt that stretched to bursting over her enormous pregnant belly supervised a toddler, who was busy drawing chalk pictures on the driveway. Mom waved. The little girl hopped up and ran toward us. "Where you going? Me go."

"Lela, come back here." Her mom waddled after her. She scooped up the little girl two seconds later. "Sorry about that. She's my social butterfly. Absolutely no fear of strangers."

"She's a doll." Chance waved. "Bye, Lela."

Lela blew him a kiss.

We both laughed and returned the gesture. We kept walking. "Remember when—"

"Noelle loved to make beautiful flower-garden chalk drawings on the driveway?" I finished the thought for him. "She would be so upset when you came home and parked on her flowers."

"Little did I know that she would grow up to be an artist with museum pieces and gallery openings."

"I still don't know where that came from. Wasn't me."

"Or me."

A sudden need for the bathroom hit me. Followed by a growing ache in my lower back. I focused on breathing through it. Now that I knew the symptoms, there were no denying them. "We need to head back."

Without a word, Chance did an about-face. We retraced our steps with little conversation. A soft breeze rustled the leaves in the burr and live oaks. Birds chattered. Squirrels chased each other up and down spindly mesquite trees. It was a peaceful neighborhood. School would be out in another hour. First, school buses would drop off elementary school children, then middle schoolers, and finally high schoolers. My kindergarteners were already home. They'd had their snacks and were busy playing.

Did they wonder where I was?

"You'll be back teaching before you know it."

Had I mentioned Chance read me like one of those car manuals he kept stacked in the garage next to his toolbox?

We turned the corner and headed toward the winding sidewalk that led to Kristen's house. A floral arrangements van parked behind Chance's Ram pulled away from the curve and drove off. A familiar red Bug took up space next to my Equinox.

"You have company."

Mona, my Sunday school class teacher. She'd driven all the way from Kerrville to see me. Without a text or a phone call. A friend in Christ just shows up when a fellow believer is in need—that's what she would say. "A friend from church."

"That's nice of her." Chance had gone to church only when his three kids were confirmed in the sixth grade. He never stood in the way of me going or taking the kids. But he drew the line at getting up early on Sunday morning to go himself. He halted in front of his pickup. He dug his keys from his pocket. "I better get back to work." He turned and faced me. "If you need anything—"

"I know."

He edged closer until his body provided shade for me. "Would your sister or your church friend be scandalized if I hugged you?"

"Nothing shocks Kristen. And Mona loves everyone—even skeptics like you. Especially skeptics like you."

"Kristen doesn't like me."

"She thinks you're responsible for our divorce."

Both of us knew better. Chance had never pushed me to tell her what the final straw had been. He wasn't that mean. Now he snorted. "She didn't like me before. No one was good enough for her big sister, but a guy without a college education who worked with his hands? She thinks I married up or you married down."

"That's ridiculous." I laid my head on his broad, sturdy chest and closed my eyes for a second. Peace settled over me. He smelled the same as he always did, like Nautica aftershave and Ivory soap. Clean. Masculine. Solid. "Thanks for coming."

I hadn't known I needed him until he showed up. He was famous for that.

His arms tightened around me. "How about I barbecue some steaks at my place next week? Get you out from under Kristen's thumb for a few hours. Give her and Daniel some alone time."

Steak was his food group, not mine. "Make it a turkey burger at my place and we'll talk."

"I'll call you." Chance jogged around the truck and got in. The windows came down. He flashed that wicked grin and winked. "I love it when you talk healthy foods. It makes you so hot."

Hot, as in desirable. It was hard to feel desirable knowing what was coming for my female body parts, but it was nice to feel wanted, even if our marriage had ended in disaster. I winked back, but he'd wheeled away from the curb, tires squealing.

What just happened? Cancer wasn't a good reason to reunite with my ex-husband. Kristen would be the first to tell me that. We weren't getting back together. Maybe we were finally jettisoning old baggage and starting fresh. I felt lighter somehow.

Until cancer spoke up. Nineteen percent of women with stage 4 ovarian cancer survived more than five years.

Bong, bong, bong. The grandfather clock was back.

twelve

KRISTEN

I'd underestimated Sherri's support system. I clutched the beautiful flower arrangement of sunflowers, daisies, purple asters, yellow roses, and white daffodils while ushering my sister's church friend into the house amid Scout and Dash's vociferous welcome.

"Hush, you two, hush, back up. This is Mona, Sherri's friend. Let her get through the door." I waded past the unrepentant canines, angling for the hallway. "They don't bite. They love everyone." Kind of like Sherri's friend, who took her brotherly and sisterly love very seriously. "Sherri's taking a walk, but she should be back any minute. Why don't we go to the kitchen so you can put the food on the island."

Sherri knew I could handle Mona, whom I'd met a few times, in small doses. Her God's-got-this philosophy tended to get under my oncologist skin. I'd watched too many patients who prayed their socks off, only to wither and die because the available drugs couldn't eradicate their disease. Why did God save some patients and not others? Why not save Mom? *Answer me that, Mona, and maybe I'll consider returning to church.*

Smiling that beatific smile of the blessedly saved, Mona nodded. She was a pretty, plump woman with chubby cheeks and dimples that

117

probably resulted in her getting her face pinched by well-meaning adults when she was a kid. "I love puppies. I have three of my own. And two cats."

Mona rose several notches in my estimation. I hustled into the kitchen without tripping over the dogs, who insisted on escorting us. Her huarache sandals clacking on the floor, Mona followed close behind, despite lugging a small cooler, a foil-covered casserole dish on top of the cooler, a canvas bag, and an oversized leather purse with a manila envelope sticking out from the top.

I settled the arrangement on the breakfast nook table, stifled the urge to peek at the envelope to see who'd sent it, and turned to help her with her burden. "It was so nice of you to bring a meal all the way from Kerrville. It really wasn't necessary. My husband loves to cook and I—"

"No worries, seriously. We always do meals for our members who are in treatment, have surgery, or are experiencing other kinds of medical challenges. It's what we do." Mona settled the cooler on the island, along with the canvas bag and her purse. She pulled the manila envelope out and set it aside. "I'll just put the lasagna in the refrigerator."

I opened my mouth to respond, but she kept going, giving me instructions for heating the lasagna while she unloaded from the cooler a salad, dressing packets, and a cherry cheesecake. A loaf of French bread came from the canvas bag. "Sherri can give me a call when you finish the lasagna. I'll pick up the casserole dish. No rush."

A sixty-mile trip each way from San Antonio to Kerrville and back. "That's incredibly kind of you. I'm sure Sherri will want to deliver it the next time she comes up to Kerrville for something she needs."

"We're family. Sherri's church family. That's what we do." Mona grabbed a napkin and dabbed at a tomato sauce stain on her pink GOT JESUS? T-shirt. "I'm sure your church family does the same."

That last sentence wasn't entirely declarative. It held a question. I had a church family, didn't I? The last time I'd been to church was for Brielle's confirmation in the church Daniel attended with his family. He'd made sure both girls attended growing up. My attendance had been sporadic at best. "I'll see what's holding up Sherri."

Pausing only long enough to shoo the dogs out the back patio door, I double-timed it back to the front door. Sherri stood on the sidewalk, watching Chance drive away. She had a curious look of longing on her face. "Sherri, you have company."

"Coming."

After one last look at Chance's Ram disappearing down the street, she turned and trotted up to the door. "Where's Mona?"

"In the kitchen. Planning how to best save me."

"All the more reason you should've stayed with her."

"Hardy-har-har."

Sherri ducked past me. I followed her. In the kitchen she folded Mona into a hug that involved much back patting and lasted an eternity. Finally, they broke apart. Mona outlined the meal she'd brought. Sherri expressed her appreciation much better than I did.

I turned to leave them alone.

"Don't go, Kristen. The class sent something else for Sherri, but in a very big way, it's intended for you too."

I paused. I could use all the help I could get. So could Sherri. These were kind, well-intentioned folks with an established pipeline to the Big Guy. Prayer might not always help, but it certainly never hurt. I slipped into a chair and waited.

Mona pulled a blanket covered with red and pink hearts from the canvas bag. She held it out to Sherri. "This is a gift from the class. We've heard it's often cold in the treatment facilities."

Did her class think Sherri and I would share the blanket? The image of us in a tug-of-war over it in the infusion room flitted across my mind.

Sherri folded the gift against her chest. She lifted it to her face and rubbed her cheek. "It's so soft. Thank you so much. I'll be back to class soon, but tell them I said thank you, please."

"I will. On Sunday we passed it around the class and prayed over it. We prayed for miraculous healing, if that's God's will. We prayed for your doctors and nurses and staff at the clinic, for a treatment plan that works, for peace, comfort, and God's presence throughout your treatment." Her tone earnest, expression solemn, Mona's gaze traveled to me and back to Sherri. "We prayed for your family because we know that they received your cancer diagnosis too. All of them, but especially you, Kristen, are going through it with Sherri."

"Thank you so much. I so appreciate those prayers." Sherri's voice quivered. More hugging ensued. "Y'all are the best. I don't know how anybody gets through these trials without faith."

People had all sorts of ways for dealing with it. Some positive. Some not. Mindfulness was a big deal these days. With yoga. Support groups. Therapy. Special diets and heavy-duty exercise. Acupuncture and herbal medicines.

"We prayed, Kristen, for your endurance, strength, and perseverance, for peace and comfort." Mona eased away from the hug. Sherri turned to face me, but she kept one hand on Mona's arm. "With what you two went through with your mother, we know it's even harder than it might be for others."

They knew about Mom? An unreasonable anger reared its fierce head. "You know she died, right? Even though I prayed and prayed and prayed, she died."

Even if Mom hadn't made sure we went to church as often as she was able—when she wasn't working on Sunday or the old clunker with a hundred thousand miles on it didn't break down. Then Sherri started working in fast food with Sunday shifts. Still, I clung to the idea that prayer could save Mom like a kid clinging to a piece of driftwood in a tsunami.

Sherri stepped toward me, her back to Mona, and held out the blanket. "Feel this. It's a comfy fleece. Isn't it nice? Isn't it wonderful that they're praying for us?"

Her tone was sweet, but her scowl told me to hold my tongue. I swallowed the angry accusations, sharp as scalpels, and dutifully ran my hand over it. "Soft. Very nice. And I do appreciate the prayers."

I wanted to believe they would make a difference for Sherri. That she would be one of the patients God deigned worthy of His healing power. He was the Great Physician. Why He saved some and not others remained the sticking point. *Explain me that one, Sherri. Why did Mrs. Cranston in apartment 3B down the hall survive her pancreatic cancer, but Mom died from her breast cancer? We prayed just as hard as her daughters did.*

As an oncologist, I knew all the scientific reasons why patients' cancer responded differently to treatments. The problem was prayer was supposed to overcome all those obstacles, and God could fell cancer with His mighty right hand. Simple as that.

So why didn't He do it for Mom? Would He do it for Sherri? I couldn't count on it. No one could.

Not now, Sherri's expression said. *Not now.*

"Don't you want to see who sent you the flowers?" My bland tone was perfect despite the deep gouges inflected on my throat by those knives. "It's a gorgeous arrangement."

The two women swiveled to stare at the clear glass vase filled with a spring bouquet as if they were noticing it for the first time. Sherri wrapped the blanket around her shoulders and went to the island. A second later she opened the small, white envelope. "I knew it." Grinning, she waved the card and sniffed the flowers. "Mmm. They're from my teacher friends at school. They're such a great bunch."

Sherri rarely had a negative word to say about her school or her colleagues. Another reason I tended to think of her job as idyllic. Not a disgruntled teacher among them.

"That was nice of them. You'll have to tell them the flower shop did a really nice job." I stood. "I need to get back to my office. I'll leave you two to catch up."

"Wait. You have to see what Shawna and Nikki sent with me." Mona picked up the manila envelope and waved it around. "I stopped for them on my way out of town."

These were two of the other kindergarten teachers at Sherri's school. "Of course."

Sherri opened the large manila envelope and turned it upside down. A landslide of homemade cards covered with childish crayon drawings cascaded on the island. "Oh my goodness." Her eyes bright with tears, she dropped the envelope. "Aww, my students made these."

"They certainly did." Mona preened as if she personally had overseen this project. "Aren't they precious?"

They certainly were. Crayoned wishes that Mrs. Reynolds feel better. Drawings of her smiling face on a stick body. Purple, pink, and red flowers on yellow construction paper. "I have an old bulletin board of Brielle's. We can hang it in your room so you can display them."

"They'll cheer me up every time I read them." A tear teetered, then trailed down Sherri's cheek. "I already miss them. Every year I think I have the best, cutest kids ever, and every year the new bunch outdoes them."

Even after thirty-plus years as a teacher, my sister still adored her job. She never considered moving up to principal or an administrative job. She loved her students too much. "They're lucky to have a teacher who cares so much."

Sherri sniffed and grabbed a paper napkin from the holder on the island. She wiped her nose. "Thanks for bringing these over, Mona. I so appreciate it."

"Anything I can do to help." Mona hugged Sherri once again. "Call me anytime, night or day. And don't forget to log on to Zoom for class on Sunday morning. They're still streaming the church service at eleven live, so you won't miss a thing."

One of the few pluses of the post-pandemic world. Churches had embraced online worship. Not that I had partaken.

"It's not the same, but it's better than nothing." Sherri swiped at her nose and blotted her cheeks again. "You better get on the road. You'll want to get home in time to have supper with your hubby."

I slipped from the room while Mona raved over the Crock-Pot her husband had given her for her birthday. Supper would be ready and waiting when she arrived home.

Mona had done her duty as a middle school English teacher for twenty-plus years. No wonder she clung to her faith. It was the only way anyone survived those years—especially with twenty-five at a time in her classroom six times a day.

"Kristen."

I paused once again in the doorway and glanced back.

Mona smiled at me. "Just know our prayers aren't one and done. We're still praying and we'll keep praying. Count on it."

"Thank you."

I meant it. Now my voice quivered like that fourteen-year-old girl when she cried out to God to save her mother. I wanted to believe. Otherwise, Sherri's recovery rested on an imperfect medical science that had only a slim chance of saving her. But I'd prayed before and it had made no difference whatsoever.

I fled.

thirteen

SHERRI

"I'm a grown woman. I pay my own way."

Kristen scowled at me. I scowled back. The infusion room nurse who'd introduced herself as Melanie hunched her shoulders as if ready to duck and run for cover. This conversation had started as soon as we left the Texas Cancer Care Clinic financial counselor's office and continued while we waited to be called in to the infusion room. We were sisters. We knew how to wring every drop of drama from an argument.

"I know that. I'm just saying Daniel and I would be happy to help out. As a loan, if you can't see your way to accepting a gift."

If the thought of my first chemo treatment didn't make me nauseated, the payment plan I'd just signed had done the trick. The school district's insurance was decent, but I hadn't made a dent in my annual out-of-pocket deductible, even with all the scans. I was sure my mouth dropped open and stayed there when the counselor showed me my treatment plan's cost. This didn't include the surgery and hospital bills coming in three months. The counselor helped me apply for a rebate for the Avastin. That helped. The rest she broke into payments. I considered myself thrifty. I now needed to get even thriftier.

"I have savings. My car is paid for. My only debt is the house. You've got two kids in college. Can you say the same?"

Kristen dropped my enormous chemo care bag on the visitor chair next to the first open recliner in the infusion room. "Okay, you've made your point. Let's move on."

"Yes, let's. Go to your office. See patients. I don't need babysitting."

"I'm not babysitting you. I'm keeping you company. Most patients bring a friend or family member. It's not a sign of weakness."

This argument would be harder to win. I sat. She didn't get that I didn't want an audience for this cancer "rite of passage." The first treatment. The coffee I'd drank at breakfast sloshed in my stomach. I hadn't even started the treatment and I already felt nauseous.

"Are you sure you're okay?"

Kris dealt with this all the time. But not with her sister as the patient. She needed reassurance. I could at least do that for her in exchange for all she was doing for me. "I'm fine, sis. Sit down. Relax. Take a load off. It's just chemo. We'll pretend I'm getting a new hairdo, mani, and pedi."

She groaned. "You had to go there. If I said that, you'd be all over me."

The new hairdo was coming any day, thanks to the Taxol. I'd dutifully read the chemo education stuff as directed before signing the form acknowledging that I knew my care was palliative, not curative. That I knew the treatment would not cure my cancer, only prolong my life, if it worked. I'd read Dr. Pasternak's patient treatment plan that described my condition as "guarded."

Highly treatable, my foot.

I understood my long-term prognosis. Making me sign what essentially was a liability form to that effect was like driving a dozen eighteen-wheelers filled with salt into a wound the size of Texas.

My phone dinged. A text from Noelle.

Good luck today. Thinking positive thoughts. Max & Gracie send kisses. Followed by a long line of emojis.

She'd attached a video of the kids blowing kisses and shouting, "Love you, Gramma!"

Thanks. Love y'all too. Give them kisses and hugs for me.

I added my own line of emojis. I sucked in air and surveyed the room.

Most of the patients were lying back in their chairs. Many had blankets pulled up around their necks. The elderly man across from me slept. The gray-haired woman wearing granny glasses sitting in a visitor chair next to him worked a crossword puzzle with an ink pen—inspiring immediate awe.

The twentysomething woman in the next recliner wore a bright-pink ball cap and earbuds connected to an iPad in her lap. A woman who had to be her mother read a John Sandford novel. I immediately peered, trying to see which one. The new Virgil Flowers book. I liked her already.

Kristen hadn't mentioned people-watching as a possibility in taking my mind from the fate that awaited me.

"I'll go make sure Dr. P. put in your orders. She's famous for forgetting." If Melanie found treating a relative of one of the clinic's oncologists nerve-racking, she didn't let it show. "Your labs are in. They're fine. It'll take a bit to get the drugs out from the pharmacy, but I can go ahead and access your port. I'm sure if you have any questions, Dr. Tremaine will answer them. But I'm here if you need me."

She scooted away and returned several minutes later with the packet needed to access my port. Kristen had prepared me for this. The poke from the big Huber needle. I closed my eyes. Once a week for three weeks on, one week off, for three months, then surgery, then three months of the same chemo routine. I did the math in my head.

Eighteen lab pokes. Eighteen port pokes. Eighteen times in a chair in the room with its ninety recliners taken by patients in every stage of living with or dying from cancer.

The lidocaine cream had done its numbing work. Kristen also had showed me how to apply it at home and cover it with a piece of plastic wrap instead of gauze, which would only soak it up. It paid to have someone in the know around.

"Not too bad, right?" Melanie attached a catheter from a bag of clear liquid hanging on the IV pole to the port. She stripped off latex gloves and dropped them into the wrapper with the cotton swabs used to clean the area around the port. "This is just a saline solution we'll use to flush your port between drugs. As soon as your premeds come out, I'll be back."

Kristen pushed the recliner down so I could lay back. "I'll get you a pillow. If you slept like I did last night, you might be able to take a nap after Mel gives you the Benadryl. Settle in and relax. With this many patients, you can imagine how backed up the pharmacy gets. It'll be a while before your drugs come out."

I hadn't slept much. Or at all. Shivering, I grabbed my blanket and my book. I got comfortable. Or a reasonable facsimile thereof. I had only a few pages left of *The Sentence*. I wanted to savor them. Kristen returned. She stuck the pillow behind my head. Her hand rested on my shoulder. "I can't stop thinking about how this must've been for Mom. Who went with her that first time? Not Dad. Why don't I remember?"

Because Mom had gone to great lengths to shield her younger daughter from the reality of her disease for as long as she could. And I helped her do it. Kristen was just a kid. The infusion room's cacophony faded away, replaced by the sound of Mom's labored breathing.

The hospice nurse checked her catheter. She adjusted her meds. "It won't be long now." She squeezed my shoulder and withdrew.

"It was probably Tricia. Or one of Mom's other friends from work.

I know the church down the street brought us some meals. I think I remember one of them offering to drive her."

We only attended church sporadically as we got older and took weekend jobs, but the white-haired outreach ladies came by regularly to check on us. The memory always stayed with me.

"That homemade chicken pot pie was sooo good." Kristen rubbed her flat belly. "And the apple pie. And that big pot of chili with home-made cinnamon rolls. Wow."

"Yep. We were eating high off the hog for a bit there." The phrase was pure Mom. She'd grown up somewhere around Cotulla, ranching country, dirt poor, the daughter of an oil field worker and a waitress. "Tricia's chicken-and-cheese enchiladas were mighty tasty too."

"You should've told me she was dying." Kristen leaned closer. Her voice dropped to a whisper. "I should've had a chance to spend more time with her. She kept pushing me away."

Here in a crowded treatment room? Now? Now she wanted to talk about it? "Kristen—"

She swiped at her face with her sleeve. "Never mind. I shouldn't've said that. You've got enough on your plate."

"Mom wanted your high school years to be as normal as possible."

"Normal?" Scowling, she snorted. "I used to pretend Kathy's family was mine. She was my best friend. Her dad was a banker. Her mom was a housewife. When we had sleepovers, her mom would braid our hair and show us how to put on makeup. She was the one who told me I should be a doctor. She said I could be anything I wanted to be. No one had ever told me that before."

Mom was busy dying, and Dad was a no-show. I'd been busy being a high school student, wage earner, nurse, and stand-in mother and father. Hot tears burned behind my eyes. "I'm sorry," I whispered. "I did the best I could."

"It was never your fault. I would never blame you," she whispered. "I felt so guilty for even thinking about wanting a different family.

Like a traitor. I didn't know she was going to die. She kept saying she'd be fine. So did you."

"She was so sure she would beat it. She insisted she would." The fierce determination never left her, not even in those last days. When her oncologist told her she had no other options left, she sought a second opinion. It wasn't any better. "I think if things had been different financially, she might've lived longer. She could've gone to Houston to MD Anderson."

"If Dad had stuck around and got a real job, you mean." Icicles hung from the words. "You wonder why I can't forgive him. Now you know."

With a quivering smile, Kris adjusted my blanket over my arms. It was such a maternal gesture. My throat ached. *There's no crying in baseball or cancer.* I drew a breath. "We'll be okay. I'm not Mom. We have family. We have each other. So much has improved since then. You said so yourself."

"It has. It definitely has." She shrugged as if shaking off a heavy winter coat. "Do you want some coffee? I need another shot of caffeine."

I was still back to those days when I found tufts of Mom's blonde hair on the bathroom floor. When I had to dig clumps of hair from the clogged shower drain the three of us shared. Watching her rush to the kitchen sink to vomit in the middle of a meal of microwaved chicken tenders, mac 'n' cheese from a box, and apple slices. Kristen handled the tenders. I made the mac 'n' cheese. Mom insisted on slicing the apples. "No, no coffee. I've got my water."

"I'll powwow with Tasha and Shay, if I can catch them between patients. I'll be back." She did her best Arnold Schwarzenegger imitation. "That's a promise."

"Tell them you're coming back to work full time on Monday."

"We'll see."

She had to have the last word. I leaned back, but I still didn't open my book. Suddenly so weary, my arms were too heavy to hold it up. I closed my eyes.

"I don't know how I lost so much weight." The high voice held surprise and pique. I peeked to my right through half-closed eyes. The speaker was a petite woman drowning in an enormous crocheted blanket. "I got a haircut, but I don't think that was it."

"Unless your hair weighed an awful lot," her nurse opined. "Like five pounds a lot."

They both giggled. I almost joined them.

"She's had three boob jobs." This from a precious older lady in a bright-yellow shirt who was embroidering a small baby quilt while a big bag of red fluid emptied into her vein. She spoke to an equally cute white-haired lady in a matching shirt. "I'm sure he'll pay for another one."

"Those jobs are expensive." The nurse pushing buttons on the IV pump jumped in. "You have to maintain them."

"He's her third husband. He's rich, and he's ten years older than she is," white-haired lady number one explained. "I guess he thinks it's worth it to give her anything she wants."

She laid aside her sewing. She opened a small red cooler and extracted sandwiches. One went to her companion. A few seconds later the smell of tuna wafted past my nose. My stomach clinched. I began composing a list of dos and don'ts for chemo days. *Don't number 1: No noxious-smelling foods, perfumes, or aftershaves.*

Do number 1: Provide your neighbors with scintillating conversation to which they can listen and escape their own thoughts for a few minutes.

Melanie was back. "I have your premeds. Are you ready to get this show on the road?"

"Yes, please." *No, no, no.* I swallowed tears. My voice shook slightly. *There's no crying in baseball or cancer.* I heaved a breath. "Let's get it over with."

"Are you scared?" Her smile held sweet sympathy. Sadness in her eyes suggested she'd seen a lot. Why choose oncological nursing? Not the time to ask. "It's okay. We'll be right here, taking care of you the whole time."

"I'm glad my sister took a hike."

"Why?"

"She has enough on her plate. She doesn't need to see me cry."

"It'll be our secret."

She asked me to confirm my name and date of birth. I did. She hooked me up. Beeping started down the row. She dashed away. The nurses must hear that sound in their sleep. I laid back in the chair and stared at the small bag hanging over my head. The drip, drip, drip was slow but steady. *Slow and steady wins the race.*

I closed my eyes and saw Noelle, Cody, Jason, and the grandkids, then Kristen and Chance. Their faces hung suspended like portraits in my mind's eye. *God, let me win this race.*

fourteen

DANIEL

The fruits of my labor—so to speak. The leftover teriyaki and brown rice smelled good even before I covered the stoneware bowl with a paper towel and slid it into the microwave in the firm's break room. A silver lining in Kristen's decision to see patients at Sherri's insistence was that I had taken over the cooking again, which meant leftovers to be enjoyed on long workdays.

Kristen hated sitting still, doing nothing while Sherri received chemotherapy. Sherri simply wanted to read and sleep. Especially now that she was into her second month of treatments. Three weeks on and one week off was brutal, and Sherri preferred not to have her sister watch her suffer.

I didn't want to be stuck in the middle, so I tried to stay in the background. Kristen plied me with instructions on what foods to prepare. Fish of any kind was out. The smell nauseated Sherri. Lots of fresh vegetables, sautéed, not raw—she was susceptible to germs—and plenty of fruit. Constipation from the steroids and the anti-nausea meds was a challenge. Diarrhea from the anti-constipation meds. Nothing acidic or spicy—mouth sores.

I scrolled through recipes on a wholistic cancer treatment website.

A *ding* told me an email had arrived. I switched. A client in Boerne. Multitasking was my middle name.

"Something smells good. Garlic, ginger, and . . . hmmm, soy sauce, a hint of apple cider vinegar, chicken maybe." Her head up, sniffing, Pilar padded barefoot into the break room. She wore a still-fresh white sleeveless blouse and navy pencil skirt after a long day of on-site meetings with clients. "I'm betting you had chicken teriyaki for dinner last night. Am I right?"

"Quite the discerning nose you have." I laughed. When was the last time I'd laughed about anything? "I went light on the garlic, though, and watered down the low-sodium soy sauce, heavy on the ginger—it's good for nausea." The microwave dinged. I removed the steaming bowl. "Even so, it's good, if I do say so myself. There's plenty. I'll share if you're interested."

"I'm a connoisseur of Japanese cuisine, but I totally appreciate the effort to make a dish healthier. I brought Asian turkey lettuce wraps. We can go halfsies." She removed a clip from her hair and let it slide down her back. "How's your sister-in-law doing?"

"It's rough. Not just because of the chemo, but it's the not working that's really driving her nuts." Sherri's job as a teacher gave her a reason to get up every morning. Now she had far too much time to think about her disease. "We're praying she'll be able to go back to work in the fall."

"That probably seems like a long way off." Her face full of sympathy, Pilar pulled a long, flat glass storage container from the refrigerator. "I don't know what I'd do if I couldn't work. I'd go crazy."

"Me too. I think we're the only two people left in the building." I selected two plates from the cabinet and placed them on the round table closest to the windows that overlooked the San Antonio River Walk. "Why are you still here? You don't have to prove to me that you're a gung-ho, hardworking addition to my staff. I've already seen that."

"Contrary to what you may have heard, I'm not a brownnoser."

She smirked, then shrugged. "To be honest, I'm still getting used to living alone. Going home to an empty condo isn't all that appealing. And I like being here. I'm excited about the new Belmont residence project."

We chatted about the initial design for this home that was situated on a sloping hill with north and east facades so the homeowners would have sweeping views over the hillside and nearby woods. Pilar waxed eloquent about her first solo project with the firm. "It's fun seeing you be so enthusiastic about a project," I said.

She put a bowl of the turkey filling in the microwave. "Why? Don't you get excited about your projects? You sounded over the moon about the education building."

"I do, but not the same way, not anymore. I've been doing this a lot of years. So has Matt. I like seeing my younger coworkers get enthused about projects."

"You make it sound like you're a zillion years older than I am." The tantalizing scents of pickled ginger, soy sauce, garlic, and chili pepper sauce floated in the air. "So what's the deal? Why are you here so late? You're the boss."

"I have work to do." True, but not the reason I was holed up in my office well past six o'clock. "I get a lot more done when no one is around to bug me."

Pilar paused, serving spoon in the air, eyebrows arched. "Would you rather I bow out?"

"No, no, absolutely not." Heat burned my face. My response was way more adamant than intended. "I mean, you have Asian wraps. You're not going anywhere before you share them."

We settled into chairs in front of the window. Conversation died away, but the silence wasn't uncomfortable. Her wraps were excellent. My teriyaki wasn't half bad, if I said so myself.

"A dime for your thoughts. I like to allow for inflation." She nudged a container of fresh fruit salad toward me. "Why so pensive?"

"Just enjoying the food."

And the company. I grew up in a big family. Eating alone was unheard of. These days I came home to find Kristen had thawed one of several dishes I'd made and frozen for Sherri's benefit. The two had eaten early and were out walking the dogs. Or Sherri couldn't eat and Kristen was in her office working—or still at the clinic. I admitted to eating out of a container standing at the kitchen sink on more than one occasion.

"Uh-huh. That's okay. I'm just happy to have someone to eat with." She put the last wrap on my plate. "I come from a big family. I never learned to like eating alone."

Then she launched into a detailed description of her meeting with our Belmont residence owners, including their eccentricities. I countered with a riff on what it was like to work with a city department and two different grant agencies involved in funding the education building. Red tape long enough to wrap around the Pentagon.

Darkness blanketed the River Walk. The food was long gone. My phone dinged. A text message from Maddie just saying hi. The sensation of a longing sated by sharing good food and excellent conversation with an intelligent woman disappeared, replaced with startling, ugly guilt. Had I been doing something wrong? Was it possible to do something wrong without realizing it?

What if Maddie had called and I'd answered? She would've asked what I was doing. Would I have told her the truth? Yes, of course. It was completely innocent. So why did I feel guilty? "I'd better get going."

"Yeah, so much for getting work done. Sorry about monopolizing your time." Pilar jumped up. She grabbed our dishes and took them to the sink. "I'll clean up. You should get home."

"No way I'm letting a junior subordinate—especially a woman—wash my dishes at work." I tried to take the sting from the words with a laugh. It fell flat. "Can you imagine how that would play out in the #MeToo headlines?"

Pilar's whole body went stiff. "Right." She clipped the single syllable so sharply it could cut like a razor. "You do yours. I'll do mine."

The task was accomplished in complete silence so loud it hurt my ears.

fifteen

SHERRI

The invitation read You're invited to a Bald Is Beautiful party. Bring your sense of humor. Hair optional.

My sense of humor tacked firmly in place, I straightened my shoulders and opened the door. Nikki, Lori, and Shawna stood on Kristen's porch. All three were dressed in teal T-shirts and leggings—the color for ovarian cancer awareness. My colleagues-slash-friends came loaded with appetizers, gifts, and bottles of bubbly stuff. A neighbor walking by might think a party of some sort was getting underway at the Tremaine house. Something fun.

It would be fun, period. End of story. Put up or shut up. And all that jazz.

I shoved my thinning hair from my face. Half a dozen strands entangled in my fingers came away. My stomach rocked. The less hair I had, the more my reflection reminded me of Mom with her fuzzy head. I gritted my teeth and smiled. "I'm so glad you could come."

Ignoring Dr. P.'s instructions to steer clear of people while my white blood cell count and neutrophils hung out in the basement, I hugged each one of them. They'd driven together from Kerrville to cheer me on—or cheer me up—while my hairstylist made a special house call. "I love all y'all."

"How are you doing?" Nikki stepped in first. "How are you feeling?"

If I had a dollar for every time I got asked this question, I'd be on a plane to Aruba. "I'm hanging in there."

"You look ma-va-lous!" Shawna did her best Martin Short imitation. "I expected to find you all skin and bones, child. You've even got boobs."

She meant it as a compliment. People had this made-for-TV-show image of emaciated cancer patients wasting away to nothing. The steroids made me so hungry I wanted to open the refrigerator, prop open my mouth, and inhale everything in it. I'd gained eight pounds and counting. I puffed out my cheeks and stuck out my chest. "Thanks. I think."

The hugs felt good. The miasma that had enveloped me since I started chemo in February dissipated, overcome by their familiar scents of lilac, roses, and vanilla bean. Friends were better medicine than the Zofran or Ativan Dr. P. offered me.

"We're so proud of you." Lori kissed my cheek with an overdone smack. "You are such an inspiration."

How did a person respond to that? What was inspiring about getting cancer and being treated for it? I was just trying to muddle through. *They mean well.* Mom's voice drowned out the prickly answer that came to mind. "Thank you. You're sweet."

"We come bearing gifts." Shawna held up two bottle of sparkling cider—one grape, one apple. "Do we know how to party or what?"

"Actually, we didn't know whether you were supposed to mix alcohol with whatever drugs you're taking." Nikki, who bore a large cheese and cracker tray, squeezed past me. "Besides, we have to drive back to Kerrville after this."

I didn't know about other elementary school teachers, but these women knew how to party without getting wasted. As the former wife of a sober alcoholic, I'd never lifted the self-imposed prohibition against alcohol in the house. Fortunately, neither Kristen nor Daniel imbibed much. "Y'all are the best."

Lori handed me a container that clearly held an ice cream cake. "We thought about bringing healthy snacks, but then we decided this was not the day for that."

"Like I said. The best."

"Where are the dogs?" Shawna was the animal lover and practically a charter member of PETA. "I want to scratch between their cute ears."

"Cleo's hiding in her room, and the dogs are enjoying a day at their favorite doggie spa."

They really did like their doggie day care, so I was determined not to feel guilty about taking over their domain for a day. We tromped in a line to the formal dining room where my hairstylist, Charlie—short for Charlene—had already set up the tools of her trade at a folding table suitably distanced from the big oak table that had been moved up against the wall so food could be served buffet style. Kristen had set up a Crock-Pot filled with queso alongside a basket of tortilla chips, guacamole, salsa, a veggie tray, a fruit tray, salads, casseroles, and an assortment of gluten-free stuff I hadn't bothered to identify. A plethora of desserts awaited in the kitchen.

Daniel was busy adding more folding chairs around card tables covered with teal tablecloths. He was a born host, something Kristen was not.

The Sunday school crowd, a punctual lot when food was involved, had arrived ten minutes earlier. They were top-notch in the food department, given the hundreds—if not thousands—of church potlucks they'd arranged over the years. They milled around, alternately chatting and munching. I didn't have to make introductions of my teacher friends. They mostly knew each other, paths crossing at either church or school.

"I think everyone's here." Everyone but my kids. The noise level hadn't abated one iota. I employed my wolf whistle. That worked. "I think everyone's here, so help yourself to food and we'll get this show on the road—"

The doorbell chimed. I sought out Kristen with my gaze and cocked my head in that direction. She shook her head. "I'm stirring the queso. I don't want it to burn. Daniel's getting more chairs. You better go."

I counted heads. All the invitees were here. Poor timing for a delivery. I trudged back to the door and peered through the beveled oblong glass. Not a delivery. I shrieked and flung the door open. "Noelle, you're here! How can you be here?"

She threw herself into my arms. Her arms tightened around my neck. She smelled faintly of stale airplane and Taco Bell. "Mom, it's so good to see you."

"Hey, what am I, chopped liver?" A goofy, self-satisfied grin stretched across his face as Chance wormed his way through the door. "Doesn't the chauffer get some of that loving?"

I smacked his arm. "How could you not tell me she was coming?"

"If I told you, it wouldn't be a surprise."

I gave him a heaping helping of hug. The two of them were awfully proud of themselves. Tears made it hard to see them clearly. I swiped at my face. There was something different about them. Both wore ski caps. In April. "What's up with you two? Bad hair day?"

"One, two, three," they chanted. Off came the ski caps. "Ta-da!"

Their clean-shaven heads glistened. Noelle's long chestnut hair was gone, revealing a lovely shaped head. Her brown eyes were huge. She wore a teal T-shirt that read FIGHT LIKE A GIRL. Without hair, Chance could be Vin Diesel's doppelganger. Not as muscular, but close. "You guys." I choked on a sob. "You didn't have to do that."

"We're your support team." Noelle dug into the duffel bag that hung from her shoulder and produced a packet of tissues. We each grabbed one. "I know it's easy to say, but it's just hair. It'll grow back. You know how fast my hair grows."

"But your hair was so beautiful." I hugged them both again and came back with Noelle's tears on my cheek. "You're both blessed with nice faces. I'll be Mr. Magoo."

"You will not." Noelle tucked her arm through mine. "I'm guessing from all the cars parked up and down the block, your guests are waiting for you. Let's rock."

"Wait. There's someone else, though." Chance grinned and flapped his arm, pointing toward the porch. "Come on out, Grandpa."

With a sheepish grin on his clean-shaven face, my dad shuffled into view behind a metal walker. He hadn't stopped with shaving the deep grooves on his face. His bald pate shone in the afternoon sun. He'd done his version of dressing up in khaki pants and a white-collared shirt. He hesitated at the door as if waiting for a formal invitation to enter. "Hey, blondie."

Would wonders never cease? I bit my tongue for a second, trying to make sure I hadn't said those words aloud. Chance had gone out on a limb with this invite. Kristen was likely to take a chain saw to that limb. My ex-husband bent closer. "He called me at the office. Apparently, he got my business number from the internet. He wanted to know what I was doing to take care of his sick daughter."

I stifled a groan. "He knows we're divorced."

"He does."

"I can get a taxi home if you don't want me here." His voice gruff, Dad jerked back a step. "I don't want to be where I'm not wanted."

Chance's thick eyebrows got a workout. "It's up to you, babe."

Babe. It had been a long time since I'd been his babe. I'd reached out to Dad first. He'd reciprocated. Wasn't that what I wanted? When should he get to know Noelle and his other grandkids? If not now, when? At my funeral? "Come on in, Dad. How are you doing?"

"I should be asking you that question." He shuffled into the foyer and offered me a one-armed hug. He needed the other one to make sure he didn't fall on his face. "Do you like my new do?"

"It suits you." I swatted away memories of how Mom had looked when the last wisps of her once-beautiful mane had fallen away. Where had he been then? "Everybody's in the dining room."

"This is a highfalutin house Kristen's got here." Wonder tainted with a smidgen of envy filled Dad's voice. "That husband of hers must be doing good."

"Kristen's an oncologist, Dad. They're both doing well in their careers, and they earn every penny, you can be sure of that."

"Must be to buy a fancy place like this."

I shut my mouth and the door at the same time. Instantly, the door chimes sounded. Good grief. Now who? I tugged the door open. Brielle and Maddie.

"Girls! You're here."

"Team Teal Tremaine reporting for duty. We love you, Auntie."

"Yeah, we wanted to be here for you." Maddie made it a group hug. Her brunette hair that hung nearly to her waist swung out like a rippling curtain in a breeze. Brielle's curly hair, a natural platinum for which older women paid big bucks, bounced on her shoulders. Such beautiful hair. Except for the blue eyes, Maddie was a female version of Daniel. Brielle took after her mom. As different in looks as they were personalities. "We brought five kinds of bagels from Nona's Bagel Shop."

My favorite bagels and one of the few foods I could eat postchemo that didn't threaten to come back up. "You win the award for best nieces ever."

They hugged and whooped it up with Noelle and Chance. I introduced them to the grandfather they'd never met. Brielle's mouth dropped open. Maddie actually took two steps back. Kristen had made it a point not to paint their grandfather as an ogre, but neither had she built him up to be more than a man who had little to do with our upbringing.

"You're Grandpa Roy?" Brielle, who was the most like her mother, recovered first. "The baseball player."

Thank goodness she didn't use the adjectives Kristen most often attached to Dad's playing career—*mediocre wannabe*.

"Once upon a time." Dad let go of his walker long enough to make a quick pretend swing of the bat. "You two are the spitting image of your mother at your age."

Not really. I bit my tongue again. No smart aleck remarks today. "Let's move the meet and greet into the dining room. Everyone's waiting."

We trooped into the dining room where more hugs, exclamations, and explanations ensued. Noelle could stay for only one night. Her babies, including Zach, needed her. Maddie and Brielle had driven in from Austin together and would stay the night as well. They were planning a full-scale sleepover / pajama party complete with sleeping bags. I'd take what I could get from all three.

The moment I'd been dreading had arrived.

Charlie patted the chair's seat. "Come on, sweetcakes, I promise to be gentle." People who've seen the old Sally Field and Julia Roberts movie *Steel Magnolias* would immediately make the comparison. My hairstylist was Dolly Parton's hairdresser character, Truvy Jones, incarnate. A Louisiana drawl that could turn howdy into a six-syllable greeting, blonde hair that added a foot to her height, and an hourglass figure topped with a double-d bosom.

She bundled my hair on my head with duckbill clips, tucked tissue around my neck, and covered me with a plastic cape. "I'll cut it short first and then break out the shaver."

Kristen brought me a glass of iced tea and a toasted cinnamon-raisin bagel slathered with cream cheese. Maybe I should've taken the Ativan. "Thanks, sis."

"It'll grow back. I promise." She leaned closer. "How did Dad end up here?"

I glanced across the room. Dad was talking Maddie's ear off about who knows what. She tugged her phone from her back pocket and took a selfie with him. Then the three granddaughters crowded in for a foursome shot. The blissful look on his face matched the smile on theirs. "He tracked down Chance, allegedly to make sure he was taking proper care of me."

Kristen kept her back to the crowd. Her glare was for me alone. "You invited him into our lives, remember?"

"I don't regret it."

The *snip, snip* of shears moved closer to my left ear. Hair tickled my cheek. My nose itched. I rubbed it. Bits of hair landed on the plastic cap. I closed my eyes.

"We'll talk about this later, sis."

I opened my eyes. Kristen's glare had disappeared. She sighed. "Sorry. Hang in there, okay?"

"Do I have a choice?"

"I better refill the tea pitcher."

She headed for the table and picked up the pitcher. Dad scooted his walker in that direction. Kristen turned her back on him and strode into the kitchen.

Baby steps. I didn't have the energy to play United Nations peace negotiator. Not today. I scooped up a handful of hair and let it slip through my fingers. The wisps floated to the drop cloth, golden blonde and silver that disappeared against the white cotton canvas. I'd never been pretty like Kristen. My hair was my best physical feature. Vanity, pure vanity. I wasn't particularly well-endowed in the boobs department. I'd once thought I might marry again. I'd tried dating a few times, mostly men from church. A schoolteacher didn't meet many single men through work. No one clicked like Chance. He'd been it for me, and I'd messed it up.

I thought I had time.

Please, God, let the chemo work. I'd reached the bargaining stage.

God, work Your miraculous healing in me. You are the Great Physician. I'll study my Bible every day. I'll teach Sunday school. I'll volunteer for VBS and Under the Bridge.

God must've received a lot of prayers like this over eternity. People like me who always believed but just never hunkered down to build a relationship. I did Sunday school, Under the Bridge, Vacation Bible School, and youth group with the kids. I believed. That was enough, right?

A sudden fierce jolt of anger shook me to the bones. Like an earthquake splitting me in two: the part that loved God and believed He was good versus the part that was furious with Him. That part wasn't interested in bargaining. Fake faith, like fake news. God couldn't answer my prayers because He knew I didn't mean them. What I really wanted was to ask Him why He allowed this to happen to me again. Hadn't my life been hard enough? Wasn't losing my mother to cancer enough? Wasn't an absentee father enough? This part was growing so big it threatened to jump the divide and slay the other part.

I crossed my arms and shook my head. No fist-shaking allowed in public.

"Hey, sit still, hon. These scissors are sharp."

Forcing myself to hold still, I managed to gulp down tea without moving my head. Outwardly immobile and inwardly seething, I chewed on my lower lip. *Get a grip. Just get through it.*

Considering the clumps of hair on my pillow and the massive piles in the shower, I expected shaving what was left of my hair to take about five seconds. But no. It took forever. The pile of silver-streaked blonde curls on the drop cloth under my chair continued to grow. The lump in my throat grew in tandem. The clipper's buzz reverberated in my ears, worse than the shrillness of a dentist's drill. My body shuddered.

"Hang in there, Mom." Noelle pulled a chair up next to me. She took my hand. "Do you want to watch in the mirror?"

"No, but thanks."

Charlie chatted about her divorce, her kids, her grandkids, Texas politics, and the state of the world. Fortunately, Noelle handled any necessary responses. I practiced deep breathing. The nausea, food tasting like wood, mouth sores, insomnia, alopecia—the medical name for hair loss—and fatigue would be worth it if the chemo worked. The steady drop in my tumor markers, the notoriously unreliable CA-125 blood work, offered hope.

But I'd been disappointed—a weak word for the anguish that accompanied Mom's last days—before.

And even if it did work, how long would my body hold the cancer at bay? Even if I reached that glorious plateau named N.E.D., cancer would find an end run and return—we had no way of knowing when.

"I'd rather have thirty minutes of wonderful than a lifetime of nothing special." The line from *Steel Magnolias* still resonated more than thirty-five years later. *You and me both, Shelby, you and me both.*

"Done." Charlie squeezed my shoulder. She reached past me and picked up a big-handled mirror. "Are you ready?"

My throat closed. I nodded. Charlie handed me the mirror like a maître d' offering a bottle of his finest Dom Perignon. Blood pulsed in my ears. My jaw hurt from clenching my teeth. My eyes burned. I forced a smile and took it.

Mr. Magoo didn't stare back at me. More of a portrait of my dad when he was my age. Except I had no eyebrows or eyelashes. I was a hairless albino. My nose was either regal or oversized, depending on who did the critiquing. My cheekbones were high, like Noelle's, but I had old-lady skin and my neck waddle seemed so much more prominent. I had a big head, and it was so white it could blind a person.

"You're beautiful." Noelle snapped a photo with her phone. "I told Cody and Jason I'd text pictures in our group chat."

"Wait, wait."

A bag of Tootsie Pops in one hand, Chance squeezed past the

women milling around the table. He pulled out three chocolate-flavored lollipops. I forced a smile. He was trying so hard. I ripped the wrapper off and struck a pose. "Who loves ya, baby?"

He and Noelle struck the same pose, lollipop to one side. "Telly."

It was a line from the ancient detective series *Kojak*, featuring a handsome, devil-may-care Telly Savalas, who made bald sexy long before actors such as Bruce Willis or Dwayne Johnson did.

He also said, "We're all born bald, baby," which made him my hero on this day. Even if it was hyperbole. All three of my children were born with varying amounts of hair. Jason had earned the nickname Spike because his hair stood up all over his misshapen head.

Most of the people in the room were old enough to get the reference, with the exception of Brielle and Maddie. Noelle knew it only because it had been a line her parents had revived at odd moments when she was growing up. Chance would pretend to be miffed when I said Telly instead of Chance. The good old days. *"I'd rather have thirty minutes of wonderful than a lifetime of nothing special."*

So we hammed it up for the phone cameras, laughing, joking. Our thirty minutes carved from reality for the metaverse where everyone was happy, happy, happy.

Noelle used to have a T-shirt that read I WANT THE LIFE EVERYONE ON FACEBOOK HAS.

Bong, bong, bong. The grandfather clock's never-ending strikes filled my ears. *Bong, bong, bong.*

I would take this moment in time in my life and hang on to it for all it was worth.

sixteen

KRISTEN

"Are you okay?"

Daniel's solicitous tone only added to my exasperation. He'd followed me into the kitchen, where I'd come to escape the hullabaloo in our dining room for a few seconds. To be alone, in other words, long enough to sort out my feelings about Dad being in my house after all these years. Because Sherri had cancer. Because she might die. None of us had said those words aloud, but they were in the fine print of each and every day. He hadn't shown up when Mom faced the same probability. Maybe he was trying to do better. That was good, right? So why was I absolutely furious that he'd had the audacity to show up at my doorstep as if our visit to the center represented a clean slate? It did not.

None of this was Daniel's fault. Sucking in a long breath, I busied myself refilling the tea and lemonade pitchers. "I'm fine. I just needed a second to regroup."

"Maybe see this as an opportunity for reconciliation." Daniel's hand rubbed my back for one scant second. He reached past me and pulled a glass storage container filled with cut fresh veggies from the refrigerator. "Maybe try communicating how you feel to him so you can shed some of the feelings you've been dragging around like baggage for the past three decades."

"So now you're my therapist?" I set the lemonade pitcher down hard. Liquid sloshed over the top and splashed the counter, me, and the floor. I closed my eyes and counted to ten. "I'm sorry. I didn't mean to snap at you. It's not your fault."

"No, but I can take it if you need to vent." Daniel wet a washcloth under the faucet and wiped the counter. Cleaning up my mess. "I'm just saying, you're wound up tighter than Big Ben. Wouldn't it feel good to tell him how you feel in a constructive way?"

"Feel about what?"

We both turned at the sound of Dad's raspy voice. He sounded like the pack-a-day smoker he'd once been. Of course a bad habit would be the thing we had in common. His walker thumped on the floor as he worked his way to the island crowded with bags, boxes, and carriers used by the church women to transport their dishes.

I took the washcloth from Daniel and knelt to wipe up the lemonade on the floor. "We'll have to mop. This is a sticky mess."

"Anything I can do to help, Krissy?"

He wasn't going away. "You can start by not acting like the girls' favorite grandpa. That award goes to Daniel's dad, Leonard. You know him. Oh, right. I forgot. You didn't come to my wedding." I stood and shot him a scowl that should've fried him to a crisp. "You've never met my husband's family. Until today, you'd never met Maddie and Brielle. Do you know what Maddie is short for? Of course you don't—"

"I'll take the beverages out to our guests."

Daniel grabbed the pitchers and hotfooted it from the kitchen. Smart man. Dad stood there, worn and pathetic, until his son-in-law was gone. "It's Madeleine. I even know how to spell it. I also know Brielle's birthday is March 2 and Maddie's is January 6."

"How? How do you know?"

"Tricia used to send me notes, clippings from newspapers, birth announcements, and such before she moved to Florida with her husband." Now he looked pleased with himself. Pleased because an old family friend reached out to him—not vice versa.

"That speaks well of Tricia. Not of you. You knew you had granddaughters, but you never wanted to know them, at least not well enough to make an effort. You never wanted to be their granddaddy in any real sense of the word. They'd never even seen you until today."

"And that's my fault?" He managed to sound wounded. Him. Wounded. "You made it clear you didn't want nothing to do with me."

"Do you even understand why?"

"You don't know nothing about how things were with me and your mom. You think she was a saint, but she wasn't."

"Don't you dare! Don't you dare stand here and talk trash about my mother." My blood pressure shot into the stratosphere. My heart threatened to burst from its cage. The urge to throw a plate or a glass or a knife at him gripped me. I grabbed the edge of the island's butcher-block top and held on, willing my hands to behave themselves. "Mom raised us. She fed and clothed us. She taught us right from wrong. She taught us to be decent human beings. She provided for us the best she could while you did nothing."

Dad folded into himself like a crushed, empty box waiting to be thrown into the recycle bin. "I don't know what she told you, but she didn't want me around. *She* told me to get lost. *She* kicked me out."

Easy for him to say. Mom wasn't here to verify his version of their marriage's collapse. "If that's true, then she had a good reason. And it doesn't mean you no longer had financial responsibilities for your children. It doesn't mean you were no longer our father."

"Do you know how much semipro baseball players made back in the day? Even today it's diddly-squat."

"So maybe you should've taken a hint and found a real job."

Dad hunched over the walker. He hung his head and studied his feet. He had that hangdog expression down to an art. "I thought I might coach, but that didn't pan out either. I didn't have much education, but I did work. Loading docks, convenience stores, delivery truck driver. I worked. It just didn't pay squat. I could barely make rent. How was I supposed to pay child support? Your mom never asked me for nothing either. She didn't want nothing from me. She made that clear."

Slash, slash, slash. I didn't need a knife to poke a hole in his dreams. That delusional balloon had deflated long ago. Who was I to rub his nose in it? "Say all that is true. If Sherri hadn't knocked on your door in February, would you be here today? Would you ever have reached out to us first? Be honest."

"I don't know." His raspy voice got raspier. He shook his head. "I knew you didn't want me around. It's hard to go where you're not wanted." He waved his arm around, the flabby underarm flapping. "You've got a good life here with your nice house and your pool and your rich in-laws. It's easy for you to paint your family history any way you want. That makes it hard for an old sinner like me to come knocking."

"You really want me to feel sorry for you?" I stopped, gritted my teeth, and practiced my counting again. "The first steps have been taken, thanks to Sherri. Today is about her. Let's just move past this for now. Go out there and be with her. That's why you came here. Leave me out of it."

Dad stared at me for several seconds until his stillness became unnerving. Finally, he shrugged. "For now."

With as much dignity as he could muster, he manhandled his walker in a one-eighty turn and trudged from the room.

I breathed in and out. My phone dinged. Who was texting me now? Not work. *Please don't let it be a patient.* It was Sherri.

> My last wish is that U spread my ashes over the Grand Canyon—while parasailing.

She was nuts. Truly nuts. And she was making me nuts. They all were.

I want U to spread my ashes from the top of the Empire State Building—after you scale it on the outside.

I leaned against the sink on my elbows and let my head drop. A big, racking sob burst from deep in my chest. Okay, I could do this. I washed my face with cold water. With each splash I washed away the grimy remnants of my conversation with Dad. Then I took my own advice and went back into the living room.

The party was still in full swing. A Tootsie Pop hanging from her mouth, Sherri grinned and winked at me from her spot behind a huge pile of gifts. She knew she was making me crazy. She held up a black Stetson cowboy hat. "From Cody. He FedExed it."

"It's you."

She worked her way through dozens of gifts that included beautiful infinity scarves, a rakish beanie, skin products, spa gift certificates, fuzzy socks, aromatic oils, and a multitude of other thoughtful presents. She had good friends.

Finally, the guests began to melt away. They had long drives back to Kerrville, and most of them had to work the following day. Dad angled for an invitation to stay, but Chance did a good job of reading the room. He ushered Dad out the door with the promise to be on call for transportation in the future. Sherri promised to visit him soon at the center. I promised nothing.

That left Sherri, Noelle, and the girls. "Why don't you and Noelle go out on the patio and catch up. Daniel, the girls, and I will clean up."

"I should clean up." Sherri surveyed the table of dirty dishes, piles of discarded wrapping paper, and the mother lode of gifts. Her face was gray with fatigue under the beautiful batik-design scarf

Nikki, a breast cancer survivor, had shown her how to wrap around her head and tuck in. "This is my mess."

"No way. Daniel and I hosted the party in my house. Our cleanup." I took her arm and propelled her toward the kitchen. "Noelle, keep your mom company. You two only have twenty-four hours to catch up on all things grandbabies. Sherri, the girls will stash your goodies in your room and let Cleo out."

"What she said." Daniel picked up a chair and folded it as if to underscore his point. "The cleaning detail reports for duty."

Sherri gave in. I followed her into the kitchen and shut the French doors behind them.

To work. At least I had the company of my daughters for a little longer. I didn't get to see enough of them. The naysayer in my ear asked, *Whose fault is that?* I mentally shot back, *Go away.* I didn't let the jerk spoil my moment when Maddie and Brielle pranced into the kitchen carrying dirty dishes.

"Where do you want the Crock-Pot, Ma?" Brielle held it out so the hardened queso wouldn't soil her T-shirt. "This is some good stuff, but it turns into concrete when it dries."

"Let's put everything in the dishwasher that we can reasonably cram into it." Daniel followed behind them, carrying a stack of serving plates. He and I saw eye to eye on this practice. Wash as little by hand as possible. Less water waste, as long as the dishwasher was full when we ran it. "That's the best way to get all that dried food off these platters too. They sat out too long."

He placed them on the counter, picked up a washcloth, and wiped his hands. "Are you girls spending the night?"

"Of course we are." Maddie's tone suggested his question was silly. "It worked out really well having Aunt Sherri's get-together today. We'll get to hang out with Noelle, and we're here for both special occasions—if you can call shaving your head a special occasion."

"What are you talking about?" A serving platter in one hand,

I turned around in time to see Maddie throw her arms around Daniel's waist and plant a kiss on his cheek. "Don't you girls have class tomorrow?"

"We're playing hooky."

Brielle added her hug to Maddie's. They always had been the fearsome threesome. Daniel spent so much more time with them than I did when they were small. I made all the special occasions, but he was there for the day-to-day stuff.

She gave me a puzzled frown. "We figured you had something planned."

"Planned for what?" As soon as the words were out of my mouth, it hit me. I put out both hands as if I could snatch them back. "I mean, of course, your dad's birthday."

Daniel disengaged from their hold on him. "Don't bother, Kristen. It's obvious you forgot."

"No, no, I didn't. I'm just tired, that's all."

He tossed the washcloth in the sink. "I'm not a six-year-old. I don't expect a big shindig for a birthday. It's just another day."

"No, it's not." Brielle planted her hands on slim hips and glared. "Especially not the big five-oh. Seriously, Mom, how could you?"

"How could you not remind me?" Neither daughter had reached out to ask what I was doing. Nor had his mother, the Martha Stewart of parties big and small. "You could've helped me. I've been up to my eyeballs with work and Sherri—"

"So now it's our fault? It's Sherri's fault?" Maddie's tone scorched my eyebrows. "We assumed you had it handled because you didn't ask for help. We bought gifts—"

I hadn't even bought a gift. Hadn't even thought about a gift. How could I have so totally forgotten my husband's milestone fiftieth birthday? It had fallen on the same day in April every year of the twenty-four years we'd been married and the two we dated. "You know I'm a terrible party planner—"

The girls talked over each other. "You're a terrible—"

"I guess now you'll forget our—"

"Enough. Enough." Daniel clapped hard once. "Stop. I don't need y'all fighting about this. I told you it was no big deal. My mom wants us to come over for dinner tomorrow night. She figured we wouldn't be doing anything. I forgot to tell you, Kristen, so I guess that makes it my fault."

Daniel hadn't forgotten. Angela likely told him she and Leonard hadn't received an invitation to a birthday party and asked why not, knowing full well why. Instead of calling me to forestall this catastrophic lapse on my part, she'd let it play out. Angela loved being right about these things. Giving her the satisfaction rankled, but she was absolutely right this time. "It's not your fault." I moved toward him. "I'm so sorry, Daniel. I'll do better, I promise."

"No, you won't." His expression turned bleak. "But like I said, it's no big deal. It's just another day. I have a big meeting with a client in the morning. I'm tired. I'll put the chairs and tables in the shed in the morning when I let the dogs out. Which reminds me, maybe the girls can pick up the dogs from doggie day care."

"Of course, Daddy, we're happy to do it." Her eyes smoldering, Maddie tossed her long hair behind her shoulder. "Anything to help."

He hugged both girls, offered me a curt nod, and strode from the room.

Maddie and Brielle adopted the same hands-on-hips posture. The same looks of disappointment and disgust marred their faces. Maddie dug her phone from her pocket. "I'll call Grandma."

"I'll tell Sherri and Noelle. Maybe Noelle can stay another night." Brielle moved toward the doors to the patio. Maddie followed. They were talking to each other, not me. "Grandma and Grandpa would love to see her."

"Girls—"

"We'll let you know what time, Mom." Maddie opened the French doors. "Maybe you can carve out an hour or two from your busy schedule to attend."

"I'll do better—"

The doors closed. My head pounded. Tears pooled in my eyes and my throat ached. "I'm sorry."

The words reverberated in the sudden stillness. Dirty dishes on every counter. An open dishwasher. Sticky lemonade drops on the floor. My kitchen was a mess. So was my life. No amount of trying seemed to fix it. All the balls wouldn't stay in the air. They weren't balls anymore. They were finely sharpened swords that threatened to eviscerate me when I failed to catch them.

I trudged to the doors and peered out. Maddie perched on the end of a chaise lounge occupied by Noelle, who had her face raised to the warm sun well into its evening descent. Every nuanced aspect of the patio reflected Daniel, from the recycled pervious pavers to the chaise lounge chairs made from FSC-certified eucalyptus with weathered gray finishes and mesh seats strategically placed under an enormous heritage live oak. The live oak tree's branches spiraled out over the zero-entry, irregularly shaped moss pool that was more like a pond designed to fit between the trees he'd been determined to save.

Every piece of furniture had to pass his test: sustainably sourced, certified nontoxic, and certified by the Fair Trade Commission. One of the companies he particularly favored went so far as to purchase and plant trees for every purchase made of their products. Doing his part to protect the earth that our daughters and grandchildren would inherit from us. When he put it that way, I had come on board without a squeak over the substantial additional costs incurred. These projects made Daniel who he was. It was why I loved him.

My lack of attention to detail didn't change my love for him. Surely he knew that.

I left the kitchen and darted up the stairs to our bedroom. The bamboo blinds were drawn. It was dark and cool. "Daniel."

No answer.

My eyes adjusted to the dark. I could make out the sheets that covered his supine body. I moved closer. "Daniel, I know you're not asleep. I'm sorry. Really I am."

Nothing.

I smoothed his tousled hair. "Forgive me."

He rolled over, his back to me. "Don't I always?"

Yes, he did. "I'll do better."

He sighed. "No, you won't. Good night."

I stood in the dark for a long time, listening to him breathe. Him refusing to speak. Me refusing to leave.

The stalemate that our marriage had become.

seventeen

SHERRI

Swish, swish, swish, spit. A concoction of warm water and baking soda definitely wasn't my choice of drinks on a blistering hot Fourth of July day. But gargling with the homemade mouthwash was better than the "Magic Mouthwash" swill Dr. P. had prescribed for mouth sores. The sores made it hard to eat. I'd gained weight because of the steroids, so I wasn't in danger of wasting away. Still, it wasn't any fun.

I spit into the sink one more time and straightened. A bald lady with dark circles around her eyes, a deep chemo flush across her cheeks, and patches of dry skin on her forehead stared back at me in the mirror.

Daniel was in the backyard grilling tilapia for fish tacos, while the girls and Kristen splashed each other in the pool. He had sweet potatoes fries in the air fryer and homemade ice cream waiting in the fridge.

The girls had talked them into driving over to a spot later where we'd be able to see the fireworks display at Six Flags Fiesta Texas. I didn't have the heart to tell them I'd probably sleep through most of the show. I was coming up on my sixth and last cycle of chemo, and it was kicking my butt.

Suck it up, buttercup. My image's snarky tone suited my mood. I loved my sister's family. I was blessed to be here with them. But what I really wanted was to be with *my* kids and more importantly—no, I wouldn't say that out loud—my grandkids.

My phone played a few notes of Coldplay's "Humankind." Noelle. My daughter had an uncanny way of knowing when I was missing her. I snatched it up. FaceTime. "Hey, daughter of mine, how's the Fourth of July celebration going?"

"We're headed to an Independence Day celebration at the park in a few minutes." Noelle's voice wafted my way, but she didn't have the camera turned on herself. "The kids wanted to wish you a happy Fourth before we go."

"Aww. Where are my little goobers? I can't see them."

"Here they are."

The phone's camera slowly panned around Noelle's cluttered living room until it landed on my grandchildren. Gracie and Max were dressed in red, white, and blue down to the bows in Gracie's blonde curls and the laces in their Converse high-top sneakers. But that's not what caught and held my gaze. Gracie's red T-shirt read BIG SISTER in white letters. Max's blue T-shirt read BIG BROTHER in white letters. Gracie, who looked like a mini Zach with blue eyes and dimples, held up a hand-lettered sign that read, I VOTE FOR A BABY SISTER. Max's sign read, I VOTE FOR A BABY BROTHER.

The meaning sank in immediately. I almost dropped the phone. "Noelle! You're pregnant!"

Whooping and hollering, the kids dropped their signs and danced around the room. Noelle's yes was barely audible over their racket. "You're the first to know—after Zach and the kids, of course. They're a wee bit excited about it."

"I can tell." I put the seat down on the toilet and sat. "When is he or she due?"

"In late March." Noelle turned the phone camera so I could see her face. She was grinning. I could see so much of Chance in her when she smiled big like that. "But you know how it is. Both these little heathens were early. Are you in the bathroom?"

"I am. I was gargling when you called. Congratulations! That's the best news I've had in forever."

"Why? What's wrong?" Her smile disappeared. "Did you have a scan?"

"No, no, not that. Not yet. Not until August. I just meant I miss you and the boys. I love your aunt Kris, but I'd rather be there watching the kids eat Popsicles and watermelon and twirling sparklers."

"I'll send you lots of pictures."

"I know you will." But it wouldn't be the same. "Are you having morning sickness?"

"Yep. That was the kicker. I was late, but I thought surely I didn't get knocked up that fast, so I waited to do a test." She'd retreated into what had been a formal dining room that she'd turned into a study with a desk, a reading nook, and a coffee bar. I could still hear the kids, only now it sounded as if they were wrestling. "Then when I couldn't stand the smell of coffee and I puked my brains out after eating a bagel for breakfast, I figured there was no doubt."

"What does Zach say?"

"If he were here right now, finding the kids trying to thrash each other, he'd probably be saying 'what were we thinking,' but mostly he's on board."

"I'm so happy for you."

"Now you have something else to look forward to. Besides going back to work in September, I mean."

A litany of questions wove themselves in and out of her statement. Would I be able to go back to work in September? Would I come for a visit? Would I be around for the baby's birth? I wished I could categorically state that yes, I would, and for this baby's first steps, her first words, kindergarten, high school graduation, and beyond.

No one could do that, of course, but least of all someone with cancer. No matter how good the prognosis. And mine hadn't been great. "I am looking forward to going back to teaching, but I'll look forward to March even more. I'll try to get up there for a visit. Hopefully for Thanksgiving. If not, Christmas."

Said with all the bravado I could muster. Noelle needed that assurance. And so did I.

"Good. I can't wait." She glanced over her shoulder. "Sounds like Zach's back. He went to pick up hot dog buns. I bought the dogs and forgot the buns. Anyway, I'll send you bunches of photos later. Don't tell Dad. The kids want to do it. But you can tell Aunt Kris and Uncle Daniel. Tell them we say hi and all that."

"I won't and I will."

"Love you, Ma."

"Love you more. Tell the goobers I said bye."

"I will. If I don't kill them first."

And she was gone. I stared at the black screen for a few seconds longer. I scooted forward until I was close enough to lean my forehead on the granite-topped vanity. It was cool on my warm skin. Time to gird my loins, so to speak, buck up, pull up my big-girl panties, and all that stuff. About eight months until the baby's due date. Not that far off. I'd be around for it. Surely, I would. *Right, God?*

The silence wasn't quite silent. It sounded more like, *We'll see.*

Yes, we would.

I stood, straightened the infinity scarf wrapped around my head, and went to share my good news with my sister and her family. I would stay awake for the fireworks after all. Such good news was worthy of a celebration.

eighteen

SHERRI

Put-up-or-shut-up day. That's what I called it. Three months of chemo, check. Debulking surgery, check. Ovaries, uterus, fallopian tubes, cervix, omentum—gone. Even my poor, unsuspecting, wrongly accused appendix—gone. My surgeon said he threw the appendectomy in for free. Three more months of chemo, check. Finally. August had rolled around. Now I could get on with my life. Or not.

Dr. P. called it a consultation. Whatever she called it, she'd better hurry up and get her behind into the exam room before I ran screaming into the hallway like Shirley MacLaine in *Terms of Endearment*. I'd waited long enough for the CT scan results. Two days. Forty-eight hours with dread planted on my shoulders, its thick, hairy arms wrapped around my neck choking me, whispering in my ear, *Be afraid. No, it'll be okay. I'll be fine*, I countered. *No, you won't. You won't live to see that new grandbaby. Yes I will*, I stubbornly fought back.

If it was good news, I could go back to teaching when school started in two weeks. If it was bad news, I faced a new chemo regimen with the job of trying to eradicate platinum-resistant ovarian cancer. According to the internet research I'd been doing against my better judgment—and Kristen's—it was the most intractable, untreatable form of the disease.

162

It wouldn't happen. Not to me. Not to Kristen. *Right, God?*

Shivering, I zipped up my hoodie. I shuffled the note cards my Sunday school class made for me, reading through them. Each contained a scripture intended to comfort me. The Bible said "do not fear" three hundred sixty-five times, one for each day.

Oh ye of little faith.

I'd tried to memorize some of them, but chemo brain fuzz made it impossible.

Finally, I settled on Psalm 23. I'd memorized it for a Vacation Bible Camp as a kid. It stuck with me when nothing else did. *"Yea, though I walk through the valley of the shadow of death, I will fear no evil . . ."*

It didn't work. My mind kept zooming around my brain like a hamster on steroids. *What if, what if, what if?*

"No matter what happens, you still have options. Remember that." Kristen took my hand and rubbed it between hers. "Your hands are icy. Next time, we bring your mittens along."

I didn't dare open my mouth. I might scream. Doctors knew these were among the worst days in the lives of their patients. Not as bad as diagnosis day, but bad. Yet they kept them waiting. It was a form of institutionalized torture. I nodded.

She'd insisted on coming with me. Just as she'd insisted she and Daniel were good after the fiasco of the birthday forgotten in the midst of planning my Bald Is Beautiful party in May. Never mind the walking-on-eggshells atmosphere that had permeated the house every day since.

I needed to be okay so I could go home to my house and my job. So they could have their house and their lives back. *Please, God, if not for my sake, for theirs.*

The door opened. Not Dr. P. Her transcriptionist. I sank back in my chair. The knot in my throat choked me. Still, that meant Dr. P. wouldn't be far behind.

"She's on her way." She scooted her office on wheels into the corner and took a seat. "She had to do a peer-to-peer for another patient."

I don't care. I want my results now. Now! Now! I gritted my teeth. My jaw hurt. My legs demanded I stand and pace. The exam room was too small. I could go out in the hall. No. I shoved aside the urge. She'd be here any minute.

Any minute. Any minute. I stared at the door, willing it to open.

Kristen and the transcriptionist commiserated. Their words were gibberish. I needed a translator.

The door flew open. Dr. P. dashed in. "Sorry, sorry. It's been a crazy day." She plopped into her chair, holding a sheaf of papers against her chest with one arm. The radiologist's report. My lab work. The tumor markers. My heart pounded in my ears. My blood pressure had been through the ceiling when Shay took my vitals. Now it had to be through the roof of a two-story house. I couldn't catch my breath. Kristen gripped my hand so hard it hurt.

"Good news."

The blood pounded so hard in my ears, I couldn't be sure I'd heard right. My breath caught in my throat. "What?"

Dr. P. held out the report. "No evidence of disease, my friend." Her smile would've lit up the scoreboard at the Alamodome. "The chemotherapy eradicated the masses left over after your debulking surgery."

I shook my head, trying to clear the dissonance. Air hissed. My worry and angst and anxiety and stress leaked away. I laughed. Kristen jumped up. She pulled me to my feet. We hugged hard and long.

I broke away and turned to Dr. P. "Can I hug you too?"

"Of course."

We hugged some more.

"Okay, my friend, now we talk about what's next." She pointed to my chair and took her own seat. "Maintenance."

"For how long?"

"Until there's progression."

"I told you that, remember?" Kristen's hand covered mine again. "The days when we just did surveillance are over. We have good options now for staving off a recurrence. We need to use them."

The bubbles of joy floating around me popped, one by one. "Right. Of course. I knew that. It's just hard to wrap my head around doing this for the rest of my life."

"That's understandable. There's the thing. You live in a new world now." Her smile held patience and caring so profound, it almost broke down the dam that kept me from bawling. "You can't go back to that old world, but you're in a good place in this one."

"I know. I'll try to focus on that. I promise." The important thing was that I could go back to work. Back to my house. I might not recur for a year or two years or more. No one knew for sure. "What did you have in mind for maintenance?"

"PARP inhibitors are the preferred frontline maintenance drug now." Dr. P. pushed her glasses up her nose. She leaned forward, elbows on her knees like she always did when preparing for a serious discussion. "The upside is you have the BRCA 1 mutation and olaparib—its trade name is Lynparza—is particularly effective for women like yourself. It comes in pill form so you don't have to come to the clinic for treatment. Just for labs and periodic checkups with me."

"Yay. And the downside?"

"The side effects can be severe. We'll tinker with the dose to try to minimize those effects as much as possible. You'll continue to take the medications for nausea in particular."

"What other side effects are we talking about?"

"Much like chemotherapy. Fatigue, diarrhea or constipation, low neutrophils, low red and white blood cell counts, low platelets, anemia."

"I'll deal with them. I really don't care. I'm going back to teaching."

Kristen stirred next to me. "I don't know, sis. The risk of sickness and infection is the same—"

"I do know. I'm teaching. I'm N.E.D. I'm not putting my life on hold any longer." I stood. "In fact, I'm going to your house right now to pack and pick up Cleo."

"That's fine." Dr. P. spoke gently. "I'll put in the order for your prescription. As soon as it's approved and you start taking it, we'll set up a schedule for labs and exams. The drug is quite expensive, but you're eligible for the manufacturer's co-pay assistance. It shouldn't cost you a thing."

Another upside. "Thank you, thank you, thank you." Still light-headed with relief, glee, disbelief, and sweet release, I rushed to the door. I had a life to live. "Are you coming, sis? I've got places to go."

Kristen exchanged another hug with Dr. P. "I'll keep you posted," she told her colleague. "If we have trouble getting approval on the drug, I'll get back to you."

"'I'll get back to you.'" I shook my finger at my sister. "You'll be busy taking care of your paying patients. They'll be pleased to have 100 percent of your attention from now on."

Until next time. She didn't say the words, but her haggard face spoke for her. There would be a next time.

So be it. Until then, I was like a singing bird who'd escaped from her cage. I would fly away to the highest branch and sing my heart out until caught again.

nineteen

DANIEL

I hadn't lost my touch. I stepped back to survey the scene I'd created. A lacy tablecloth purchased new for this special occasion covered the primitive reclaimed oak table that seated eight. Silver candleholders held white taper candles with perfect elegance. I'd laid out our vintage cobalt-blue Fiesta dinnerware place settings for two on white place mats. Matching napkins puffed up on the plates. Crystal wine glasses hugged the edge of the mats. Three dozen red roses graced the center of the table. I adjusted the volume on the stereo. Kristen's favorite jazz artist, John Coltrane, played her favorite instrument, the saxophone, on low.

Dash and Scout watched from their side-by-side spots near the bay window. Occasionally, one or the other would raise his head to peer at me quizzically. "I know. I'm not usually so fancy, but twenty-five years deserves fancy, don't you think?"

Dash cocked his head and yawned.

"Okay, so you're not impressed. She will be, I promise."

I straightened the white eight-by-eleven envelope decorated with a silver bow next to Kristen's place setting. The big, romantic gesture my dad had recommended last winter. I'd pulled out all the stops for our silver anniversary. I could count on one hand the number of couples our age we knew who were still married at this milestone marker.

Sure, there'd been plenty of bad days, especially recently. But today I was ignoring them. This muggy September evening we would start fresh. She'd see how hard I was trying. She'd try too. That night of Sherri's Bald Is Beautiful party, she'd stood in our bedroom and insisted she loved me.

That memory had carried me through three more months of Sherri's treatment followed by three months of Kristen catching up on all the work she hadn't done while helping her sister navigate in the cancer world.

Satisfied with my work, I returned to the kitchen to check on the food. I grabbed pot holders and opened the oven door. The tantalizing aroma of Italian stuffed shells wafted through the air. The cheese on top bubbled a beautiful golden brown. She'd ordered shells on our first date at a hole-in-the-wall restaurant on San Antonio's northwest side. She was just starting medical school. I was a newbie junior architect at a firm where I planned to pay my dues until I could start designing the kind of buildings I truly longed to create.

It seemed like a long time ago.

I glanced at my watch. Ten 'til six. She usually made it home by six these days. Knowing what today was, she wouldn't be late. She'd assured me before she left the house this morning that she would be here. She would not be late. No way she'd forget. She'd promised to do better that night in our bedroom. After all these months, how she defined that still remained unclear. I'd given her the benefit of the doubt over and over again. That was what we did. The pattern was set.

I passed the time adding butter and garlic powder between the partially sliced pieces of French bread. I wrapped it in foil so it was ready to go into the oven as soon as Kristen walked through the door. The green salad with fresh cherub tomatoes, black olives, peppers, a sprinkle of shredded Parmesan, and cucumbers was ready to be tossed.

The homemade lemon-and-olive-oil vinaigrette was chilling. The tiramisu—purchased from Paesanos—would remind her of the one we'd shared on that first date. I'd let her have the last bite.

Six o'clock. The clock in the breakfast nook tickled loudly. I turned down the oven so it would keep the shells warm without overcooking them. I cleaned up my prep mess and loaded the dishwasher. It would be nice not to have to do it afterward. I hoped to be otherwise occupied.

Six fifteen. I turned off the music. Coltrane was starting to annoy me.

Six thirty. I poured myself a glass of red wine. I wasn't much of a wine drinker. Especially red wines served at room temperature. My lips puckered. I poured it down the kitchen sink.

Six thirty-eight. I called her. No answer. Left a voice mail. "Dinner's ready. I hope you're on the way."

Six forty-five. I texted her.

The shells are getting dry. Are u on yr way?

No answer.

Seven o'clock. I turned off the oven, removed the shells, covered them with foil, and stuck them in the refrigerator. The foil-wrapped bread followed.

She'd forgotten. Or she'd simply been too busy with a patient. Either way, it didn't matter. I'd had enough of playing second or third or tenth fiddle. I could call again. I could text again. Normally, that was what I did. Now it seemed tantamount to begging for her attention.

No more begging. No more pleading for a smidgen of her time. Time was precious. If anyone knew that, Kristen did. Yet she continued to flagrantly disregard its passage when it came to our relationship.

Would she miss me if I simply walked away? The disfigured, barely recognizable truth buried under years of making excuses for her stared at me like a succubus suddenly appearing in the mirror.

Seven ten. I stomped up the stairs to our bedroom. The dogs followed me around, still looking puzzled. They recognized the duffel bag. They weren't happy when I traveled. "It's okay, guys, we'll share custody. I'll see to it."

Neither dog appeared mollified. Maybe it was my tone.

Seven twenty-five. I surveyed the toiletries stuffed into my bag. I had everything I needed, at least for a start. I'd get the rest later. I trudged downstairs and scanned the great room. It looked different through the lens of leaving. I loved this house. I loved the people who lived in it. The people and the hounds.

I knelt and hugged the hounds. Dash whimpered low in his throat. Scout yipped. "I know. It sucks, right?" I stood. "No worries, guys, I'll figure something out. I promise."

Seven forty-five. I added food and water to their bowls in case she didn't come home at all this evening. She occasionally spent the night at the hospital, knowing I was around to take care of Dash and Scout.

If it came to it, would Kristen give up custody? I honestly didn't know. She'd never had pets as a kid. I'd never not had them. Dogs were my idea. When she'd realized how short their lives were, she'd balked at adopting new ones after our first dog, Walter, a sixty-pound rescue mutt who thought he was a lapdog, died at the ripe old age of twelve. *"Why keep doing that to ourselves?"* she'd asked through tears.

Because dogs, unlike humans, loved unconditionally.

Eight o'clock. I walked out.

twenty

KRISTEN

I hugged my patient's husband. I needed it as much as he did. He broke away, turned his back, and put both beefy hands on his wide hips. We stood outside his wife's ICU room. We were alone—accompanied only by our grief, his anger, and my guilt—now that the hospital's doctor had walked away, leaving me to deal with the aftermath of my patient's sudden, horrific demise. Daryl Sedaris leaned forward, his chest heaving. I laid a hand on his arm. "Is there someone I can call for you?"

He jerked from my touch and turned to face me. Tears dripped from his chin. "My mom and dad are on their way." He swiped snot on his sleeve. His hoarse voice broke, and he swallowed a sob. "I have to call her parents. They're in Cincinnati. I should've called them sooner, but I thought she'd . . . the surgeon said . . . you said—"

"These kinds of fistulas are so rare, and the sepsis that sometimes results from the repair surgery can usually be treated successfully." My mind traveled back to that day in my office in February when I told this man and his young, blooming-with-health wife, mother of two-year-old Shiloh, that her uterine cancer was highly treatable.

The drug regimen I outlined was standard of care, although one of the IV drugs was fairly new. The percentage of patients experiencing a fistula during clinical trials had been less than a third of a percentage point. I hadn't mentioned its more serious side effects at all. Those would be covered by the chemotherapy education—before the patient signed the liability release form and started treatment. "I'm so very sorry for your loss."

Words always failed in these situations. The English language failed. No words could convey the depth and breadth of the hole in my heart that kept getting bigger with every lost patient. Claire Sedaris, age twenty-six, had called me from home three days earlier complaining of severe abdominal pain, fever, and feces coming out her vagina. Classic signs of a gastrointestinal fistula. I urged her to go immediately to the emergency room. I called ahead to get her admitted stat. I met them at the hospital. I did everything I could until I had to step aside and let the surgeon take over.

That surgeon had successfully repaired the hole in her bowel. Unfortunately, sepsis set in almost immediately. It raced through this young woman's body like an unrelenting firestorm. Antibiotics didn't touch it. Two days later this vibrant, marathon-running, vegan, physical therapist mother and wife was dead.

"The treatment was supposed to save her life, not kill her."

Anger burned the words to a cinder. His tone, his face, his body posture reeked of anger at a boiling point, threatening to spill over and scald me. Anger was easier to handle than grief.

"That's the tightrope we walk with cancer treatment. The drugs' side effects are often as dangerous as the disease, but not treating the cancer at all surely leads to death as well."

"It sucks. *It sucks!*" His big hands fisted and unfisted. He wanted to hit something or somebody. He wanted to lash out and make others hurt as much as he did. I'd seen it all before. Felt it myself. His greatest fear had been realized so suddenly, he hadn't had time to ease into the possibility and begin to think about what his life would be like without the woman he loved. "And Shiloh. How will I tell Shiloh?"

He sank against the wall. A passing nurse slowed and stopped. I shook my head. She moved on.

I grappled for words, any two or three or four that I could string together in some semblance of comfort when there was no comfort to be had. "She'll have you. You'll have your family to help raise her."

"Little girls need their moms."

A movie clip resumed in my head as if it had never stopped playing.

Sherri and I stand in front of the hole in the ground, staring as the plain wooden casket is lowered. The wheels squeak. The only sound on a breathlessly hot July day. I sweat through the black cotton blouse Tricia bought for me, along with a black skirt. I didn't want to wear black. Mom's favorite color was blue. Tricia said no, not for a funeral. Why did it matter? Only about twenty people attended the funeral, and they all knew Mom liked blue best.

Sherri's hand creeps into mine. Hers is slick with perspiration. She squeezes. I don't squeeze back. I can't. I can't move. I can't speak. I'm frozen, caught like an actor with stage fright forced to go onstage without knowing my lines or where to stand. It's happening to someone else. Not me. Mom will get up in the morning. I'll toast bagels for breakfast. Sherri will slather them with cream cheese. Mom will add the strawberry preserves. Our own little assembly line.

"Strawberries are good for you. Antioxidants," she'll announce like she does every time. "You should always have fruit for breakfast."

We'll laugh. Sherri will say something sarcastic: "Sure, Ma, like ice cream is good for you because it has milk in it. All that calcium and vitamin D. We should have ice cream for breakfast."

"It's hot enough. Maybe tomorrow," Mom will say.

We'll laugh some more.

The kitchen will smell like coffee and toast. It'll smell like love.

You can't be dead, Mom. You can't. We need you. I need you. You can't go. Come back. Come back.

Tricia takes my other hand. They drag us away. They're not being mean. They just know we can't stand here forever, no matter how much we insist.

It didn't matter. We visited her simple, twenty-four by forty-eight gravestone once a month for years. Until we moved to Austin for college.

When was the last time I visited? I couldn't remember.

This man was right. It sucked. Eventually, it would stop sucking so much. But not completely. Never.

"Children are amazingly resilient," I whispered. Mostly because they didn't have a choice. "You'll raise her right. You'll help her remember her mom."

He covered his face with both hands. They did little to muffle his sobs. Tears dripped between his fingers. They dropped onto the carpet, leaving tiny darkened spots on the gray Berber.

"Daryl!"

A tall, muscular woman dressed in leggings and a T-shirt advertising a triathlon raced into the room, followed by a massive man who was the picture of what Daryl would look like in twenty-five years. Daryl's hands dropped. He straightened. The newcomers enveloped him in a hug.

My cue to withdraw. I slipped away before Daryl would be forced to introduce me as the oncologist who killed the love of his life.

I gritted my teeth and breathed deeply and slowly through my nose as I trudged through the hallway, took a crowded elevator to the parking garage, dug through my bag for my keys, opened my door, and slid in. I leaned my forehead against the wheel, hands at two and ten.

Only then did I cry.

Crying was a luxury I rarely allowed myself. When I decided on medical oncology as my specialty, I knew what was ahead of me. I did rotations in pediatric, radiological, medical, gynecological, hematological, and surgical oncology. The rates of burnout, depression, and even suicide were high in my field for good reason. I didn't care. I'd stayed ahead of the latest developments in my field, read all the studies, did research of my own, headed clinical trials, attended conferences, presented at conferences. I'd tried hard at being the very best. There would be breakthroughs. People would not only live longer, but they'd be cured.

Sometimes that was true, but not often enough. Not nearly often enough. I hadn't done enough. I hadn't been enough. Not for Claire Sedaris.

I would also be a wife, mother, sister, and friend. Women could do it all now, couldn't they?

Enough. I straightened, took a deep breath, and grabbed a tissue from the console. I blew hard. Enough feeling sorry for myself. Time to go home and regroup.

A shower and a good night's sleep was my focus. The thought of food turned my stomach. Hopefully, Daniel hadn't made dinner. Tomorrow I'd eat a bagel and cream cheese in Mom's honor.

Food. Daniel.

No, no, no.

twenty-one

KRISTEN

No, no, no. Daniel.

I dug through my bag and found my phone.

There it was. One missed call. One text.

I read. I listened.

No, no, no.

I glanced at my phone.

Eight fifteen.

Not that late. Not so bad. We could still eat. I didn't even have to wrap the certificate I bought for him that would fund the planting of five hundred trees in Mozambique, Kenya, Madagascar, and Nicaragua. He would love it. Plus, it was proof I hadn't forgotten. Right?

I glanced down at my wrinkled white linen blouse and navy pants. No time for a shower and dressing more appropriately for a romantic anniversary dinner. Daniel wouldn't care. He'd never cared about outward appearances.

I hit the ignition button. Told OnStar to call him. It rang and rang. *Pick up, Daniel. Pick up.* "This is Daniel Tremaine. I can't take your call right now . . ." Voice mail. I smacked the wheel. "Daniel, I didn't forget. I promise. I'm just running late. I'll explain when I get there. Happy anniversary! Don't start without me."

That last part was meant to be funny. Funny ha-ha.

I made it to the house in under thirty minutes. The stars were aligned. No cop saw me blow through a stop sign, make an illegal U-turn, or exceed the speed limit by twenty miles an hour.

The house was dark. Candlelight, maybe? Romantic mood lighting, possibly? I didn't bother to pull into the garage or plug in. Later. I grabbed my bag and let myself in. "Daniel! Daniel?"

Scout and Dash met me with their usual joyous, rousing chorus of barks, yips, and licks. "Hi, guys. Where's Daniel? Where is he?"

Was it my imagination or did their expressions dim? They continued to circle, dance, and welcome but with less vigor.

"Daniel?" I dropped my bag and keys on the foyer table and kicked off my flats. "I'm here. Happy anniversary!"

No answer.

I sped into the grand room. Empty. Dining room next. I halted.

He'd laid the table out with great care. Lacy tablecloth, our wedding dishes. A massive bouquet of red roses in a gorgeous cut-glass vase had a starring role in the center of the table. Crystal wineglasses waited to be filled.

My throat tight, I moved closer. A large white envelope decorated with a huge silver bow lay next to one of the place settings. Daniel had written my name in his careful block print. "Oh, Daniel, I'm sorry."

How many times had I said I was sorry today?

Scout whined and nudged my hand with his wet nose. "I know, boy. I messed up. Again. Where is he?"

Not in the kitchen. It was spotless. Leave it to Daniel to clean up his own mess, even when I screwed up. Maybe he needed to decompress and went out on the patio. I threaded my way through the chaise lounges and stood on the moss pool's edge. The wind had shifted to the north. I shivered and crossed my arms. Crickets chirped. A frog croaked. Dash raised his head and sniffed the air. "Where is he, Dash?"

No answer.

He wasn't upstairs in our bedroom either. The comforter was mussed. Like maybe he sat there for a moment, thinking. I opened his closet door. I never went in it, so it was hard to tell if anything was missing. A lot of empty hangers, but then it was Thursday. Most of the week gone. We did laundry on Saturdays. Or he did.

An empty spot opened up on the floor next to his neat rows of slip-on shoes, flip-flops, a wide assortment of sneakers, and a pair of slippers—a gift from one of the girls—he'd never worn. That open spot. His duffel bag. The one he liked to use for travel because it was small enough to take on board a plane but big enough for a weeklong trip. It was gone.

A headlong rush to the bathroom confirmed my suspicion. His toiletries were gone. Even the Polo Maddie had given him for Christmas.

"Daniel!"

Stupid to call his name when he'd so obviously and blatantly vacated the premises. My image in the mirror shot me an accusing glare. I shook my head. "I know it's my fault, but I didn't do it on purpose. He should've given me a chance to explain."

My friend in the mirror rolled her bloodshot eyes and snorted. *He's heard all your excuses before. You couldn't even show up for your twenty-fifth anniversary.*

I ran both hands through my hair made wild by a day of increasingly stressful developments. "I showed up!"

Two hours late. Without a call or a text. Without answering his call or text. What do you expect? That he'll wait for you forever?

"He always has."

That's his point. He's spent twenty-five years waiting for you to put him first. Not all the time. Just once in a while. Just on these special occasions.

"My patient died. It was my fault."

My voice cracked. Resorting to emotional blackmail had always been unnecessary with Daniel. He never wanted to feel like a whiner. He never wanted to be the kind of spouse who complained when his wife had such an important career. People's lives depended on her. And the last thing he wanted to do was make her cry. His tender heart couldn't take it.

I'd used that get-out-of-jail-free card one time too many.

I hit his name at the top of my favorites list. *Come on, come on! Pick up, Daniel.*

Voice mail. "Daniel, I'm sorry. Please call me back. I'm so sorry. Let's talk. I can fix this."

I hung up and texted him.

Come on, Daniel. Call me. Please.

I can't talk to u right now. I'll say things I shouldn't

I'm sorry. My patient died.

I'm sorry your patient died

Come home.

No

Where are you? I'll come to u.

No

Can't we talk?

No. Not tonight. Be sure u open the envelope on the table. u should know what you'll be missing

Just talk to me.

Night

Daniel?

No response.

I sped down the stairs into the great room. The envelope was light. *You should know what you'll be missing.* Right now, I was missing my husband. I dropped into the chair and turned the envelope over in my lap.

Just open it.

I tore off the top and withdrew a sheaf of pages on a travel agency letterhead. An itinerary. Plane tickets. Hotel reservations. Excursions.

A trip to France in the spring. Two weeks. One full week in Paris.

The honeymoon we never took. We couldn't afford it, then we had kids, then our careers took over our lives.

The trip of our dreams went from being a belated honeymoon to a bucket list item.

"Oh, Daniel." My eyes burned with unshed tears. They wouldn't fall. They knew it was all my fault. Tears wouldn't make it better. I clutched the papers to my chest. "I'm so sorry."

I called his number. Voice mail. "Daniel, I love this. I love you. Please call me."

I hung up and texted him.

The best anniversary gift possible. thank u. I love it. I love u. Call me. Please.

He wouldn't. He'd made that clear. Not tonight. Maybe not ever.

I tottered up the stairs and into the bedroom. Without removing my clothes, I pulled back the comforter and slid under it. I curled up in a fetal ball. "I'm sorry," I whispered into the inky blackness.

I know you are. Sorry isn't good enough. Not nearly good enough.

My phone dinged. A text. Daniel. I fumbled it from the charger, dropped it, hung over the edge of the bed, and retrieved it.

> Happy anniversary! I hope you and Daniel are having a
> lovely evening. Here's to many more

From Sherri. I threw myself back on the pillows. I couldn't tell her what a failure her sister was.

> **Thanks. Talk to u tomorrow.**

Tomorrow I would figure out how to get him back. Scarlett O'Hara had nothing on me. I closed my eyes and waited for morning.

DANIEL

"Stay at Mom and Dad's house."

"I'm not a kid, Andrew." I rubbed my burning eyes. "I can't go running home to Mommy because I had a fight with my wife."

"You're not running home. You're regrouping." My brother was doing his version of counseling. He was good at it. He and his wife had done couples' counseling off and on for years. "You're asking—demanding—that your wife invest some time and effort into your marriage. That's not too much to ask."

"Sherri has cancer. She may die. Kristen has her hands full."

"That doesn't mean she can abdicate from your marriage."

I'd called Andrew because I knew my brother would tell me what I wanted to hear. "I'm not being selfish?"

"You're the least selfish person I know. You're the Mother Teresa of the Tremaine men."

"Let's not get carried away."

"Come stay with us."

"You have a full house." And I didn't need my brother's wife

181

serving me soup like I was sick—heartsick. "Besides, you're almost an hour from my office downtown—ninety minutes during rush hour. I'm better off here."

"Where's here?"

"A motel that rents suites by the week or month."

"That's crazy. You can afford a nice hotel. Why not treat yourself? You're punishing yourself, aren't you?"

"No. I'm trying to be economical." Besides, it was just until I found an apartment or, even better, a house I could rent. Until I could buy my own house. My stomach dropped. Was I really considering giving up the house I'd built with Kristen? Would she even want it? *Slow down, just slow down.* "It's just for a while until I figure out what to do."

"Okay, but you're always welcome here. You know Dad would love to have you at the ranch. Mom would love it if you stayed at the house."

They would make it too easy for me to bail out. They'd both want to give me advice. Dad would invite me on a hunting trip. Mom would cook all my favorite dishes while she gave me more advice. Leaving a marriage and breaking wedding vows wasn't supposed to be easy. It wasn't supposed to happen at all. "I know. I have to sleep. I have a site meeting with a client in the morning."

"Call me if you need anything."

"Will do."

"I mean it."

"Thanks."

I put the phone on the charger and leaned back against the too-soft pillows. The Econo Lodge suite smelled like Fabuloso cleanser and lemon furniture polish. The mattress had a sunken spot on the side I always slept on. I scooted to the other side. Another crater the size of someone's overly large behind. I stood, pulled back the comforter, and slid under the sheets. The digital clock on the nightstand glowered at me: 11:05 p.m. A whiff of bleach stung my nostrils. I was so used to eco-friendly cleansers I'd forgotten how harsh commercial ones smelled. Pipes creaked. Water dripped from the bathtub faucet, a steady, irritating *drip, drip, drip.*

I rolled over on my back and stared at the ceiling, replaying the texts exchanged with Kristen. Her patient died. A young mother and wife. Of course she had to stay with the husband. Of course she did. Anything less would be inhumane. *I didn't mean to be. I hadn't started out this way. I love you, Daniel.*

I'd withheld my love from her for the first time in twenty-five-plus years. Did that make me a monster or just lonely? Was I being selfish? Would leaving home make me less lonely?

The constant sound of traffic rushing by on IH-10 East should've been soothing. An eighteen-wheeler's airhorn blasted the silence. A horn blared in response.

It was the loneliest sound in the world.

twenty-two

SHERRI

The smell of whiteboard marker in the morning was invigorating. The smell of vomit, not so much. As a kindergarten teacher, sometimes I had to take one with the other. "It's okay, Sonya. Miss Lucy will walk you to the nurse's office."

I patted the five-year-old's hunched shoulder. She hiccupped a sob. "I sorry, Miss Reynolds." She swiped her runny nose with her sleeve. "I told Mommy my tummy hurt. She said she had to go to work."

Then she leaned over the trash can I'd grabbed after the first round and vomited a second time. More sobs. "I sorry, I sorry."

Gunnar, who sat on the first row within splashing distance, groaned. "Eww, gross."

His classmates tittered.

"It's not funny." Haley, who sat behind him, kicked his chair. She and Sonya were best friends this week. "She doesn't feel good."

"It stinks." Gunnar held his nose. "So do you."

"All right, kids, that's enough. We don't need a running commentary." I swallowed hard against my own nausea. The PARP inhibitor so far refused to relent on this side effect. I drew a breath and breathed out through my mouth. "It's okay. These things happen."

Some teachers railed against parents who sent children to school knowing they were likely sick or getting sick. When my kids were young, I empathized with their dilemma. Mine stayed home only if they were vomiting, had a fever, diarrhea, or any combination thereof. I had a responsibility to my students. Parents needed to work, so their children had to come to school, tummy ache or not. "I hope you feel better, sweetie. Miss Lucy, could you tell Mr. Tom we need a cleanup in room K2?"

My trusty teacher's aide nodded. "Will do. I'll be back as soon as I get Sonya situated."

"Good. You should be back in time to lead them to the cafeteria." Thank goodness. We all needed a reset.

Lucy picked up the trash can—just in case—and took Sonya's hand. "My turn to monitor the lunchroom. Enjoy your lunch."

I would if I could get this smell out of my nose. To that end, I opened the windows that lined one wall of the classroom. A nice September breeze wafted in. "Okay, class, where were we?"

"Show-and-tell." Haley's hand shot up. "My turn, my turn!"

Their homework had been to bring something to show that began with a *B* and be prepared to tell us something about it. "Go ahead, Haley."

The freckle-faced girl grinned. She was missing both her front teeth. She pulled her backpack onto her desk and unzipped it. "This is my friend Boo-Boo, the bunny."

Out popped a large white rabbit that immediately peed on Haley's desk.

Mr. Tom, the custodian, took care of the mess. Lucy returned, and then it was lunchtime. Time did fly when you were having fun. I snagged my lunch cooler and headed to the teacher's lounge. I settled at a table occupied by Nikki and Shawna, who were commiserating over their students' learning loss over the summer. Now they were playing catch-up. I pulled out yogurt, strawberries, almonds, and a sleeve of Ritz crackers. My stomach rocked. *Come on, not now.* I practiced breathing exercises.

"You do such a beautiful job with the kids." Principal Neil Dodson paused next to our table. His remark was directed at me, totally ignoring the other two teachers within earshot. "Especially all things considered."

"Thank you." *I think.* Was that a left-handed compliment? "What do you mean, all things considered?"

"With your condition and all."

My condition and all . . . my cancer. "My condition's fine." Other than nausea and low blood cell counts, my maintenance drug had been far easier to tolerate than chemotherapy. Plus, oral pills meant I didn't have to go to the clinic to be treated so often. My energy was back. I was jogging again, taking a spin class, and trying out yoga. I considered myself blessed. "I think I have more energy than some of my kids."

"Good, good. You're such an inspiration to us all." Neil jerked his head toward Shawna and Nikki. "Right, y'all?"

Nikki winked at me. "Such an inspiration."

"Such an inspiration." Shawna tossed a mini rice cake at me. "I bow at your feet, oh great one."

Neil frowned. "No need to be sarcastic. Teaching a roomful of kindergartners while fighting cancer is quite a feat in my book."

I wasn't fighting anything. I was living with it and being treated for it. No punches thrown. "Thank you, Neil."

With one last frown for my colleagues, he wandered away.

"You guys! He means well." Most people did. They either didn't know what to say, or they had outdated notions of what cancer patients should act and feel like. "At least he doesn't run the other direction when he sees me."

Since I returned to teaching this fall, some of my colleagues seemed to disappear whenever I entered the room.

"You're right." Nikki deposited an enormous peanut butter cookie on my napkin. "My apologies."

"To Neil, not me." I nudged the cookie back toward her. "Maybe you should give it to him instead."

"Not happening. That would be a waste of a homemade cookie." She grinned. "I'll split it with you."

"No way! I want the whole thing." I snatched it from the jaws of a hungry teacher in the nick of time. "I wish I could be more inspirational. Now that I'm N.E.D., all I can think about is when is it coming back. I lay awake at night doing the what-if thing. It's driving me nuts."

"I remember those days." Nikki patted her flat chest. She'd decided against surgical reconstruction after her breast cancer bout. "It's been five years, and supposedly I'm past having to worry about recurrence. But there are still times when fear sneaks through the back door."

"The Bible says *do not fear* 365 times," Shawna and I chorused together, doing our best Mona imitation. "One for each day."

"We're so blessed to have her as our Sunday school teacher." I decided to do dessert first and took a big bite of cookie. It was a while before I could finish the thought. "I remind myself of when she asked me if I thought God was still good. If the answer is still yes, then I have to trust that He has a plan for me."

"So when's He going to let you in on this plan?" Shawna slurped what was probably her third Diet Dr Pepper of the day. By dinner-time, she would've finished off four or five. "I love Mona to death, but sometimes her Sunday school answers irritate me."

Sunday school answers. *God's got this. God has a plan. God is good. God can bring good from all things.* All true, but not helpful when a person grappled with why one cancer patient lived and the daughter of the folks sitting in the same pew didn't. They prayed just as hard. They believed just as much.

Mona said some of our questions wouldn't be answered until we arrived in heaven.

That I believed.

We finished out the day without further incidents—if I didn't count Boo-Boo pooping on a beanbag during reading time. On my way home, I stopped at the church to drop off a bag of clothes for the Under the Bridge ministry for people experiencing homelessness. Who should be in the foyer but Mona.

"Were your ears burning?" We hugged. "Shawna, Nikki, and I were talking about you over lunch."

"I thought I felt a twinge. I'm glad I'm interesting enough to be the topic of your conversation." She curtsied as dainty as a ballerina, despite her lovely girth. "Anything I can do for you today?"

Mona always asked this question. I'd never heard her ask for anything in return. "No, I'm fine."

"You don't look fine." Mona took the bag from me and hoisted it into the bin left by the church's kitchen door for this purpose. "You look tired and flummoxed."

As a former middle school English teacher, Mona liked to bring out the big-guns vocabulary. She never pulled punches when voicing her opinions either. I picked up a pair of sandals that had fallen onto the floor next to the bin. "Thank you so much for those kind words."

"You're welcome. I calls them like I sees them." She cocked her head toward the workroom that held supplies, staff and lay leader mailboxes, and the copier. "Step into my office."

This was supposed to be an in-and-out stop, but no one in her right mind said no or not now to Mona. I followed her into the workroom and plopped into the closest chair. She checked the outreach committee's box, then turned to face me. "What gives?"

"Katie Carmichael died yesterday."

"I know. We're organizing the food for the reception after the funeral next week." Sadness sparred with a brisk no-nonsense, can-do attitude. "Her Mother's Day Out kids are making cards for Bob and her two boys."

"She was only thirty-nine. She taught at Mother's Day Out. She taught Sunday school. Her husband is in the faith band. They never miss church. It had only been five or six months since her diagnosis."

"Brain cancer moves fast, so I'm told." Mona slipped mail into her oversized bag and fixed her clear-eyed gaze on me. "It's hard for all of us when we lose a sister in Christ and member of our church family, but I imagine it's even harder for someone like you who's dealing with a similar situation."

I lined up a dozen Magic Markers in a single row. "The entire church prayed for Katie. We have some powerful prayer warriors in this church, including you."

"We do." She sat across from me. "Come on, girl, spit it out."

"She died in six months."

Her gaze bathed me in kindness. "And?"

"I'm still here. Katie's not. It doesn't seem right. In fact, it sucks." I teetered on the edge of admitting my lack of faith to one of the most ardent believers I'd ever known. "Bob has to be asking himself right now why God answers some prayers and not others. Why He saves one person and not the other."

"I think Pastor Joel would say God answers all prayers, just not the way we want Him to." She picked up my row of markers and tucked them into a pencil box in the middle of the table. "I won't give you the ultimate healing pitch—"

"Thank you."

"I don't know why some people are healed and others aren't. But the question remains the same. Do you believe God is good?"

"Most of the time." I sucked in a breath and let it out. "But sometimes, in the middle of the night, I wake up and stare at the black darkness and wonder if He's even there. Even real. If He even cares."

"Me too."

"You do?"

Mona leaned closer as if about to share a secret with me. Her face crinkled in a conspiratorial smile. "I'd wager that every Christian does. They just won't admit it."

I closed my eyes and opened them. "Good to know. I'm just glad I'm not the only one."

"Me too." She shrugged with a philosophical air. "I figure once we finally see Him face-to-face, we can get our questions answered once and for all. In the meantime, we have to hang on, even in our unbelief."

Not always an easy thing to do. An ache in the vicinity of my lower back made it harder. Every little ache, every little pain, and I was sure the cancer was back, growing inside me, threatening to take over. "So you think we're getting through those pearly gates even though we're so riddled with uncertainty?"

She grabbed my hand, closed her eyes. "Lord, forgive us in our unbelief. Give us the faith we need to survive this day and every day. Amen." Her eyes opened and she glanced at her watch. "Welp, I have to run, my dear. I put together chicken-cheese enchiladas last night. I just have to pop the dish in the oven so it'll be ready when hubs gets home. You're welcome to join us."

Smiling, I shook my head. Mona was a force of nature. "Thank you, but I have chores to take care of this evening and school tomorrow."

On top of that, I would be busy surviving this day and every day after it.

twenty-three

KRISTEN

Fifteen patients down, five to go. I desperately needed a second wind. Not sleeping at night since Daniel walked out—more likely ran out—was taking a heavy toll. The fact that he refused to answer calls or return texts only reinforced the drowning sensation that overwhelmed me in the middle of patient exams. My eyes were gritty. My head throbbed. A sour feeling now lived in my stomach. I grabbed my bottle of tea and slipped out the clinic's back door to the employee parking. After a quick survey of the lot, I settled against a wall behind a Suburban that would block patients driving by from seeing their oncologist taking a smoke break.

Oncologists knew healthy living didn't translate to no cancer. So why not have a smoke now and then? For me, now and then meant once a day. Twice if it was a bad day. Okay, three times tops. It was my one vice. I'd quit. Eventually.

"You too, huh?"

I jumped, tucked my hand behind my back, and turned. Arina—or as Sherri liked to call her, Dr. P.—approached, a small pocketbook in hand.

"Oh, it's you." I took a long draw and let the smoke curl out of my nose. "Great minds think alike."

Arina lit her cigarette and leaned against the wall. "Others might contest the great minds part." She grinned. "It's been a day."

"Yep, for me too."

"At least the end is in sight." She contemplated the glowing end of her cigarette. "Only two months to go."

"What do you mean?"

"I guess you haven't heard." She raised her face to the afternoon sun and closed her eyes, a big smile stretched across her mannish face. "I put in my papers. I'm retiring."

"What? No way!" I coughed out the smoke I'd just inhaled. "You're kidding, right? Arina, you're not much older than I am."

"That's sweet of you, my friend. I'm ten years older than you and aging faster."

That made her fifty-eight. Way too young to retire. "Even so, why so young?"

"For one thing, the stress is killing me." She held up the cigarette. "Exhibit A. Sergei wants me to quit smoking. I can't do one without doing the other."

"Your patients. They love you. They depend on you." The thought hit me like a bullet between the eyes. "Sherri loves you."

"I love my patients too. But I love my husband more." Her face softened and she became more attractive. "Sergei is six years older than I am. I want us to have time together. A lot of time. We're building a house in the Blue Ridge Mountains in North Carolina. Plus, we have the cabin in Washington State. What's the point of having these places if you never get to enjoy them?"

Was that first part a not-so-subtle jab at me? She couldn't know about my split with Daniel. I loved my husband as much as she loved Sergei. Her husband was an oncologist. He understood her workload and her priorities. He understood in ways Daniel never would.

Plus, she had a built-in pressure valve that I didn't have. "You go on vacation every three months." Her contract with the practice contained this caveat. A week—nine days with weekends—off every three months for her mental health. "Isn't that enough?"

"Apparently not. Every time I come back, I count the days until the next time. I love hiking and birding with Sergei. He loves to cook for me. He wants to have a big garden and two more dogs. Maybe even a cat."

They could do all those things around San Antonio. No need to quit. "You have a garden. Sergei cooks. You hike the greenway trails. You have two big dogs already. What's the problem?"

"Spoken like someone who drank the oncologist-is-God Kool-Aid." She sucked on her cigarette and created a perfect smoke ring. "You know, this field ages us ten times faster than any other. Sergei says we should start living our bucket list now before the stress kills us. That means camping in at least one national park in every state of these great United States of America."

Daniel was nowhere near retirement. He couldn't afford to take a vacation every three months—in terms of time off work or the expense. Neither could I. At least there we were on the same schedule. Thank goodness. "I'm just surprised."

"I don't know why. I've been saying it for at least two years."

"Exactly, but you never actually did it." I stubbed out my cigarette, picked up the butt, and put it in the plastic bag I kept in my purse for that purpose. "When will you tell your patients?"

"This week."

She followed my lead, adding her butt to my bag. I held the door for her and we went inside. "But you can tell Sherri if you want."

"No way. I'm not doing your dirty work for you." Sherri would be devastated. Patients often became emotionally attached to their doctors, especially the ones who successfully brought them through horrific treatments for deadly diseases. "Don't be a coward."

"She has you. She'll be fine. You can help her select a replacement. Dr. Rodriguez already knows her from doing her surgery."

So reasonable and rational—which meant nothing in the face of the irrational belief that your doctor has kept you alive and without her you'll die. It didn't make sense, but cancer did that to people. Another reason I didn't foresee an early retirement in my future.

"There you are. I should've known." Her tone accusing, Shay marched down the hallway toward us. "The hospital called about Mrs. Brice. Dr. Rodriguez is looking for you to talk about possibly having Mrs. Detweiler do radiation, and Mr. Denman has a question about swelling in his feet."

"All that in the ten minutes I was outside?"

"All that and then some." Shay motioned toward the exam rooms. "Mr. Reeves is next up, exam room 2."

Ten minutes and all hell broke loose. What would happen if I were gone nine days every three months? Or simply retired and didn't come back? I loved Daniel. Forgetting his birthday was bad. Being late to our anniversary, terrible. But in many ways, understandable. Somehow, I had to make him see that.

First, I had to get him to talk to me. Soon.

Right now, I had patients to see. I hustled to the exam room, but my mind kept reviewing Arina's reasons for retiring young. They had a nice ring to them. But they didn't stand up to the work that still needed to be done. I needed time to work my way into clinical trials. To make an impact. A bigger impact than treating one patient at a time.

Arina wanted more time with her husband. She wanted to hike, swim in the ocean, zip-line, camp in Yellowstone. With Sergei.

I had my own bucket list. With Daniel. Later. I wasn't through conquering cancer and saving patients. There would be time for trips to Paris later.

Seriously? Who are you kidding?

Mom's voice.

No guarantee of a future filled with trips to exotic locales existed.

As the saying went, I could get hit by a bus tomorrow. So could Daniel. Or I could be diagnosed with breast cancer, like one in three of my fellow women would be. Or he could get prostate cancer, so common in men.

Could, would, might, who knew? Only God knew.

So did that mean I should throw in the towel? No. There would never be enough time. Retiring would always be out of the question because time would always be in short supply.

twenty-four

SHERRI

I followed Cammy, Dr. P.'s medical assistant, down the hallway to the exam room like one of my eager-beaver students who wanted to be first in line in the cafeteria. Anything to get this over with. Missing another day of school sucked. November was a short month with the Thanksgiving holiday coming up. Subs couldn't be trusted to keep up with my lesson plans. These kiddos were expected to know how to read by the end of the year, and it was my job to teach them. Even if I felt like ground hamburger some days.

The scan wasn't that worrisome, not really. My CA-125 was up but still within the normal range. It had been only three months. The PARP inhibitor gave some women with my genetic mutation as much as two years without progression. Sure, some only got six months. That's why it was called an average. I'd been telling myself that since the CT scan two days earlier.

Cammy and I discussed the pros and cons of low-carb diets while I was weighed—down two pounds for the second visit in a row—and she took my vitals. Blood pressure 150 over 90. "Stress will do that," she commiserated. She told me about her little boy's first basketball game. We compared notes on the books we were reading. Cammy was good at distracting.

"She has two patients ahead of you." Dr. P.'s medical assistant didn't do the "be right with you" thing. She knew better. "So it'll be a bit. I'm sorry."

Did she know the results of my scan? Probably.

"I brought my book." I was reading William Kent Krueger's new Cork O'Connor mystery. If that didn't keep my attention, nothing would. "If you could turn up the heat, that would be great."

"I wish I could." She grimaced. "It's November; winter is just around the corner, but in the clinic we're still running the AC. I hope you brought a sweater."

I had.

She left me alone. I donned my sweater. Instead of reading my book, I googled *ovarian cancer recurrence*. Like I hadn't done that before. *Web*MD was my best friend. I turned the phone facedown. I didn't need to search anything. I was fine. I'd refill my prescription for the PARP inhibitor and go on my merry way.

I had Thanksgiving decorations to make for my room. Lessons to share with my students about the pilgrims, about blessings, about what really was served on that first Thanksgiving. What had been the real role of Native Americans in that celebration. My little ones would use blunt scissors and construction paper to make pilgrim hats and Native American headbands with feathers. We'd carve pumpkins. I'd bring toasted pumpkin seeds and pumpkin bars for our Thanksgiving feast.

I couldn't recur this soon. Not with my entire church family praying for me. Not with all my colleagues praying. My family—the believers, of course. My social media friends.

How many prayers did it take? Was there a threshold? God already knew what I wanted. I wanted one question answered: What does God think I need? Mona's pep talk resounded in my head. If we were healed, we would stay around, spreading the love of Jesus in the world. If God chose the "ultimate healing," we'd go be face-to-face with Jesus, the Big Kahuna, Himself. What could be better than that?

I believed all that. I did. But it wasn't a win-win for my kids. For Noelle and Zach's new baby, who wouldn't know his grandma. I wouldn't know him—or her—either. It wouldn't be a win-win for Kristen, who would go through the anger and pain and suffering of losing another loved one to cancer. Despite her best efforts, she would feel guilty.

Don't use me to hone the character of the people I love, God, please.

Who was I to tell God what to do? *It's only a request, God, a suggestion, if You will.*

I needed to know which way it would go. The not knowing made me crazy. If I knew, I could just get on with it—whatever *it* was.

The more I tried not to think about it, the more I thought about it. Round and round and round. Conversations in my head on repeat. Sleep was the only time they stopped. Then I dreamed about chemotherapy. Always with Dr. Pasternak taking care of me. Always waiting, waiting, waiting.

I apparently trusted her.

So trust her now.

The door swung open. Finally.

Nope. Kris barreled into the room. She had a stain on her blouse, red-rimmed eyes, and hair that needed a good trim. "Hey, sis. I saw Arina in the hallway. She has one more patient, then you're next."

"What are you doing here?"

"Moral support."

"We talked about this. I'm fine. No matter what happens, I'm fine."

"It's good to be positive." She plopped down next to me. "My patients with positive attitudes always do better."

"Why are you here, really?" A horrible thought struck me. My left leg bounced. "Did Dr. P. ask you to come? What did she tell you?"

"No. She wouldn't do that." Kris's scoffing tone matched her frown. She put her hand on my knee, stilling my leg. "Not unless you agreed to it."

Right. Right. "You should be seeing patients."

"I am. This is my lunch break."

"You better not be keeping anybody waiting on my account."

"I'm not."

"So I've given it some more thought, and I want my ashes spread from the Great Wall of China—after you walk the whole thing."

"Oh, please. Have you noticed that our relations with China are not particularly good these days—what with the whole Taiwan thing?"

"You mean you won't fulfill your dead sister's last wish?"

"No problem. I want my ashes sprinkled on Mount Everest. You're the marathon runner. You can hike the highest mountain in the Himalayans, no problem."

"No problem." *Was* a marathon runner, not anymore. "So. Moving on. Have you talked to Daniel?" Might as well address the giraffe in the room. She wouldn't; therefore I would. "Did you call him?"

"I've called him numerous times. He has stopped picking up. Instead, he's showing up at the house and taking stuff when I'm not there."

"Stuff? Like what?"

"Clothes and stuff. At least he sends me texts informing me when he's going to take the dogs."

"Poor Dash and Scout. They must be so confused. Like kids whose parents are fighting." That reality was far too familiar. My kids had seen right through Chance's and my efforts to hide our deteriorating marriage. They'd dealt with splitting their time between two households like souls old before their time. "Where does he take them? Where's he living?"

"He didn't say, but I figure it has to be the ranch on the weekends. It would have to be someplace like that to take the dogs. Maybe his parents' during the week—the ranch would be too far a drive when he's working."

"Maybe you should go beyond apologizing and show him you can do better. You know, walk the walk for once."

"Seriously, I did. I offered to go to couples counseling."

I already knew the answer to my next question, but I asked it anyway. "And what did he say?"

"He asked me when."

"And?"

"Why are you doing this? I told you what happened. Why rehash the rehash?"

"Because until you prove to him that you intend to make your marriage a priority, he's not coming home."

"I'm in line for a job I really want. I've been trying to move into doing more research for a couple of years now. The opening is coming up. He knows that—"

"Once again, your career is more important than your marriage."

"Doing something concrete and real to find more and better treatments for cancer like yours isn't something you say no to. Daniel knows that."

"He also knows that he's unhappy and lonely. So go ahead, cure cancer, just don't expect Daniel to hang around waiting while you do."

"He's trying to save the world by designing zero-carbon footprint houses and I don't complain—"

"Not the same and you know it."

"It's a double standard for women—"

The door swung open. "Hello, hello, my friends."

"To be continued."

Kris sat back and crossed her arms. "You have enough on your plate without solving my problems—"

"Girls, girls." Dr. P. shook her head. "You remind me of my sisters and me. We fought like alley cats, but if anyone messed with us . . . whew, there was hell to pay."

"Sorry, someone got up on the wrong side of the bed."

"Moving right along." I elbowed Kris. She shut her mouth. I focused on Dr. P. "You have my results?"

"I do." Two syllables delivered in a neutral tone. She sat down with a sheaf of papers in front of her. "The scan showed progression. Extensively. The retroperitoneal lymph nodes are larger, and three more have popped up. There's a small mass in your left lung and in the pleural lining. Masses on your liver and the gastrocolic omentum."

No easing into it. Rip that bandage off.

The words sucked the air from the tiny exam room. The *boom-boom-boom* could only be the beating of my heart. Darkness shrank my peripheral vision. Purple spots danced in front of my eyes. Kris's cold hand covered mine. I stopped shaking my head, only just realizing that I was doing it so hard my brain hurt. "That can't be right. This drug is supposed to be the latest, greatest."

"You have high-grade serous ovarian cancer." Dr. P. leaned forward, elbows on her knees, squinting at me over her bifocals. Her let's-get-serious pose. Her Russian accent got thicker when she was serious. "We now know it's platinum resistant. That makes it even tougher to treat. It narrows our options, but we're not *out* of options."

Kris let go of my hand. I floundered, disoriented. Her arm came around my shoulders and drew me closer. Nine months of hoping and praying and pretending to be fine, determined to be fine, believing in God and medicine.

"Your CA-125 was up, but not drastically." Dr. P. sighed. "I'd hoped it was an anomaly."

I'd joined the 10-to-15 percent club. My mouth was so dry I couldn't form a response. I tugged from Kris's grip. I needed my water bottle. I gulped down half a dozen swallows. *Okay. Okay. It's okay.* I managed a shaky laugh. "At least I can stop taking the PARP inhibitor. No more wearing the stupid patch and throwing up my supper. What now?"

"You still have options."

"You said that. Be specific." I gripped my hands in my lap. "Please."

Her voice droned. Kris's responded. Back and forth. They were laying it out. Clinical trials. Other nonplatinum standard-of-care regimens. Options. I listened. I heard the words, but as much as I wanted to understand, my mind refused to absorb them.

Instead, it reached back four years, selected a movie, and hit Play. I stood in a labor and delivery room at a hospital in Chicago. Bright lights. Sweat soaked Noelle's hair. She cried. Zach laughed and cried with her. I cried—I cried at the birth of every grandchild. Zach took Gracie from Noelle's arms and handed her to me.

She weighed so little. She squirmed. Her tiny fists batted the air. Gracie had a bruised, flattened nose. Her tufts of damp hair stuck up willy-nilly. She opened her mouth and wailed in her distress at being so rudely introduced to a cold, brilliant world. My heart expanded until my body fought to contain it. I loved this little one so much it hurt. Every bit as much as I loved each of my children. The heart had an infinite capacity for a mother's love. For a grandmother's love.

I promised to introduce her to all my favorite books. I promised to teach her all my favorite Bible songs. I promised to watch her favorite animated shows with her over and over again. Play with Barbies. Study the moon through a telescope. Collect shells on the beach. Eat watermelon and corn on the cob. Play baseball. Tell each other secrets. I promised all that and then some.

I hadn't been able to travel to Chicago for Max's birth. I'd arrived a few days after. The same sensation had overtaken me holding his sturdy body while rocking in the same rocking chair I'd used for all three of my kids. I made the same promises. Just as I had with Jason's and Cody's children.

Soon there would be another baby joining Gracie and Max. Babies should have grandmothers. As many of them as humanly possible.

"A clinical trial it is. When do I start?"

"I'll put a call in to my colleague Dr. Capstone this afternoon." Dr. P. removed her glasses. This was serious. She never took her glasses off. "I want to get you situated with him as quickly as possible. I'm retiring next month."

"What? No, no! Oh, Dr. P." Tears bubbled up. I gritted my teeth, but the tears refused to be denied. *There's no crying in baseball or cancer.* Yes, there is. Today there is. I gritted my teeth and forced my lips to form the word. "Congratulations."

The delivery lacked sincerity, but it was my best effort. Dr. Pasternak patted my knee. "You'll be fine. Dr. Capstone is an exceptional physician with twenty-plus years of experience. His clinics are coordinating participation in more than ninety clinical trials right now. He'll pair you with the one right for you."

I cleared my throat. "But he still won't be you."

"No, he'll be better. I don't do clinical trials or research. He's what you need at this stage of your treatment."

Logic didn't apply to my feelings of abandonment. The feeling she was a traitor, abandoning ship when the going got tough—tougher. Ridiculous, but a person couldn't help the way she felt. "Good to know. Do I wait to hear from him or call for an appointment?"

"His scheduler will call you. I promise."

She stood. I stood. She held out her arms. I walked into the hug, however begrudgingly. A person didn't turn down a hug. Especially from this woman. Her hugs were monumental. "Congratulations," I whispered. "Happy retirement."

"Thank you." She stepped back. "You'll be fine. You have Kristen to steer the boat."

"Gee, thanks. No pressure." Kris took her turn at getting a hug. "You're not retiring yet, and I still know where you live."

A sensation of floating, like the earth had lost a portion of its gravity, assailed me. I'd lost my mooring. "We better get going, Kris.

Dr. P. probably has packing to do." I pasted a grin on my face. "She's a short-timer."

"Your sister will keep me posted."

Would she want to know how the story ended for her patients? Or would it be better to imagine that all of them reached that magical realm of N.E.D. and stayed there? Did she prefer to imagine me dancing the night away with Ned?

If I were her, I would. "Sure, I'm sure she will."

On that note of complete insincerity, we parted ways.

twenty-five

SHERRI

Chance's shiny Ram sat in my driveway when I pulled up in front of the house. My poor, pitiful house. About to be abandoned again. He shut off the mower and waved. A surge of nostalgia sucked the air from my lungs. The orderly lines across my yard had once been the lines he created on the lawn we shared for so many years. He used to do the same thing with the vacuum back in the day when we had carpet. An almost-date with my ex-husband would be nice—until I told him my news.

I got out of the Equinox. The scent of fresh-cut grass enveloped me. The scent of family and home. This would be the last time Chance mowed this year. Maybe the last time ever. *Stop.*

"Hey, Sher, how's it going?" He pushed the mower to his truck and heaved it into the bed. His bicep muscles and pecs bulged under his white T-shirt. "Are you ready for a Chance-certified best turkey burger in Kerrville?"

My stomach rocked. My fingers touched the patch on the back of my arm like a talisman. It would take a few days for the PARP to leave my system. "Sounds good. You brought your grill, I take it?"

"It's on the patio already. I watered your plants and pruned your flower garden while I was back there." He lifted his Cowboys cap and brushed back hair damp with sweat despite the fall air. "I also threw down some winter fertilizer. You're set until spring."

Bong, bong, bong.

The grandfather clock stuck his nose in my business on a daily, if not hourly, basis now. *If I was around in the spring.* I didn't share that thought with him. "You're too kind, yard man."

His mirrored sunglasses hid his eyes, but his grin suggested he didn't mind the moniker. "Make that yard man and chef. The baking potatoes are already in the oven."

"Bacon bits, shredded cheddar, sour cream, and chives?"

"You have to ask?"

He followed me into the house. Cleo met us at the door—met Chance at the door. He was always her favorite. She did loop-de-loops around his legs. He picked her up. "What can I say? She knows a good man when she sees him."

"Traitor." I dropped my bag on the couch in the living room. "I'll open some windows. Might as well let that fall air in. We have so few days when we don't have to use the AC or the heat."

"Let me do that."

"I'm not an invalid. Go check to see if the grill is ready."

Chance did as instructed. It took all my strength to shove the two windows open. I leaned my head against the cool glass and rested my eyes.

"Are you okay?"

I turned. Chance stood in the doorway. Fear etched lines around his face and eyes, then disappeared behind a forced smile. I nodded. "Fine. That was quick. What can I do? Make a salad?"

"Already made. I can't put the meat on until the potatoes are almost done. You mentioned something about boxes in the attic. Do you want me to get them down now?"

"Yes, please."

I stood at the bottom of the pull-down stairs in the hallway and listened to his boots stomping above me. "They're next to the Christmas tree bag!" I yelled. "Right next to the stack of plastic containers of decorations."

"I see them. There's like four big boxes. All of them?"

"Yes, please. Plus the two that have PHOTOS written in marker on the outside." One box for each of the kids. Baby books, report cards, school pictures, artwork, trophies, medals, memories. And a much older box for Kris and me. "Be careful up there."

Chance appeared at the opening. Dust floated in the air, illuminated by the hallway light. "Are you sure if I hand these down to you, you'll be able to wrestle them to the floor?"

"I'm not decrepit." Not exactly. I still managed thirty minutes of chair aerobics and another thirty of spinning most days. Some days I even walked with Shawna and Nikki after school. "Bring it on."

They weren't that heavy. Mostly, he slid them down the wooden steps, and I simply guided them to the floor, one at a time, and pushed them aside to make room for the next one. Cleo sniffed them for rodents, then settled on top of the first box as if claiming her domain. Chance clomped down the steps backward, giving me a nice view of his backside. He definitely wasn't showing *his* age.

"What is all this stuff?"

"Memory boxes."

He sneezed into the crook of his arm. "Dusty memories. Let's leave them until after we eat."

I took this as permission to leave my news until after we ate as well. Despite the low nausea, I not only ate half the monster turkey cheeseburger but a portion of the loaded baked potato and a few bites of salad. Chance demolished a T-bone so barely cooked it bled red. I pretended not to notice when he fed bits to Cleo, half hidden on a chair pushed up to the table.

Chance's presence grounded me in the era when Saturday nights during the summer were barbecue nights. He'd fire up the charcoal grill to make hot dogs for the kids and burgers for us. French fries, salad, and ice cream for dessert. To this day, the scent of grilled hot dogs made me think of all the times I cut the dogs into little bites for fear the kids would choke on them. I cut grapes in half all through their grade school years until Chance made me stop.

"Where'd you go?" Chance held out the ranch dressing. A creamy buttermilk taste that never failed to remind me of him. "You didn't hear a word I just said."

"Just pining for the days when my biggest worry was making sure the kids didn't choke on a piece of popcorn."

"Trips to the movie theater turned you into a basket case. Hot dogs and popcorn."

"Remember when Jason stuck a bean in his nose?"

"And Cody fell off the top bunk bed and broke his wrist."

"I think there was one stretch where one of us went to the ER at least once a month for four months."

"Even that wasn't as hard as watching them walk out the door to drive to school on their own for the first time."

"Or the fiftieth time." Chance dabbed a chunk of steak in A.1. sauce. "You were a good parent. You are a good parent."

"So are you."

"They turned out great, so I guess we did all right."

His smile was better medicine than anything that came in pill form.

Stuffed to the gills, I begged for a rain check on the chocolate cheesecake he'd picked up from the H-E-B bakery. "I couldn't eat another bite. Later, please."

"Later, but I'm holding you to it." He leaned back in his chair, wiped his face with his napkin, and burped gently. "I might have to loosen my belt. You don't know what you're missing with my steaks, girl."

"Some things don't change. That's the same broken record you've been playing for the last thirty years."

"We had some good times, didn't we?"

I rolled a cherry tomato to the center of my plate with my fork. "Until I ruined it."

"I can't pretend anymore that it was all your fault."

"Mostly my fault." I picked up my plate and reached for his. Shaking his head, he pushed my hand away. "My mess. I'll clean up."

"No way. You cooked. I clean." Not that Chance had done any cooking during our marriage. Only barbecuing the meat. But things were different now. We weren't married. He'd done something nice for me. "Go put on some music, relax. I'll take care of this."

"We'll do it together." He picked up the condiments and headed for the refrigerator. "It'll take half the time."

"Who are you and what have you done with Chance?"

"I wasn't that bad."

"I can count on my fingers the few times you loaded the dishwasher during our marriage." I scraped the plates into the sink and ran the garbage disposal. "I was in charge of grocery shopping, cooking, laundry, housecleaning, and all three kids."

"You make me sound like a lazy lump-on-a-log." He stowed the leftovers in the fridge until it was time for him to take them home. "I started and ran a business in those days. I also took care of all the yard work, installed ceiling fans and electric garage doors, fixed stopped-up toilets when Jason dumped toilet paper rolls in the commode, and changed the oil in both cars."

"You did." And I taught twenty kindergarteners five days a week. But that was water over the dam. It seemed like a long time ago. "We both had our hands full. I guess that's why the marriage failed. We didn't make it a priority."

"Is that what's happening with Dan and Kris?"

"Pretty much." I hated watching Kris flail around like a sailboat without a sail. I understood better than most how guilty and ashamed she felt. How certain she was that it was all her fault. I prayed hard every night that her marriage didn't end like mine. "Kris wants to fix it, but Dan isn't ready to forgive her yet."

"I guess we know how that goes."

Our gazes ran through a maze of painful memories and met in the middle where healing had occurred. "I hope it doesn't take as long for them to figure out how to make it right."

"Me too."

"I wash; you dry."

He obliged. Chance found his way around my small kitchen with ease. He also serenaded me with John Mellencamp's "Jack & Diane" using a spatula as a mic with "Pink Houses" as an encore. His theory that we would do the work in half the time went out the window when I joined him for a duet of "Stand Back" and "Edge of Seventeen" by Stevie Nicks.

I was breathless from laughing by the time the impromptu musical portion of the evening ended. He had a great baritone. I couldn't carry a tune in a bucket. "Thank you for not plugging your ears."

"Cleo carries a tune better than you do." He stuck the last pan in its cabinet. "Whatever happened to our CD collection?"

"You took it with you when you left."

"Huh. I don't remember that."

He probably didn't remember much. He'd fallen off the wagon for six months after our divorce. Another heartbreaking development laid at my feet. "Do you even have a CD player?"

He shrugged. "Spotify is my best friend these days."

"Figures."

He made decaf coffee and we traipsed into the living room where he'd positioned the boxes in a row in front of the couch with the coffee table situated so I could lay out the contents. "Do you mind if I stay?"

"Of course not." I accepted a mug from him and set it aside. "I wish you would."

"Why are you doing this right now?"

Because I might not be able to do it later. Because I didn't want them to have to sort through stuff after I died. "Because I plan to make scrapbooks for each of the kids. I'll give them their baby books, a scrapbook, and a photo album. It's time to get this stuff out of my attic. Let them store it in their attics."

"There's four boxes."

"I want to make one for Dad. A gift of seeing what we accomplished in his absence. Making memories in retro, I guess."

"That's mighty big of you."

"It's past time to let go of old grudges."

"I'm proud of you for being so grown up." He waved his hand at the boxes. "It's a huge undertaking."

I ducked my head and focused on using scissors to cut the packing tape open on the first box. My back twinged. I sucked in a breath. Time for more painkillers. No, not in front of Chance. "Turns out I'm about to have a lot of time on my hands . . . again."

"What are you talking about?"

"I don't want to spoil the evening. We're having such a nice time."

Chance gently tugged the scissors from my hands. "Tell me."

So I did.

"Oh, man. I'm so sorry." Chance encircled me in a hug so big and so tight no monsters could get at me. I leaned my head against his chest. His heartbeat steadied mine. "I've been reading up on treatments for ovarian cancer. Clinical trials are the way to go."

This guy who never read anything had been slogging through cancer-treatment articles. My kind of love language. Tears threatened. I closed my eyes and fought them back. "That's what my oncologist and Kris say."

"You're lucky to have your sister help you navigate this, but it has to be scary." He kissed the top of my head. "It scares me."

"I wish I could say it'll be okay—"

"I wish I could say it to you." His arms tightened. "I wish I could fix it for you."

"There's no way around it, just through it." I touched the wispy hairs on my forehead. They were just getting long enough to curl. "You have copies of my living will and the medical power of attorney where you can get to them, right?"

"Blondie—"

"We have to have this talk. Don't make it harder."

"Okay. Maybe it would be a good time to rethink the DNR."

"No, all the more reason to have one. You know how I feel about being kept alive by machines." Mom hadn't wanted it. I didn't want it. I didn't want it for my kids. "I've already told Kris about the cremation plan. I'm still deciding where I want my ashes spread."

"Still leaning toward Machu Picchu?" He didn't laugh. We'd tossed around crazy ideas when we bought the plans way back when. When we were young and healthy. I never thought I'd live forever. Mom's death taught me that. Chance had been more optimistic. He'd grown up with both sets of grandparents still alive. "I'm thinking Old Faithful at Yellowstone."

"I can see that. Wyoming is definitely your vibe."

"Noelle won't be happy. She'll want a place she can visit."

The ache in my heart was worse than unbearable. This must've been how Mom felt. Leaving her two kids, knowing how they would grieve. "I'm doing my best to hang on. That's why I'm skipping the standard-of-care stuff and going straight to a clinical trial."

"When do you go to the clinical trial place?"

"Day after tomorrow. That's the earliest they could get me in."

"I'd like to go with you."

"You don't need to do that. I don't want you taking off work for it. Kris is already doing that."

"I want to feel like I'm doing something."

"You are. Right now."

We leaned back against the couch. Chance pulled a crocheted afghan from the back and tossed it over me. I relaxed against his solid frame. Just for a little bit. Just a few minutes with an unexpected and undeserved anchor in the storm. Cleo hopped up on the couch and joined us. Her purr was as soothing as ocean waves on a quiet night at the Gulf Coast.

"I should pack," I whispered. "I need to put Cleo's stuff in the car."

"I'll do it in a while. I'll lug the boxes out too."

Reluctantly, I sat up and let the blanket slide down. Cool night air sent shivers up my arms. "I just want to take a quick peek before you do that."

"Gotcha." Chance glanced at his phone. "That should probably be soon. You still have to drive back to Kris's. You're gonna be alone and tired. Not a good recipe."

"I'm a big girl." Even if I didn't want to be. "I've done it a million times."

Opening the first box was my version of time traveling. Noelle's baptismal dress, her first pair of shoes, her favorite dolly. The deeper I dug, the more the memories filled the movie screen. I held up a purple Barney the dinosaur. "Remember how obnoxious that music was?"

He hummed repetitive bars of "Clean Up" in the same singsong way that the kids had in their day care days.

"Stop, stop, stop." I pulled out Golden Book editions of *The Three Billy Goats Gruff*, *The Gingerbread Man*, and *Little Red Riding Hood*. "I have to send these to Noelle."

"It would be cheaper for her to buy them on Amazon."

"Not the same. Not the same at all."

"I know." He pulled out her baby book. "You spent so much time on hers."

"And less and less with each succeeding baby. I don't think there's anything in Jason's."

Next came pictures of her day-care classes and then her early artwork, carefully preserved in plastic sleeves. Fingerpainting, macaroni art, paper plate art, a calendar made in kindergarten featuring art for each of the months. "She was a good artist, even then." I snatched a tissue from the box on the table and dabbed my nose. "Look at this family portrait. She gave me a belly bump because I was pregnant with Jason that year."

"And she caught my beard and Alabama waterfall stage perfectly."

"You had such pretty hair. All my friends were jealous." An ache of longing thrummed in my chest. I put my hand over my heart. It beat a sad, sad song. "We had some good times, didn't we? Before I screwed everything up."

"Speaking of letting go of grudges, I've done that. You can stop punishing yourself now." Chance slid an arm around me and pulled me closer. "Don't send the books. Tell her you need her to come home for a visit. She can bring the kids. You need to see them."

My throat closed. I leaned my head on his shoulder. "They can't know."

"They have a right to know. FaceTime is a poor substitute. You want Gracie and Max to know you."

Fatigue claimed me. I closed my eyes.

Chance took the family portrait from me. "Come on. I'm putting you to bed. You're not driving back to Kris's tonight."

"I have to—"

"I'll let her know." He helped me to my feet. "I'll sack out in the guest room."

"There's no need for you to stay."

"Don't argue. Sleep."

I pulled my pill bottles from my bag and went to the en suite bathroom.

"What's all that for?" Chance stood in the doorway, his expression somewhere between protective and scared. "You were never much of a pill popper."

"I'm still not. It's just an overachieving ibuprofen for pain, an allergy pill, and something for my acid reflux."

"You're in pain? When did that start?"

"Just lately. It's not bad, but it wakes me up sometimes, so this is just me being proactive."

He nodded but didn't look convinced.

"Are you going to watch me brush my teeth and help me put on my pj's?"

His smile rueful, he shook his head and retreated. I took care of business and trudged into the bedroom. He was still there. "Don't worry. I'm just tucking you in."

It was nice. He was nice. He pulled the comforter up, touched my cheek, and kissed my forehead. "Sweet dreams." He lingered in the doorway. "Promise me you'll think about what I said about the kids?"

"I will," I whispered. "Tomorrow."

Later, around midnight, I woke up. *Bong, bong, bong.* That infernal clock awakened me. Worst-case scenarios on repeat. The hamster on the wheel went round and round. What if this? What if that? Not even Cleo's steady purr near my head could drown out the ugly possibilities.

I needed the dang clock to shut up.

I needed human contact. Tears wanted to have their way with me. I gritted my teeth. Feeling sorry for myself in the dark was no better than doing it in broad daylight. One truth was abundantly clear. In the final analysis, whether God healed me here or decided on the ultimate healing, I wasn't ready. Dread cloaked my body, accelerating my heartbeat. To fade from existence like dead trees felled in their prime. If there was no God, no Jesus, no afterlife, then there would be nothing at all.

What if we were kidding ourselves?

God, help me in my unbelief. That's it. That's my prayer. Don't give up on me. Please.

A shiver ran through me. The sheets were cold. The room cold. My body heat wasn't enough to keep me warm.

I rose and stumbled from the room and across the hall. Chance had left his door open. Moonlight cast a glow through the windows he'd left open. He always liked a cold room for sleeping. His form didn't move under the comforter. I slipped under it and curled up close to his back.

After a few seconds, he rolled over and put his arm over me. I slept.

twenty-six

KRISTEN

Déjà vu all over again. Not exactly. Without Daniel's steadying presence, the news of Sherri's recurrence had me tottering around, weak-kneed and dizzy. Spinning in circles, unable to stop. Sherri had no clue. Thank God, she had no clue about the gut punch her scan results represented. Her prognosis had plummeted from guarded to terminal. As in shrinking from five years to two years on the upside. Six months to a year on the low side.

Unless we found a clinical trial that worked. I slid under the comforter and pulled it up to my chin. A college degree, medical school, internship, residency, specialty, twenty years in the field of oncology, and I still couldn't save her. *What's up with that, God? Tell me, wasn't Mom enough? What do You want from me?*

No answer.

No surprise, considering how rarely I spoke with the Big Kahuna. Only when I wanted something. Why would He deign to respond then?

I stacked up pillows on either side of me like a fort. With the comforter pulled up over my head, I hunkered down in the dark, hiding from the truth. It wasn't the same without Daniel next to me, his breathing steady, his body warm, if distant. Twenty-five years. I didn't know how to sleep without him by my side, doing that little *snort-snort-wheeze* snore he did.

Now he'd taken the dogs, leaving me without their soft, humming canine snores, whimpers, and legs running in their dreams. His note said he would return them on Monday.

Not Sunday. If he returned them Sunday night, I'd be here. He'd rather wait until I left for work on Monday. Only I wouldn't be going to work on Monday. Instead, I'd be Sherri's wingwoman for her appointment with the oncologist who founded a clinic that specialized in Phase I clinical trials. Arina had called him while we sat in her office. I agreed with her thought process on this one. Phase I trials were open, first-in-human trials. Every patient received the trial drug. No double-blind studies. No secrecy. We would know almost immediately if the drug was working.

Sherri had moved back in without a fight. Clinical trials were time-consuming, at least at the beginning. A lot of hoop-jumping with scans, blood work, sometimes eye exams, EKGs, and MUGAs. She needed to be here in town. Another leave of absence from her beloved students.

Dread, much like the feeling of walking through a spiderweb, hit me. Would she ever teach again?

I threw back the comforter and knocked down the pillows. *Breathe. In and out. In and out.*

The silence mocked me. It was too quiet. Too quiet. I needed Daniel.

Daniel.

I grabbed my phone from the charger. I held it to my chest. *In and out. In and out.* Would Sherri say that contacting him now was a form of emotional blackmail?

It was eleven o'clock. He'd be sleeping. I just wanted to hear his voice.

Voice mail would pick up. Unlike me, Daniel was good at letting voice mail screen his calls at night. I couldn't afford to do that. My patients needed me.

Which was how we'd arrived at this point. I touched his number. It rang. Voice mail, just voice mail. I'd be satisfied with hearing his recorded voice.

"Kristen, what's wrong?"

Sleep made his voice husky.

"What makes you think something's wrong?"

He cleared his throat. "It's after eleven. Why aren't you asleep?"

"I miss . . . the dogs. Can you bring them back tomorrow instead of Monday morning?"

Liar, liar, pants on fire.

"You woke me up because you want the dogs back?" Sleep faded away, leaving behind irritation and resignation. "Seriously, Kristen. Don't make them a bone of contention between us."

"No, no. I'm not trying to do that—"

"I have to sleep. I'm having breakfast with the girls at Mom's in the morning at the crack of dawn."

The girls were in town and they hadn't called me? Hadn't told me?

"Daniel—"

He'd already hung up.

He'd managed to slip in that tidbit about the girls just so I'd know where they stood with this separation. I hadn't told them. They didn't need to know, if it was temporary. And it was temporary. I kept telling myself that.

The fearsome threesome rides again.

Why was it that I could never admit to Daniel that I needed him?

Blood pounded in my ears. I threw the phone on the bed and leaned against the pillows. *Because you always knew he'd leave you.*

Stupid. In twenty-five years he'd never left me. Not until I deserved it. Even when I'd deserved it.

You always deserved it. Also, you always knew he would leave sooner or later. Dad did.

There it was.

"Stupid." Even my voice sounded lonely in the stillness. "Now I'm talking to myself."

Early breakfast or not, the girls would still be up on a Friday night. I opened the text thread that included the three of us. It had been three months since our last group text. Celebrating Sherri's N.E.D. announcement.

Hey, how are u doing?

I waited. No answer. I counted one thousand one, one thousand two . . . to thirty seconds.

Come on. It's Friday night. I know you're up.

The girls always made fun of me for texting in complete sentences with punctuation. The sure signs of an old person.

No response.

Maintaining radio silence?

Come on, girls. Don't be mean. It's disrespectful to ignore your mother. The seconds ticked by.

Bunking at Gma's
I figured. Your dad said u were in town.
You talked to Dad?
Just now. Sort of.
Why didn't u tell us he moved out?

Why didn't you tell me you were in town?

No response. Ticktock, ticktock.

U 1st

Finally. I paused, my index figure poised over the letters. The girls also made fun of me for not using my thumbs to text. I was just as fast, maybe faster, with my point-and-stab approach.

I didn't think it would last.

Not this long for sure. He'd make his point. I'd beg forgiveness. He would give it because that was the way he was built.

U forgot yr 25th anniversary

Anger emojis filled a row on the screen.

They'd remembered. Still, did they have a right to be angry on Daniel's behalf? Or was this more? Years of being angry, like their dad, and not letting it show because, after all, I was saving lives? Or trying to.

I know. I blew it big time. I apologized. I don't know what else to do.

Yes u do

That was Maddie. The daughter studying to become a psychologist one day.

I said I'd go to couples counseling.

In spring

Really? Did Daniel have to tell them everything? My head throbbed. I rubbed my forehead with the heel of my hand.

Have lunch with me tomorrow.
Shopping with Gma, then to play downtown

Of course.

Then Sunday.
Have to get back. Exams, jobs
Don't make me the bad guy without hearing my side of the story.
Don't stick us in middle

Maddie was right. They didn't deserve this. At least they were young adults already out of the house, living on their own. Not a first grader who cried herself to sleep after her dad didn't make good on his promise to teach her to throw and catch and to coach her baseball team.

Give Dash and Scout a hug for me.
U probably miss them more than u do Dad

That was Brielle. She was more likely to react emotionally. To strike back when hurt.

I miss all y'all.
Night
Night.

I grabbed the closest pillow, wrapped my arms around it, and buried my head in the soft material. It smelled of Daniel's eco-friendly apple cider vinegar and citrus shampoo bar. It was expensive stuff. Daniel said it was worth it not to pollute the world more than it already was. Classic Daniel. I inhaled. Daniel always smelled so peaceful. He had an even keel about him that I lacked. His stoicism to my chaos.

"I need my dogs." Again with the talking to myself. I threw my legs over the edge of the bed and stood. "I get to talk to myself if I want. Who's going to know?"

I stomped down the stairs.

Footsteps sounded. A cabinet door closed. I wasn't alone. Sherri had spent the previous night in Kerrville, and I'd left the TV on all night so the house wouldn't seem so empty. Pathetic as it sounded. "Sherri?"

"Out here."

Suddenly cheered, I traipsed into the kitchen. Sherri was bent over, head in the refrigerator, her derriere sticking out. She wore sweats and fuzzy purple slippers. Her baggy sweatshirt featured a scowling Garfield the cat.

Cleo lay on the island, curled up, sleeping. The audacity of that cat. At least Sherri had her warm, furry companion. "Holding the door open doesn't make the contents magically change."

Sherri straightened and frowned. "I thought you would have more flavors of ice cream."

"Six flavors aren't enough? You depleted my supplies your first visit. I haven't restocked." I went to the drawer and grabbed a handful of spoons. "Besides, I bet if I peeked in your freezer right now, you wouldn't have any at all."

"I keep fudge pops in my freezer at all times."

"The forty-calorie ones? That's not ice cream. That's frozen chalk masquerading as ice cream."

"I also have strawberry frozen yogurt and orange sherbet." Her voice full of self-righteousness, Sherri filled her arms with ice cream cartons in various sizes from half pints to half gallons. She scooted to the island. "Whoa, cold, cold, cold! Your flavors are variations on a theme: chocolate fudge brownie, chocolate chip cookie dough, chocolate therapy, rocky road, mint chocolate chip, super fudge chunk, s'mores. It's all chocolate. Your favorite."

Cleo rose, stretched to three times her normal length, turned her nose up at me, and strolled to the edge of the island. She jumped down with all the grace of a lioness. Cats were so snotty. As a dog person, I didn't get it. "What's your point?"

"What about Daniel's favorite?"

"Daniel likes chocolate too."

"He likes whatever you like, you mean." Sherri opened each carton with methodical precision. She selected a spoon and perused her options with almost comical deliberation. As if she didn't intend to sample all of them. "What are you doing up at this hour?"

"I thought some herbal tea would help me sleep."

"Yeah, right." Sherri snorted. She slid the Blue Bell Rocky Road carton closer. "You were lying in bed contemplating what life as a divorced woman would be like. You decided you would consume everything in the refrigerator because what did it matter if you blimped out? No one would ever love you again anyway."

Ouch. She didn't have to be so cavalier about my life. "Was not. Did not."

"I've been there, done that. I know exactly how it feels. I can do ten verses of the woe-is-me song with the best country songwriter out there."

I selected the half gallon of super fudge chunk and settled onto the closest stool. "It feels like . . . the end of the world. Like, how did I get here? Like, it's not fair. Was I supposed to deny my patient's husband basic compassion? 'Sorry, I know your wife is dead, but I've gotta go. My husband made stuffed shells and garlic bread. He thinks I should show up for our anniversary.'"

"Thing is, you didn't even have that conversation in your head. You didn't remember about the anniversary until it was all over. Besides, you're still making it Daniel's fault." She dug a spoonful of ice cream from the carton and surveyed it, waiting, I imagine, for it to melt a little. "Does it even occur to you that Daniel has his own likes and dislikes? I bet he likes other flavors of ice cream. Have you ever asked him?"

"Let's talk about something else."

"You mean like my prognosis going from bad to worse?" Wincing, she rubbed her lower back with her free hand. Time for more ibuprofen. "No, I don't think so. I'm eating ice cream because some woman on my Facebook group for ovarian cancer survivors told me if I'm still eating sugar, I'm basically killing myself. No wonder I'm stage 4. No wonder I'm platinum resistant.

"According to this whack job who I'm sure means well, I need to do a cleanse, adopt an intermittent fasting regimen, remove all carbo-hydrates from my diet, and build myself a sauna so I can do a sweat at least four times a week. Oh, and I forgot the CBD and essential oils. I decided it would be easier and cheaper and more satisfying to consume large quantities of sugar until I collapse and die posthaste. I figure, what a way to go. Death by chocolate therapy." She finally ran out of air.

I shook my spoon at her. "How many times have I told you to stay away from those groups, sis?" In the old days, patients went to their medical school graduate doctors for medical advice, not websites or social media where crackpots slash well-meaning individuals loved to share their wealth of unfounded medical advice with patients desperate for a way to stave off the seemingly inevitable end.

"You've eaten healthy your entire adult life. You've exercised regularly. You take vitamins. You don't drink alcohol. You don't smoke. You get all your regular checkups. You still got cancer. It's nothing you did or didn't do. You even took oral contraceptives, had multiple children before age thirty, and breastfed them. You did all the things researchers say might help you not get ovarian cancer. You still got it."

"So you're saying I should've had more fun while I could because running 5ks and eating salmon, kale salad, and superfoods like blueberries didn't make one iota of difference?"

Her dour expression made me laugh.

"No. Being healthy and in good shape physically means you're in a better position to fight the disease."

"And yet, an effective drug for eradicating platinum-resistant ovarian cancer doesn't exist."

"Don't wave the white flag yet. Like Arina says, you have options." The cold ice cream eased the ache in my throat, but only for a few seconds. "I'm proud of you for agreeing to a clinical trial. Your participation will help other women down the road—women like my girls and yours. That's important work. Don't lose sight of that."

Which was why I wanted—needed—to engage in cancer research. If the job came through, I had to take it. I shouldn't have to choose. A clinical trial was a win-win for Sherri and for the women who came after her. One of my patients benefited from a trial to the tune of two years without progression. That drug was making its way through the FDA approval process.

"It's hard, though, because there's no way to know if a first-in-human trial drug will be effective. Why not sign up for a trial for a Phase III or IV drug, where there's a solid chance it'll help?"

"Because not every participant gets the trial drug in later phases. Everyone gets at least standard of care, which is good, but in double-blind studies, not even your doctor will know which arm of the study you're in. I've watched patients go downhill fast, and there was nothing I could do about it."

I didn't choose oncology to sit around and watch my patients expire.

"I'm so blessed to have you as a sister." She set her chocolate therapy spoon aside and moved on to the brownie fudge. "Thanks for taking me in. Again."

"I'm happy to do it." My voice wasn't much steadier. I couldn't imagine her alone in her house tonight, staring at the ceiling, writing the script for the last days of her life in her head. "We'll get through this together."

"So, how about the Amazon Rainforest? You can take a boat ride through alligator-, snake-, and piranha-infested waters to just the right spot to spread my ashes." She licked her spoon with a satisfied grin. "Sound good?"

"I'm thinking the Bermuda Triangle would be the perfect spot for my ashes." Two could play this game. It actually helped in a perverted upside-down-world way. "It's the perfect metaphor for my life right now."

"You'd go so far as to die in order to not talk to Daniel?" Sherri pointed her spoon at me and rolled her eyes. "Not happening. You will not be allowed to chicken out. You need to have a face-to-face with Daniel in neutral territory. Agree to counseling ASAP. Get on your knees and beg if that's what's required."

Easy for her to say. She hadn't taken Chance back. Or had she? "I guess Chance didn't get on his knees and beg you to take him back."

Tense exchanges at the gas grill, the scent of chicken and beef fajitas wafting in a soft May breeze. Kids dancing through a sprinkler, screaming and laughing. The taste of cilantro, onion, and serrano pepper from Sherri's pico de gallo on my tongue. Salty tortilla chips. The visceral memory swam to the surface. Daniel, the kids, and I had been present when the final straw broke the camel's back in Sherri's marriage. A screen door slamming. Sherri in the kitchen, crying over a Crock-Pot of queso.

"You might have forgiven him, but you didn't forget. Obviously."

Sherri's spoon clattered on the butcher-block island top. She grabbed a napkin and wiped away droplets of ice cream before they could stain the wood. "You've got it backward. I begged Chance to take *me* back. He's forgiven me, but it's taken a lot of years for me to mend that fence."

"Is that how you ended up spending the night with him last night?"

"It's not what you think. He's a friend—a better friend than he ever was a husband. I'm not blaming anything on him. I wasn't a great wife either. I deserved the divorce."

"You? What did you ever do to deserve a divorce?" The thought boggled my mind. Ms. Christian churchgoer who never missed a Sunday service, Sunday school, Bible study, and a plethora of what she called "servant opportunities" over the years.

I switched to chocolate chip cookie dough. "You were Supermom, Superwife, and Superteacher. You could've crossed the Atlantic doing the breaststroke. I could barely keep my head above water doing a dog paddle in a plastic blow-up pool."

Sherri's cheeks turned a fiery red. They matched the ugly red blotches on her neck. "I never wanted you to know." She stabbed at the ice cream with her spoon. "But now I realize I can't go to my grave letting you think Chance was the bad guy. I've compounded my big sin by basically lying by omission about it."

"First of all, you're not going to the grave anytime soon." The big lie we tell ourselves in oncology in order to keep from curling up in a fetal position under the bed. "Second of all, what are you talking about? You're the most perfect Christian woman I know."

She shook her head hard. "No human being is perfect. Period. Only Jesus. I did something. Something awful."

Cleo, who'd visited her food bowl on the off chance more food had magically appeared, ambled over to Sherri's feet, then leaped onto her lap. Sherri dropped her spoon. She hugged the cat to her chest. "Cleo knows and she still loves me. That's why I love animals."

"Don't leave me hanging, sis. Tell me. I'm the worst sinner in the world, so you won't get any guff from me. Seriously."

"Not the worst by a long shot. I committed adultery."

The words hung in the air, like electricity after a lightning bolt in an electrical storm. Not possible. My worldview shifted on its axis. Its tether slipped loose and the world floated away. "What? When? Why? I don't believe—"

"I know, I'm Miss Goody Two-shoes." Bitterness stained her words. "That's what Chance said. Miss Holier-Than-Thou. Miss Kindergarten Teacher. I can give you the dozen excuses I threw at Chance. Each worse than the one before."

"I don't need to know the gory details . . . Okay, so yes, I do. What would make you do such a thing?"

"Haven't you ever felt like life is just passing you by? My life was so mundane. ABCs. Colors and shapes. I was lonely. Chance was never home when he first started his construction business. I felt . . . undesirable after my third baby. All lumpy and stretch-marked. I couldn't lose the weight. I spent every day, all day, taking care of kids—mine and everyone else's. You name it, I could rationalize it to the nth degree."

"Who?"

"A divorced father of one of my students. It only happened once."

"Wow. Once. It's not like you had an affair then."

"I slept with someone who wasn't my husband. That's one of the big ten thou shalt nots." Her gaze dropped to the ice cream that had just begun to melt. Her expression morose, she stirred. "It's the one reason actually cited in the Bible acceptable for divorce. Infidelity."

"I can't wrap my head around it."

"Neither could Chance."

"How did he find out?"

"I told him."

"Why? To hurt him? You should've talked to me first." Like I had any experience in this realm. I was too busy for one man, let alone two. "I would've told you to keep your guilty conscience to yourself."

"I couldn't tell you. I couldn't tell anyone. Only Chance. He was the one person I could be honest with. He deserved to know."

"And he reacted by divorcing you."

"Yep. I don't blame him. It took him a long time to forgive me, but he has. That's why I had to tell you. You can't blame him for any of it."

"You wouldn't have done it if he'd been paying attention."

"I spent a lot of years telling myself that. But I know better. If I needed his attention, I should've worked harder to get it." She kissed Cleo's face. The cat's purr provided background music to this heart-to-heart. "Which brings us back to Daniel."

No, it didn't. Daniel was a male version of Sherri. He wouldn't cheat on me. His code of ethics wouldn't allow it. "Daniel's not having an affair."

"You didn't think I would either. But the bigger issue is that you are."

She was nuts. I didn't have the time or the inclination. "You're delusional. I'm not."

"With your job. With your patients. If you don't fix this now, he'll find someone else. Men don't do alone well. Daniel's attractive, and he's in good shape. He's smart, kind, and he has good manners. He owns his own business and is successful. He's lonely. He's the lottery jackpot of men. You can bet plenty of women are waiting to step in."

I didn't need the recitation of Daniel's good qualities. I'd fallen in love with them—minus the business. "Thanks for the pep talk."

"I'm a divorced fifty-two-year-old woman who hasn't had a date in recent memory. I'm dying of cancer—"

Fear shot like adrenaline through me. She did not just say that. She hadn't read the script. I hadn't spent my entire life in the field of oncology only to lose another person I loved to cancer. "No, you're not—"

"Don't be me. Fix this thing with Daniel. Don't let anything get in the way of your marriage—not your job, not your patients, and definitely not me."

"You're not in the way."

"Kris."

"Whatever." Time to change the subject. "How did you keep going to church after what you did?"

"That's the beautiful thing about God. He's sovereign and just. He's also gracious and merciful. I repented and begged forgiveness. He forgave me and sent me on my way, with the directive to sin no more. And I didn't—not that sin anyway."

Life was so black-and-white for believers. "As simple as that."

"As simple and as hard."

Hard because humans weren't as forgiving as the big I Am.

Sherri rested her head on her arms and closed her eyes. I stood and went to her. "It's okay. It'll be okay." I rubbed her shoulders. "No matter what happens, we're in this together."

"I'm so tired." Her eyes were closed. "Maybe I can sleep now."

"Come on. I'll get you some Advil and tuck you in."

"The ice cream."

"I'll take care of it."

"Like you're taking care of me."

"Something like that."

"Tomorrow, you'll call Daniel."

"Promise."

For all the good it would do me. Unless Daniel had embraced the message about forgiveness, it seemed unlikely. He was only human.

twenty-seven

DANIEL

The call wasn't unexpected. Kristen called every few days. Apparently, she hadn't heard that the definition of insanity was doing the same thing over and over and expecting a different result. I let the call go to voice mail. A few seconds later a cricket sounded. Sure enough, a text.

I know you're screening my calls. Please call me back.

I studied the artist's renditions of my proposal for a ranch house near Comfort on my computer screen. Beautiful, simple lines. Built into a hillside with sweeping views from floor-to-ceiling windows. Rain-collection barrels. Metal roof. Solar panels. Limestone steps down to a plateau where we would build a pergola surrounded with native plants. Stone seating. LED lighting powered by more solar panels.

"I'm walking over to Best Mugs and Muffins to pick up our order for the staff meeting tomorrow." Pilar stood in the doorway. With her long hair in a ponytail, she could pass for a college student. "Can I get you anything? They should have pumpkin spice bread, unless they've sold out already. That stuff goes fast."

"I need to stretch my legs and blow out the cobwebs." I turned off the monitor and stood. "I'll walk with you."

"I'll get my purse and sweater. Meet you at the door."

I was halfway across the broad expanse of reclaimed oak floor when Matt stuck his head out his doorway. "Where're you going?"

"With Pilar to get some muffins and coffee. She'll need help carrying the order for tomorrow."

"I'm sure she can handle it." Rubbing his neck, Matt craned his head from side to side. "I thought you were up to your neck finishing the Comfort house."

"My brain hurts. I need to recalibrate it."

"Uh-huh. You need to recalibrate something."

"What's that supposed to mean?"

Pilar traipsed into view.

Matt shrugged and disappeared into his office.

What was that all about?

I held the inner door for Pilar. She held the outer door for me. On the street a cool fall breeze greeted us. I immediately felt better, liberated. Fall was a short season in San Antonio, but it was my favorite. The sun warmed my face without burning it. Everyone seemed more at ease after a blistering-hot summer.

"Are you still staying at the Econo Lodge?" Pilar sidestepped a guy on a skateboard followed by another one on an electric scooter.

"Yep. I kind of like the smallness of it now." The so-called suite with a microwave, sink, and minifridge rented by the month. They even had a laundromat on-site and a Denny's across the street. "Plus, someone else cleans it for me."

She laughed. "Good try. I bet they don't use the eco-friendly cleansers you favor. Or the bedding or the furniture. That alone is making you crazy."

No one was saying much. But all my coworkers knew I'd moved out of the house. I spent a lot of time at the office or at the gym. Matt and my brothers agreed I should stay at Mom and Dad's or at the ranch. I went out to the ranch on the weekends when I had the dogs. Otherwise, I was baching it.

Pilar spent more than her share of time at the office as well. She had joined a gym and a running group, but that didn't seem to keep her fully occupied. I found myself sitting in her office at all hours of the night, discussing everything from impressionist art to pop culture to debating *Star Wars* versus *Star Trek*. She was all about *Star Wars*. I was a *Star Trek* guy—specifically Captain Picard and *The Next Generation*.

"Would I be out of line to ask if you wanted to see a movie or just get a slice of pizza some evening? I found a good place for Chicago-style pizza." Pilar pushed Walk at the crosswalk. A futile gesture. I was almost positive the button actually kept the walk sign from lighting up. "We both need to get out of the office. Instead of having all those debates in the same old space, why not find a new view? Just as friends."

She'd given this pitch some thought. Like a presentation to a potential client. The caveat had been an afterthought, however. As if delivering the pitch and hearing it spoken aloud had made her realize there was a key issue with her proposal.

I might be living alone, but I was still married. "It's a nice thought."

"But . . ."

"But I'm your boss and I'm married, and one thing tends to lead to another. Or so I've been told."

"That's what I figured." She shrugged those elegant shoulders. "You don't believe men and women can be friends?"

"Sure. If they're both single, though. And on the same rung of the corporate ladder."

"Yeah, you're right."

An awkward silence ensued.

We picked up our pace past the fountain. A man was throwing

bread on the pavers, attracting a swarm of pigeons. A woman was sleeping on a bench, a straw hat covering her face. And a preacher was reading Revelation at the top of his hoarse voice.

"It's just that . . . I know it's none of my business . . ."

When people said that, it meant they were about to make something their business. "Go ahead. Dig that hole."

She ducked her head. Her ponytail swung back and forth. She studied the permeable pavers under her black flats. "When I left my husband, it was for good. I wasn't punishing him. I knew it was over. He knew it. I don't get that vibe from you. I just wonder how long you intend to punish your wife. How long are you going to punish yourself?"

"I'm not punishing her or me."

"Are you sure? You're living in an Econo Lodge, for Pete's sake. You come to work every day looking like it's another terrible, horrible, no good, very bad day. Are you sure your name isn't Alexander?"

"Very funny."

"Do you miss her?"

"Of course I do."

"Or do you miss the idea of being married and living in a house with a pool and dogs and watching Jon Stewart with your wife?"

"We never watched Jon Stewart together or apart."

"You know what I mean."

I did know. I held the bakery door open for her. She slipped past me, smelling of patchouli. A scent I thought had gone the way of hippies and the sixties. Even perfumes could go retro.

She inhaled and sniffed the air. "Cinnamon rolls. I can't bear it. Gingerbread. Pumpkin bread."

"You got all that from one sniff?"

"How have you not noticed this nose?" She pointed with a nail painted pearly white. She did have a rather pronounced nose, but not unattractively so. "I can identify essential oils at one hundred paces."

I gave her my business credit card and let her do the ordering while I grabbed a seat next to a window so I could watch folks wandering in and out of San Fernando Cathedral, one of the oldest churches in the country and a beautiful example of Gothic architecture.

Was I punishing Kristen?

A guitar riff reminiscent of Bryan Adams's "The Boys of Summer" emanated from my phone. A photo of Kristen and the girls on Mustang Island appeared. I glanced out the window again to study two little kids wading in the fountain, their faces filled with delight. They grew up so fast. I stabbed the green circle. "Hello."

"Thank you for answering."

"I figured it was that or get a new number."

"Would you do that?"

"No. Of course not. What's up?" Not quite the same as "what do you want" but close. I knew what she wanted. I just couldn't give it to her. I'd come this far. I had to see this to the end. I couldn't be the one who always gave in.

"I asked the girls what day they were coming home for Thanksgiving. They said they weren't."

Thanksgiving was the one major holiday we'd kept for ourselves all these years. We did Christmas Eve at home and Christmas Day at my parents'. New Year's Eve at my parents' annual bash with fireworks. July Fourth at my parents'. Kristen wanted one day in which we could have our own traditions, just us. I hadn't blamed her. "They always come home for Thanksgiving."

"Apparently, not this year. Not unless you'll be there."

Ah . . . Maddie and Brielle were playing marriage counselors. Get their parents in the same room. Force them to confront their problems. Voilà. They live happily ever after. Like a Lifetime Original Movie.

"I don't think so."

"Daniel, please. Don't do this to me."

"It probably surprises you to know this isn't about you. It's about me."

Pilar placed a steaming mug of coffee in front of me. Best Mugs and Muffins lived up to its name. The rich aroma sent me hurtling through time to the year I'd given Kristen an espresso machine for her birthday. I like a dark roast, but not the kind of double shots she drank to stay awake while she studied for her final exams. She was the smartest, most focused, most determined woman I'd ever met. For some reason, she chose me. I could never figure that out.

I picked up the heavy earthenware mug and sipped. Stevia and almond milk, a touch of cinnamon and pumpkin spice. "Kristen?"

Pilar's carefully plucked eyebrows rose. She stood and started to move away. I touched her sleeve. Her face filled with such sympathy. I shook my head and pointed to the chair.

She sat.

"I've told you what happened that night, Daniel." Kristen's voice cracked. "I've apologized. I've promised to do better. I know I've said that before, but I can't start to make it up to you if you won't come home. If you won't even see me or talk to me."

I stared at the simple silver band on my ring finger. "I'll talk to the girls."

"Does that mean you'll come home?"

"It means the girls and I will be there for Thanksgiving dinner."

"Thank you," she whispered. "It'll be good. It'll be a nice family dinner."

"The girls told me about Sherri. I'm sorry."

"She's hanging in there. The girl's got grit."

"I'm sorry this is happening again." I was one of the few people who knew how much this development chipped away at Kristen's determination to stop cancer from hurting anyone she loved ever again. God complex or not, Kristen had devoted her life to the notion that she personally would trounce this disease and send it whimpering back to whatever black hole from whence it slithered. "I'm glad Sherri has you."

"Thank you."

The barista shouted out a customer's name for pickup. Once, twice, three times. A guy dropped his *Express-News* on the table and rose.

"Where are you?" Kristen's tone took on a wary note. "I thought you would be in the office."

"At Best Mugs and Muffins. We're picking up treats for tomorrow's staff meeting."

"We? Why are you and Matt running errands? Don't you have gophers for that?"

I rubbed my forehead. I had said *we*. I had nothing to hide. I wasn't doing anything wrong. So why the throbbing over my left eye? "I have to go."

"Oh, it's not Matt, is it? It's okay. You don't have to tell me." Now her tone said she was imagining all sorts of things. I didn't owe her an explanation of an innocent run for baked goods. Let her imagination run wild. "It's none of my business, is it?"

Yes, it was. We were still married. "I have to go."

"Sure. What time on the twenty-fourth?"

"In time for the parade, of course."

A soft laugh. The surliness gone. "Of course, what was I thinking? See you then."

For better or for worse. No, that was a different concept for a different time.

Pilar placed a warm, gooey cinnamon roll with a dab of butter melting over the thick layer of icing in front of me. "This calls for a celebration."

More of a question than an affirmation. "No, it was me being a jerk and then feeling guilty and giving in. I always give in." I took a bite. The sweetness couldn't allay the bitterness on my tongue. "I want my girls to have Thanksgiving at home like we always do. Like nothing has changed. Because nothing has changed. Apparently."

"Matt and Colleen were going to invite you to their place for Thanksgiving."

"Because they feel sorry for me."

"Because they're your friends and they hate seeing you like this." She peered into her coffee as if reading her future there. "I haven't known you very long, and I hate seeing you like this. I never thought of myself as someone who would step into a gap between a husband and his wife, but I never imagined feeling such a . . . I hate to use the word *attraction* because that's not what this is about. . . . I like you. I worry about you. I know you're not interested in me, so don't feel like you've done anything wrong, please."

The chatter of the other customers, clanging of cutlery against china, and soft jazz floating from overhead speakers disappeared. We could've been absolutely alone in the center of one of the ten largest cities in the country. Her cheeks were scarlet, her dark eyes downcast. She hadn't done anything wrong either. "Just so you know, if the situation *were* different, I would be interested. Just so you know."

Our gazes locked. Her expression lightened. She smiled. "It's a pretty darn good consolation prize."

"Eat your cinnamon roll."

I ate every last crumb of mine. So did she, starting with the center piece and working her way out. I'd never seen anyone eat a cinnamon roll that way, and I told her so.

"It's my favorite piece."

"Which is why you're supposed to leave it for last so you can savor it."

"You never know what life will bring. Maybe you'll have a stroke and die before you get to the best part." Her grin broadcast a deeper meaning. "That's why I'm into immediate gratification."

I ate the center. The most gooeyness, the most cinnamon, the most sweetness. I could see her point. "We'd better go. Matt will wonder what's happened to us."

"I think Matt has a pretty good imagination."

Turns out she was right. Back at the office, Matt beckoned me into his office only minutes after our return. He'd helped himself to a banana-nut muffin, which I pointed out was meant for the staff meeting.

"I couldn't wait."

Immediate gratification. "What's up?"

Matt rose and shut the door to his office. A sure sign he was about to meddle where he didn't belong. "So does Kris know about Pilar?"

A cold chill prickled up and down my arms. "What are you talking about? There's nothing to tell."

"Oh yeah?" He plopped in his chair, leaned back, and tented his stubby fingers. "All those late nights in the office. Every other sentence out of her mouth when we play poker starts with 'Daniel says.' I know you and Kristen are having a tough time. Living with such an incredibly dedicated physician isn't easy. I understand that. But you're still married."

"There's nothing going on between Pilar and me."

"Seriously?" He jerked his head toward the door. "Some of our coworkers have noticed. I walked into the break room this morning and heard them speculating about it."

"I think I'd know if something was going on between us."

"To quote my wife, 'There are physical affairs and then there are emotional affairs.'" Matt folded his tent fingers and sat up. "You, my friend, are having an emotional affair. What say you to this charge?"

"I say you're full of it, as usual."

"So stop hanging out with her. Go home to your wife. Work things out. That will have the added benefit of removing an office romance from the gossip gristmill and force Pilar to get on with her life as well. If you're not having an affair with Pilar, you won't miss those meetups, or will you?"

Like crazy. As much as I missed sleeping next to my wife?

I opened my mouth, then closed it. "You don't know what it's like. I'm not asking Kristen to give up her career. I love how smart, dedicated, persevering, stubborn, and determined she is. I'm just asking for a sliver of her time for us before we're two strangers living parallel lives under the same roof."

"Have you told her that?"

"I've tried. She always says the same thing. She'll do better." I scrubbed at my face with both hands. "But she never does. In fact, she takes on more responsibility. She's Sherri's navigator, and she's still seeing patients full time. I think she's even considering getting more into the research side."

"Man, I'm not disagreeing with you." Matt picked up a pen, set it down, and shrugged. "You deserve your wife's attention. Having an affair is not the way to go about it. You'll drive the wedge so far between you, there may be no bridging the gap."

"Have you ever considered it?"

"Are you kidding? I can barely handle one woman. What would I do with two?" He snorted. "Besides, Colleen wouldn't allow it. Having an affair isn't going to make you happy. It's going to make you even more miserable because you're not that guy. You're too honorable for a sleazy affair."

Was I? The truth was, I'd given it more than a little thought on those long nights in the too-squishy double mattress listening to the IH-10 highway sounds at 3:00 a.m. and someone with a heavy tread pacing in the room overhead. Water heater clinking. Water dripping in the bathtub. "I'm not having an affair. Cheating on my wife won't make me happy. I get that."

"You're not listening. You don't have to sleep with a woman to be involved with her. Colleen was really clear about that. Like she wanted me to get it too. She asked me which one would she hate more—me having a physical relationship with another woman or an emotional connection with that woman."

Both would hurt. But Matt—or Colleen—had a point. "I'm going to the house for Thanksgiving. That's the best I can do for now."

"Good for you, bro. It's a start."

Maybe. "You know about Sherri?"

"Yeah. Andrew told me. It sucks."

We commiserated in silence for a few minutes.

"That's another good reason to spend the holiday with your wife and kids. It may be Sherri's last one. Kris will need you."

Matt wasn't above a little emotional blackmail. Except Kris rarely needed me. "It's not Sherri's last Thanksgiving. Kris won't allow that."

"That's a big boulder on some fairly small shoulders."

"I know, but I'm not sure she'll let me help her carry it."

"My two o'clock is here." Matt stood and came around his desk. He stuck his hand on my shoulder and squeezed. "I'm rooting for the two of you, buddy."

Then he was off to greet his customer. I heaved myself from the chair. He was right. No throwing in the towel. I headed for my office. Pilar passed me in the hallway. She smiled. "Captain Janeway is better than Picard any day."

"No way." I smiled and kept walking. "Just because she's a woman." Friends could banter. Couldn't they?

twenty-eight

SHERRI

The new kid on the block. Like starting a new school in the middle of the semester. I sat on the recliner in the infusion room for my first clinical trial treatment. A nurse joked with her patient. A bald, wrinkled woman hooked up to an infusion pump ate Cheetos with an equally bald, wrinkled man who periodically handed her a large Styrofoam cup with the words BIG GULP scrawled across it. A middle-aged husband and wife team watched TV on an iPad, the sound of canned laughter spilling across the room. I counted twenty-two chairs, about half of them occupied, compared to the ninety-plus at the Texas Cancer Care Clinic. More intimate, one might say.

"Hi, Ms. Reynolds, I'm Jana. I'll be your nurse today." A cute, pregnant brunette in navy scrubs rolled a cart carrying a portable electrocardiogram machine with one hand and a vitals basket on wheels with the other toward me. Talk about ambidextrous. "Would you like a pillow and a blanket before we get started?"

"I brought my own blanket." I tugged the prayer blanket my Sunday school class had given me from my bag. "But I will take a pillow, please."

"We keep our blankets in a warmer, just so you know." Her mask hid her lips, but her eyes suggested a smile. If it weren't for the baby bump, she'd look fourteen. "Are you sure?"

I was sure. The blanket anchored me in the prayers of some of the most powerful prayer warriors in my world. Jana brought me the pillow. Then she proceeded to untangle the umpteen number of lead wires that constituted the EKG. "It takes longer to straighten these buggers out than the EKG does." She rolled her soft brown eyes. "I keep thinking there should be a way to keep them in line, but we haven't figured it out.

"We'll do this before and after the treatment," she added. "I'll get your vitals, do a blood draw, and by that time your drugs should be out from the pharmacy. Then I'll access your port and we can get started. We'll do another blood draw after the infusion. And vitals again, of course."

"I was wondering why you can't do the blood draws from my port?" I didn't want to get a reputation as a complainer right off the bat, but my veins were like Swiss cheese after jumping through hoops with blood work and a heart diagnostic screening over the past week. "The phlebotomist already poked me once for lab work before I saw Dr. Capstone. She had to dig around to get a vein that worked."

"I'm so sorry, but the study protocol doesn't allow us to do these specific draws from your port." Jana truly did sound sorry. But it didn't help much. "They don't want the draw to be contaminated. We'll leave the needle in so we don't have to poke you again after treatment."

I bit my tongue to keep from snapping at her. *Don't shoot the messenger.* "They told me when I got the port that it would be my best friend. That it could be used for everything."

Empathy oozed from her pores. "I know. I hate hurting my patients. I wish there was some way to avoid it, but the study folks don't give us a choice. In this case, it's understandable. We don't want the data to be corrupted, do we?"

Welcome to clinical trials, in other words. Patient comfort wasn't a high priority. They probably thought of patients as subjects. Not people. Whatever it took as long as it worked.

I laid back so she could attach the sticky electrodes to my chest and stomach. Jana muttered to herself as she figured out which lead wire went to which electrode. "I think I've got it." She straightened and gave a victory air punch like an athlete celebrating a win. "I have to do three of these thirty seconds apart, so try not to move until I tell you I'm done."

I closed my eyes. The murmur of half a dozen conversations poured over me. A woman's voice. "I told Mom if this trial doesn't work, hospice is next for me. She got all upset at me for saying it, but it's true. At a certain point you have to face facts."

A woman answered with something indistinct but bland.

From another direction, a man's voice held quiet, professional-sounding concern: "I think it's time to consider hospice. We're not able to control her pain adequately with oral medications. She's no longer able to walk on her own. She's not eating. We'll need to do a catheter shortly."

"You don't have to list the reasons, Doc . . ."

I opened my eyes. A doctor I hadn't met sat on a stool on wheels talking with a man seated in a visitor chair next to a woman so covered with blankets I could barely make out her face. She seemed to be sleeping.

Ten minutes in and I'd already heard the word *hospice* used in two different conversations. I held my breath against a sudden surge of tears. *Suck it up, blondie. It is what it is.* I hated that saying. Like everything happens for a reason. Tell that to parents who'd lost children in school shootings. Or the victims of a serial rapist. Was there some grand design that made their suffering "worth it"? Nowhere in the Bible did it say everything happened for a reason.

"Alrighty then. I'm done." Jana unhooked the lead wires. "I'll leave the stickies until we do the second set of EKGs." She quickly finished the task and moved on to temperature, respiration, and blood pressure. She was an efficient nurse. "Next up, the catheter for your blood draws."

More teeth-gritting ensued. Jana had a surprisingly good technique. She chose a vein close to my wrist. That area tended to be more tender, but she didn't have to dig around or poke me a second time. I appreciated that. She cocked her head. "Whew! I'm in."

She made quick work of the blood draw, then hopped up from her stool. "I'll check on your drugs. If you need anything, just give a shout."

I thanked her, but she was already zipping toward the pharmacy window across the room. I tugged my book from my bag and settled in. Before I could open it, my phone dinged.

Kris. She had dropped me off on her way to the Texas Cancer Care Clinic for a meeting.

> I got hung up talking to the practice manager after the meeting. I have to take care of some work she handed me. I'll probably be another hour.
> **I told u no need to come. pick me up when I'm done**
> And I said you're full of it.
> **No u are**

Sisters knew how to bring out the best in each other.

> I'll bring Chick-fil-A.
> **Ok. You're forgiven for hovering**

Chick-fil-A's waffle fries could make up for many transgressions. She would split herself in two trying to be all things to all people. Except Daniel. What work had the practice manager handed her? Would it be another excuse for not going to marriage counseling until the spring? Did she want to be divorced and single at fifty? I'd walked that road. Reinventing myself as a single woman was no fun.

My phone rang. FaceTime. Had to be Noelle. I hated to reject the call, but I had no choice. Unlike the folks watching TV with no earbuds, I didn't want to bother the people trying to sleep. I texted Noelle instead.

Sorry at clinic. First clinical trial day
Whoops. Max wanted to tell you no more diapers. Potty-trained. Finally. Daytime, anyway. Also counted to 10

Lots of emojis followed.

Yay! Tell him Grandma says high five & big

My own slew of emojis followed.

FaceTime later. Fingers & toes crossed that all goes well
Thanks. Later

I opened my book a second time. The patient in the recliner to my right, a man with a belly as big as my pregnant nurse's, began to snore. It was a snore for the record books. With a vibrato that would make an opera singer proud and an occasional snort that suggested disdain over a not-so-funny joke.

Reading through it would require laser focus and earmuffs.

Jana reappeared, carrying a basket filled with three bags of clear liquids. I raised my eyebrows and cocked my head toward the snorer. Her eyebrows rose and fell. "He's in a lot of pain. He doesn't sleep much at night. We gave him pain meds and Benadryl. We'll let him sleep as long as possible."

The rest of the story. Knowing what others were suffering through helped put my puny symptoms in perspective. "Poor guy."

Jana accessed my port, we went through the usual drill of name and date of birth, and then the *tick-tick* of the infusion pump started.

"We're doing the steroids first, then the anti-nausea meds. That'll take about thirty minutes." Jana studied something on the infusion pump, smoothed the tubing, and stepped back. "Then the study drug. That will take about ninety minutes, so it'll be about two hours, then the EKG, blood draw, and vitals. Two hours and fifteen minutes, give or take. Is someone picking you up?"

"My sister will be here in a little bit. She wants to hang out."

"If you need anything, just wave me down."

She had three other patients, one with a container of at least eight or nine blood draw tubes waiting to be filled. Clinical trials were labor-intensive for the nurses. I didn't envy the physical and emotional investment they made in each patient. So similar to Kristen's.

Speaking of which. Kristen trotted down the hallway past the water and coffee station toward the infusion room. She was loaded down with Chick-fil-A bags and two drinks. Her face was flushed, but she was smiling. Not something she did much these days.

I cleared one of the small flat "tables" attached to the arm of my recliner. "Why so chipper?"

"Your grilled chicken sandwich, waffle fries, and tea, madame." Her grin widened. She pulled up a chair and took the other "table" for her usual—a breaded chicken sandwich with pickles, fries, and a Diet Dr Pepper.

She smelled of cigarette smoke.

"So much for quitting."

"Quitting?" She gave me her best quizzical look. "I'll never give up DP."

"You smell like cigarettes."

"Sorry. It was a crazy morning. Exciting, but crazy."

Not crazy like mine. There's crazy, and then there's crazy. "Exciting? What happened? Did the practice manager decide to move on?"

"No. The board finally made a decision. That position I told you about is mine. I'm the clinic's liaison between our research arm and this clinical trial clinic. Texas Cancer Care Clinic is beefing up its research budget, and I'm going to be a part of that."

She spit all that out so fast she was breathless.

"Wow. That does sound exciting." I unwrapped my sandwich. The scent of grilled chicken permeated the air. I opened a ketchup packet for my fries, using the time to measure my words. "Will you cut back on your patient load then?"

"Oh no. We're revamping my schedule so I can be here at this clinic for meetings every Friday morning. I'll do more televisits. I can do those late afternoon, early evening."

"Do you hear yourself?"

She doctored her fries with ketchup. "What?"

"What happened to marriage counseling and making your relationship with Daniel a priority?"

"Don't you get it? It's my chance to not just treat patients like you with existing regimens that eventually stop working. It's a chance to help develop drugs with fewer side effects and greater efficacy. To save lives."

"I understand—"

"There you are, Kristen." Dr. Capstone trotted across the room. He never strolled. He always did double-time as if there weren't enough minutes in an hour. In his business there weren't. He'd started this clinic and then added ones in Austin and Dallas. Now his dark-brown eyes beamed. "I heard you were in the house. I just got off the phone with the powers that be. It sounds like we're in business."

Kristen wiped her hands on a napkin and stood. "I'll be right back, sis. I just want to confirm a few details with Richard."

"Sure. No problem."

This was my sister's life. Trying to balance the drive to change something that couldn't be changed—our mother's death—no matter the cost to herself or those around her. This was her choice. I couldn't stand in her way any more than Daniel could.

"Your sister's an oncologist?"

The snorer next to me was awake.

"She is."

"Lucky you."

Lucky me. Not so lucky for Daniel.

twenty-nine

KRISTEN

My turn to set the table with wedding dishes, silverware, and silver candleholders. This time the taper candles were orange, the tablecloth golden brown. No, it wasn't a romantic dinner for two, but it might be just as important. I surveyed the place settings: a design of fall leaves and apples on the place mats; burnt orange and earthy brown cloth napkins in wicker ring holders; and a woven cornucopia basket filled with gourds, squash, and small pumpkins as the centerpiece.

The aroma of turkey roasting floated into the dining room. The kids didn't know how lucky they were that Sherri knew how to cook a turkey. And make cornbread dressing—Daniel's favorite—gravy, and homemade cranberry sauce. Guilt pinched my arm hard. With the steroids and low blood cell counts came insomnia and fatigue. I'd fought against putting her to work in the kitchen, but she insisted. I did all the chopping and mashing and basting. We agreed to cut a few corners—pumpkin and pecan pies from Bill Miller and brown-and-serve rolls. Sherri liked to bake but didn't have the stamina for it anymore. I sucked at it.

Everything had to be perfect. Not only were the girls coming, they were bringing their boyfriends. Following tradition, I'd convinced them to come over in time to watch the Macy's Thanksgiving Day

Parade. We would eat around one o'clock, in plenty of time to cheer on the Cowboys in a game against their divisional rivals the New York Giants later in the afternoon.

The agenda was set.

"You'll need one more place setting."

I turned to face Sherri, who stood in the doorway, wiping her hands on a dish towel. The trial drug didn't cause alopecia. It might only be cosmetic, but the hair curling around her ears was good for her morale. Her CA-125 was down, still not in the normal range but down. The last CT scan indicated no progression. The lymph nodes hadn't shrunk either. But we still called it a win and celebrated with Whataburgers.

Her face was pasty white and puffy against her maroon blouse and black slacks. She'd gained several pounds—not a bad thing. Despite food tasting like cardboard and never-ending nausea, she had a raging appetite brought on by the steroids.

I whirled and counted again. "Daniel, you, me, Maddie, Brielle, their boyfriends. That's seven."

"And Dad. You forgot Dad."

I advanced on her. "I can't forget something I didn't know. Since when is Dad coming?"

"Since I arranged for VIA Trans to pick him up, bring him, and return him later this evening."

"You knew I wouldn't do it, and Daniel won't do it without my blessing."

"I would've popped over there myself, but I knew you were stressing about the cooking."

"You should've asked me."

"I can't have my kids and grandkids here. Chance is visiting his parents in Fort Myers. Dad's all the family we have left. Humor me."

She didn't blatantly play the cancer card, but she came close. Her kids would come. They'd want to spend as much time with her as possible, if they truly knew how dire her situation was. But she refused to tell them. Her woebegone expression, complete with lower lip extended, said all that and more. I went to the hutch and collected the items to set another place.

"Thank you, sister of mine."

"You're welcome." I managed not to sound like a sore loser. "He sits by you."

"No problemo."

With any luck the girls would arrive first. They seemed enchanted with their newfound grandfather. So where were they? I already had the TV on. The preparade gabfest had started. NBC's Savannah Guthrie and Hoda Kotb bantered like crazy. They would run out of small talk before the first marching band hit the parade route.

The doorbell rang. Dash and Scout dashed toward the hallway, while Cleo slunk toward the bedroom.

"Here we go." I put my hand close to my mouth, blew, and sniffed. Did I smell like cigarettes? No, the Shalimar—Daniel's favorite—I'd spritzed on my wrist after a long shower and careful application of my makeup was still just right. I smoothed my damp palms over my black slacks and checked to make sure I hadn't dripped grease on my blue blouse. I'd changed my clothes four times. We normally wore sweats and football jerseys, but today I needed to knock some socks off. It felt like they were company coming for a visit. The boyfriends *were* company. I'd never met either one.

"Are you going to get that?"

"I think I'm having a moment." I bent over and put my hands on my thighs. "I may hyperventilate."

"Do what Dr. Capstone tells me to do. Think happy thoughts." Did Sherri see Mom's face in the mirror? She had that same ethereal skin as Mom did. "Remember how blessed you are to have your girls and your husband here, even under these circumstances. I'll check on the turkey. Go let our guests in."

I did exactly that. It took several minutes with the dogs barking and everyone talking at once, but eventually we sorted it all out. Maddie's boyfriend was a premed student named Josh. Psychology and medicine would go well together.

Brielle's boyfriend, Chad, was majoring in Middle Eastern studies. He spoke Farsi and Arabic. He wanted to be in the Foreign Service or a UN translator. An interesting choice for Brielle, who was studying early childhood education. She'd wanted to be an elementary school teacher for as long as I could remember.

Daniel mostly directed his salutations to the dogs, who nearly knocked him over in enthusiastic delight at his return. He knelt and embraced them both. His head was down, hiding his expression.

Hugs for both girls, handshakes with the boys. Nodding, Daniel sidestepped any direct contact with me.

Somehow I managed to herd them into the grand room—or maybe Dash and Scout did the herding. I'd set out cheese and cracker trays, chips and dip, and pickle rollups. "Don't eat too much. Turkey and all the trimmings are served at one o'clock sharp."

"I can't wait." Brielle wore a gorgeous cardigan set in a soft burgundy. No sweats for her either. "I skipped Grandpa's chocolate chip waffles this morning so I'd have room for everything."

"And I have a hollow leg." Josh patted his flat belly. The boy—young man, really—could've walked out of a modeling catalogue. Tall, but not too tall. Blond. Paul Newman bedroom eyes, perfect teeth. And smart. Premed students had to be. "As a poor premed student, I stuff my face anytime home-cooked food is on the table."

"It smells wonderful. I've been smelling that aroma in my dreams for the last week." Maddie shook off a purple jacket, revealing a maroon dress belted at the waist with a full skirt. With her matching lip gloss and curves, she was a throwback to the movie stars of the fifties. A throwback to her grandmother. "Did you make the cranberry sauce from scratch, the way I like it?"

"Absolutely. Grandma Angela's recipe all the way." Including the two cups of sugar. Daniel could never know the truth about one of his favorite holiday dishes. "We also made your dad's favorite cornbread dressing."

Daniel picked up the remote. He turned up the sound. "The parade's about to start, guys. They have some new balloons this year."

I bit my lower lip to keep accusatory words from bursting forth. If he intended to ignore me all day, why come?

For the girls, of course.

"Where's Aunt Sherri?" Her expression sympathetic, Maddie squeezed my arm as she brushed past me. "I want to give her a hug."

I tugged her back. "Let's stick to air hugs. Her counts are low. We're practicing social distancing today."

"Should we even be here?" Brielle scooped up her coat. "I didn't even think of that."

"I'm fine, girls. No need to freak out." Sherri strode into the room exuding energy. She'd changed into cherry-red slacks and a crisp white blouse. She wore a cute flowered hairband that showed off her curls. She'd even done up her face with enough makeup to mask her pallor. "Ignore your mother. She's a worrywart. Bring on the hugs. They're the best medicine you can't buy."

More introductions. Hugs all around. Sherri even hugged Daniel. He hugged her back. My concerns duly noted and discarded. Sherri grilled the boys on their intentions with her nieces. Soon they were laughing over the anecdotes she pulled from a store of memories from our childhood that I mostly didn't remember. Then she segued into stories about the girls when they were little. They always involved both Daniel and me as a team united against two wily little terrors.

Daniel's gaze skittered away. He knew what she was doing. So did I. "I better put the rolls in the oven."

"I'll do it." Sherri jumped up. "Take my seat."

On the love seat. Next to Daniel. "You've been cooking all morning. Take a rest."

"I feel great, sis. Sit, sit." She dashed away like a track star on steroids.

This was what I wanted, right? Our family together on one of our favorite holidays. Food, family, and football. I sat. Daniel squirmed away. I placed my hand, fingers splayed, on the space between us. "I don't have cooties, I promise."

"It's not cooties that worry me."

Maddie and Brielle made a big production of pointing out their favorite balloons to the boys. I leaned closer. "Isn't it nice to have us all here together under one roof?"

"On Saturday, Maddie and Brielle go back to Austin." He leaned away from me. "I'm not living here by myself—or with just my sister-in-law—again."

"I'll be home more during the holidays. Especially since . . ." My voice cracked. I swallowed a sudden, hard knot of tears. This could be Sherri's last Christmas. I almost said it aloud. This was not permitted. Negative thinking did no good whatsoever. "It'll be fun to have everyone together for Christmas."

His expression softened. "Do you think Sherri's kids will come home?"

"I hope so." The words sounded more fervent than I'd intended. "It would be nice."

"It would." He glanced toward the girls, then back at me. "You'll be taking some time off then?"

Daniel had an uncanny ability to read my mind. I grabbed a toothpick and stabbed a hunk of honeydew melon. I nibbled. When I was sure my voice would cooperate, I shook my head. "I'll be off the week of Christmas, of course, but until then it's full steam ahead. You remember the research position I told you about? The board confirmed my appointment—"

"I should've known." Shaking his head, Daniel snorted. "Not even your sister dying—"

How dare he? Couldn't he see? This was a way of finding the new treatments women like Sherri needed in order to survive ovarian cancer. "Don't you say that. Don't you dare say that."

The girls' chatter with their boyfriends ceased. The banal give-and-take of the parade commentators droned on. Brielle and Maddie both shot us searing scowls. I forced a smile. "Sorry, we were just debating whether the Cowboys will make it to the playoffs this season."

And if they believed that, I had some oceanfront property in Arizona I wanted to sell them.

"No one in their right mind would bet on the Cowboys this year." Josh rolled his eyes and shrugged. "It's a building year."

A Cowboys fan. Maddie had done well.

The doorbell rang. Never had a diversion been more welcomed. "I'll get that."

Daniel's frown could've fried an egg.

More deep-breathing exercises. I shooed the dogs back and opened the door. Dad bowed with a courtly air that matched his gray suit and tie. He'd gone all out. His effort had the desired effect. He was trying so hard. "Come in, Dad. Daniel and the girls are in the great room."

"What a funny name for a living room. Fancy." He pushed his walker, outfitted with green tennis balls on the front legs, past me. "Did you get it from one of those DIY shows they have on the Magnolia Network?"

"You watch home-renovation shows?"

"The old broads at the center are always talking about them while they play bridge and pinochle. Like they can do something fancy with their little apartments."

"Daniel's an architect, as you know. He designed this house. He decides what the rooms are called."

"He seems like a nice guy. You did good."

If I used Dad as a yardstick, any guy with a pulse who stuck around would be top-of-the-line. I swallowed the thought. Too bad I'd never acquired a taste for alcohol. This would be a good time for a shot of whiskey. "Everybody's watching the parade. The girls will be excited to see you."

"You always watch TV on holidays? I could've stayed home and done that."

I ignored the question. His walker thumped against the floor. I slowed my steps to match his lift-and-set pattern. He wore cyclist's gloves. A discordant accessory. "Why the gloves?"

"I lean too hard on the walker." His tone was rueful. "My palms hurt. I'm getting calluses. My physical therapist recommended them."

The sympathy that welled up in me couldn't be denied. It had to be hard for a former athlete who prided himself on his physicality to adjust to being unable to hide his infirmity. So-called able-bodied people saw the walker before they saw the person. Walker equaled old age. Walker equaled disabled. And a society that worshipped at the feet of youth and perfection pitied people with disabilities. "Are you doing all your exercises?"

"Every day. I'd be walking with a cane now if my physical therapist wasn't such a pessimist."

He thumped faster as if to prove his point.

"You'll get there."

I showed him into the "fancy" room and fled to the kitchen. Her face flushed from the oven's heat, Sherri lifted the turkey from the oven and set the pan on top of the stove. "It's done. I'll move it to the platter so we can get at the drippings and start the gravy. Can you cover it with foil?"

"Yes. Dad's here."

"Good. We're all here. How are you and Daniel doing?"

"He's mad."

"You told him about the research appointment?"

"I did. He didn't take it well."

She shook her head. "What did I tell you? What did you expect?"

"That he'd understand how important this is. It's bigger than me or him—"

"Or your marriage. That excuse obviously has grown thin."

Brielle slammed into the room. Her face was red. Tears wet her cheeks. "Mom, what did you say to Dad?"

I rushed to meet her, reached out. She backed away as if I'd mentioned COVID-19. "What's the matter, honey? Why are you crying?"

"What did you say to him?" She put both hands on her hips and stared at me. Her normally soft voice rose to a pitch so sharp it hurt my ears. "He's leaving. He's leaving!"

"What? No, no." I shot past her and ran down the hall to the great room. "Daniel? Daniel!"

Maddie stood in the middle of the room. Josh was helping her put on her coat. "He's gone. He said to tell you he took the dogs. You're the most selfish person in the world." Her scowl left scratch marks on my face and heart. "I don't know how Dad even married you. Or why you had kids. You don't think about anybody but yourself."

"That's not true—"

"Don't talk to your mom like that, child." Dad was still standing, hunched over his walker. "Krissy, you should go after—"

"Shut up, Dad. This doesn't concern you."

"I'll see what's cooking in the kitchen." His tone was surprisingly kind. "Maybe Sherri needs my help."

"I can give you a ride home," Maddie called after him. "You don't have to stay here."

"That's okay, sugar." He patted Brielle's shoulder as he passed her. "I'm used to family fights on holidays. It was one of the few things the Millers did well." He kept walking.

"See, you can't even show respect for your own father." Maddie's blue eyes were bright with tears that didn't fall. "You're like the antithesis of a role model. Like the opposite of what I want to be." She jerked away from Josh's attempt to put his arm around her. "You're the reason I'm never getting married or having kids."

"What? You're not?" Josh's mouth dropped open. "I—"

"Shut up, Josh." Maddie shoved past me. "If you guys want a ride back to Grandma's, you'd better get moving."

Brielle grabbed her coat from the rack near the arched doorway. "Wait for me, sis." She didn't meet my gaze as she shrugged the coat on. Chad stood awkwardly, hands at his side, his cheeks bright red as if waiting for her to notice him. She didn't. "I can't stay here another second."

She paused a few feet from me, her gaze directed somewhere over my shoulder. "Just so you know, when I get married, I'm going to stop working. I'll have babies and my job will be to take care of them and my husband. He'll never feel like Dad feels right now."

Chad nodded at me as he followed her out. His expression was a version of *I wish I was anywhere but here.* "It was nice to meet you, Dr. Tremaine. I mean, you know . . ." His voice trailed away.

"I know." I gathered up my tattered dignity and scooted after them out the front door and into the driveway. "Don't leave, girls! Please, don't leave. The turkey's ready. Sit down. We'll talk this out."

"There's nothing to talk about." Maddie slid into the Prius Daniel had insisted on buying her for her twenty-first birthday. "Not to Bri and me. You should be talking to Dad."

"I will. I'll talk to him. I'll get him to come back."

"No you won't." Brielle wiped her nose with a sodden tissue. Chad opened the door and she folded herself into the back seat. "You didn't see the hurt on his face. He's done, Mom. He's done with you. I don't know what you said, but you broke his heart."

Maddie's window whirred down. "And now you've broken our hearts." Her voice cracked. "Happy frickin' Thanksgiving."

The window whirred back up. The engine turned over. Then they were gone.

I don't know how long I stood there in the middle of the driveway, alone. "What just happened?"

I stared at the empty street. All up and down the block people were inside, sitting down to Thanksgiving dinner, laughing, talking, watching football, saying prayers of Thanksgiving, eating too much, loosening their belts, taking naps, and reminiscing about holidays past.

Sure, not all of them were Norman Rockwell dinners. I had vague memories of those arguments Dad had mentioned. Those still, tense meals when the turkey tasted like sawdust, Mom burned the rolls, and the piecrust turned out as hard as cement. Dad sat in front of the TV watching football, empty beer bottles covering the coffee table like a crowd of ne'er-do-well friends who'd outstayed their welcome.

My hands shook so hard I had trouble hitting his name under favorites in my phone. It rang, rang, rang. Voice mail. "Talk to me, Daniel. You keep leaving. Isn't our marriage worth a knock-down, drag-out fight? Can't you tell me how you feel instead of walking away? You're no better than my dad."

I hung up before my voice broke into a million little pieces. What a stupid message. It would only make him madder. No getting it back.

Please ignore the last part of that voice mail. You're making me crazy. I know I make you crazy. Isn't that because we love each other? Don't walk away. Talk to me. Yell at me. Scream. Just don't walk away. Please.

Then I waited, my gaze glued to that rectangular screen, hoping, holding my breath.

Nothing.

Darkness crept into my peripheral vision. Purple dots danced there. I gasped for air.

The girls. I switched to our thread.

I'm so sorry. I didn't mean to spoil our Thanksgiving. I love you guys so much. I love your dad. I'm trying to do the right thing for everyone. Give me a chance to explain. Please.

I waited.

Nothing.

"Come inside, sissy."

I couldn't turn around. Sherri would see the guilt and defeat in my face. I swallowed against a tidal wave of tears. If I started crying now, I'd never stop. "Maybe I'll take a walk."

"Come inside. I called Gardenside Manor. They said they're happy to accept a donation of the turkey and fixin's to go with what they're serving. We can eat with Dad's neighbors and friends. They're having games afterward. A lot of those folks have no one visiting them today. They'd love the company."

"I don't want to talk to people." I didn't want to talk to anyone ever again. My legs gave way. I sat on the steps. "What have I done?"

"You've made a mess." Sherri joined me. "As you know, I'm familiar with these kinds of messes. They can be fixed, but forgiveness takes time. It takes time to rebuild trust."

"Is it so wrong to want to fix a bigger problem?"

Sherri's arm came around my shoulders. She leaned her head against mine. "No. But nothing you do will bring Mom back—"

"I'm not trying to—"

"Yes, you are. You're still that fourteen-year-old girl watching a casket being lowered into the ground and wanting her back so bad you dream about it."

"I love Daniel." Why I felt the need to whisper this truth was beyond me. I cleared my throat and spoke up. "I love Daniel. I want him back so bad I dream about it."

"He loves you, too, or this wouldn't be killing him."

"Why does he keep leaving then? Why doesn't he stay and fight for our marriage?" I undid my clenched hands one finger at a time. "Mom died. Dad left. Daniel leaves. Everyone leaves."

And Sherri might be next to leave. I didn't have to say it. She had to be thinking it too.

She rubbed my back in a soft, reassuring circle. "Daniel is trying to make a point. Surely you can see that? Why would he stay when you don't pay attention to him when he *is* here? You want him to be here when it's convenient for you—not when he needs you to be present. Totally present."

Harsh. My sister knew how to deliver a knockout punch. I scooted away from her. "That's not true." My voice was weak in my ears. "When I'm here, I'm here."

"Except when you're on your laptop reviewing patient plans or answering emails or responding to texts. When was the last time you went anywhere with Daniel? When was the last time you went to church with him? When was the last time you snuggled in the morning instead of jumping out of bed to run to your laptop?"

"All right, all right, just shut up already. You're not helping."

"I'm sorry. I'm not trying to make you feel worse. But I've been on Daniel's end of this scenario. I know how painful it is to be left to watch TV alone, eat dinner alone, sleep alone. To parent alone. It's the loneliest place on earth."

"You're my sister. You're supposed to be on my side."

"I *am* on your side." She elbowed me in the ribs. "That's why I'm saying all this. I want you to be happy. You love Daniel. He loves you. But it takes two to make a relationship work. Daniel can't do it by himself."

"How can we fix this if he keeps leaving? He's just like Dad."

"Dad's here now. He's trying. He's waiting for you to try too."

"She's right." Dad's walker thunked onto the porch. I swiveled and stared up at him. He squinted against the early afternoon sun. "I don't know about you two, but I'm hungrier than a bear just waking up from a long winter's nap. Let's head back to the prison. I heard there's gonna be some card games this afternoon. A couple of those women are serious card sharks."

"We can't solve all the world's problems right now." Sherri stood, dusted off her behind, and held out her hand to me. "But we can help some folks celebrate Thanksgiving."

I took her hand and she pulled me to my feet. "You're a terrible poker player."

"It don't matter." Dad whipped his walker around and headed inside. "Those dirty old men will be happy just ogling you two."

"Oh, now that's a lovely thought." Sherri followed him. "I better put on a turtleneck."

"Why deprive them?" I dredged up a watery laugh. "They have so little joy in their lives."

Through no fault of their own. If joy was missing in my life, it was my fault. Sherri was right. I had work to do. I wanted to start now. Instead, I would eat pumpkin pie and play cards.

thirty

DANIEL

Thanksgiving was for giving thanks. Hence the name. Bitterness left a foul taste in my mouth. My jaw hurt from gritting my teeth every time my phone rang or dinged with texts from Kristen and/or the girls. Walking away felt good and bad, right and wrong, necessary and horrible. The soupy mixture of emotions roiled in my stomach. More teeth gritting to keep from hurling out the window.

Dash woofed softly and nudged me with his snout. "I know. I can't walk into my parents' house full of rancor toward my wife and spoil everyone's Thanksgiving." I took one hand off the wheel long enough to pat his furrowed brow while stopped at a light at Bandera Road and Loop 1604. "Just give me a minute. I'll get my act together before we pull into the driveway."

Kristen was so oblivious. How could she be so out of sync with me? Or me with her? Had we ever even been in the same universe? I craned my head side to side and rolled my shoulders. My head pounded. Finally, the light changed and I jolted forward.

Scout joined Dash in a follow-up woof, as if not convinced. "I'm fine, guys. I promise. We're fine. I have plenty to be thankful for, including you. I'm thankful I have parents who will welcome me showing up at the last minute with no prior notice. They'll be thrilled to see me. What's more, they'll be thrilled to see you. Not everyone can say that about their parents."

I pulled into the long, circular driveway behind Leonard's Ram, William's Tahoe, and Andrew's Blazer. My hybrid was dwarfed and out of place. I barely had the door open to let the dogs out when Maddie's green Prius slammed to a halt behind me. "Make that me and four more mouths to feed. This won't be fun, boys. Back me up, okay?"

Maddie popped from the car ahead of Brielle and the boyfriends. They'd left Kristen sitting at a table set for eight with only her dad and Sherri for company. Empathy tried to trick me into feeling sorry for her. And guilty. Uh-uh. Not this time. "You girls didn't have to leave." I spoke first. I was the father. I should take the high road. "You could've eaten with your mother. This is between her and me. Not y'all."

"Oh, right. We're just supposed to pretend like we're fine while our parents are headed for divorce." Maddie spit out the words with a venomous glare. "What did she say to you, Dad, that made you walk out on our family Thanksgiving?"

I studied the driveway pavement. Our pact never to fight in front of the girls had been broken in a most spectacular way. "It's complicated."

"Seriously? Life is complicated." Maddie's hand went to her chest in the vicinity of her heart. "I don't get it. You and Mom never fought when we lived at home. You have—had—the perfect marriage when we were growing up. What is going on?"

Then she burst into tears. Josh reached for her. She pushed away and tried to rush past me. I didn't let her go. I tucked her into my arms like a child with her head against my chest. "I'm sorry, ladybug. I'm so sorry."

Her cheeks wet with tears, Brielle stumbled toward me. I made room for her. The two boys stood still, arms dangling at their sides. "I'm sorry, guys, we're not really this dysfunctional. This probably will go down as your worst Thanksgiving ever, and I'm truly, truly sorry for that."

"Naw." His expression rueful, Chad shoved his overlong sandy-brown bangs from his eyes. "I've had worse. Y'all got nothing on my family. Really."

Josh said nothing. He surveyed the street like a trapped animal searching for a way out. They'd all come to San Antonio in Maddie's car, at her insistence. She was her father's daughter when it came to fossil fuels.

I leaned in close to my girls and whispered for their ears, "This has nothing to do with you two. Your mother and I love you very much. We'll figure this out. I promise."

"What did she do?" Brielle raised her head. Her voice quivered. "Is she . . . having an affair?"

"No. No! Nothing like that." I tightened my hug. The things going through their minds were obviously far worse than the truth. "I need more of her time. I need for us to be a couple more and not just two people living in the same house, occasionally eating a meal together. I'm tired of being married and still being lonely."

The tables turned. The girls hugged me. They stopped crying. *Thank You, Lord, for that.* Maddie turned to their guests and invited them into my parents' home. "Y'all must be starving."

The boys looked suitably relieved. My mother must've heard the commotion when they and the dogs trooped into her foyer to be met by Dash and Scout's sister, Luna, who greeted them like the family they were.

Mom bustled into the living room holding a dish towel. Her face bloomed with delight. "You came after all. Excellent. Excellent. Madeleine, put your guests' coats in the primary bedroom. Brielle, show them to the backyard. Your uncles are warming up for the big football showdown after we eat, which will be in about forty minutes. Luna, Dash, Scout, out back with Brielle."

She knew how to direct. Everyone did as they were told—even the dogs.

Nothing fazed my mother. In this case, she likely anticipated the outcome of Kristen's ill-fated attempt to recreate vintage family Thanksgiving holidays at our home. She kissed my cheek and immediately wiped off a smudge of her red lipstick. How many women prepare a holiday meal fully made up and wearing a matching pearl necklace and earrings?

I opened my mouth. She shook her head and placed her index finger across my lips. "No explanations necessary. Your brothers will be thrilled. More players for the football game."

"I'm sorry to dump five more mouths to feed on you at the last minute."

"You know your dad. He's smoked a twenty-five-pound turkey, air-fried another one, and I've got a third one in the oven. The daughters-in-law brought their favorite sides. We've mashed a massive twenty-pound bag of potatoes. We made all the pies yesterday—two each of pumpkin, pecan, and sweet-potato-praline, plus pumpkin and lemon bars for the heathens who don't care for pie. There'll be enough for everyone to take home leftovers."

Take home leftovers. For me that meant the minifridge at the Econo Lodge. I dodged the thought. "Sorry about the dogs. I just wanted some time with them. I wasn't thinking straight—"

"No apologies necessary. Dash and Scout are welcome anytime. You know that. Help your sisters-in-law set up another card table and bring in four more chairs. Your girls and their gents will have their own table." My brothers' wives were old hands at handling my mother's holiday extravaganzas. "It'll be cozy. Those boys are adorable. That Josh is a keeper."

I rubbed my forehead. "Everything is a mess."

She took my arm and led me toward the kitchen. "Let me get you some Tylenol for that headache and a nice glass of sweet tea."

I sank into a chair at the table in the breakfast nook and concentrated on regrouping. Not spoiling another Thanksgiving dinner had to be my first priority. Mom handed me the headache remedy and her fresh-brewed sun tea so sweet it made my teeth hurt. "I know something about being married to a polar opposite."

My mother had never complained to me or my brothers about married life with my dad. She would consider it a form of high treason. Still, the marriage had to feel sometimes like wearing too-tight cowboy boots. "You never complain, though. You always seem so happy."

"Your dad loves hunting, fishing, camping, Westerns and action movies, George Strait and Willie Nelson, and reading Craig Johnson's Longmire mysteries. His idea of dancing is the two-step. There's nothing wrong with any of that." She opened the oven door and peeked in. "It's done! Doesn't it smell heavenly? I love the theater. I love concerts at the Tobin Center and the Majestic Theater. I read historical fiction, and my favorite movies have plot and dialogue and actual character development. We're about as alike as miniature poodles and German shepherds. We're the same species, that's about it."

"But you get along."

"Like you, I'm the one who does the adjusting. Once in a great while I go to the theater with friends. I took my granddaughters to see *Hamilton* and *The Nutcracker*. When he goes on hunting trips, I fill up on plays and concerts with friends. I get to control the remote and I pick the music on the car stereo."

"When he comes back?"

"He controls the remote and the car stereo."

"It's different—"

"Because I'm a housewife and I never worked outside the home, as they say now? It's out of vogue, I know, but he's the head of my household and my heart." Wearing a flowered apron over a pale-blue dress,

269

she was the epitome described by her philosophy. "That doesn't mean I shouldn't be allowed to express an opposing opinion or pursue my interests. Your dad knows where I stand on every decision he makes that affects me and our family."

"Kristen's career is important."

"I agree. Just as important as yours in this day and age. But so is your happiness. You know, I believe in those sacred wedding vows. I believe in doing everything possible to make a marriage work."

"I hear a *but* in there somewhere."

She picked up a pile of pot holders and paused in front of the massive gas stove. "I'm also a mother whose heart hurts when her son is so obviously unhappy."

She wasn't a kumbaya, hold-hands kind of person who showered her children with physical affection, which made her admission all the more touching. I took a long swallow of tea and cleared my throat. "I'll be fine."

"I know you will. One way or another." She lifted the turkey from the oven and set the pan on trivets on the island. "Just don't waste too much more of your life living in limbo. Figure out specifically what you want and need from your wife. Then spell it out for her. If she can't get on board, then you need to do what you need to do. Life is so short, and you're such a good man. You deserve to be happy. You deserve to be treated better. You're a catch. And I'm not just saying that because I'm your mother."

She slapped the pot holders on the granite countertop. "There. I've said my piece. Your father says we should stay out of it, but I know he agrees with me on one thing. You deserve a woman who remembers your birthday. After all, it has fallen on the same date every year you two have been together. That should be the bare minimum in a marriage. Don't you think?"

One time. One time in a twenty-six-year relationship Kristen had forgotten. Under trying circumstances. I didn't begrudge her that one.

The totality of her neglect equaled a far greater sin in my book. Her decision to accept the post as clinical trial liaison was the last flurry of snow necessary to trigger the avalanche that buried our marriage.

"I better go get the table and chairs." I stood and kissed her cheek. "The turkey smells wonderful. Thanks for the support."

"Anytime. You're my favorite son." She laughed that trill of a ladylike laugh that so amused my dad. "Don't tell the others I said that."

I would never. I was sure she told them the same thing regularly.

Alone in the massive storage closet, I leaned against the wall and drew a long breath. The scent of Kristen's Shalimar—a sensual blend of jasmine, roses, vanilla, and balsam notes—filled my nostrils. I breathed out and let it go, along with all the memories of swaying to Coltrane, curled up in bed on a rainy Sunday morning, and kissing in a dark movie theater that it evoked. All gone. "Okay." I tugged my phone from my jeans pocket and punched in the number.

Pilar answered on the first ring. "Daniel? Happy Thanksgiving! You're the last person I expected to hear from today."

"Happy Thanksgiving."

"You don't sound so happy."

"Working on it." I straightened. "How is Thanksgiving at the Caine residence? Is Matt pontificating about what the colonists and the Wampanoag Indians ate in Plymouth in 1621?"

"He did mention something about venison and most of the women being dead, having died that first winter in the New World." She laughed softly. "But Colleen says we're having turkey since they had tons of wild turkey in the region as well. She also drew the line at making pumpkin custard in the pumpkin shell because they had nothing to make the piecrust with. Is that why you called? To see what was on the menu here?"

"Yes . . . no. I mean I was thinking about what you said once about doing stuff as friends."

I sounded like the tongue-tied goober I'd been in high school.

"Yes, I remember that." A quizzical tone mixed with a touch of amusement in Pilar's voice. "Did you come to a different conclusion upon further thought?"

"Do you like horseback riding?"

"I don't know."

"What do you mean you don't know?"

"I grew up in Chicago, Daniel. I didn't see a lot of horses on Lake Shore Drive."

"Right, right. Maybe I could teach you. How about that?"

Her light breathing filled the space for a few seconds. "Horses are really big."

"Big and beautiful, and you'd be perfectly safe with a guy like me who started riding them when he was still in diapers."

Noise sounded in the background. "I'll be right there." She was obviously talking to someone else, not me, although the thought that she might rush over to start horse riding lessons right now had a certain appeal to it. "I have to go. Apparently, my nonexistent talent as a wide receiver is urgently needed on the football field. But call me later. Tonight. We'll lock in a time for horseback riding lessons."

"Good. Good."

"I'm glad you called."

"Me too."

She hung up. I heaved a breath. The start of something. It might be salve on a wound that had to heal before I could move on. So why did I feel like a traitor?

I stared at the phone, at the numeral 6 on the phone icon. Six missed calls, or maybe three missed calls and three voice mails. Three texts.

I shoved the phone back in my pocket, picked up the table in one hand and two chairs with the other. They weighed less than the suitcase of mixed emotions balanced on my shoulders.

thirty-one

KRISTEN

Gathering around a bio-ethanol fire in a pseudo-fireplace didn't have the romantic holiday ring to it that a fragrant mesquite fire would have, but it still reminded me of Daniel. I could still hear his adamant speech on burning wood in an urban area. Big no-no. I turned it up a bit for more warmth. Forty-five degrees in San Antonio was fireplace weather. Perfect for Christmas decorating on this second week of December.

"At least you still have a chimney. I'm sure Santa appreciates Daniel's concern for the environment, but he still needs the traditional fireplace." Dressed in teal sweats and fuzzy white socks, Sherri sat cross-legged on the rug surrounded by stacks of childish artwork, photos, baby books, and mementos. Cleo was curled up at her side, asleep on top of Noelle's favorite childhood blankie. "Do you miss having a real wood-burning fireplace?"

"Not really. It's so much easier to start this fire." I knelt on the floor across from her and picked up a drawing of several people with big faces and small stick bodies. Noelle had scrawled her name in purple crayon across the bottom, along with the words MY FAMILY. "Before we built this house, I almost set the old one on fire. Daniel actually forbade me from messing with it."

Saying Daniel's name without a quiver in my voice deserved a medal and applause. Communications between us had ceased almost completely since the Thanksgiving fiasco. I'd tried calling and texting to no avail. I'd considered showing up at his office, but I didn't want to embarrass him—or myself. I didn't even know where he was staying.

"I always let Chance do it. It seems to appeal to men's inner caveman. Like barbecuing and shooting off fireworks. Something about playing with fire." Sherri took the drawing from me, admired it, and placed it on the keep pile. "How did you almost catch the house on fire?"

I groaned. Admitting this stupid mistake was hard for a highly educated medical professional who prided herself on being relatively smart. "I cleaned out the fireplace. I put the ashes in a paper bag."

Sherri chuckled like she knew what was coming. Dark circles accentuated her blue eyes. The steroids were wreaking havoc on her system the day of and the day after treatment. She'd graduated from ibuprofen to hydrocodone for a back strain she'd suffered while teaching. At least, that was what she'd claimed. I wanted to believe her. Otherwise, the pain was cancer-related and not a good sign. If it weren't for zolpidem, she'd be up all night.

"The ashes were cold, right?"

"Not completely. Apparently, I put the bag in the trash can. A few minutes later I smelled smoke. Then the smoke alarms started going off." The memory still rankled. I hung my head in remembered shame. "I had to use the fire extinguisher to put out the flames."

Sherri hooted and clapped. "Whoops. I suspect Daniel didn't take it well."

"It scared him more than anything. He announced very firmly that he was in charge of all fires in perpetuity."

We both laughed. If only her laugh could be bottled. It would cheer up the most entrenched negativist. She held up a drawing of a horse and a little boy in cowboy boots and a cowboy hat bigger than his body. "Noelle wasn't the only one who could draw growing up. Cody did this one."

"I love that you're doing these memory boxes for the kids. I know Noelle will appreciate it. The guys maybe not as much, but they'll be fun to show to their kids and wives. If Jason marries again."

My sister had bought four decorated photo boxes that fit inside bigger boxes where she planned to add scrapbooks and mementos such as medals, trophies, toddler-sized baseball mitts, favorite stuffed animals, and other trinkets she'd saved over the years. Putting the gifts together was a labor of love. She'd been consumed by sorting, arranging, and building the scrapbooks for a few weeks now. Her plan to give one to Dad was irritating at first, but it gave her joy, so who was I to scoff? It might make him feel even guiltier about abandoning us. In that case, it would serve a purpose totally different from the one Sherri intended. No sense in spoiling her vibe.

She placed one of Jason's fourth-grade report cards on a page across from a photo of his baseball team that year and a class photo. "I hope Jason does. I don't want to think of him going through life alone."

"He's young. He'll find his soulmate yet."

"How about you? Any sign your soulmate is softening yet?"

Our music playlist on Spotify segued from a jazzy rendition of "Jingle Bells" to a more traditional version of "Joy to the World." I rose and went to the stack of Tupperware containers on the couch. My back to my sister, I perused the plastic box that held the homemade ornaments. I selected one Daniel made as a teenager—a miniature wooden sled with a boy belly flopped on top of it. He'd painted it so perfectly. That the fragile ornament had survived all these years boggled the mind. Like our marriage. "Nope. The girls are thawing, though. Brielle texted me today, wanting to know what to get you for Christmas."

"It would be a better sign if she asked what to get *you* for Christmas."

Maybe, but any communication was better than the radio silence they'd maintained for more than two weeks. Every day that went by broke another piece of my heart. Only a massively busy schedule of patients and coordinating the clinical-trial partnership had kept me from sinking into a morass of depression. Decorating the Christmas tree without them was an exercise in keeping a stiff upper lip. Sherri thought it would help us get into the holiday spirit. If it helped her, I was game.

I hung the ornament on a branch not far from a beautiful sand dollar painted with a delicate poinsettia that had been a gift from Maddie a few years back. Then there was JESUS IS THE REASON FOR THE SEASON tiny book ornament Daniel had tied to one of my gifts the first year we dated. And the Christmas tree constructed with cinnamon sticks and buttons Brielle made in preschool.

And on and on. Every ornament brought with it a bittersweet memory of Christmases past.

"You'll make new memories with the girls and Daniel this year." As usual, Sherri was adept at reading my mind. "Christmas is a forgiving season. You'll see."

"From your lips to God's ears."

I stood back and viewed my work of art in progress. The strings of sparkling, colored lights were crooked. That had always been Daniel's job. I had too many globe ornaments up high. But then we always kept them away from the bottom because one powerful swipe of Dash's or Scout's tail would see them flying. Which would have been a good reason to have their tails docked, the norm with their breed, but Daniel refused, saying they weren't show dogs and should remain the way God made them.

Daniel fought for the things he believed in. Was he through fighting for me?

"I miss the dogs." Daniel had taken custody again this weekend. The poor pooches must be so confused with this constant back and forth. I also missed Daniel, but that went without saying. "Even their bad breath and doggie farts."

"They'll be back tomorrow night."

If only that went for Daniel as well.

"So I've been thinking." Sherri paused while she moved around a photo of Noelle in a ballet tutu performing onstage with an honor roll certificate from the seventh grade. A confirmation booklet finished the double-page spread. She leaned back and studied the results.

"You've been thinking. That must've hurt."

"Ha, ha. I've been thinking. I want my ashes scattered from the Eiffel Tower. Paris is supposed to be beautiful in the spring."

"Only if you scatter mine from the viewing platform of the Arc de Triomphe."

"I'm being serious." She picked up a huge valentine made from red construction paper. One of the kids had decorated it with white lacy cutouts. Sherri held it to her heart. "Aww, Jason made this in second grade. He wrote LOVE YOU FOREVER, MOM on it. He was such a sweet kid."

She gave the heart its own page in Jason's scrapbook. "Anyway. Did you know there are three levels where you can stop to enjoy the view? The first one you can walk up three hundred sixty steps or take an elevator. There's a gift shop, a cafeteria, and a restaurant, plus an outdoor terrace space."

"You've done your research." I didn't tell her I knew all of this because Daniel and I had dreamed of visiting Paris. That he'd actually bought the plane tickets. Then I'd blown it. "But surely you don't want me to spread your ashes from the first level?"

"No, of course not." She scooped up a handful of popcorn from the enormous bowl on the coffee table.

I'd made it the old-fashioned way in a big pot. Buttered, of course. The scent always reminded me of Mom and popcorn Friday nights when we stuffed our faces and scared ourselves silly with the old reruns of *The Twilight Zone*.

Sherri wiped her greasy hands and mouth on a napkin. "That is so good! I think you've perfected your technique. The second level is another 355 steps up or an elevator ride. I expect you to take the stairs. It has the same amenities as the first level, except the viewing platforms allow you a lovely view of Notre-Dame, the Louvre, and Basilique du Sacré-Coeur. I expect you to visit all of them after scattering my ashes."

"So the second level is it then?"

"Oh, heavens no. The top level reaches an elevation of 276 meters. Fortunately for you, there are no steps, but the website calls it 'an exhilarating elevator ride from the second level.' In fact, it says 'visiting the top level is one of the most thrilling things to do in Paris, but it's not for the faint of heart.'" Obviously pleased at herself for remembering all of this, she grinned at me. "You're not faint of heart, are you, sister of mine?"

"Of course not. So why are we talking about this tonight while you're making Christmas presents and I'm decorating the Christmas tree? It's a bit morbid, wouldn't you say?"

"Because." She sipped her apple-cinnamon-spice tea and placed the BEST MOM EVER mug gently back on the coffee table. "Because I don't think the study drug is working. Plus, it's not morbid. Remember the reason for the season? What better time to think about it than when we're celebrating Jesus' birth? It's nice to think of resting in a place where romance is in the air every spring. People in love visit Paris. It's beautiful and historic. It's perfect."

"Let's go back to the part where you think the drug isn't working."

I set the angel tree topper back in its tissue. An all-consuming dread ballooned in my stomach. Bitter bile burned the back of my throat. "You haven't had a scan yet. Your tumor markers have risen, but only slightly. What makes you say that?"

She patted her belly. "The nausea and indigestion. The shortness of breath. You know how it is, though. Every little pain and the cancer is growing." Her hand moved to her lower back. "Only this time we're dealing with a first-in-humans trial drug. We really don't know if it'll work at all."

"The drug made it to Phase I because it worked in the laboratory setting."

"I get that." She picked up a photo of Jason in a football uniform holding his helmet. "I waver between trying to be positive and trying to be realistic. I tried just taking ibuprofen last night to sleep. It wasn't enough. That doesn't seem like a good sign."

"Have you told Richard—Dr. Capstone?"

"I will when I go in for my appointment on Friday."

"No. Call tomorrow morning. ASAP. You don't want to wait around."

"It's not that bad—"

"Any new symptoms should be reported immediately."

"Okay, okay." She leaned back against the couch. Cleo rose, stretched, then slipped onto Sherri's lap, where she curled up and closed her eyes. Cleopatra, Queen of Cats. What a life of leisure.

Focusing on the specific symptom allowed me to push away a feeling of impending doom. Like I was about to fail an exam or lose a race. She was right. The symptoms didn't bode well. So this drug didn't work. There were other trials. Other drugs. She had options. Standard of care. This was one of those times when being an oncologist and family of a patient was a double-edged sword. I knew too much to hop on the "you can beat this" bandwagon. I also knew enough to be comforted knowing new treatments were in the pipeline.

Keeping patients—Sherri—alive until they were made available to them was crucial.

"That's enough scrapbooking for tonight." I told Alexa to stop the music. She complied without argument. "Which movie do you want to watch first?"

The stack of DVDs included *Elf, The Santa Clause, Miracle on 34th Street, A Christmas Story, Home Alone, How the Grinch Stole Christmas, The Holiday, Jack Frost, It's a Wonderful Life,* and *A Christmas Carol.* The collection had grown each year as the girls grew and their tastes changed. Some of the old standbys were still around, such as *A Charlie Brown Christmas* and *Rudolph the Red-Nosed Reindeer,* but I couldn't bear to place them on the stack tonight. Not when I was decorating without them.

Sherri crawled up on the couch and tugged the crocheted blanket down from its back. "You pick."

"*The Holiday* it is."

"I knew you'd pick that one."

"You did not." Neither of us was a traditionalist when it came to Christmas movies. We tended toward the rom-coms in all things. "You thought I'd choose *Jack Frost.*"

"Uh-uh. You still have a crush on Jude Law."

"He has aged well, don't you think?"

"Better than we have."

We giggled like adolescent preteens. I started the movie and climbed under the blanket with her. It was like climbing into a time machine and traveling to when we were kids. When Mom popped the popcorn and Sherri made cocoa from scratch. I was in charge of the movies we rented from Blockbuster.

"Let's stay up all night watching movies like we did when we were in high school."

"Works for me." I tugged the blanket over my knees. "Stop hogging."

Sherri pulled the popcorn closer. "Stop hogging the corn. We need Milk Duds and Sour Patch Kids and Skittles."

"I have a stash of M&Ms in my office. I'll get them and sodas in a while. Now hush, the movie's starting."

It was just like high school. Perfect in that moment when all the outside forces couldn't penetrate the fort we'd built just for the two of us.

Just this one night.

thirty-two

DANIEL

The rap on the door sounded like a gunshot in the silence. I jumped and spilled my coffee on my shirt. It dripped on my keyboard. "Dang it." I took two strides to reach the tiny kitchenette counter for napkins. Another rap. "Coming." I sopped up the coffee, dropped the napkin in the trash can, and strode—again two strides—to the door. I peered through the peephole.

Pilar.

I backed away and quickly scanned the room. The hotel maid had come and gone earlier. She'd taken care of my empty take-out cartons and overflowing trash can. The room might be pitiful as a full-time residence, but there was nothing blatantly embarrassing in sight. I opened the door. "Hey."

"Hey." She tossed her keys from one hand to the other and craned her head to scan the room behind me. "I hope it's all right I stopped by without calling first."

"Sure. Come on in." I stepped aside and caught a whiff of patchouli as she passed me. A lot nicer than the cleansers the maid used. "Have you recovered from the horseback riding lesson?"

She wrinkled her nose and rubbed her backside. "I'm still sore, but I thought I did pretty well for a city girl."

She had. Even though she'd professed to being absolutely petrified for the first half hour. Gradually, she'd relaxed enough to try a canter. "Are you here to sign up for another lesson?"

"Maybe next year." Her tone said *or maybe not.* She glanced around the room. Two chairs, one full of books. A third chair at a small desk. A bed. Not a lot of choices for sitting. She remained standing. "Actually, I decided since you introduced me to something you did growing up that I should return the favor."

Something in her impish grin told me this was about getting even. I slid the books to the floor and offered her a seat. She shook her head. "No time to waste. Come on, don't you want to know what I have planned for us today?"

"Today?"

"I know I should've called, but that would've given you the chance to think of an excuse."

So she was planning something she knew I wouldn't jump at. "Okay, I'll bite. What's on today's agenda?"

"Ice skating. I love ice skating. We used to go to different city parks in Chicago to skate all the time growing up. They were mostly free if you owned your own skates, which we did."

"Which I'm sure was fun, but there's no place to ice skate in San Antonio." Thankfully. "It's sixty-two degrees out today, in case you haven't noticed."

"Oh, but there is a place." She grinned like a kid about to lick an ice cream cone. "Don't you read the newspaper or watch the news? The Rotary Club got a bunch of sponsors and created an ice rink at Travis Park for the holidays."

"I see." I did. I saw myself falling on my behind in front of this graceful woman—repeatedly. I'd never even been good at rollerblading as a kid. "I don't know. I brought home a lot of work. Besides, I don't have skates."

Home. Talk about a slip of the lip. Like this tiny beige room with beige curtains and mass-produced abstract art on the walls, with its minifridge and microwave passing as a kitchenette, was home.

"Nobody owns ice skates here." She waved away my objection with one hand. "So they rent them. Convenient, huh?"

"Like I said, I brought home a lot of work—"

"Excuses, excuses. You're a big chicken."

"What are you, twelve? I'm immune to the double-dog-dare peer-pressure tactics."

"Come on. It'll be fun. I'll teach you. Just like you taught me to ride a horse." She flapped her arms like wings and bawked like a chicken. "Bawk, bawk, bawk."

So maybe I wasn't immune to peer pressure. Thirty minutes later we were downtown, donning ice skates with at least a hundred other people—mostly excited kids wearing stocking caps and Christmas-themed T-shirts. I had to admit the Rotary Club had created something magical at this historic old park. People screamed with laughter. It was . . . Christmassy.

Caught up in the moment, I laced up my skates and headed onto the ice, leaving my qualms behind. Pilar tied her hair back in a red ribbon. She wore black skinny jeans and a red Rudolph sweatshirt. I had the prettiest partner on the ice.

She grinned at me. "I told you it would be fun."

"It is." I lost my balance and landed on my rear end before the two syllables were completed. The ice was hard and unforgiving. "Ouch."

A bunch of kids whizzed by, laughing. At least they didn't point and snicker.

Pilar didn't laugh, but it was obvious she was stifling an explosive chuckle. She extended her hand and pulled me to my feet. "Bend at the knees and keep your arms out in front of you." She demonstrated. "If you feel like you're going to fall, put your hands on your knees. That'll stop your momentum."

I followed her lead. A few more tries and I had an awkward skate, skate, glide, flap-my-arms-to-keep-my-balance routine going. "Hey, I'm skating."

"You are indeed." Pilar skated around me and then did a fancy twist and twirl. "I knew you could."

It *was* fun. As the day flowed into evening, hundreds of twinkly white lights lit up in the gathering dusk. Strains of "White Christmas" floated in the air courtesy of a jazz trio. A local restaurant sold hot chocolate, tea, and coffee, along with pan dulce and churros.

For the first time this year, the Christmas spirit caught up with me. Pilar tucked her arm in mine and we circled the rink together. We stopped near the edge. She snapped a few selfies of us.

"You're a natural." Her face glowing with the cool air and exertion, she tucked her phone away and repositioned her arm inside mine. "Admit it. You're enjoying this more than horseback riding."

"Sure, I like it, but nothing is better than horseback—"

"Mr. Tremaine! I thought that was you. Hi."

I turned at the sound of a familiar voice. It took a minute to place it. Shay McCullough. Kristen's medical assistant. She skated to a neat stop in front of us, along with her little boy. Brian? Billy? Bryson. That was it. Bryson. "Hi, Shay."

"It's been such a long time. Merry Christmas! You remember my son, Bryson?"

"I do. I do. He's a foot taller. He favors you, doesn't he?"

"He does. We're here with Tasha. You know, Dr. Tremaine's PA, and her kids."

Shay glanced from me to Pilar, her expression expectant. Curious. My mind froze as hard as the ice under our feet. The pause grew awkward. Pilar stepped forward and held out her hand. "I'm Pilar Lozano. Daniel and I work together."

"Nice to meet you." Understanding flitted across Shay's face. She shook Pilar's hand. Her cheeks, already pink from skating, turned red.

"Well, we better get moving. Our tickets expire in fifteen minutes, and Bryson is determined to do as many loop-de-loops as possible."

"It was nice to meet you, Shay. And you, too, Bryson." Pilar waved as they skated away. "Happy holidays."

I heaved a breath. My legs were frozen under me. *Move, move.* Finally, I managed to skate toward the exit.

"Daniel. Daniel! Wait." Pilar followed me off the ice to the first open bench. I plopped down on it and went to work unlacing my skates. She settled next to me. "Daniel, what's going on?"

She touched my hands to still them. I studied her fingers. Long, slim, nails painted mauve. No rings. Classy like the rest of her. I couldn't for the life of me speak.

"Okay, I'll go first." She removed her hand and sat back. "You're embarrassed and worried that your wife's coworker saw you on a date with me. She'll tell Kristen and you're worried how she'll react. Or maybe you think it's a good thing. Maybe you think she'll finally wake up and realize you have other options and get her act together. Is that it?"

Shaken by her accusatory tone, I straightened. "No, no. I wouldn't use you like that."

"I should hope not." She broke eye contact. Her gaze shifted to the rink, where skaters zoomed by, laughing, breathless, happy. "You can't use me as a substitute for your wife and then run and hide when someone you know sees us together. I don't deserve that."

"No, you don't. I'm not running or hiding."

"Then what are you doing?"

I tugged the skates off and set them aside. Giving myself time to organize my thoughts. They milled about in total chaos. I pulled on my Nikes and tied them. Now that the sun had sunk behind the tall downtown buildings, the air was cold. I shivered. "I don't know. I'm sorry. I thought we could have something. I enjoy talking shop with you. I enjoy having interests in common. I thought having a partner who shared my interests would be so great. I could envision us visiting historical architectural sites in Europe and Greece. And designing and building beautiful edifices together."

"As friends or as more?"

"I thought . . . I wanted it to be more."

"But?"

"The fact is, you don't get to pick who you fall in love with. Sometimes you don't have much in common with a person except a love that simply refuses to relinquish its hold on you."

"I know." She patted my back. It was such a kindly gesture. Pilar was a kind woman. "I know. I wish I'd met you before you married her. I would've given her a run for the money."

"And my life would've been very different. I just want you to know, I never meant to hurt you. You've been through so much with your divorce—"

"No worries. I think I've always known you were already spoken for. It's just taken longer for you to figure it out."

"I'm sorry."

"Don't be. Come on. I'll drive you home."

Home. Back to the dismal Econo Lodge room. Sitting on a park bench with a friend and colleague watching families skate seemed so much more appealing. "At least let me buy you a hot cocoa and a churro for all your trouble."

"You're not afraid we'll run into someone else you know?" Pilar smiled wryly. "Apparently your wife's PA is around here somewhere."

"If we do, I promise to do better."

"You mean you'll actually introduce me instead of dying of embarrassment and turning into an ice sculpture before our very eyes?"

"I'm sorry."

She took my hand in her warm one and squeezed. "Me too," she whispered. "Me too."

thirty-three

SHERRI

Joy to me. Joy to the world, true, but at that brilliant, shiny moment in time in my brother-in-law's church, I selfishly took all the joy for me. I would share it with Jesus later. With Max on my hip, I raised the candle high in unison with a packed sanctuary of Christmas Eve worshippers. Ignoring an annoying shortness of breath, I sang the familiar words with gusto. Max jabbered his version of the hymn's lyrics. Noelle put her arm around me. I glanced down the pew. Noelle, Gracie, Zach, Chance, Jason, Cody, Cais, Xander, Lucas, Daniel, Maddie, Brielle, Dad, and Kristen. Daniel's family crowded the two rows in front of us.

For one night, all drama had been set aside. Or maybe it was for the one-hour service. I caught Kristen's gaze. She lifted her candle higher. That she deigned to sit next to Dad—that she'd come to the service at all—spoke of her willingness to try. What better night to mend old wounds than the celebration of our Savior's birth?

No drama would be allowed to taint my joy tonight. My children and grandchildren—minus Jason's sweet Chloe, who was in Dallas with her mother—were here together with me. Celebrating Christmas with me. *Thank You, Jesus.* The joy was so exquisite, so intense, it almost hurt. I had to squint at the soaring stained glass window with its dove rising above the flames behind the pastor's pulpit. Its brilliant, joyful colors blinded me.

The song ended. Candles were extinguished. The pastor's benediction urged us to go forth and spread the joy of Jesus Christ in the world. Again selfish to the bone, I simply wanted to spread it in my own family for just this one season.

"You're so beautiful. Your cheeks are rosy. You've put on some weight." Her baby bump preceding her by a foot, Noelle took Gracie's hand and followed me into the aisle. "You're glowing. I'm so thankful the trial drug is working."

Bong, bong, bong. That infernal grandfather clock started up again. Noelle didn't need to know the rosy cheeks were the result of steroids. Or my suspicions that the drug wasn't doing its job reinforced by the growing ache in my lower back that even hydrocodone didn't entirely eliminate or the low-grade nausea that took away my appetite. The steroids were responsible for my face's round, full look. "Thank you, honey. It's the sheer happiness at having all three of my kids and most of my grandkids together for Christmas."

"Open presents?" Max clapped in delight at his own idea. "Now."

Noelle laughed. "Not until tomorrow—"

"After Santa comes." Gracie tugged at Max's tiny boat shoe bought for this dress-up occasion. "We have to go home and go to sleep so Santa can come."

"Presents."

"We'll open one present." I kissed his chubby cheek with a flourish. "We have to put out the cookies and milk for Santa."

"Cookies. Want cookies." Max was all about sweets. Noelle had caught him helping himself to the peppermint candy cane cookies she and Chance made the previous day. Along with gingerbread men, sugar cookies that we'd all decorated, and Chance's special cinnamon-flavored peanut brittle. Max did his puppy dog eyes thing. "Granmol, baby eat cookies."

"You're not a baby." Gracie rolled her blue eyes in her best big-sister style. "You're three."

"Tree." Max held up the requisite number of fingers. "Tree. Me baby."

Max likely would need speech therapy in the future. I hugged him close. His solid little boy body was warm. He smelled of cherry yogurt and Teddy Grahams he'd eaten during the service. "Definitely cookies. And hot chocolate. Right, Mommy?"

Noelle nodded, but she mock scowled at me. Grandmas were allowed to spoil kids while mommies had to wrestle them into bed despite sugar overloads. "Yes, but like Gracie said, you have to go to bed soon or Santa won't be able to come."

We joined a steady stream of worshippers out the double doors, through the narthex, and into the parking lot. Stopping every few feet to exchange pleasantries with members of Daniel's church, who exclaimed over how cute the kids were and welcomed us to their service. South Texas hospitality at its best.

Mother Nature had given us the gift of a cold, clear, starry night with a brisk north wind. South Texas so often failed to provide us with the necessary winter weather. Balmy December nights could make it hard for some to get into the Christmas spirit. We'd grilled plenty of fajitas on Christmas Eve over the years. This year I was so full of Christmas spirit, my eyeballs were floating in it.

Back at the house, Noelle, Cais, Jason, Cody, and Zach insisted on taking over kitchen duties. In lieu of a big sit-down feast, we'd decided on a smorgasbord of goodies on which we could graze throughout the evening. Chips and queso, tamales, a fruit tray, jalapeño poppers, veggies and dip, beanie-weenies, charcuterie boards filled with crackers, cheeses, pickles, and deli meats. Spinach dip and crackers. Mexican five-layer dip and chips.

And of course, every imaginable Christmas cookie and candy we'd spent the previous week making. Adult libations, eggnog, hot cranberry-spice punch, and chocolate milk—a special request from Cody's boys.

While my kids and their spouses arranged the feast, Daniel turned on the fire in the fireplace. Brielle and Maddie took Dash and Scout with them and disappeared into a bedroom, likely to call and chat with their boyfriends, both of whom had decided to hang in there despite the Thanksgiving debacle.

I settled onto the couch with my grandkids gathered around for the traditional reading of *The Night Before Christmas*. My kids had been able to recite the story from memory by the time they announced they were too old for its reading. I took my time, using all my best voices. Relishing these moments that might never come again.

Bong, bong, bong.

Gracie laid her head on my shoulder. Xander leaned into me to better see the illustrations. Before it was over, Max crawled off my lap and onto the floor to take the Little People Mary and Joseph on a donkey ride to the nativity scene stable. The nativity scene had been a part of every Reynolds Christmas since Noelle started walking. She and her brothers had spent hours playing with the donkeys, sheep, wise men, and oxen. Every year when it came time to pack up the decorations, we had to hunt down Mary, Joseph, and baby Jesus, usually tucked under a blanket in Noelle's room or riding high on one of the boys' toy bins.

Traditions. Maybe this would be the year I gave the nativity scene to Noelle for future Christmas traditions at her house.

"'Happy Christmas to all and to all a good night.'" I closed the book and leaned back. Xander sighed. "Grandma, what's a sash and why did he throw it up? It doesn't sound like something good to eat."

I stifled a chuckle. "A sash is a curtain. What the writer meant was he opened the sash."

"Whew! Good." Lucas took the book from me and opened it to the page in question. "I didn't know why some guy threw up on Christmas Eve. No one wants to puke on a holiday."

"Or any time. Puke is gross." Gracie shuddered. "It tastes bad."

"Indeed. On that note, we should put out the milk and cookies for Santa." I swallowed the laughter that burbled up. "Which cookies do you think he'll like?"

"First, we get to open a present, Grandma. You said so." Xander slid off the couch onto his knees and frog-hopped over to the tree. Gifts were stacked up high all around it. With this many people under one roof, the sheer number of presents guaranteed a massive haul of trash to the curb in the coming week.

"First get something to eat. Then put on your jammies. Then we open a present. One present." I held up one finger.

Max held up two fingers. "Two, Granmol."

"Nope. Just one." I grabbed him up on my lap and tickled his belly. "Just one, Maxwell."

"Two, two, two." He giggled so hard he hiccupped. "Two."

"One. Go on, get going."

A strategy designed to ensure these tasks would be accomplished with a minimum of fuss. Like dangling a carrot, it worked. They rushed off to find their moms and dads, chattering about what they wanted Santa to bring them.

Dad shuffled across the room from the recliner where he'd been watching with a benign expression. He plopped down next to me and patted my knee. "You're in your element, blondie."

"I am a kindergarten teacher, after all." Even if I hadn't taught in months. Shawna, Nikki, and Lori had brought me a shopping bag full of handmade cards and gifts from my students the previous week. Then they'd taken me Christmas shopping. The Christmas displays, music, and hustle-bustle made it so much easier to get in the mood. My friends even knew how to gauge my waning strength and brought me home before I dropped of exhaustion in the maze of toy aisles. When had it become so difficult to pick out gifts for kids? "I hate that they live so far away. They grow up so fast. They'll be teenagers before I know it."

My voice petered out. Would I be here to see them start high school, graduate, go to college, and marry?

"I'm the one who missed out." Dad nudged me with his elbow. "It's too late for me to get it back. I'm the one who's too old. You'll be around for many more years. I feel it in my old bones."

How wonderful it would be if his old bones could predict my future. I nudged him back. "Good try, Dad. You're too stubborn to check out anytime soon."

"Even so, I missed not only the years when I should've been there for you and Krissy but all the years when your kids were growing up. I'm thankful they had Daniel's and Chance's families. They got at least one set of decent grandparents. I'm sorry, Sher. I haven't said it before and I should've. I'm so sorry I was such a sorry son of a gun for a father and grandfather."

"Apology accepted." I leaned against him and inhaled his scent of Drakkar Noir. It sent my mind racing after memories of ice cream cones at Dairy Queen, playing catch in the backyard, and at least one long car ride to Mustang Island. "You're here now. Brielle and Maddie could use another grandpa right now, and these little rugrats aren't too young to learn about the importance of baseball in righting the world's wrongs."

"It just so happens they're all getting baseball gloves and balls from Grandpa for Christmas. Even Brielle and Maddie. The girls are getting an invitation to take me out to the ball game at Wolff Stadium when the Missions' season starts in April."

What a great way to start to build memories with Kristen and Daniel's girls. Too bad mine didn't live close enough to make those memories too. "I'd like to get in on that action."

"You've got it, girlie." He struggled forward on the couch and grabbed his walker. "I'm gonna get me some grub. Should I bring you a plate?"

"I'll get it for her, Roy." Chance loomed over us. He had two glasses in his hands. "I come bearing eggnog—the alcohol-free kind, of course."

I took his offering, and he gave Dad a hand getting up. After Dad tromped toward the dining room, Chance took his place on the couch. "How are you doing?"

"Great. I'm doing great. I never imagined having all the kids here for the holidays. I assume you had a hand in arranging this."

He gave me his best *aw-shucks* grin and ducked his head. "Me, Kristen, the kids, we set up a text group so we could figure out all the details as far as who arrived when, who needed rides from the airport, where everyone would stay, all that logistical stuff."

"You done good."

Chance took my hand and intertwined his fingers with mine. "I'm glad. It's kind of my Christmas present to you. I mean, you're still getting something wrapped up in a bow, but I figured this was what you would most want."

"You figured right. Everything I need is right here."

"Good. You deserve a happy Christmas and New Year after the year you've had." He stood. "I'll be right back with our food. Don't let anyone take my place."

The way he said it made me feel like a high school girl holding a seat in the cafeteria for her boyfriend. I giggled. "I promise."

He put way too much food on my plate. I started with the desserts and worked my way back to the veggies, dip, and tamales. My stomach didn't want to eat much these days, but Chance's presence somehow made it easier. What I lacked in appetite, he more than made up for, demolishing four tamales, a huge pile of chips and queso, two sandwiches, and at least one of each of the desserts.

"If you were one of the kids, I'd tell you to slow down before you make yourself sick." I laid my plate on the coffee table. "You'll have to undo your belt pretty soon."

"I'm wearing my buffet pants." He grinned the same grin I saw on Cody's and Jason's faces when they talked about fast cars, football, and grilling. "They're also old man pants, you know, with the elastic in the back."

"You're kidding me, right?"

"Yep, just kidding. I've lost some weight this past year. They're just big."

It had been a hard year for him too. A cancer diagnosis wreaked havoc on the entire family. It was hard to believe it had been almost a year since my diagnosis. "I'm sorry it's been so hard. I'm just glad we're all together. You appreciate holidays so much more when you truly in your gut realize there's no guarantee we'll all be together for another one. People know that, yet they still take it for granted."

"I know I do." His expression pensive, he rubbed his thumb across the back of my hand. "I'm sorry I took you for granted, babe."

"Nothing you did deserved what I did. I'm the one who should keep apologizing until the end of time."

"I hate that I made you feel neglected and lonely. Having been on my own all these years, I totally get now what loneliness feels like."

I squeezed his hand. "I'm sorry. It's my fault you ended up divorced. I hate it."

"My fault too. I could've forgiven you. We could've gone to marriage counseling like you wanted. My pride was hurt. I wanted you to hurt as much as I did. So I cut off my nose to spite my face."

"If it's any consolation, it hurt a lot. I don't think there's anything besides my mom's death that has hurt more."

"It's not a consolation. I'm not proud of the way I acted. All I did was end a marriage worth saving."

Worth saving. I had always thought so too. Knowing he felt the same way smoothed away the rough, hard scars that lingered all these years. If only we'd had this conversation earlier. Now it was too late. Too late. "You could've remarried. Why didn't you?"

A bittersweet smile flitted across his face. "Aww, babe, you know why."

"No, I don't. Why?"

"Because I never stopped loving you."

Tears burned my eyes. I swallowed hard. "I love you too," I whispered. "Always."

He leaned closer. His lips brushed mine. "Merry Christmas, babe."

"Merry Christmas." I wiped away the tear that managed to escape despite my best effort to corral it. "Merry Christmas."

thirty-four

SHERRI

The moment of truth. Time for the big kids to open their presents. The little kids had opened their one present. Then they made a plate of cookies for Santa and arranged it on the coffee table with a glass of milk. Max proceeded to help himself to one of the decorated sugar cookies and eat most of it before we noticed. He'd fallen asleep on my lap watching *A Charlie Brown Christmas*. Zach and Cody herded the other kids into their sleeping bags in their respective bedrooms. The noise level dropped by 75 percent.

Kristen asked her kids to help clean up the kitchen, giving me the space to have this time with mine. I called them all together and made the announcement. "I want y'all to open your gifts from your dad and me tonight since Jason is headed to Dallas at oh-dark-thirty in the morning."

Chance lifted the boxes from their hiding spots behind the tree and deposited them in front of Dad, Cody and Cais, Noelle and Zach, and Jason. I had wrapped the boxes in vintage Santa paper and added oversized bows with handmade name tags. A labor of love down to the last detail.

"Ah, Ma." Jason had his open first. He removed the lid and lifted out the scrapbook. His cover featured a blown-up photo of him on his sixth birthday, missing his two front teeth, wearing his Superman cap, Spider-Man boxer shorts, and nothing else. "What is this?"

"Your superhero phase. You were sure you had superpowers." Noelle giggled so hard she snorted. "Remember when you climbed up on the garage roof? You were planning to fly off and save the world."

"It's a good thing I caught you before you tested that theory." Chance ran his hand through his hair. "Why do you think I turned gray so young?"

Jason slowly turned the pages. Day care musical programs, macaroni artwork, kindergarten report card, T-ball team photos, photos of sandcastles at the coast. Swimming in the backyard blow-up pool, memento after memento, photo after photo. "I can't believe you saved all this stuff."

"Chloe will get a kick out of seeing it, too, I bet." I exchanged smiles with my youngest son. He'd never been one to hang out with his mom. He was my independent soul who couldn't wait to get out on his own. But I always knew he loved me, and he knew I loved him. We communicated on a frequency that didn't involve a lot of words. "Maybe you can make room for the scrapbook in your carry-on bag. I'll hang on to the rest of the box until you get a deployment stateside. You can share it with Chloe and tell her how much Grandma loves her and misses her and wants to see her soon."

"Will do. We'll FaceTime tomorrow. I know she'll want to ask you a million questions about what I was like as a kid."

He stopped at a page that held a prom photo. He wore a black T-shirt designed to mimic a tux, black jeans, and black high-top Converse sneakers. His date had made her dress from T-shirts bought at a Goodwill store. She chose army boots to complete her ensemble. How my antiestablishment son ended up in the military remained one of the great unsolved mysteries of the universe. "I wonder what happened to Sheila. She was a free spirit."

Unlike his wife, who'd decided she didn't like traveling or being a military spouse about a year into their marriage. In her defense, she was very young and, like Jason, an introvert who didn't make friends easily. Once Jason made a friend, however, he was a friend for life.

"I heard Sheila moved to San Diego, created her own natural-wear fashion line, and opened a CBD store." Cody held up his scrapbook, open to the page where I'd attached his leaving-the-hospital photo. "Dang, I was a handsome dude, even then."

"If you like bald, chunky Buddha-shaped guys with red faces and flat purple-and-blue noses." Cais elbowed him. "You're lucky I didn't know you then. And that I'm not so shallow your misshapen face would deter me from seeking out the real you."

"Hey, I've seen your baby photos, woman. Both our boys took after you at birth, and I still hung around."

They laughed. Cais planted a kiss on her husband's cheek. He mussed her hair. Nine years into their marriage and they were still plainly in love.

She kept turning the pages, laughing, pointing, and teasing. All three kids joined in the jaunt down memory lanes that I'd taken when I assembled the books. Exactly the reminder I'd sought of what wonderful times we had as a family all those years. Beautiful times. Not idyllic. Not perfect. But tight-knit, loving, got-your-back times.

I tore my gaze from the kids to check on Dad. He sat in the love seat that had been pushed to one side to make room for the seven-foot Christmas tree and the gifts that surrounded it. He bent over his open scrapbook, head down so I couldn't read his expression. I got up and went to him. "Dad? What do you think?"

"This is . . . I'm so . . ." He cleared his throat. "I'm sorry I wasn't here for the games or the programs or the graduations. I don't deserve these memories. Keep them for Kris and y'all's kids."

"They have their own memories. This wasn't about making you feel guilty." I sat down next to him and pointed at one of Kris's basketball team photos. She knelt on the first row with the YMCA twelve-and-under league championship trophy at her side. Her grin was a carbon copy of the one Dad used to have when the Rangers won a big game. And for him, they were all big games. "I wanted you to have a chance to share those memories. Better late than never, wouldn't you say?"

His Adam's apple bobbed. He cleared his throat. His hands smoothed the Most Valuable Player medal I'd glued to the page by its ribbon. "She picked basketball because I didn't keep my promise to coach her baseball team. I was such a fool—"

"She was a standout power forward all the way through high school. She could've played college ball, but she wanted to focus on academics." I touched his knobby fingers covered with gray hair and age spots. "It's that making lemonade from lemons thing—she made gallons of it, vats of it. Kris is wired that way. With singular determination, just like you were when it came to baseball."

He leaned forward and picked up the photo box. "I haven't even looked at these yet." His voice dropped to a hoarse whisper. "I'm gonna wait until I get back to the prison. If that's okay."

"It's more than okay. If you ever want to talk about them, I'm here."

His hug was quick, hard. He leaned back and stared into my face. "You have your mom's eyes and nose. But more than that, you've got her sweet spirit. She put up with so much from me. I took her for granted. Then she was gone and I couldn't face you girls. I'll go to my grave regretting that."

"Let it go, Dad. I have. Kris will. Eventually."

"Mom, who was a better student—Noelle or me?" Cody had his hand up in the air like a kid in my classroom. "I had the most straight As, right?"

The argument was on. I went to mediate. "In middle school, maybe, but Noelle had you beat in high school. Not that it was a competition. You both did well—you all did well."

"Naw, you had it right the first time." Jason shrugged. "We all know I hated school."

"But your grades were good. You were just bored." I patted his army regulation-cut hair. "You hated the basic courses because they were too easy for you."

"Teacher's pet," Cody and Noelle chanted in unison. "Mom's favorite."

Not true. I favored all three of my kids. Each in their own way. I went back to my spot on the couch where Cleo was curled up on a pillow, surprisingly comfortable with the chaos. She knew family.

Chance plopped down next to me. He glanced at his watch. "I better go. It's a long drive to Kerrville. I'll be back early in the morning to make the waffles and squeeze the orange juice."

"I wish we had room for you to stay here—"

"It's okay. I have to check on the dogs and make sure they have food and water."

Chance's two rescue pit bulls were almost as spoiled as Kris and Daniel's dogs, currently hunkered down in the kitchen gnawing on their vet's-choice rubber chew bones. Even they were allowed to open one gift on Christmas Eve.

"See you tomorrow."

"See you tomorrow." This time his kiss lasted longer. He tasted sweet, familiar, and yet new and exotic. "Sweet dreams."

I broke away and glanced toward the kids. They pretended not to notice their parents engaging in embarrassing PDA. After that kiss, I wasn't sure I'd sleep at all. "See you tomorrow."

Gradually, one by one, everyone slipped off to bed. I didn't want to go to bed. I didn't want to sleep. I wanted this evening to last and last. Brielle and Maddie took Dad back to Gardenside Manor and then went to Grandma Tremaine's. They would spend Christmas Day with Daniel and his family.

I switched to *A Miracle on 34th Street*. The adult kids brought out the Santa gifts and arranged them around the tree. Then we stuffed stockings with small gifts and candy just like Chance and I did when they were little. Finally, I hung candy canes on the tree.

Zach, Cody, Jason, and Cais bowed out at that point. I hadn't seen Kristen or Daniel in a while. Noelle and I had the living room to ourselves. She curled up on the couch next to me. "Did I see you and Dad kissing, by any chance?"

"I plead the fifth."

She laughed. "You two getting back together would be the best Christmas gift ever."

"Oh, honey, don't get your hopes up. I'm sure it's the holiday and having you kids all ove—"

"Don't blame it on us. That definitely wasn't a sweet holiday kiss I saw."

"We'll see."

She tossed a pillow at me. "We will indeed, Mother."

I tossed the pillow back. She grabbed it and hugged it close for a second. "You didn't open a present," she said.

"You know me, I'm a traditionalist." I liked to open everything on Christmas Day. "I'm happy with my peanut brittle and fudge."

Which had been tucked in my stocking so it wouldn't be empty on Christmas Day.

"I have a present for you that doesn't require opening."

"Okay. What kind of gift is it?"

"The kind of gift that means you'll have to get used to the pitter-patter of little feet all over the house."

I already had this gift and it was perfect. "Having you here for the holidays is the best gift I could ever have received."

"I hope you still feel that way when we're still here a month from now."

"What do you mean?"

"I mean we've made arrangements for the kids and me to stay." She set the pillow aside and smoothed her hands over her belly. "Aunt Kris helped me find an obstetrician here. My records have been transferred. Zach will fly back to Chicago on New Year's Day. He'll come back and forth when he can and in time for Ainsley's birth. We drove down here in my car so I'll have transportation."

My mouth opened, closed, opened. I was speechless. Literally. A rare occurrence according to Chance, Kris, and my friends. "I can't . . . seriously . . . you . . . did you say Ainsley?"

"I did." She rubbed her belly again. "We're having another girl. We decided against a big gender reveal."

The possibility of them staying had never entered my mind. How could it? How could she? It was too much to hope for. "How? Where? You have a life—"

"Aunt Kris is totally on board with it. We'll mostly stay here, but we'll also spend some time with Dad in Kerrville. If you feel like a break at your house, we can stay with you there too."

"But what about your art projects?"

"Finished or on hold. I planned to take a hiatus when Ainsley's born anyway."

"But Zach and your obstetrician—"

"Mom, Zach's a big boy. He knows how important this is to me. I want to have the baby here so you can be with me, like you were with Gracie. I have an appointment with my new obstetrician on the second of January. This is my third kid. I know what I'm doing."

I remembered feeling that way when Jason was born. I finally had the hang of things. "I'm overwhelmed."

"Don't be. It'll be fun."

Fun didn't begin to cover it. The gift of time. Every morning I could open that gift again. I swallowed back tears. "More than fun."

"Don't cry, Ma."

"I can't help it. I was doing my best to live in the moment, to cherish every single minute without thinking ahead to saying goodbye again. I'm so relieved, so excited—"

"You might feel differently after a few of Max's tantrums. Or Gracie's nagging. When she wants something, she never gives up. And the questions, oh my goodness, the endless questions."

"I can't wait!" I threw my arms around her in a hug that would've won a Super Bowl of hugs.

"Whoa!" Noelle drew back. "Ainsley is kicking like an all-star soccer player. Good grief. It must be all the sugar from the peanut brittle I ate." She tugged my hand over her belly.

Little Ainsley's kicks landed squarely in the palm of my hand. "Wow, she's busy, isn't she?"

"I hope she wears herself out, or I won't sleep tonight."

"Speaking of which, you'd better get some sleep. You know the kids will be up at the crack of dawn." I leaned close to her belly. "Good night, Ainsley. Sleep tight."

"Good night, Mom." Noelle hoisted herself from the couch. "Pretty soon I'll need a crane to get up." She giggled. "I already can't see my feet."

I followed her down the hallway toward the bedrooms. "I can't believe you're staying."

"Are you happy?"

"So happy I won't be able to sleep a wink tonight."

"Merry Christmas."

"The best ever."

She eased open the door to the bedroom she was sharing with Zach and the kids. "'Night."

"'Night." I stood there for a long time after she closed the door, simply basking in the warmth of knowing there were good, good days to come. No matter what came next.

"Happy birthday, Jesus," I whispered. "It's not really fair. I'm getting all the best gifts."

I didn't think Jesus minded. He was that kind of guy.

thirty-five

DANIEL

The flames flickered, crackled, and caught in the oval bio-ethanol chiminea. The fire was smaller than a wood one, but it produced no smoke and added no pollutants to San Antonio's smog. Like the environment was the most important thing on my mind on Christmas Eve. I was nervous. Like a guy on his first date. Why? The first notes of the King & Country song "God Only Knows" strummed in my head. Probably because it had been more than three months since I'd been alone with my wife. I straightened and stepped back. "That's better. Are you cold?"

"I can feel the heat." Kristen leaned back on the pool lounge chair. She held a Santa mug of cocoa in both hands. She'd changed from the form-fitting red dress she wore to church into black leggings and a long red, black, and gold plaid shirt. "I'm glad it's cool this evening. It feels more like Christmas."

Twinkly white lights and fresh, live garland strung on the pergola added to that festive feel, along with huge potted poinsettias placed between each of the pool chairs. "Y'all did a nice job decorating inside and out. Plus, having a house full of kids and grandkids helps." I took a seat two pool chairs down from where she sat. "Noelle's kids are so cute. That Max is something else."

"Xander is identical to Cody when he was that age. They're all cute." She sipped her cocoa. "I wonder how long it'll be before we have grandkids."

"Maddie says she's not getting married or having kids." I wanted those words back. They came precariously close to broaching the subject of the Thanksgiving blowout. "But Brie wants a bunch, so hopefully that'll even out."

"So I guess Maddie told you about the argument we had after you left on Thanksgiving."

Ad nauseam at my mother's house the next day. "Let's not get into that tonight, okay?"

"Okay." She stirred the miniature marshmallows in her cocoa for a few seconds. "Thank you for coming tonight."

"I did it for the girls." I could've gone to Mom and Dad's house, but forgiveness and healing had to start somewhere. What better time than Christmas Eve? Plus, the girls were the ones who suffered the most if we started forcing them to choose where to spend their holidays. "I want them to have really good holidays this year—regardless of our differences."

"Me too. I appreciate that you probably would rather be at your parents' house."

Not really. Watching my brothers with their wives only served to highlight my aloneness—to me and to them. They all walked on eggshells around me or gave me pep talks at every turn. "Maddie was right about one thing. She said I shouldn't have left without saying anything. It was . . . cowardly."

"You don't like confrontation. You never have."

"Which is how we ended up where we are. Maybe if I'd said something earlier, things would be different." I picked up my mulled apple cider. The scent of cinnamon set the memories in motion— every Christmas growing up, every Christmas with Kristen. Cinnamon evoked happy times. Happier times. "I don't want to be a whiner. Or the guy who stands in the way of his wife's career. Especially when it involves saving lives—"

"Trying to save lives."

"Knowing how hard that is with cancer patients makes me feel all the more guilty."

"You have nothing to feel guilty about. I know I need to find a better balance." Her tone suggested she regretted the situation. That was a start. "Since Sherri's diagnosis, I've felt like everything is spinning out of control."

Her voice quivered. My arms had a mind of their own. They wanted to wrap themselves around her. A fierce pain ripped through me. *You can't have it both ways.* It was like Pavlov's response. She needed me. I needed to be needed by her. Old habits were hard to break. "I'm sorry it's hard. So she's not doing as well as she wants everyone to think?"

"No. I don't know. She doesn't think the study drug's working because she's having some pain and bloating. She's lost her appetite, which means she's losing weight. Her tumor markers haven't come down. Dr. Capstone says we haven't given the clinical trial enough time to do its job. We have to follow the study protocol. Which means waiting until the next CT scan the first week of January."

"So don't borrow trouble." Easy to say. Hard to do. "Sorry. That's such a stupid thing to say. The not knowing must be agony."

"She's giving her kids memory boxes for Christmas with scrapbooks full of mementos and photos."

Wonderful gifts under any circumstance, but the worry in Kristen's voice was justified. "She's saying goodbye, isn't she?"

"It feels that way. Prematurely too. If Sherri gives up, she'll be more likely to succumb sooner."

Succumb. Kristen chose that word because she couldn't bear to say the word *die* in the same sentence with her sister's name.

She swung her legs off the lounge chair so her boots were on the pavers and she could face me. "Now I know what my patients go through. I always thought I did, because of Mom, but I was a kid then. I didn't really go through it, not the way Sherri did. She knew when Mom came home from the hospital that last time that she'd come home to die. She didn't tell me. Neither did Mom. They let me think she came home because she was better. I could see she was getting sicker and sicker, but I guess I was in denial. I went to school and played basketball and went to the movies instead of spending every minute I could with her.

"Then one day Sherri sat me down on the couch in the living room with the hospice nurse. Together they told me I needed to go in her bedroom and say goodbye. I was so mad, so angry, so furious— none of those words begin to describe how irate I was.

"I told myself they were wrong. Mom wouldn't die. She wasn't a quitter. She'd survived being abandoned by my dad. She'd raised us alone. We were the three amigos. She was a superhero. Her superpower was the ability to make everything all right even when it wasn't."

I didn't say a word. I didn't dare interrupt the flow. Under the twinkling Christmas lights, brilliant against a starless, cold night sky, Kristen spoke into the darkness as if I wasn't even there. She wasn't telling me. She was telling the world. Telling God how angry and abandoned a fourteen-year-old girl had felt at losing her mother to cancer.

"I'm not sure she even knew I came into the room. I sat on the edge of the bed and took her hand. I squeezed it, but she didn't squeeze back." Kristen stared down at her own hands in her lap, but it was clear she didn't see them. "She smelled like baby wipes and rubbing alcohol. Her face was skeletal. Her breathing rattled in her chest, but her hair had started to grow back."

Kristen's fingers went to her head. She touched her blonde locks. "She had gray curls. Like the ones Sherri has now."

I couldn't take it. I stood and walked to the pool's edge. I stared up at the starry sky. I breathed. In and out. I went to sit next to her. "I'm so sorry." I put my arm around her. "Let it out. It's the only way through it."

Tears trickled down her cheeks. She swiped at them. "I begged her to open her eyes and talk to me. I begged her not to die. I told her I needed her to live."

"But she didn't."

"She didn't even move. I stuck a cassette tape I made of her favorite songs in the boom box. We used to sing along to George Strait's 'You Look So Good in Love' and 'Amarillo by Morning,' Dolly Parton's 'Jolene,' and Waylon Jennings's 'Good-Hearted Woman.' Sherri came in and sat next to me." Kris sniffed. I handed her a napkin. She wiped her face. "We held her hands and sang songs for a long time. I kept thinking she would open her eyes and start singing along. That she'd belt out Johnny Cash's 'Jackson' or Loretta Lynn's 'You Ain't Woman Enough.' But she didn't. She died just after midnight without ever waking up."

Kristen leaned her forehead against my chest. I held her close. Her body shivered, but it wasn't from the cold. "I can't go through that with Sherri. I just can't. Sherri loves her God so much. What kind of God makes a person go through this twice?"

I grew up in church. I had years of sermons and Sunday school and youth group and Vacation Bible School. Yet all I could come up with were churchy answers. Sunday school answers. Nothing that would help a woman so gutted by pain she could barely hold up her head. "I wish I had an answer. I wish I could take this pain away. I wish I could suffer it for you."

"I know you do. That's the kind of guy you are." She raised her head and heaved a sigh. "I keep telling Sherri to hang in there, not to give up, that she still has options, and she does. But I also know that time will run out. Eventually. I'm hoping we find a clinical trial that works and if we do, that could buy her a year or two years. Maybe by that time a new treatment will be available or another trial that buys her six months, a year, two years. That's the way it works with late-stage metastatic cancer. Buying chunks of time until time runs out. Every time there's progression, she'll have to make the decision about whether to keep trying."

"Sherri's a smart woman. She knows what to expect." How I wished she didn't. "Ultimately, it's her quality of life that counts. She'll have to decide when to stop. And you'll be there to hold her up when that time comes. So will Chance. So will her kids. You won't go through it alone."

"I know," she whispered. "I know and I'm sorry. I shouldn't be dumping all this on you on Christmas Eve of all times."

"No, don't apologize. This is the first time in twenty-five years you've talked to me about those days before your mother's death and how you felt. That's huge. Thank you for sharing it with me."

"I know I have a lot of work to do before we can be together." Her chin quivered. "Just please promise me you won't totally walk away. Don't leave me for someone else, please."

"I won't." No need to tell her about my discovery. I couldn't leave her for someone else. My head might want to run as far and as fast as possible from Kristen, but my heart had dug in its heels and refused to budge. "I promise."

"I'm holding you to that promise." She pulled away and stood. "Thanks for being such a good listener. Now you should go home." Her cheeks reddened. "I mean to your parents' home. Your nieces and nephews will be up at the crack of dawn."

"I wish . . ." I don't know what I wished. We'd never spent Christmas Day apart in all the years of our marriage. That the girls had chosen to spend it with me and my family—by all rights, Kristen's family too—gave me no joy. My throat hurt. My chest ached. "I'm sorry . . ."

"I'll be fine. I'll have a full house."

Full of Sherri and Chance's family. But still family.

"I forgot. I have your Christmas present under the tree."

"You'll never find it under the massive stacks of kid gifts." I tugged her gift from my jacket pocket. I held it out. "Wait until tomorrow to open it."

"Why?"

"Because I couldn't take it tonight. Okay?"

It was God's honest truth. This schism, this great divide was as much my fault as hers. I loved holidays. I loved family. I loved Kristen. But to give in now would be to go back to where we were three and a half months ago. To undo the statement I'd made. I couldn't do that.

She studied the slim box wrapped in silver Christmas wrapping paper I'd picked out from my mom's stash. I'd added a glittery white bow almost as big as the box. "Okay. I'll wait. Until you're gone."

I laughed. So did she. Kristen was worse than the kids when it came to waiting to open gifts. She demanded hints. She hunted through closets, peeked under beds, and eavesdropped on conversations, trying to find her presents. I had become quite adept at outwitting her. Mostly by leaving the gifts at Mom's or one of my brothers' houses. "Do you want me to turn off the fire before I go?"

"No, thanks. I think I'll stay out here awhile longer." She laid the box on the chair and tucked her hands under her armpits to warm them. "I don't want Sherri to see that I've been crying."

"She's probably in bed. But okay, I understand that."

I stared at her boots. Her hand touched mine. "It's Christmas, Danny."

Kristen was the only one who ever called me that. No way I could resist. "You're right."

She stepped into my arms. I kissed her softly like I'd never kissed her before. Like the arguments and anger and hurt had been erased for this one single kiss. We were just a man and a woman finding solace in a storm not of our making. She drew away. Her eyes were huge and wet with tears. "Tell everyone I said Merry Christmas. I'll text the girls in the morning."

Every muscle in my body thrummed with the need to stay, to walk with my wife up the stairs and into our bedroom. To lay down together in our bed. To wake up tomorrow to a new day together. "Will do." My voice was raw, hoarse. "Merry Christmas."

She stared up at me. She took my hand. "Stay."

"I can't."

"You won't, you mean."

"Just like you won't step back from your job. You said yourself you haven't figured out how to balance your career and your family. I can't play second chair in the orchestra anymore."

"You said you were glad I told you about my mother and how it affected me. Yet you don't seem to understand how it connects to who I am now. I'm doing this for her. For Brielle. For Maddie. For Sherri. For Gracie. For Ainsley. For their daughters and granddaughters. They're all at greater risk because they have a history of cancer in their family. Breast cancer and now ovarian cancer." She'd found her voice, her steady voice, her doctor voice, the one that knew she was right. Always right. "It's not fair to make this your hill to die on. Not right now. Not when I'm trying to save Sherri."

She'd brought out the big guns. The ones that always made me stand down in abject surrender. The ones that made me feel like a selfish jerk. Not this time. "This battle doesn't rest on your shoulders and your shoulders alone. Scientists and doctors and researchers have been trying for decades to find a cure, to even find treatments that don't poison their patients. You won't find the answers on your own. You're good, but you're not that good. Nothing you do will bring your mother back. You cannot save Sherri. The tools you need don't exist."

I had to stop. I had to breathe. I sucked in air and exhaled. Kristen simply stood there, shoulders back, eyes shining, not bothering to contradict or intervene. "When will the time be right to step back and let someone else carry the load while you use your precious time for the people who love you right now, right here?"

"You're right. I know you're right." She hunched her shoulders. Want and need warred with habits almost impossible to break in her face. "I want to do better. I will try to do better. I promise. But you have to tell me what it is you want from me. To give up my job? Are you asking me to stop being me?"

"No, no, of course not."

"Then what specifically do you want? Tell me, because I honestly don't know how to fix this."

She was right. I'd spent years bottling up my unhappiness. Did I expect her to figure it out by osmosis? Through telepathy? I sat and drew her down next to me. "I want to eat dinner together three or four times a week. I want to have a date night once a week. I want you to go to church with me and out to eat with my family afterward. I know that last one is a big ask, but you might find something there you've been missing all this time. I want a real, true vacation every year. I want to talk about something besides work and household stuff . . ." I ran out of breath.

She didn't answer. We sat there, side by side, but a million miles apart. Finally, I stood. "Or we can go on like we are now for a little longer and I'll figure out what's next for me."

I started for the French doors.

"Danny, wait." She popped up and grabbed my arm. "Wait. Nothing you're asking for is out-of-bounds. I'm just out of practice." She slid her arms around my waist and hugged me. "Can we start with counseling? You pick the counselor. I'll call and make the appointment the first week in January."

"Promise you'll show up?"

She held up two fingers. "Scout's honor."

"You were never a Scout."

She smiled. "But you were, so you know what it means."

"Okay. I'll hold you to it."

"Can we seal it with a kiss?"

Small steps. "Don't worry about the gift under the tree. You just gave me the best Christmas present possible."

I kissed her thoroughly, deeply, then backed away. "Remember, there's more where that came from."

She simply nodded.

Humming "We Wish You a Merry Christmas," I left. While I still could.

KRISTEN

"Merry Christmas." I didn't need the fire after all, but it was too late to call Daniel back. I heaved a deep breath of cold air and waited for the heat that enveloped my entire body to wash away.

"More where that came from." I just had to rewire my entire brain. He wasn't being unfair, not really, but how could I change course now, with Sherri's life hanging in the balance? I could try, but I also had to consider the possibility that I could make a difference in women's lives now and in the future. Daniel had his calling in eco-conservation. I had mine. No one asked him to give up trying to create an equitable balance between the earth and its inhabitants who were wreaking havoc, destroying the environment, and sucking up its natural resources with no thought for their children, grandchildren, and future generations.

Still, his kiss, his touch, the warmth in his eyes that had been missing for so long I could barely remember—these things couldn't be ignored. This was the Daniel who served me breakfast in bed every morning of our honeymoon. The man who brought me flowers for days after we found out we were pregnant. The guy who gave me foot rubs and back massages throughout both pregnancies. The man whose kiss still made it hard for me to walk a straight line.

For the first time I wanted off the roller coaster, but I couldn't allow this feeling to stand in the way of doing my job. For a little longer. For as long as it took to walk Sherri through to the other side to where she would be N.E.D. Where she would go back to work as a teacher and be a mother and a grandmother.

Please, God. I know I don't have the right to ask You for anything, but they say You're merciful, kind, and full of grace. Please let Sherri live.

Sucking up to God when I needed something from Him. Again. Had I even prayed as a kid before Mom got sick? I didn't know. Mom's death was a ten-foot-high fence erected on my timeline. Much of what happened before it—with the exception of Dad's periodic presence—was hidden behind the fence.

Suffice it to say, I had no right to ask for anything, but I was sure God got that all the time. People who waited around until they really needed something to chat Him up.

Sorry, God. I can't even say I'll try to do better, because I'm not sure I will.

Was I testing God to see if He would do as I asked in order to bring me into the fold? Even I knew those tests never ended well.

I settled on the lounge chair and leaned back with Daniel's gift in my hand. It was easy to tell he'd wrapped it. Daniel was much better at wrapping than I was. Which made it easy for me to palm the job off on him every year when the kids were little. He didn't mind. He put on a Christmas movie, especially *A Christmas Carol* or *It's a Wonderful Life*. Then he spread out all his supplies on the coffee table, leaving room for his hot toddy and an assortment of Christmas cookies and candies, preferably frosted gingerbread men, brickle, and haystacks, his favorites. All he asked was that I be in the room while he did it.

All he wanted from me was simple conversation.

He asked so little.

That kiss. When I met Daniel, I had more experience with kissing than I cared to admit. I'd made the rounds in high school and college. A good therapist would've likely suggested I was seeking to fill the hole left by my father's abandonment and my mother's death. Whatever the case might have been, I was one of those girls who "got around." Even so, or maybe because of my experience, Daniel's kisses were spectacular. That's when I recognized that the key to truly wonderful physical affection was caring. Bereft of an emotional connection, the physical was an empty exercise. Daniel taught me how wonderful true connection could be.

I asked him once about his experience with women prior to me, thinking he must've been experienced. He laughed so hard he cried. A nerd. Awkward. A doofus. He was so hard on himself. Of course he did whack me with a two-by-four the first time we met. There had been no place to go but up.

My throat started to ache again. Nope. No more. I heaved a sigh. *Get it together.* I carefully unwrapped his gift without tearing the paper—following in his footsteps. Daniel liked to reuse paper or find another use for it. A velvet jewelry box appeared along with a small white note card with Daniel's tight, precise script on it. BALL'S IN YOUR COURT. Signed *D*.

Simple, clear, yet cryptic. Could it be both? I wouldn't know until I opened the gift.

I held the box close to my heart for several seconds. Blood pulsed in my ears. My heart banged against my chest. I'd bought him a 1953 first edition hardback of *The Future of Architecture* by Frank Lloyd Wright and *The Architecture of Trees* by Cesare Leonardi and Franca Stagi. Both nice. He would like them. Books were his thing. I'd put a lot of thought into my gift.

Jewelry was personal. Intimate.

I could never get it right.

I could hear him now. *This isn't about getting it right. A gift from the heart is all I want. A gift you picked out.*

And yet this felt like a test—one that I'd failed.

Open it. Just open it.

Inside on a silk bed lay a sterling silver rope necklace bearing two hearts curved together in an infinity symbol. Elegant. Beautiful. Simple. So Daniel.

The message *was* simple.

I closed the box, leaned back, and stared at the starless, infinite sky.

No matter what happened, one simple truth remained.

Daniel loved me.

thirty-six

SHERRI

Mr. Reality, my old nemesis, showed up dark and brooding on my doorstep on January third, belatedly welcoming me to the new year. He'd dropped out of sight while my family circled the wagons around me for the holidays. Or I'd been too busy to dwell on his constantly lurking shadow. He accompanied me while I skipped my beloved bagel with peanut butter and a big honking mug of coffee, even though the instructions for my CT scan said I didn't need to fast. My stomach disagreed. Mr. Reality was my backseat driver on the trip to the imaging center.

Noelle and the kids had accompanied Zach to the airport this brilliantly sunny winter day. Cody and his crew had hit the road on New Year's Day. Kristen had a meeting with her clinical trial folks. That left me and Mr. Reality on put-up-or-shut-up day for my clinical trial study drug.

I was fine on my own. A big girl. A full-grown woman. I gave Mr. Reality the cold shoulder and shut the curtains to the tiny dressing room so I could remove my bra with its metal clasps. I knew the routine. No necklaces, no zippers, no metal of any kind. Leggings and a T-shirt. Then I followed the technician into the cold, cold imaging room and assumed the position on the table that would roll into a doughnut.

"*You still have options.*" I silently repeated this mantra chanted by Dr. Capstone and Kristen at my last appointment. "*You still have options. You still have options.*"

The turtles swimming in a blue pond on the ceiling mural smirked. *You again?* This was my fifth CT scan in under a year. Still, I squirmed, attempting to get comfortable lying on my back with both arms above my head. The imaging technician tucked a pillow under my head and a foam inverted V pillow under my knees. Both helped.

"Let's get you hooked up to the IV." The technician, a friendly guy wearing a HEROES WORK HERE button, had a grizzled face with a salt-and-pepper five o'clock shadow. Not a newbie, which worked in my favor. He gently repositioned my arm out flat and rubbed his fingers over the patch of skin near the crook of my elbow. "You said you were a hard poke. I can see that. Is the other arm better?"

"No." I stared at the turtles. Did turtles get cancer? "The other arm is worse."

He handed me a red rubber heart. "Squeeze it until the needle is in, then relax. I'm going to tighten this rubber tourniquet. I don't mean to hurt you, but the tighter the better."

The usual spiel. *Breathe in, one-two-three-four. Hold for a one-two-three-four count. Breathe out, one-two-three-four.* He hit the vein on the first poke. No digging around. "Gotcha."

We sighed at the same time, then laughed.

"I hate that part of the job. I'm sure you're not a fan of it either."

"I hate being such a big baby about it."

"Considering what you're going through, I can understand that little things add up." He tucked the catheter tube through my fingers and placed my arm back over my head. "I'll take a few shots to make sure we're good, then I'll pop in to start the contrast."

I could've reeled off his spiel for him. A few seconds later, my chariot-aka-table slid into the doughnut. At least I wasn't claustrophobic. I closed my eyes. *Don't think. Don't think. Don't think.* The technician's disembodied voice commanded me to hold my breath. A few seconds passed. "You can breathe."

Then I was out of the doughnut again, peering at my turtles for moral support. *You're doing fine, blondie.* The technician returned. "Contrast going in. Remember, you'll have that warm feeling in the nether regions like—"

"Like I might pee my pants." I finished his sentence with much less diplomacy than he would've. Maybe I'd done this one time too many. "Got it."

He chuckled. "Another couple of minutes and I'll have you out of here."

And he did. "When do you see your doctor?"

"My appointment is Thursday."

Two days hence. In the cancer club to which no one wanted to belong, this little purgatory, this Bermuda Triangle, this camping on the banks of the Hades River was one of the greatest causes of *scanxiety*. I had yet to find a way to combat it.

"Good to know. He'll have your report by then."

His expression revealed nothing. Did the technicians know what they were seeing? Surely they did. But they didn't have the previous scans up to compare to see if tumors had shrunk or progressed or if new ones had popped up. Even if he knew anything, he couldn't tell me. I chewed my lower lip. *Don't embarrass yourself by asking.* That was Mr. Reality's contribution to the internal conversation. The urge to pepper the tech with questions ballooned. *Just give me a hint. A peek at the results. An insider's tip.*

"So, did you see anything interesting?"

The technician's smile faded, replaced with a sweet concern. "I'm sorry. I don't read the images. That's the radiologist's job. She'll forward the report to your oncologist."

"I know. I know." I heaved a breath. "I just thought you might . . ."

"No worries. Lots of patients ask, but I'm not a doctor. I don't have your medical history at my fingertips. It's best to wait for the radiologist's report."

Oh so gentle, so diplomatic. "Of course. I know that. I'm just skittish today."

"With good reason."

What did that mean? I pondered *"with good reason"* as I slipped into the changing room to put on my bra. A woman my age shouldn't gallivant about in public without one. *"With good reason."* He saw something. Or he was simply being kind while being evasive.

Two days until I'd know which it was. Two days . . . 48 hours . . . 2,880 minutes . . . or 172,800 seconds. At least I would be asleep for about sixteen of those hours. Thanks to zolpidem.

Those two days passed in a blur of grandma joy. Max, Gracie, and I created dinosaurs and flowers with homemade playdough. We bundled up in coats, mittens, and stocking caps—at least I did, the San Antonio winter was balmy for my Chicago-born grandkids— and walked the dogs. Or the dogs walked us. I ignored the shortness of breath that accompanied more than a few steps. And the backache that came with it.

We built tents with chairs, sheets, and blankets. Once the magic structure was complete, we huddled underneath it and played library, taking turns as the storyteller at story hour. Max took his naps on the couch with Dash as a pillow. Noelle painted our fingernails and toes purple. She dyed my hair teal for ovarian cancer awareness and texted photos to Cody and Jason, who were duly impressed by their mother's coolness. She wielded her phone camera with the determination that Zach should miss nothing in this period of separation. What she didn't text him she posted on Facebook. Cais posted pictures of the boys playing basketball and driving with the remote-control cars I gave them for Christmas. What had families done to stay in touch before the advent of social media?

We baked three kinds of cookies. Despite my constant companion nausea, I ate all three kinds, all the while maintaining a studied indifference to the passage of time. Ignoring the *bong, bong, bong*. Ignoring the painful backache. Even the nights blurred with the help of my trusty sleep aid and Cleo's steady purr in my ear.

Finally, the hour was upon me. Upon us. The results would affect everyone in my family. Kristen insisted on going with me. Noelle would've gone, too, if it weren't for the kids. I counted it a blessing she couldn't.

Dr. Capstone did a better job than Dr. P. of moving quickly to join us in the exam room, the usual sheaf of papers in his hand. A bigger sheaf than a CT scan warranted. He didn't have Dr. P.'s serious talk pose or her bifocals, but the same kind expression on his face was a dead giveaway.

"You have the shortness of breath, pain, and the nausea for a reason." He scooted closer on his handy stool. "The scan shows growth in the enlarged lymph nodes and the masses in your left lung. Additionally, we're seeing a new small mass in your large intestine. Fluid is noted in your abdomen—which explains why you're having difficulty eating, nausea, shortness of breath, and back pain."

Fluid building up in my abdomen. It would have to be drained. It would keep returning. End stage. "You mean ascites."

"Yes." His brown eyes filled with compassion. He pushed his wire-rimmed glasses up his nose. "Remember, you have options. Other study drugs can eradicate the ascites as well as reduce the masses. At the very least, they could result in a stable disease."

He no longer suggested these as-yet-unnamed drugs could eradicate the disease all together. No more N.E.D. for me.

Bong, bong, bong.

"Could I see it?" Kristen held out her hand. Dr. Capstone handed her the report. She studied it as if seeking a different result. Her free hand covered mine. "It's not what we wanted, sis, but you still have options."

If I heard that statement one more time, I would run screaming from the room. I was caught in an endless loop. Either I stayed on the roller coaster or I jumped off. Neither offered the kind of life I'd once had and longed to have again. "Could you be more specific, Dr. Capstone?" I asked through clenched teeth. "Include a reality check, if you don't mind."

"I'm not giving up on you." He produced another blue folder like the one he'd given me on my first visit to the clinic. A new clinical trial. "This study involves immunotherapy—"

"Clinical trials haven't shown good results for immunotherapy in treating ovarian cancer." Kristen intercepted the folder. "You don't have anything more promising?"

"This trial couples the immunotherapy with a chemotherapy drug." Dr. Capstone didn't seem to mind her abruptness. "The results have been promising. Of course this is a Phase I first-in-humans study. We could refer you to another clinic with Phase III and IV studies, but it would take time."

"And they're double-blind studies."

"They are. Neither the patient nor doctor knows if you'll get the study drug."

Like playing Russian roulette. I put my hand to my mouth. Coffee sloshed in my stomach. My clenched jaw ached. Everything ached. "If I don't do the study, what then?"

"Then we would need to talk about hospice."

"Sherri, you can't give up—"

"It's not about giving up, sis. It's about deciding how I want to spend this time." I put my arm around her. My turn to comfort my sister. I'd been down this road before. She'd done it with patients, but

I'd lived it with Mom. "What about standard of care? I haven't tried Doxorubicin yet. We could do it with Avastin."

"You could." Dr. Capstone took the study from Kris and set it aside. "That regimen is only effective 30 percent of the time, and then only in keeping the disease stable. The side effects are significant, especially for a patient who is as immunocompromised as you are."

Hair loss, nausea, mouth sores, neuropathy, extreme fatigue, low blood cell counts, diarrhea. Same song, fiftieth verse. I lowered my head into my hands. *Think. Think. Pray.* The words wouldn't come. *God, help me.*

It was enough. I raised my head. "I'll review the new study and come back tomorrow to sign on. How long is the washout period?"

"Three weeks—"

"Three weeks without treatment?" Kristen shook her head. "That's unacceptable."

"We can't start Sherri on a new drug with the old one still in her system." Dr. Capstone's voice was soft, low. "You know that, Kristen."

"I do." Her voice shook. "Sorry, I do."

"Don't be sorry." He stood. "You'll need to do the end-of-study lab work and EKG, Sherri. Review the new study. Bring your questions tomorrow. We'll talk then."

"Will do." I summoned my positive face. "Thank you for your help. Thank you for trying."

He'd dedicated his life to finding new, better treatments for cancer. He lived with the victories and defeats every day. Just like Kristen did. They were heroes. "Can I hug you?"

His face reddened. "You may."

"You win some, you lose some," I whispered. "Thanks for not giving up on me."

"You don't give up."

It wasn't about giving up. It was about making sure my time was well spent. Whatever time I had.

thirty-seven

KRISTEN

The wheelchair sitting in the middle of my living room was like a loudspeaker blaring in my ears. *This is real. It's happening.* I smothered the urge to clap my hands to my ears. *Shut up. Just shut up.*

"Why are you standing there, staring?" Sherri put her arms over her head and stretched in her favorite nesting spot on the couch where she kept her now-retired chemo blanket, her TBR pile of books, and her iPod with her playlist of favorite songs. She fumbled with buttons on a coat now at least a size too big. "Are you about to haul off and sock someone?"

"Nope. Just contemplating how we'll get you off the porch in this thing."

Chance and I had discussed building a ramp via text. He and some of his construction crew could do it—but not until the following week.

"I'm capable of walking down the steps. You jumped the gun with this buggy." She grinned and tugged a stocking cap over her sparse hair. "By itself it probably doesn't weigh much."

She was determined to ignore the fact that she'd fallen in the bathroom the previous evening. The bruise on her cheek and her sore arm notwithstanding. "Why wear yourself out so early in the day? Don't you want to conserve your strength for the playground?"

Still grinning, Sherri shrugged. "I guess it's lucky I've lost some weight then."

There was nothing lucky about her weight loss. I helped her stand, totter two steps, and plop into the chair. Three weeks without treatment had allowed her symptoms to worsen. Eating had become more difficult. Pain more prominent. Her bowels and bladder stopped working properly. Instead of starting the new trial, she'd spent the next two weeks in the hospital having surgery to remove a tumor blocking her intestines and treating a bladder infection that refused to relent. A procedure to remove the ascites in her abdomen had temporarily relieved her nausea and bloating. Until it built up again.

Then Richard had given us the talk.

The hospice talk. Six weeks to six months without further treatment.

So much for not giving up on Sherri. So much for still having options.

I said no. Sherri said yes to limiting treatment to that which would keep her comfortable. She hadn't even hesitated. Not even for my sake. Or the kids' sake. Nothing I said changed her mind. Nor did Chance's laments. Cody and Jason had argued at first, but something Noelle had said in their lengthy evening phone calls had changed their minds. Jason had brought Chloe for a weeklong visit earlier in the month. Both he and Jason had family emergency leave approved and available.

"Come on, smile." Sherri poked me with her skinny index finger. "I'm happy to be home—in your home. It's a good day, sissy."

"Me happy too." Max, her number-one supporter and constant sidekick, hopped from the couch and climbed into her lap. "Baby ride too."

"I'm happy too." Sherri, ever the teacher, corrected him. "I want to ride too."

Max wrapped his arms around her neck and crowed, "I happy too. I ride too."

"Good job."

"Max! Mom, don't let him sit on you." Noelle strode into the room already cloaked in her coat and knee-high boots. "Max, get down and walk next to Grandma."

"He's not hurting anything." Which meant the hydrocodone and anti-nausea meds were doing their jobs adequately. Sherri clasped her arms around Max and nuzzled his neck. He giggled. "Where's Gracie? Let's roll. My hot rod is hopped up and ready to race."

Gracie trotted into the room. She carried her coat and Max's, which she handed to her mother. "Grandma, do you need mittens?"

She'd turned into a little Mini-Me since Sherri's return from the hospital. Noelle had explained in the simplest of terms to both kids why Grandma was in the hospital. Gracie, at five, understood more than little Max. She pushed the protein shakes and Pedialyte, asked Sherri if she needed another pillow, and straightened the blankets without being asked. She also took it upon herself to feed Cleo and help me change the litter in the cat's box.

"I've got them." Sherri held up the thick woolen mittens one of her church friends had knitted for her. "Let's go. Time's a wastin'."

That was her mantra now. No time to waste.

I hated this. My phone dinged. Daniel wanting to know how she was doing today. He and the girls texted and visited regularly. I gave him an update.

If u need anything . . .
Thanks.

Our weekly counseling sessions were going well—if you liked the pain of picking a scab off a sore over and over again. Daniel had unloaded plenty those first few sessions. I was still figuring out how to open a vein and bleed for a complete stranger.

It would be worth it in the end. At least, that's what I kept telling myself.

We headed to the neighborhood park with the wheelchair and both dogs in the back of Noelle's Dodge Durango. The brilliant early March sunshine was deceitful. It promised warmth, but a cold north wind had its way with us as soon as we started along the trail with the dogs leading the way. After an abbreviated hike, the kids abandoned us for the playscape. Sherri didn't seem to mind. Her cheeks grew rosy. She took photos of the kids playing and Noelle, her belly ginormous now, swinging. She texted them to Zach, who was due for another visit in two days.

I settled onto a bench next to her chair. She glanced at me. "Come on. Don't be a party pooper. Listen to them laughing. Isn't kid giggling the best?"

"It is." I stuck my gloved hands between my knees to warm them. The wind took my breath hostage. "It's a beautiful day."

"Do me a favor."

"Anything."

"Live in this moment with me. Stop brooding about what-might-have-been. Or what-will-be. This is our time now. It's all we're getting." She raised her face to the sun and took a deep breath. "I love this time of year. It's crisp. It's clean. It's crazy beautiful."

"I can't help it. I want more time."

"Remember what Mom used to say? You get what you get and you don't throw a fit."

Only she'd been referring to store-brand sneakers and cheap backpacks. "And then she died."

"She did, and we survived." Sherri's voice became low, soft. "We went on and lived our lives."

"I don't understand how you can be so . . . calm about it."

"I don't have a choice. I'm not trying to be kumbaya or Pollyannaish." She put her mittens to her cheeks and rubbed. Her eyes were so blue against the sky and her white skin. Mom's eyes. "I either live the beliefs I've professed my entire adult life, or I fall into an abyss of darkness from which there's no coming back. I choose hope—not that I'll be healed here on earth—but that the best is yet to come."

When had she turned that corner? How had she gone there without me? Was I supposed to be learning some lesson from this travesty of loss? Wasn't Mom enough?

I studied the leaves swirling across grass brown and dead from a long, dry winter. "I'm glad you can cling to your beliefs." I'd had many patients who never came to terms with their impending death. They spent those last few weeks, days, and minutes scared out of their minds of a great unknown, afraid of the imagined abyss that awaited them. I didn't want that for Sherri. I owed her my strength and support. "How's your pain? Do you need your pills?"

"Sissy, you have to come to terms with this. I don't want to leave behind a sister who's bitter and angry and sad—"

"I can work on the bitter and angry part, but it's too much to ask me not to be sad."

"I get that, but don't be sad for me. No more pain, no more sorrow, no more tears. Scripture promises us that, and God knows how much I need that."

"I know. I really do know."

"This isn't on you. You couldn't heal me. No one could. So no guilt. Okay?"

I forced myself to meet her gaze. Pain had etched new lines around her eyes and mouth. Her cheeks were sunken. Dark rings like bruises surrounded those cobalt-blue eyes.

"I'm good. The acupuncture and massages are helping."

"You sound surprised."

"No, not that they help, but that you suggested them."

"I'm for anything that helps." The palliative doctor and her buddy the nutritionist had been surprisingly helpful as well. I would remember to refer more patients to the clinic's palliative-care team in the future. "How about something to drink? I brought coconut water, a strawberry smoothie, and a chocolate protein drink."

She snorted and pantomimed sticking her finger down her throat. "The first thing I'm doing when I get to heaven is eating a large everything-but-the-kitchen-sink pizza with Mom. I'm having coffee and a toasted whole-wheat raisin bagel with cream cheese for breakfast. I bet she has them every morning. No more worrying about our weight."

"What makes you think there'll be food in heaven?"

"Are you kidding? God made us. He made food. He knows a good thing when He sees it."

"I'm glad you're so interested in food." I pointed toward the parking lot. "Chance is here. He's bringing lunch."

Not that Sherri would be able to eat much. Her bag bypassed her blocked intestines, but she had to eat soft, low-fiber foods. "Unless it's peanut curry and fried rice, I'm not interested."

"Even if it's Chick-fil-A and waffle fries?"

She cocked her head as if contemplating. "I might be able to manage a fry or two."

No, it wasn't nutritious, but getting her to eat anything at all was a win. "Let's eat at the pavilion."

It was a raucous meal filled with the kids—young and old—spouting tall tales about how many waffle fries they could eat in one sitting, who had the best record for number of sour pickles eaten, and who could burp the loudest. Just to be clear, that last argument was between Max and Chance. And Chance won, totally oblivious to Noelle's disgusted shouts of "stop, you heathens." Fortunately, no other families were seated at the nearby tables to witness our vulgar table manners.

"Time to hit the road." Noelle nudged wrappers and milk cartons toward Gracie and Max. "Throw your trash away so we can get going. It's nap time."

Her gaze slid toward Sherri, who frequently spent much of the day sleeping now.

"No, Mommy." Max's lower lip extended. His big blue eyes teared up. "Pay more. Pease. Pay more."

"Please, Mommy, can we play a little more?" Gracie picked up her trash and Max's. "Just fifteen more minutes. Please."

"Please, Mommy!" Sherri parroted her grandchildren. "Fifteen more minutes, pretty please with sugar on it?"

Noelle glanced at me. I nodded. "Fifteen minutes, but not a second more. Grandma Sherri is tired."

"Am not!" She scoffed. "Just because *you're* tired."

Noelle at thirty-eight weeks pregnant didn't get much sleep. She had good reason to be tired. I was tired. I didn't sleep much either. When I did, my dreams were filled with open graves, funeral dirges, and rainy, windswept cemeteries. I hadn't been to the clinic since Sherri went into the hospital. Another oncologist had taken over the clinical trial liaison job. My patients had been referred out. Shay was assigned to a new oncologist who was using my office—temporarily.

Maybe. Every day it became harder to see myself simply returning to the clinic to work as if nothing had happened. As if nothing had changed.

I scooped up the trash, including the chicken sandwich Sherri hadn't eaten, and headed to the trash cans situated near the park toilets.

Chance followed. He took a last sip of his lemonade and dropped the tall cup into the trash can. "How's she doing today?"

I glanced over his shoulder toward the playscape. Noelle had pushed Sherri's wheelchair closer to the swings where Gracie and Max were swinging higher and higher into the sky. Sherri clapped and egged them on. "It's a good day."

"You can tell me the truth." His Adam's apple bobbed. He shoved trash into the receptacle with more force than necessary. "How much longer do you think she has?"

"It's hard to say, Chance—"

"The boys need to know. I need to get them here."

It wasn't that simple. Patients could be ready before their bodies were. Or their bodies would give out, but their will to live simply would not let go. "Four, maybe five weeks."

"Are you sure?"

"If you can get them home sooner, you should do it."

"Dad, Aunt Kristen."

We turned in unison at the entreaty in Noelle's voice.

Doing a strange duck walk—Daniel's dad would call it a John Wayne walk—she waddled toward us. "Umm, my water just broke."

thirty-eight

SHERRI

"Were you having labor pains?" I tried to stand. I wanted to help Noelle into Chance's truck, but my legs wouldn't cooperate. I flopped back into the chair. "How far apart are they?"

"They just started during lunch, and they're barely noticeable." Noelle rubbed her belly and leaned against the truck door. She blew out a big breath. "I thought they were Braxton-Hicks again. I'm not due for another two weeks."

She'd experienced so-called false labor pains sporadically for the last several weeks. "But you *were* dilated at your last appointment."

"Only two centimeters." She turned and reached for me. "Let me help you into the truck."

"Are you kidding? You're in labor, child. I'll help myself."

"I'll help you both." Chance strode across the grass, his long legs eating up real estate. "I got the kids buckled into their car seats. Kristen was vague on how the new seats work."

Kristen would take the kids and the dogs, drop the dogs at the house, and pick up Noelle's hospital bag, packed and ready to go since her last appointment.

"I'm in labor. I'm not an invalid." Noelle hoisted herself into the cab. "Besides, we have lots of time. Just because my water broke doesn't mean Ainsley plans to pop out any second."

Except third babies tended to come more quickly. Chance and I exchanged glances. He lifted me from the chair like I weighed no more than Ainsley would when she entered this world. I hugged his neck and planted a quick kiss on his cheek.

He returned the favor. "What was that for?"

"Early celebration. We're about to become grandparents again. How does it feel to be grandpa to six grandkids?"

"Like I should grab a cane and go to Denny's for coffee every morning with my grumpy old men club." He deposited me gently on the seat. "But that will have to wait until I pay off all my debt and convince one of my kids to take over my construction company."

Like that would happen. Cody and Cais were career military. Jason planned a career in cybersecurity when he separated from the Army at some unspecified time in the future. Noelle was an artist and a mommy. "You'll work until you drop in your steel-toed boots, you mean."

Noelle grunted. I took her hand. She squeezed mine so hard my fingers hurt. I bit my lip and bore the pain. "Get a move on, old man. Unless you want to deliver your granddaughter in the bed of this truck."

"Not happening." Noelle winced and sucked in air. "I'll cross my legs until we get to Methodist. I talked to Zach. He's getting on the next plane from O'Hare. He told me to wait for him."

A direct flight from Chicago to San Antonio took two hours and twenty-four minutes wheels up to touchdown. Zach might make it. Or not. Chance was in charge of getting him from the airport to the hospital posthaste.

A mere thirty minutes later Noelle had a wheelchair of her own and we were wheeled into her labor, delivery, and recovery room in the obstetrics unit. An anesthesiologist had been called. Noelle was a big fan of epidurals. I concurred. The L&D nurses did their thing. Noelle was four centimeters dilated. The nurse suggested she take a walk if she felt up to it. Gone were the days when women lay down and stayed down until babies were born.

"Are you up to a walk, Mom, if I push you?"

"I can push myself." I could—until my arms gave out. "Let's do a loop, and then I have something I want to show you."

She padded in skidproof socks down a long hallway, her belly preceding her by a foot. I kept up with no problem. "I'm so glad I'm here for this."

"Me too." She smiled down at me, but her eyes reddened. She sniffed. "Sorry, I'm so emotional. It's all the hormones. Don't mind me."

"I can't wait to meet Ainsley." I was plenty emotional too. Because I would witness the birth of my grandchild. Not because of time slipping away from me. The clock no longer bonged in my ears. I lived in this moment, thankful for it and every single second that followed. "I wonder if she'll take after you or Zach."

"She's in such a hurry, I'm betting she'll be like Zach." Noelle paused. She put her hand on her stomach, leaned forward, and panted. I waited. Nurses passed us by, unconcerned, intent on their tasks. Finally she heaved a long breath. "That was a good one. I think she'll be like Zach because he's always double-timing. And he was a star soccer player back in the day. Ainsley's already honed her kick plenty."

Her face a study in concentration, she paused again. She winced and panted.

"Maybe we should head back." I eyed the long hallway. "I'm pooped."

Let her think it was me. We trundled back to the room. She sat on the bed's edge and let her feet dangle. "Zach's going to be disappointed."

"He's on his way, honey."

"He's not going to make it in time."

"I'm sorry. It's my fault." I was sorry, but I also knew Zach would understand. He was a compassionate man and he would have—God willing—many years to know and love his daughter. "I'm selfish, I know, but I'm glad you're doing this here. I'll record the entire thing on my phone for him."

"Zach understands, believe me."

"He's a keeper." I tugged the bag Kristen had sent for me, along with Noelle's, from a nearby chair. "I have something I want to give you."

I handed her a manila envelope. "Open it, please."

She pulled three smaller envelopes from it. They were addressed to Gracie, Max, and Ainsley. "Mom, what is this?"

"Letters and flash drives from me to your kiddos."

"Mom." Her eyes teared up. Her lower lip trembled just like it did when she was a kid. She clutched the envelopes to her chest. "You've been saying goodbye since Christmas. You're still here."

"I wrote them each a letter telling them how much I loved them, how much fun I had with them, and talking about my dying. I'd rather leave the conversation about what happens when a person dies to you and Zach, if you don't mind." I wasn't afraid. I didn't want them to be afraid. But I wasn't sure I could have the conversation without crying. Because *I* would miss them. And once again I was being selfish. Being in their lives, watching them grow and change. Giving them sage advice about bullies, books to read, love, work, life lessons—that's what grandmas were supposed to do. I would miss out on that.

"The flash drives contain photos from our times together all the way back to Gracie's birth. It's easier to preserve than a scrapbook. Or you can make a scrapbook for them someday—in your spare time." I managed a chuckle. "With your art and raising three kids and being Zach's wife."

The days when I worked full time teaching twenty-plus five-year-olds who became like my own each school year, raised three kids, and struggled to be a wife to Chance seemed like a hundred years ago and just yesterday. The faces of little Mary and Mark, twins with identical missing front teeth and carrot-orange hair. Delia, who broke her arm jumping from the swings at recess. Christy, who could read second-grade books on her first day of kindergarten. My brain was like a yearbook filled with all the kids I'd taught over the years. From the overachievers to the scallywags to the silent, hurting, bruised kids who suspected every adult of being a potential abuser.

The yearbook shared space with the scrapbooks for my kids and the photo albums from my own abbreviated childhood. Kris jumping off the couch and hitting her nose on the coffee table at age five. She still had the tiny white scar across the bridge. The baseball games. The smell of beer, popcorn, and hot dogs still evoked memories of Dad. Painting our toes. Mom teaching us to put on makeup. Mom teaching us the two-step. Making Kool-Aid Popsicles in metal ice trays. Teaching Kris to drive. Lying on our backs in the grass and staring up at the stars late at night, trying to decide which one Mom had claimed as her own.

I was also sad for Kris and Chance and the kids and the grandkids. Sorrow would darken their world when I stepped into light. But only for a while. Every day the light would seep back in, a little at a time, in the mundane—learning to count, learning to say *please* instead of *pease*. Throwing a curveball. Learning to tap-dance or swim the butterfly stroke. Attending a first middle school dance. Earning a high school degree. Then college. Falling in love. Marrying. Life. Then death.

That's how it worked in theory. The truth was that life had all sorts of dead ends, forks in the road, detours, and potholes, like a maze that a person never quite figured out until the end popped up in the most unexpected place.

"Mom?"

I cleared my throat and took Noelle's hand. "Yep."

"I'll never let them forget you. That's a promise."

"Thank you. I'm so sorry I can't be here to do the things grandmas are supposed to do. It hurts my heart. It's up to Zach's mom now. I hope she's up to it."

"She is, but she's not you." Tears ran down Noelle's face. She swiped at them. "I know how stupid it is to say this, but I can't help it. It sucks. It's not fair. I can't do this without you."

"Yes, you can. Of that, I'm sure." I pulled myself from the chair and squeezed onto the bed next to her. "You're made to be a mommy. I'm always telling people that. I'm so proud of you. I love you so much."

She buried her head on my shoulder. "Oh, Mom," she whispered. "I love you too."

Her hand tightened on mine. She raised her head. Her hands went to her belly. "I forgot how much this hurts."

"God intended it that way. Otherwise, women would never have a second child."

"That's why He gave people like me a job." A woman wearing scrubs strode into the room. "I'm your anesthesiologist. I love my job. Patients are always so happy to see me."

I slid from the bed and got out of her way.

After that, time seemed to slow down. The monitors allowed us to watch Ainsley's heartbeat and Noelle's vitals. We also watched the clock. Timing not only her contractions but how long until Zach would arrive. Her promise to keep her legs crossed proved to be overly optimistic.

Chance was likely waiting in the cell phone lot at San Antonio International while Zach's flight taxied down the tarmac to the gate when Ainsley slipped into the obstetrician's hands with a fierce cry of either alarm or relief—I couldn't decide.

She was six pounds fifteen ounces of perfect, from the wisps of damp blonde hair that covered the translucent skin on her head down to her tiny toes. The nurses cleaned her up and laid her naked on Noelle's bare chest. Ainsley's squalls quieted. Her eyes closed.

Noelle kissed her red face and gazed at her new daughter with the same disbelief I'd seen in Chance's face when he first held Noelle. Amazement and disbelief that we as human beings had the ability to create such an exquisite child. How was it possible? Scientists could give us the cold, hard facts, but only God could make it happen.

I settled in my chair and continued to record these moments for Zach. Each one more precious than the last. Finally, a nurse took Ainsley long enough to run a few more tests, make footprints on a hospital certificate, attach a tiny ankle monitor, and then wrap her tightly in a dinosaur-decorated blanket. By that time she was awake and fussing again. Back with her mommy, she partook of her first attempt at nursing.

She came through like a champ, according to Noelle. "She knows what to do. That's half the battle." She motioned for me to come closer. "Come meet your new granddaughter, Mom. Kristen texted me. Dad's on his way up with Zach. She'll bring in the kids after Zach gets to meet her first. Then Kristen will go pick up Grandpa Roy."

Grandpa Roy. Great-Grandpa Roy. Four generations in one hospital room to welcome a newcomer to the family.

The calm before the best meet and greet ever.

I took Ainsley into my arms and walked over to the window with its view of San Antonio's downtown in the distance. Renewed vigor coursed through my body, giving me this moment with her. "Hey, wee little one, welcome to the world."

Exhausted from the work of getting dressed and her first meal, she cooed in her sleep. I tucked the blanket around her face. "Yep, you're right. It's enough to make me tired too. I'm so happy to meet you, Ainsley. I won't be around to teach you your alphabet, your one-two-threes, or read you *I Dance in My Red Pajamas*, but it's okay. You won the lottery with your parents. Your big brother and sister are pretty cool too. And your aunt Kris isn't half bad, either. The jury's still out on Great-Grandpa Roy, but I have a sneaking suspicion he's okay. I leave you in good hands, sweetness."

My tears dripped on her blankie, but she didn't mind. She knew she was safe in the arms of her grandma Sherri, now and forever.

thirty-nine

KRISTEN

A soft whimper, more of a sigh, invaded my sleep. I burrowed deeper into a dream in which I'd taken the girls to a baseball game, only it was at the old Mission Stadium. Dad was there playing center field, his chest puffed up like a champion boxer. I kept looking for Daniel. He was nowhere in sight. Brielle was crying. *There's no crying in baseball, silly.*

A cool hand touched mine. I forced my eyes open. The room was dark and warm. Sherri's fingers curled around mine. Chance had been called out to a job site earlier in the day and hadn't returned yet. Noelle and the boys were sleeping. So I'd been taking this shift. "Is the pain worse? Do I need to call the nurse?"

No answer.

Pain had taken over her body. More pain than a human being should be asked to bear. Not even morphine could totally banish it. The hospice nurse kept adjusting her doses upward, but it couldn't keep up. I preferred to let her handle the medications. As Sherri's sister, I was too close to her pain and suffering. As much as I didn't want her to go, I didn't want her to suffer. The two giants warred in my head morning, noon, and night. "Sherri, honey, what do you need?"

"I want to go outside," she muttered. "Outside."

"Sherri, are you awake?"

"Outside."

I fumbled for my phone on the wheeled comfort cart next to the bed. "Honey, it's after midnight."

"I know." A cough rattled in her lungs and caught in her throat. "We have to find Mom's star."

Mom's star. As teenagers we'd lain in the grass and stared up at the sky on those nights so long ago, whispering about boys and love and what happened after you died. Could Mom see us? Did she know I got an A in calculus, that my basketball team made it to state, or that Sherri liked Tommy Martin? Wouldn't it be cool if she could send us a note or a signal or a hint?

We could use that hint now more than ever.

"Okay." I slipped from bed, put on my sneakers, and pulled her wheelchair over to the bed. "Let's get you bundled up. We'll stick your meds in your lap."

"Unhook me."

"No. No, I'm not doing that."

"I can take it. I want . . . to be . . . awake."

I did as she asked. She'd lost so much weight, I could've carried her out to the backyard. Instead I settled her into the chair. She managed to put on her coat herself. I tucked a comforter around her legs. "Warm enough?"

"Any warmer and I'd melt." Her old self showed itself in a brief flash. "At the rate you're moving, the sun will be up before we get there."

In stealth mode, like teenagers sneaking out of the house to a party, we sped down the corridor, through the kitchen, and out the back door.

Cool, damp air and a chorus of crickets greeted us. A three-quarter moon lit our way past the moss pool to the place where the yard opened up into a grassy carpet where no trees would block our view. I stopped the chair. "How's this?"

"Perfect."

Sherri threw the comforter on the grass. She put her hands on the chair's arms and attempted to stand.

"Hey, hey! Just look up. The stars are bright tonight." I put my hands on her shoulders to push her back into the chair. The truth was, light and air pollution in the country's tenth largest city obscured much of the heavens. We were far enough away from the city center to see some stars. It would have to do. "We don't have to actually lie on the ground."

"Wuss. Are you afraid if you get down you won't be able to get back up?" Sherri shoved her body forward and toppled onto the comforter. "I'm not worried. You can pick me up."

She hadn't lost her sense of humor.

Loss.

Don't think about it.

I tugged the comforter from under her behind so I could spread it out. "Fine, but you're not sitting on the cold ground."

"Why? Are you afraid I'll catch a cold? Don't worry, cancer will kill me first." Her cackle turned into a hacking cough that segued into retching. She had nothing in her stomach. Eventually the dry heaving stopped. "Too soon for morbid humor?"

Her voice was so hoarse it was unrecognizable. I couldn't begin to respond to her gallows humor. I wasn't there. I would never be there.

I settled onto the comforter next to her. We both stretched out and looked up. I closed my eyes, took a long breath, and held it for a few seconds. *Be in the moment. Treasure this moment in time.*

A breeze riled leaves in the stand of live oaks in the distance. The crickets amped up their concert. Bright-yellow eyes peered at us in the dark, then the creature—a possum or a raccoon—scurried away. The scent of moss and wet earth wafted in the air. A moment in time.

"Do the voice."

"What?"

"Do the coach," she croaked. "For me."

"I can't."

"For me."

One more time, that's what she was saying. One last time. So I did. I sucked up the tears and the regret and the hurt and put on my Tom-Hanks-does-Coach-Dugan baseball cap. "'There's no crying in baseball. It's supposed to be hard. If it wasn't hard, everyone would do it.'"

Sherri joined me for the first few words, then her voice trailed away.

We lay there for a few minutes, breathing, being, recollecting.

"I found it." Sherri raised her arm and pointed. "See it? Right there. Next to the Big Dipper's handle."

"I see it." I nestled closer and tucked my cold hands under the comforter. "'Star light, star bright, first star I see tonight, I wish I may, I wish I might, have this wish I wish tonight.'"

I wish Sherri would live to a ripe, old age.

Was that too much to ask?

"What did you wish for?" Sherri's voice grew soft and breathless, as if she'd run out of steam. "A cure for cancer?"

That would've been less selfish. "I can't tell you. Then the wish won't come true."

"That's birthday wishes."

"All wishes."

"There's a meme that floats around on social media." Sherri paused, then breathed, a tortuous sound that hurt me in every joint and muscle. "It says why wish upon the stars when you can pray to the One who made them?"

"Maybe I'm hedging my bets. Maybe it seems as if we're more likely to have a wish upon a star come true."

"Just because you didn't get the answer you want doesn't mean God isn't real or He isn't good or that He doesn't care."

"This probably isn't the best time to try to convince me of that."

Clutching her hands to her stomach, she rolled over onto her side. Pain.

God, You're the Great I Am. You can do anything. So why don't You relieve her pain?

Stupid, stupid. Challenging God. Be careful what you pray for. You might not like the answer. He could relieve her pain by simply allowing her to die. What she liked to call the "ultimate healing." "Let me get you back inside. You need your pain meds."

"I'll see Mom in heaven . . . I want . . . to see you . . . too."

The spurt of energy that had propelled her from bed and into the dark night had dissipated. I struggled to sit up. "We should go inside."

"Tell me you'll pray . . . in your . . . unbelief."

I wrapped my arms around her and held on as if she were the rock, the anchor, and I was the drowning soul who needed saving. "I promise to try."

"I'll take it." Another ragged breath. A gasp. "You have to let me go."

"I know. It's okay. Go."

"Tell the kids."

I kissed her forehead. I memorized the feel of her warm skin and baby-soft wisps of hair, her smell of lavender and chamomile oils, and her essence of kindness, wisdom, and loveliness.

Not bothering with the wheelchair, I carried her like a small child into the house. Her eyes were closed and her breathing labored by the time I hooked up her morphine drip.

My legs didn't want to move, couldn't move. My feet weighed fifty pounds. Her cold fingers pushed mine away. *Go.*

The hallway stretched on forever. I trudged to Noelle's bedroom. It took all my strength to turn the doorknob. The night-light cast its tepid illumination over the small bodies tucked in the bed between Zach and Noelle. Ainsley whimpered in her sleep in the nearby portable crib. I touched Noelle's shoulder. Her eyes opened. She nodded. Without a word, she rose and went to wake her brothers.

Now Chance. He picked up on the first ring. The sound of air rushing and the radio playing said he was in his truck. I opened my mouth. Nothing came out.

"I'm on my way."

I whispered, "Be safe."

In other words, *Don't die trying to get here in time.*

He made it by a matter of minutes. I liked to believe Sherri knew he was there. She never opened her eyes. She didn't speak. But she knew. The people who loved her the most were there when she walked with a resolute stride into the kingdom, where she was welcomed with open arms by her Lord and Savior and, more importantly, Mom.

That's what I told myself. And then I kept my promise. I prayed in my unbelief.

forty

DANIEL

"Ten-nine-eight-seven . . . ready or not, here I come." Giggling mani-
acally, Xander shot from behind the live oak tree in our backyard in
search of the kids hiding from him. Obviously his dad had taught him
a different set of rules. No counting back from a hundred. Or down
to one. "Here I come, Gracie! I see you, Max."

I had to laugh. Even though laughing hurt on this day. No way
Xander could see Gracie or Max. They were hunkered down under
the tablecloth that covered the table of food Kristen had amassed for
Sherri's Celebration of Life. Sherri had chosen a party over a church
service. She wanted her friends and family to gather in remembrance,
not in grief. Maddie and Brielle had accepted DJ duties with a playlist
of Sherri's favorite classic rock anthems. At the moment, Fleetwood
Mac's "Go Your Own Way" rocked the yard.

Sherri always went her own way.

Getting used to that past tense would take some time.

"That Xander is a character, isn't he?" Mona, who had introduced
herself as Sherri's church lady friend, had instigated the hide-and-seek
game. She said the kids needed to know it was okay to have fun today
and every day thereafter. Smiling, she used pot holders to place a King

Ranch casserole on a trivet next to a basket of assorted bagels waiting to be toasted and topped with flavored cream cheeses. "He reminds me of Sherri. So does this casserole. She always had seconds when I brought it to our church potlucks. You'll have to try it."

"Thanks, I will. In a bit." I'd nibbled on a bagel slathered with crunchy peanut butter in Sherri's honor. She would've swooned at the variety of foods that kept multiplying as her school and church friends arrived. "I just ate a bagel."

"Of course. Just don't wait too long. It'll get cold." Mona adjusted the aluminum foil that topped her dish and placed a large serving spoon atop it. "I think I have some Sterno cups in my van. I could set up these casseroles to stay warm."

She trotted away, a woman on a mission. Mona was one of those people who dealt with grief by keeping busy and helping others. Not a bad way to go.

Grief had its hands around my neck, squeezing until I couldn't speak, let alone breathe. I'd known Sherri as long as I'd known my wife. The two were a matched set. Different in so many ways but fundamentally kind, caring, funny sisters who finished each other's sentences while keeping each other honest.

Despite my thick UT burnt-orange-and-white sweatshirt, I shivered. What I needed was coffee. Thankful for a hot drink on this blustery mid-April day, I poured myself another steaming cup of Sherri's favorite Cuban dark roast and then added a dash of almond milk and a spoonful of Stevia. My sister-in-law would've been proud of me.

I glanced around. Kristen was keeping her distance. That was so Kristen. She was determined to get through this under her own steam.

I tried to walk with Kristen through those days, to make sure she slept, ate, showered, and occasionally stepped outside for fresh air. Mostly she nodded and said she was fine. The only sign she was lying was the ease with which she handed over custody of Dash and Scout, saying she couldn't care for them while Sherri was so sick.

Chance slept in Sherri's room most of those last nights. He handled her needs until there was nothing more to do with catheters and tubes taking care of basic necessities. Now he walked across the grass toward me looking lost and bewildered. I gestured toward the coffee setup. "Can I pour you a shot of caffeine?"

He rubbed at his stubbled face with both hands and nodded. "I couldn't sleep last night." His bloodshot eyes attested to his statement. "I guess this will take some getting used to. I take the coffee black."

I nodded. Not much to say to that. I'd tried imagining this world without Kristen and my body turned icy cold, my hands stopped working, my mind froze. A hole the size of Texas opened up in my soul. I swallowed the knot in my throat and nodded again.

Chance accepted the coffee I handed him, took a sip, and surveyed the yard. Noelle sat in a lawn chair, her sister-in-law on one side, her grandfather on the other side. Roy held Ainsley with the obvious delight of a man who'd fallen in love with a tiny girl who would one day wrap him around her little finger. Noelle's eyes were as bloodshot as her dad's. Cody, Zach, and Jason stood aside talking in low voices. They'd both spent the last few weeks in San Antonio on emergency family leave.

"The boys seem to be holding up well."

"I don't think it's hit them yet." Chance's voice was hoarse. His shoulders sagged. He cupped his hands around his coffee and stared at its rising steam. "Not until they get home and realize they can't call her or text her or FaceTime her. That's when it really hits a person."

That sounded like the voice of experience. "I'm sorry, Chance."

He shrugged and cleared his throat. "I wish I hadn't wasted so much time. I shoulda asked her to marry me again. I don't know why I didn't. I was too stupid or too proud. I don't know."

"I don't believe that. I think it was more like you two were still married, especially after her diagnosis."

"We were best friends. At least she was my best friend." He picked up a pumpkin bar, took a bite, then put it down. The muscle in his jaw worked. "Kristen's taking it hard."

"I know." She wouldn't let anyone comfort her. Especially not me. It was my turn to straighten sagging shoulders. "She's trying so hard to be strong."

"Maybe you should forgive her for whatever she did or didn't do." Chance gestured toward me with his cup. "It took me forever to forgive Sherri for something because it hurt my pride bad. If I'd known she'd be gone so soon. . . ." He gulped coffee and winced when the hot liquid burned his mouth.

I had forgiven her. Every counseling session brought us a little closer to where we—where I—needed to be in order to break old patterns and establish new ones. "We're working on it."

"Good." He nodded. His Adam's apple bobbed. "I need to duck out."

His way of saying he couldn't hold it together anymore. "I'll let Kristen know."

"Tell her I'll . . . I'm . . ." He ducked his head and strode toward the gate.

Now I had an excuse to seek her out. I slipped through the French doors and glanced around the kitchen. The myriad casseroles, desserts, and other dishes delivered by friends and family covered the counters, the island, and the breakfast nook table. No sign of Kristen.

I wandered through the house, feeling like a stranger in a foreign land. Tiny superhero sneakers, Matchbox monster trucks, a stuffed unicorn with a silver horn, a binkie, a tiara, a bag of disposable diapers, wipes, a tube of something called Butt Paste—lots of small people lived in my space these days.

I squeezed by a Big Wheel tricycle, bypassed a miniature stroller that held a Curious George monkey with a plastic banana stuck in his mouth, and headed for the great room. An inquiring meow greeted me. Cleo arose from her spot on the couch, arched her long body, leaped down, and trotted toward me. I squatted and patted her sleek back. Her purr revved. "Sorry I bothered you." Did she know Sherri was gone? "I'm sorry for your loss. Do you know where Kristen is?"

She leaned against my thigh and yawned widely.

"I guess not." I stood. "Go back to sleep. I'll find Kristen by myself."

I headed down the hall that led to the guest bedroom. The sound of someone moving stopped me. I peered inside the room that had been Sherri's most of the past year. Kristen glanced up, then back at the blanket she was folding. "Hey."

"Hey." I teetered on the line between being in the room and not. "You have a bunch of guests out back."

"I know. I'll be there in a while. I want to get Sherri's things together so Noelle can take whatever she wants with her when they go back to Chicago in a few days."

"I spoke with Cleo for a minute." Dash and Scout, currently enjoying a spa day at their favorite doggie day care, had grown accustomed to sharing their space with Cleo. In fact, they seemed to enjoy her snobby airs. "What's the plan for her?"

"Sherri said it was up to me if I wanted to keep her. She's been here for so long it's her home." Her gaze pensive, Kristen stroked the blanket as if stroking Cleo's sleek fur. "But Noelle and the kids have become attached to her. They want to take her home with them. Besides, I didn't know what . . . if . . . it's your house too . . . still."

I didn't have an answer for the real question behind her words. "I like cats. You know that."

We'd never adopted cats because we figured dogs were enough. And they didn't require someone to handle litter box duties.

"Zach and Noelle will have a full SUV on the trip home." Zach had rented a U-Haul trailer to cart some of Sherri's treasured bookshelves, books, and a few other pieces of furniture from her house. Sherri had insisted it be cleaned out and the house sold before she died. "No loose ends" had been her edict. However painful. "Noelle already has her hands full with three kids, but if she wants to adopt Cleo, you should let her. I do think Dash and Scout will miss her, though."

"They'll never admit it, but I know they will." Kristen laid the blanket aside and picked up a book. A silver James Avery bookmark fell on the floor. She knelt and picked it up. "Oh no. I lost her place."

Her voice broke. I shot into the room and knelt beside her. "It's okay. It'll be okay."

Why did people always say that? It would not be okay. That was obvious.

Her expression frantic, Kristen flipped through the pages. "She always said there were more books in her TBR pile than she could ever read. Even before her diagnosis. Now she'll never know how this mystery was solved."

I wanted to say that wouldn't be the end of the world. Stupid. It was the end of the world. For Sherri. And in many ways, for Kristen. "I know."

"When she couldn't read anymore, she was ready to go." Kristen clutched the book to her chest. She nodded toward a pile of books on the nightstand next to the hospital bed. "I told her it was okay to go."

The ultimate sacrifice for a loving sister. "You were right."

"She was ready, but I wasn't." Kristen ducked her head. She stared at the rug, her gaze far, far away. "It's hard not having her to talk to. When stuff like this happens, she's the one I tell."

"I'm so sorry." There was nothing else to say. Kristen had been the one to teach me that platitudes could be more hurtful than helpful. "Come outside. Sit in the sun. Watch the kids play. That's what Sherri would want you to do. Be Aunt Kris. They'll need that."

"You always were the empathetic one."

"You use up all your empathy and nurturing on your patients. My work doesn't require that."

She eased to her feet. "It's going to be so quiet here without the kids. It sounds strange to say, but it's been fun having them here despite the circumstances. I like holding babies, kissing boo-boos, watching cartoons, and playing Uno. I don't even mind changing diapers."

"Our time will come."

Whether Kristen and I learned to live together again or continued to live parallel lives, the girls would likely provide us with grandchildren to love and share. If we were blessed.

Kristen stared at me. "Do you think so?"

She didn't want pat answers. I stood and held out my hand to help her up. "I hope so."

She took my hand and allowed me to pull her to her feet. "Do you ever pray?"

The earnest expression on her face spoke to how important my answer was. I had as many questions, all unanswered, as she did. "Sometimes."

"Does it help?"

"Sometimes."

"It doesn't help much when you don't get the answer you want."

"I'd agree with that. We're only human. I figure I'll ask God when I'm face-to-face, if that happens."

If I made it.

Together, we walked out to the backyard. I opened the French doors for her. The afternoon sun poured in. Sunlight bathed her white, tired face. She glanced back at me. "It *will* be okay, won't it?"

"Yes."

Someday.

forty-one

KRISTEN

No hole in the ground. No funeral dirges. No shivering in a rainy, windswept day. The April sun hurt my eyes as I brushed past Daniel and stepped out on the patio. Instead, Bryan Adams's "Summer of '69" blasted from the speakers Maddie and Brielle had set up in the grass. Shrieking with laughter, Gracie chased Xander around the moss pool with a water blaster. Lucas helped himself to a piece of carrot cake and two chocolate chip cookies, then scampered away before his mom noticed.

"Kristen, over here." Cais unfolded her long legs and stood. "Take my seat. I need to slow those kids down before one of them ends up in the pool."

I sank onto the lounge chair on legs weak with fatigue. Sleep still evaded me most nights.

Noelle stretched and got up. Her face—still pudgy with baby weight—was gray with fatigue. Ainsley had her days and nights mixed up. That and grief had served to turn Noelle into a walking zombie. "Are you okay with her a little longer, Grandpa?"

"Sure, sure. I could hold her into tomorrow." Dad's grin made him seem years younger. "She's comfy with her great-gramps."

"Then I'm going to run inside and pump. I want her to get used to taking a bottle for the trip home."

Dad's face turned red. "You do that, honey. I'll make sure Max doesn't O.D. on sugar."

"You should take a nap while you're in there." I cocked my head toward the house. "The kids have plenty of adult supervision."

"I can't sleep during Mom's party." Her chin trembled. "I'll bring out more food when I come back."

Angela and Leonard, who'd come and gone already, had brought an entire brisket with all the trimmings. Everyone would need to take home food. Sherri's kids would return home in the next few days, leaving me with a full refrigerator and an empty house. "You should eat yourself. You don't want your milk supply to run dry."

Wincing, she touched the tiny gold cross hanging around her neck. "I know. I know. It's just . . . nothing sounds good."

"Have a bagel in her honor."

She gave me a jerky nod and trotted away. Dad winked at me. "By the way, great-grandpas are good for letting kids eat as many cookies as they can without puking."

I had to smile. "I won't tell on you."

"How are you doing, Krissy? Hanging in there?" Dad shifted Ainsley to his other shoulder and reached across the aisle to pat my arm. "I know it's been a rough patch."

Rough for him too. He'd visited regularly during the last few months. He and Sherri watched baseball games. He provided his own color commentary. He even watched our baseball movies, starting with *A League of Their Own*. His mimicry of Coach Dugan was almost as good as mine. "I'm okay. How are you doing?"

"Snuggling babies is good therapy." He sat up. "In fact, it's your turn for the medicine."

I swiveled and held out my arms. He deposited eight pounds of cuteness into my arms. I inhaled the scent of baby. The ache in my throat subsided a little. My shoulders relaxed. She cooed in her sleep.

"I'm sorry. I'm really sorry, Krissy." Dad's gravelly voice quivered. "I apologized to Sherri before she went. I waited too dang long to do it. I wasted so much time. I missed so much."

Suddenly, I no longer needed or wanted an apology from this man. "I've come to the conclusion we all do the best we can. You did what you could." I watched Daniel pour lemonade into a cup for Max. He and the little boy high-fived. He would make a wonderful grandpa. "I've made my own mistakes and missed out too. So much. Clean slate?"

"Clean slate." He rubbed his neck and tugged at his white T-shirt's V-neck. "I promise to be around now for as long as I can."

"I promise not to be a crybaby about the past."

"It's a deal."

We lapsed into silence. The kids made enough noise for us. Shawna, Nikki, and Lori were teaching the kids to slow-dance to Eric Clapton's "Layla." The kids thought it was hysterical. Gracie insisted Daniel dance with her. He was a perfect gentleman, as usual. He was a good dancer too. An ache radiated from my chest throughout my entire body. To have his arms around me again. To dance to Coltrane. We didn't even need music in the early days.

"Do you think Sherri can see this from wherever she is?" Dad used his hands to lift his legs from the lounger and settle his sneakered feet on the pavers. "We always tell little kids who lose a grandma or a dad or a mom that they're watching over them. Do you think that's true?"

My first response was nearly, *You're asking me?* I smoothed Ainsley's silky blonde locks. Her tiny baby breaths tickled my neck. They smelled sweet like her mommy's milk. "I hope so. Sherri believed. I'd like to believe too. I'm thinking about going back to church."

"Mind if I tag along?"

Was this the famous godly plan Sherri talked about? Dad could be my company. Two people soiled with sin sitting in the back row. "Actually that would be great. You can be my buffer when the church ladies descend."

"*You* can be my wingwoman. Maybe one of those church ladies will take pity on a poor guy with a walker and fix him a home-cooked meal." He crowed at the thought. "They're always good cooks. Sometimes they're lonely too."

"Dad!"

"Lots of those church ladies are widows."

His cheeky grin surprised me. Despite his age and growing disability, he wasn't giving up on the possibility that he still had life to live. I could take a page from his book. "I'll pencil you in on my calendar."

We high-fived. Startled, Ainsley opened her eyes, but she didn't cry. She stared up at me like she knew me.

"Sherri would've loved this." Dad leaned back and stared at the sky. "Really loved it."

Look at this, Sherri, three generations hanging out.

forty-two

KRISTEN

Shabby, but not too shabby. I pulled the Leaf into the parking lot in front of a squat, square building painted a pale turquoise. Not anything like the sleek, landscaped northwest-side clinic I'd left behind after boxing up a puny assortment of personal items the day before. The sand-colored metal roof glinted in the April sunlight over stuccoed walls. A hand-painted sign read WOMEN'S AND CHILDREN'S HEALTH SERVICES. Tired-looking clunkers lined the first row in the parking lot shared with a neighboring bail bondsman office, a Dollar General store, and a pawnshop.

A pregnant woman in a hijab trudged between the cars, a toddler in tow. She paused at the double doors. A woman in skinny jeans and a neon-orange T-shirt shifted a baby from one hip to the other, then opened the door for the Muslim woman.

I popped a piece of nicotine gum in my mouth. Anything to keep from lighting up. My doctor said the physical addiction was over, but the psychological one would take much, much longer to conquer.

Just like waking up this morning and thinking I should talk to Sherri about this decision. She would know if it was the right thing to do. For a few fleeting seconds, I'd found comfort in the thought. Then I remembered. She was gone and I was still here and I had to make this decision on my own.

For the first time in my life, I couldn't rely on big sis for advice.

Here we go, sis.

I pushed through the doors to bedlam. Small children knelt around a short table, playing with building blocks and chattering in high-pitched, excited voices. Every chair was filled with women, many of them holding babies. The overflow stood. Nurses in green scrubs gave shots to screeching children. Another nurse, this one dressed in purple scrubs, distributed clipboards to the women, all of whom talked at once.

She seemed to know what was going on. I made to follow her. She turned and nearly bumped into me. "Oh, hi. Have you been here before? No?" Before I could answer she held out the last clipboard. "Fill out the forms. If you have insurance, have your card and your ID ready when Crystal calls your name. If you don't have insurance, don't worry about it. If you don't have an ID, the last sheet on the clipboard has information on how to get one."

I tried more than once to interrupt her spiel but with no effect. A screaming baby behind us probably didn't help. Finally she stopped to breathe. I jumped into the fray. "I'm Dr. Tremaine. I came to talk—"

"Speak up." She put her hand to her ear. "I can't hear you."

"I'm Dr. Tremaine. I spoke to Dr. Chavez—"

"Oh, thank You, God. Thank You, sweet Jesus." She gave the impression she meant this as a prayer of thanksgiving. The thick silver cross hanging on her ample chest gave credence to this theory. "Go through the door next to the receptionist's window. Exam rooms 2, 3, and 4 have patients waiting."

"I haven't signed a contract yet. I'm here to talk—"

"Doc, we don't have time to talk." The badge hanging from a lanyard identified her as RN Lucy. No last name. "Metro Health is having a pop-up immunization clinic today for the kids, but the women are all here to see the doctor. Doc Liv needs backup."

Doc Liv. As in Dr. Olivia Chavez? The doctor with whom I'd done a preliminary virtual interview the previous day.

Lucy nudged me toward the door. "Next time wear scrubs. You don't wanna wear your good clothes here."

On the other side of the swinging door, the noise was slightly buffered. A young guy wearing a badge that identified him as Medical Assistant Mick stuck out his hand. "You must be the new doctor. You can't imagine how happy we are to have you on board."

I shook his hand. "I need to see Dr. Chavez."

"You and everyone else." He snort-laughed. "See some of these patients and you might get a chance."

A heavyset woman dressed in the now-familiar purple scrubs shot through a door behind him. "Mick, Miss DeeDee needs samples of that nausea medicine the rep left last week. Her insurance doesn't cover it. Ask Crystal to set her up with an appointment in two weeks, but if the med doesn't help, she's to come back ASAP."

"Got it." Mick took the chart she offered him and disappeared into the exam room.

"You must be Kristen." Another handshake, this one so firm my knuckles hurt. "I'm Liv Chavez. Sorry, no time to chat. Grab a chart and take Tammy Quiroz in room 1. She came in for her annual exam and pap. However, she's pregnant. You get to break the news and do her exam."

"I thought we were going to talk—"

"No time." She propelled me with that same firm grip toward the exam room. "I hate keeping these women waiting. Especially the ones with kids. You remember how that is? I do. It sucks. We'll talk later—if you decide to stay."

Her black sneakers squeaking on the tiled floor, she grabbed a chart outside exam room 2, slipped inside, and closed the door.

A tryout? For me and for them. I was game.

Five hours later I staggered into the break room-slash-conference room where I grabbed a water bottle and plopped into the closest chair. I blew straggling hair from my eyes and sighed. My back hurt. My mouth was dry from talking so much. It had been a long time since I did that many pelvic and breast exams. Or explained the importance of regular mammograms. Or talked about birth control. Or prescribed antibiotics for an STD to a sixteen-year-old girl.

I gulped down water and wiped my face on my sleeve like a five-year-old.

"There you are." Dr. Chavez trotted into the room. With her brown hair frizzed out around her head, she appeared as frazzled as I felt. "I was afraid maybe you escaped before I had a chance to convince you to stay."

"Oh, I'm staying, Dr. Chavez." The idea hadn't fully formed until I uttered those words. "If you'll have me."

"Call me Liv. Are you kidding? We'd be thrilled. I'd be thrilled. We are thrilled." She clapped as if her words needed exclamation points. "And relieved."

"It was fun." A strange way to describe the give-and-take with patients who weren't scared out of their minds and poised to bolt the second I walked through the door. "That sounds ridiculous, but it felt good to talk to these women about how to take care of their bodies."

"It's not always fun, but it's satisfying." Liv laid both hands on the table and splayed her fingers wide. She wore no rings and no nail polish. "I'm not going to lie. There are plenty of days when we have patients who are being abused by their partners. Or they're doing drugs while pregnant. Or they're neglecting or abusing their children. Or they're simply overwhelmed because they don't have the financial resources they need to properly care for themselves and their children."

"Real-world problems."

"Yes. Exactly." She nudged tortoise shell–rimmed glasses up her aquiline nose. "I have to ask you. Why? Why give up oncology after twenty-plus years to come work at a frontline clinic? It's kind of outside your comfort zone, I would think."

"I want to help women understand their bodies better so they'll recognize when something's wrong before it becomes a life-and-death matter." This was the interview question I'd spent hours answering while I lay in bed in the dark waiting for dawn to come. "I want to help them take better care of themselves so they're less likely to get cancer. There's no stopping cancer, but there are things we can do to insulate ourselves.

"If women are better educated, they can better advocate for themselves with doctors who ignore or don't realize what these symptoms can mean. Telling women that they need to get regular screenings and avoid certain behaviors after they already have the disease is unproductive and frustrating—for them and for me."

"That's an important mission." Liv pursed her lips. She peered at me like a woman trying to decide whether to say yes to a first date. "Lofty, perhaps, but worthy. So much of what we do around here is quick, down-and-dirty treatment of symptoms. If you can hang on to that mission in the midst of the yeast infections, unplanned pregnancies, and strange rashes, more power to you. I'm right there beside you all the way."

Her forehead wrinkled as she tapped on the scarred table that might have been a yard-sale rescue. "You haven't asked how much it pays."

"I figured we'd get there eventually."

"I'm afraid to tell you. I can only imagine what you were pulling down at Texas Cancer Care." She shook her head as if to say *tut-tut-tut*. "No way we can match it."

"I don't need to make big money." I did need to help Daniel pay for the girls' college education and make mortgage payments. "I just have bills to pay like everybody else."

"This is why I've put off inviting another physician to join us. A lot of our funding comes from government grants. Some charitable foundation grants." Liv heaved a sigh worthy of an Oscar trophy. "We cobble together our budget with insurance and Medicaid reimbursements. A shoestring budget, in other words. The salaries are barely industry standard and the benefits are pitiful."

"With a sales pitch like that, I can't imagine why physicians and nurses aren't trampling each other to get through the door."

"It's better for you to come on board with eyes wide open rather than discovering after giving notice that this isn't going to work for you."

"I already gave notice." I held out my hand. "Stop trying to make me regret it."

We shook on it. Her smile transformed a plain face into a beautiful one. "Woo-hoo!" Her shout brought Mick, Crystal, and Lucy running into the room. "Folks, we've caught a live one."

What followed could only be described as a Snoopy dance à la hip-hop and variations on the two-step, polka, and waltz. Liv joined in with a salsa that she insisted on teaching me. The celebration continued with tacos, gorditas, empanadas, an assortment of hot sauces, and a large bag of sopapillas.

For the first time in forever, I relaxed.

forty-three

KRISTEN

I saw Daniel before he saw me, for which I was grateful. It gave me time to fortify my flagging resolve. He stood between two towering stone columns under the palm-thatched roof of the Japanese Tea Garden pagoda, gazing down at the bright flashes of orange koi swimming in the lily ponds below. Light flooded the gazebo on this crisp April morning. A navy windbreaker protected him from a brisk breeze, bringing with it the scent of wet earth and greenery. The normally soothing sound of a waterfall cascading down one wall of what had once been a stone quarry didn't calm my nerves. Whatever Daniel contemplated, it held him completely still and seemingly unaware of my approach. Which was just as well.

Now that I was here, my carefully rehearsed presentation had faded into a flurry of memories evoked by Daniel's mere presence. His skin's heat next to mine. The roughness of his five o'clock shadow. The silky feel of his thick dark curls in my fingers. The way his breathing slowed when he drifted off to sleep. My entire body missed him in such a visceral way that my aching throat closed. I drew a shaky breath.

"Daniel?"

He turned. "There you are."

I drew closer, close enough to see the tired lines around his mouth and eyes. He wasn't sleeping well either. "I'm sorry I'm late. Traffic was crazy."

"It's all right. I enjoy the quiet here. It's such a serene place. There's not a lot of visitors this early in the season."

"Remember when we used to take the girls to play at the playscape in Breckenridge and then push them in the double stroller all the way up here and back?"

"I do. It was fun. As long as it wasn't on a holiday weekend."

The beloved historic park was too popular for its own good.

"I brought coffee." I held up two grandes. "With real cream and sugar just for you."

"Sure. Thanks." He took the cup. "So what's this all about, Kristen? What are we doing here? You didn't mention this outing in our last session."

Because that counseling session had mostly been about dealing with grief at Sherri's death and why it was so hard for me to lean on Daniel for support and comfort. Because I wasn't sure I'd have the guts to go through with it. When the counselor had congratulated us on how much progress we'd made, I knew it was time. With the new job locked down, I had no excuse to wait any longer.

If only Daniel thought so too.

I held my breath until the inevitable wave of grief passed over me. It didn't drown me the way it had for the past month. The quiet house, the empty guest bedroom, the dearth of commentary regarding my choice of TV shows, movies, and books, the absence of a certain ridiculously demanding cat—all of it had to be endured until it became simply the norm. Until the sense that something was missing subsided.

Don't chicken out now. Her voice sounded in my head. *Come on, bawk, bawk, bawk.*

You just shush now.

I heard her voice in the silent evenings mostly. Sometimes she sounded like Mom, and I wondered if the two of them were having a good time bugging me from the great beyond. At least it gave me a sense of relief to think they weren't alone. They had each other.

Come on, sissy, stop pussyfooting around.

Fine. "I'm sorry I didn't return your calls. I needed to get my life in order before I could talk to you."

Daniel stuck his hands in his jean pockets. His shoulders hunched. "So did you? Get your life in order?"

I *had* done a lot of work, but through it all, another absence had been impossible to ignore. Day and night. Night and day. I set my coffee on the floor, then took his and placed it beside mine. I dropped to my knees on the cold, hard stone floor and stared up at him.

"Kristen—"

"Just let me get through this." I licked dry lips and drew another long breath. "I'm so sorry. I'm sorry I neglected you. I'm sorry I chose not to see how lonely you were. I'm sorry I put my patients and my career ahead of you. Please forgive me."

"Please get up." He tugged at my hands. "You don't have to get down on your knees."

"I do. I know how horribly I've neglected you. I hate knowing how lonely you've felt. I truly understand how that feels because I'm so lonely without you."

"Are you sure it's me you're lonely for?" His gaze shifted to the red, purple, and white pansies that lined the pagoda floor's edges. He shook his head. "Are you sure it's not Sherri you're missing? You haven't returned to work. When you do—"

"That's something else I want you to know. I'm not going back to the clinic."

"What do you mean you're not going back? Oncology is your life's work."

I let go of his hand and leaned back on my haunches to relieve my aching knees. "I gave notice right after Sherri died. I didn't leave them in the lurch. They'd already transferred my patients during my leave of absence."

"I thought that's all it was." His tone made the statement more of a question. "A leave of absence."

"Which gave me time to review my life and my work." I studied my hands. Hands that had cradled my dying sister's head. Hands that had massaged her back and washed and combed her wispy hair. "I couldn't keep her from dying any more than the two of us could keep Mom from dying. So much in cancer treatment has changed since then, but not enough. Thousands of women will die from ovarian cancer this year, and there's nothing I can do about it."

Daniel knelt in front of me, so close I could've reached out and touched his cheek. A sweet, sweet concern enveloped his weary face. "Honey, you can't give up. Don't give up. Not for me."

"I'm not giving up." I swallowed tears that never seemed to dry up. "I'm figuring out my priorities and how I want to live in however much time I have left. I've signed on to work at a health-care clinic for indigent women. I educate them about the importance of mammograms, do pelvic exams and pap smears, help with birth control questions, and educate them about gynecological cancers."

I ran out of breath. I'd given this speech in various iterations a few times already—to the practice manager, to Shay, to Tasha, to the patients who'd called me after learning that their temporary physicians were now permanent. To Maddie and Brielle.

"Why?"

"Because I want to catch these women before the disease claims them. I want to educate them about listening to their bodies and advocating for themselves with doctors who forget to listen to patients. I want them to know how to identify symptoms before it's too late." I couldn't do anything about family history or genetics, but I could help women increase their chances of staving off cancer in other ways.

"Preventive health care is better than waiting until they get to me and their cancer is already ravaging their bodies."

"You've given it a lot of thought."

"It's a different mindset. A nine-to-six, Monday-through-Friday job. A job with boundaries. But still a job that gives me a sense of purpose and contribution."

"No giving out your cell phone number?"

"No giving out my number." There was a price to pay for this newfound freedom. One I was sure Daniel wouldn't mind. He was that kind of guy. "Of course, it's also a substantial pay cut."

He didn't even flinch. "Money's never been an issue with us—not even when we didn't have any."

"UT's tuition isn't cheap—especially when you have two kids enrolled."

"Fortunately, we planned for it. And both girls are doing their part to help."

"You mean you planned for it and you taught them well. I'm so thankful you did." I touched the nicotine patch on the back of my left arm. "There's one more thing. I quit smoking."

"Wow. That's incredible." His dimples popped with a grin so big I almost lost my balance. "That's great news. I'm so proud of you."

"It's still hard, but I don't need that crutch anymore. I never needed it; I just refused to give it up." The desire for a cigarette at this moment was so intense my jaws hurt, but it would pass. Eventually. "I can't practice at a women's health services clinic and smoke. I understand the irony in that statement, but I'm finally ready to practice what I preach."

"Good for you." Daniel gently touched the entwined hearts nestled against my chest. "You're wearing it."

"It's beautiful." I put hand over his and held it there near my heart. "I know what it means to you. I want you to know what it means to me."

"Which is?"

"It means I don't know where I end and you begin, and I don't want to find out. I'll never take you for granted again. I know we still have work to do, and I'm more than willing to do it. I want to spend whatever time I have left—that you have left—together. Everyone pretends they have all the time in the world. You and I know we don't. I'm an idiot for wasting so much time."

"I'm glad you can see that."

His expression gave me hope. "You said the ball's in my court."

His dark eyes filled with unmistakable emotion. He nodded but didn't speak.

"Good. Because I came here today to ask you to marry me . . . again."

His eyebrows rose. Surprise mixed with uncertainty and then hope. "What are you saying?"

I let go of his hand and pulled an envelope from my purse. I held it out.

He fumbled through its contents. His hands shook. He stared at the documents, then at me. "Two first-class tickets to Paris."

"I'm saying I want to take that honeymoon you planned in September and I was too stupid to take, but we need to hurry. Take a peek at the dates."

"One week from now. For three weeks."

"One week in Paris and two weeks in the south of France. Just like we always dreamed."

"But first you want to get married . . . again?"

"Renew our vows."

"That would take some planning."

"The planning's already done. If you're willing."

He smoothed his long, thin fingers across the tickets. His gaze came up and met mine. "Of course I'm willing."

"Oh thank goodness. Otherwise, a bunch of people are going to be really irritated with me." I dug my phone from my purse and made the call. "Come on up."

It took a few moments but eventually Maddie, Brielle, who was pushing Grandpa Roy in a wheelchair, Matt Caine and his wife, and the pastor from the Tremaines' church trooped over the accessible walkway to the pagoda.

Even Daniel's family had agreed to join the wedding party. Angela and Leonard might not be my biggest fans, but they wanted their son to be happy. On that we could agree. Daniel's brothers followed their parents' example—Angela made sure of that. Not one to do anything halfway, Leonard pushed a trolley that held a large German chocolate wedding cake and a few bottles of the bubbly stuff. Everyone was smiling and looking self-satisfied.

They'd been so sure he would agree. Much surer than I was. My lungs filled with air. I breathed. My heart resumed beating.

forty-four

DANIEL

The bouquet of twenty-five red roses fit nicely in Kristen's arms. Her cheeks turned red to match when I handed them to her before we got in the rideshare car. The TSA agent at the airport actually cracked a smile as he reviewed our boarding passes and IDs before waving us through. If the agent behind the X-ray equipment found anything odd about the contents of Kristen's carry-on bag, she didn't say anything.

We made it to the gate with a few minutes to spare. Kristen perched on the edge of a chair near the counter. She was wound so tight she vibrated. She buried her nose in the roses and sniffed. "They smell so sweet. Did I thank you?"

"Profusely."

"Sorry, I'm a little light-headed this morning." Laughing, she rubbed her eyes and surveyed the crowd at the gate. "I can't believe in fourteen hours we'll be at the Paris airport. It's surreal."

Surreal, like a dream, like walking on air, all the clichés applied. I checked for the twentieth time to make sure I still had our boarding passes and passports. Kristen insisted I hold on to hers. She wasn't sure she could be trusted with them.

She pulled her already dog-eared copy of a France travel guide from her backpack. "Did I read to you what it says about the Eiffel Tower?"

"I believe you did." Also more than once while helping me shop and pack for this trip. She'd covered everything from the weather to exchange rates, to the must-see attractions such as Notre-Dame, the Louvre, and Basilique du Sacré-Coeur, to food. I settled onto the seat next to her. "But go ahead. Read it again."

"'There are three levels where visitors can stop to enjoy the view. The first one requires you to walk up three hundred sixty steps, or visitors may prefer to take an elevator. There's a gift shop, a cafeteria, and a restaurant, plus an outdoor terrace space. The second level is another 355 steps up, or again an elevator ride is available.'" Kristen stopped. "Of course, Sherri expected us to take the stairs. She was very specific about that."

"I would expect nothing less."

Her gaze went to her carry-on bag. She'd packed the requisite form and death certificate even though she was only bringing a small portion of her sister's cremated remains to France. The kids had already spread the rest from a charter boat three miles out from Mustang Island in the Gulf of Mexico. "The second level has the same amenities as the first level, except the viewing platform has a lovely view of the other attractions we'll visit afterward."

"So the second level is it then?"

"No, that would be too easy. The top level reaches an elevation of 276 meters. Fortunately—or unfortunately, depending on how you look at it—there are no steps, but it's allegedly 'an exhilarating elevator ride from the second level.' In fact, it says 'visiting the top level is one of the most thrilling things to do in Paris, but it's not for the faint of heart.' Sherri was certain I would not fall into that category."

"Me neither. I say if we've waited all this time to visit the Eiffel Tower, we should go all in."

"Thank you for allowing us to take the time to do this. It's not really a honeymoon activity. You're so kind." Her fingers went to the entwined hearts hanging from the silver chain around her neck. "I'm sorry I didn't appreciate all the ways you make room for my drama and my needs sooner."

"No more apologizing, remember?" I slid closer so our shoulders touched. She leaned into me. The enticing, familiar, yet still-exotic scent of Shalimar welcomed me home. No cigarette smell lingered in her hair. "Clean slate."

"Right." She kissed my cheek. I brushed her lips with mine. "New beginnings."

The agent picked up the mic and announced that first class would now begin boarding a flight to Chicago with a connecting flight to Charles de Gaulle Airport in Paris, France.

I stood and held out my hand. Kristen took it. Together we gathered our things and boarded the flight that would take us to a destination of our dreams—a dream we'd held on to for more than twenty-five years.

The time had to be right. The time had to be perfect. The time was now.

A Note from the Author

The Year of Goodbyes and Hellos was the hardest and the easiest book I've ever written. I remember in intimate detail what it felt like to wait in a frigid exam room, barely able to breathe, in terror until a doctor walked in and changed my life forever. Not just my life but the lives of my husband, my children, and my entire family. Everyone I loved received the diagnosis with me. In seven years I've had at least twenty-five CT scans and several PET scans, hundreds of lab draws, a few MRIs, MUGAs, ultrasounds, and a variety of other exams. Each one brings with it an anxiety and uncertainty for which there seems to be no cure. Not even a faith to which I've clung throughout the years precludes the worry and fear. I'm only human, I frequently remind myself. Fear and anxiety are human frailties.

All those thoughts, feelings, and emotions are poured into *The Year of Goodbyes and Hellos*. It's the kind of research no writer wants to do, but once she has, why not use it? Use it to examine the seismic shift in a person's very soul when her life expectancy shrinks despite every effort to stop it, when the buoyant expectation of enjoying retirement with her husband and watching her grandchildren grow up pops, shrivels, and blows away. How does one hang on to faith when prayers seem to go unanswered? Was it really faith at all or a flimsy facsimile? Writing *The Year of Goodbyes and Hellos* allowed me to work through all those thoughts and feelings. It wasn't always pleasant, but when it was finished, joy did indeed come in the morning.

While *The Year of Goodbyes and Hellos* ultimately is a work of fiction, the reality of ovarian cancer is not. I'll be in treatment for the rest of my life—with all the physical, mental, emotional, and spiritual impacts that reality implies. I can't send this novel out into the world without sharing an urgent message with my female readers. Listen to your bodies. Talk to your doctors when something doesn't seem right. Advocate for yourself. Get a second opinion if the first doctor doesn't take your concerns seriously. Here are some important facts (true at the time of publication) all women should know:

- Pap smears do not detect ovarian cancer.
- There is no diagnostic tool for ovarian cancer.
- Symptoms might include: unexplained weight loss coupled with bloating, a feeling of fullness while having eaten very little, more frequent trips to the bathroom, fatigue, back pain, and pain during intercourse. The symptoms are ill-defined and often diagnosed as other ailments first.
- Increased risks for ovarian cancer include: middle-aged or older, genetic mutations, a family history of the disease, and never having given birth, among others.
- Ways to reduce risk: maintain a healthy diet and active lifestyle, a healthy weight, pregnancy, breastfeeding, tubal ligations, taking birth control pills for five years or more. Knowing your family's cancer history, sharing it with your doctor, and getting regular checkups.

The truth is, people can do all the right things (I thought I did) and still get cancer—any cancer. But we can increase our chances of survival by staying in tune with our bodies and getting our checkups regularly. Especially pelvic exams, pap smears, mammograms, and colonoscopies. Early detection is everything when it comes to successfully treating all forms of cancers.

If you want or need more information about ovarian cancer, please check out these reputable sources online:

National Ovarian Cancer Coalition: https://ovarian.org/

Ovarian Cancer Research Alliance: https://ocrahope.org/

Our Way Forward: https://www.ourwayforward.com/

American Cancer Society: https://www.cancer.org/

Acknowledgments

I find it hard to know where to begin in thanking the people who made *The Year of Goodbyes and Hellos* possible. There are those who've supported me since my stage 4 ovarian cancer diagnosis and those who supported me in writing and publishing the story that grew from it. Both were integral parts of the whole. I look back at seven years of treatment and see it now as a form of "hands-on" research. Every appointment, every blood draw, every scan, every surgery, every health-care provider with whom I came into contact served as fodder for the big and small details needed to accurately and authentically write Kristen's and Sherri's stories.

However, there are some folks I'd like to specifically thank. First up, Dr. Irene Kazhdan. She served as my oncologist for five years. She kept me alive. Together we beat the odds that insisted most women diagnosed with metastatic ovarian cancer don't live five years. She is smart, funny, stern, a storyteller, a hugger, a dog-lover, a gardener, and as dedicated to her patients as any physician I've ever known. Yes, she's my model for Arina Pasternak.

Dr. Kazhdan retired in 2021. I hope she's enjoying hiking the Blue Ridge Mountains and sitting by the sea in upstate Washington. She deserves the rest. She left me in good hands. My thanks to

Dr. Anthony Tolcher and the staff at NEXT Oncology. They picked up the mantle with Phase I first-in-human clinical trials that have helped me continue to live with cancer while learning the minutiae of how trials are run. Research is possible everywhere!

In particular I want to thank infusion room nurse Marsha Grubbs, who read the manuscript in its rawest form and corrected medical details. Any mistakes are mine alone. Marsha, thank you for brightening the infusion room with your infectious laugh, cute sneakers, "cha-cha-cha," and occasional thumbing of the nose at "protocol."

I'm so thankful for the folks on the publishing side of this story as well. My thanks to my agent, Julie Gwinn, for encouraging me to write the story of my heart even when it meant changing genres yet again and all the challenges of selling such a change. Thanks to my editor, Becky Monds, for her kind encouragement and willingness to crawl out on a publishing limb with me yet again. Becky has edited twenty-one novels and nine novellas for me. I never cease to be amazed at her ability to see individual themes, characters, and story arcs while never losing sight of the overall story. Coming alongside her is Julee Schwarzburg, eagle-eyed line editor, who has corrected my *Chicago Manual of Style* errors and a multitude of other mistakes for all those books. If there were Olympic gold medals in editing (and patience), these two would win every time.

On a deeply personal note, I would not have survived the last eight years of devastating health diagnosis heaped on diagnosis without my husband, Tim. His willingness to become a caregiver when my ability to walk normally disappeared without warning or a clear reason grew through the difficult surgery that followed, the further loss of mobility, the seesaw diagnoses, the cancer diagnosis, the sometimes horrific treatment side effects, and never-ending uncertainty that plagues a person who has lived past her expiration date. Your love and dedication have been tested in ways I never could have imagined. You've stepped up every time—more than I could ever deserve. Our plans for our "golden years" look so very different than we once anticipated, but you have never shied away from creating a whole new look. (Thank you for Costa Rica!) Love always.

Discussion Questions

1. Kristen loves her husband and daughters, but she's also dedicated to helping her patients survive a deadly disease. She's trying to balance family and career. Do you think it makes a difference that she's an oncologist and her patients depend on her for survival? Are there times they should take precedence? Is it harder for women than men to balance career and family? Why or why not?

2. How do you feel about Daniel's decision to move out when Kristen forgets their anniversary? Do you think he's justified in feeling shortchanged by her dedication to her patients? Should he have returned home when he found out Kristen's patient died that evening? Why or why not?

3. Put yourself in the shoes of Maddie and Brielle, who often can't rely on their mother to be there for them in times of small or even big crises. How would it make you feel? Does a "higher calling" profession serve as an excuse for sometimes abdicating from parental duties?

4. Do you agree with Matt's wife's observation that a spouse can be guilty of an "emotional" affair even though it hasn't reached the physical-affair stage? Why or why not? Would an emotional affair hurt more? Do you think men and women see these two affairs differently? How so?

5. Were you surprised Sherri was the culprit who had the affair that ended her marriage to Chance? Did it seem out of character to you? How did she change and grow as a result of this grave error in judgment? Do you think Chance should've forgiven her and taken her back? Would you if you were in a similar situation with your spouse?

6. If you received a cancer diagnosis (or if you have received it), how do you think it would change your approach to day-to-day living? Or would it? Why do you think most people don't realize that time is finite and live accordingly until they or someone close to them dies "too young" or receives a terminal diagnosis? Is there value in the philosophy of "live every day as if it's your last"?

7. The "power of positive thinking" and "mindfulness" receive a great deal of attention in the treatment of difficult, deadly diseases and traumatic injuries. Do you believe positive thinking has an impact on how a person's body reacts to treatment for illnesses and severe injuries? If so, why?

8. Throughout the story, Kristen and Sherri banter over where and how they want their cremated ashes spread. Does their light-hearted treatment of this difficult subject surprise you? Why do you think they handle it this way? Do you think it's healthy? Why or why not?

9. Sherri's faith dictates that she will receive complete healing in heaven if her cancer treatment is unsuccessful here on earth. Even so, she prays God will heal her so she can have more time with the family she loves. There's a saying: "Everybody wants to go to heaven, but nobody wants to die." Do you think the desire to live longer, to be healed, shows a lack of faith? Why or why not?

10. Kristen and Sherri suffered the same losses as children, the same traumas, but Sherri grew in her faith. Kristen lost hers.

Why do you think people react differently in these sets of circumstances? Why do some become closer to God while others push Him away?

11. Do you think it would be natural for Kristen's faith to shrivel even more after Sherri's death? Were you surprised, then, that Kristen was asking questions about prayer and contemplating going to church? If you were in her shoes, would you react the same way or differently?

12. Were you surprised Kristen gave up her job as an oncologist to work treating women at a nonprofit health clinic? Do you think she made the right choice? Explain.

13. Were you surprised Daniel forgave Kristen and agreed to renew their vows? What would you have done in his shoes? Explain.

From the Publisher

GREAT BOOKS

ARE EVEN BETTER WHEN THEY'RE SHARED!

Help other readers find this one:

- Post a review at your favorite online bookseller

- Post a picture on a social media account and share why you enjoyed it

- Send a note to a friend who would also love it—or better yet, give them a copy

Thanks for reading!

About the Author

Photo by Tim Irvin

Kelly Irvin is a bestselling, award-winning author of more than thirty novels and stories. A retired public relations professional, Kelly lives with her husband, Tim, in San Antonio. They have two children, four grandchildren, and two ornery cats.

Visit her online at KellyIrvin.com
Instagram: @kelly_irvin
Facebook: @Kelly.Irvin.Author
Twitter: @Kelly_S_Irvin